MOTHER'S PEOPLE

A Tale of Courage and Grace

GALE FORBES

Readers are encouraged to go to www.MissionPointPress.com to contact the author or to find information on how to buy this book in bulk at a discounted rate.

Published by Mission Point Press
2554 Chandler Rd.
Traverse City, MI 49696
(231) 421-9513
www.MissionPointPress.com

ISBN: 978-1-958363-49-2
Library of Congress Control Number: 2022921251

Printed in the United States of America

CONTENTS

Lena

MOTHER'S PEOPLE

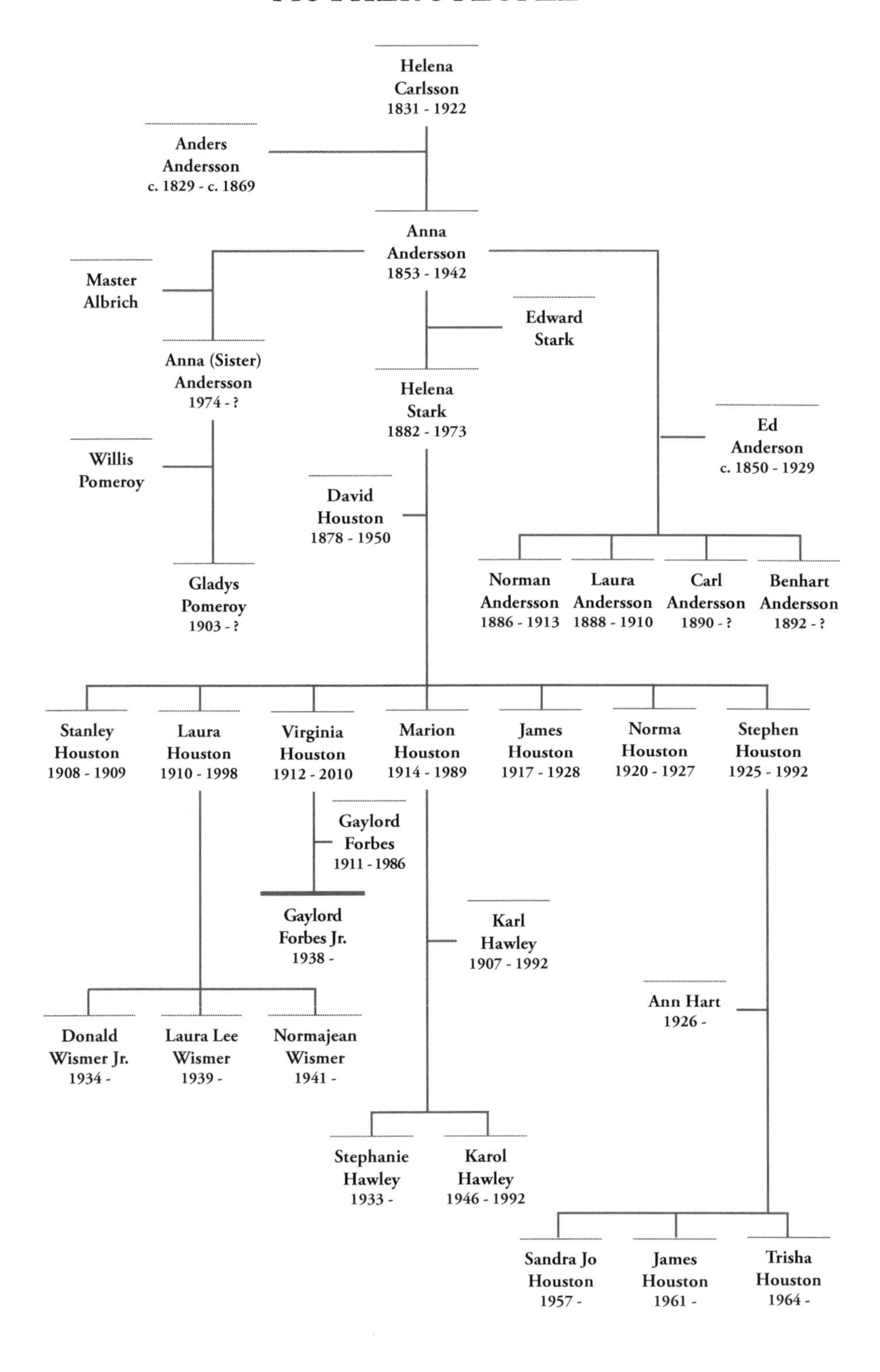

PROLOGUE

Sweden in the mid-nineteenth century floundered in the backwater of Europe's Industrial Revolution. The economy depended on farming and mining, and production was challenged by a migrant labor force that worked at southern manors during the growing season then moved to the mines in the north once harvest ended.

The Great Famine of 1841 staggered the country. Snow covered the ground until mid-summer, and then an early winter decimated the harvest. The following year, clouds poured rain and fields turned to swamps. Oats and barley drowned; potatoes and turnips rotted in mire.

Drought followed flood. Mud baked to adobe and fields turned brown under a relentless sun. Wells dried, ponds evaporated, cattle perished and famine ran rampant; dysentery and smallpox overtook villages.

The economy verged on collapse. Unemployment was rife, unwed births rampant, and Swedes fled to the New World in alarming numbers. Of the tens of thousands who emigrated to America, most left to find a better life—but two had no choice and were expelled to privation.

My great-great grandmother, Helena Andersson, and her pregnant daughter, Anna, were banished from Sweden and their manor village. They were exiled to Germany without escort, and in the ensuing eight years, made their way to America, and built an enduring American family. Mother's People *is that story.*

HELENA

March 1874, Sicksjo Sweden

SOMETHING STIRRED. SHE blinked awake. What was it? The cottage was still; the patter of rain gone. Helena got on an elbow and peered from her cubby under the loft ladder. A sliver of moonlight cast shadows across a spare room.

A gentle thunk rustled the silence. A crinkle of paper followed, then the scrape of the kettle. A rising glow from the hearth cast flickering images over rose-entwined wallpaper, an ancient chest, a small table, and her daughter at the basin, head in hands.

Was her daughter sick? Helena dug her wrap from the bedclothes; cold air crept under the quilts. Slipping on her doeskins, she pulled the chamber pot from under the bed, tucked aside her shift, and squatted. She had a busy day: the overseer was coming to inspect the cottage, and in the afternoon, she was due to check on Mrs. Olsson's new baby.

The chamber pot covered, she ducked from under the loft ladder then went to the kindling box for a lucifer. Striking match against hearth, she lifted the lamp glass and put flame to wick. Her daughter was face down at the table, head in the crook of her arm; a half-empty bowl of oatmeal sat by her elbow. She put a hand to her daughter's forehead. "Anna, honey, are you sick? Do you feel okay?"

Her daughter jerked away.

"Anna! What is the matter? Are you ill?" A chill ran through her. Was something going around? Please, God, not another plague. Six years ago, death was everywhere. Some folks in the village even came to her to beg for goldenseal or opium, thinking her midwife's potions could protect against the scourge. When the floods came, Anders, her man, set out for Stockholm in search of food. He never returned. She'd lost everyone, except her daughter and her brother, Peter, who had emigrated to America.

"Anna. Answer me." Her daughter was hunched over the table, unresponsive, as if her bones had been removed.

Anna mumbled unintelligibly, then rose on her elbows and gagged.

Helena grabbed the dishrag and pushed it to her daughter. "Anna? I didn't hear. What did you say?" She leaned close.

Anna mumbled. Helena rocked back, her eyes wide. "You're pregnant! My god, Anna!" She froze, fingers to mouth. Embers in the hearth popped and snapped, the kettle rumbled, somewhere a cockerel crowed. "I though . . . I thought you weren't going to be . . . be . . . uh, personal, until you were betrothed. Why didn't you tell me you were seeing someone?"

No young man in Anna's group of friends stood out. Perhaps she'd missed signs that Anna had a serious beau. But her daughter having a man was not bad; it was a start to a new family. And she'd be a grandmother at last. "So, Anna, tell me. Your man? Who is he?" Anna didn't move; she nudged her daughter's arm.

"Who is he? Do I know him?" She shook Anna's listless form. "Anna." Her voice lowered. "Who is he? I want to know—who is the father?"

Her daughter sat up and took a long careful breath. "Albrecht." Her head fell back, eyes transfixed, shrinking into herself the way she used to as a child when caught doing something.

Helena recoiled, her breath taken. "Albrecht?" she gasped. "Master Albrecht? The lord's son?" She stood and braced against the counter to steady herself. Anna with the master? How could that be? Chambermaids were forbidden to associate with the royals.

Her mind reeled; she turned and parted the window curtain. The cottages across Low Road were dark. Where the rain-rutted lane turned east toward the manor's wharf, Lake Hjalmapen glistened under a three-quarter moon; higher up, remnants of snow remained. The manor house on the rise was a dark outline of chimneys and gables; stone fences in the meadow floated in morning mist.

Could the master have . . . ? No. Her daughter was far too feisty to be overpowered by such a *tallow ketch*. But liquorish was another matter. The lord's son had access to many things that could lead a young girl astray. She let the curtain fall back.

"Anna." She nudged. "Anna, did he . . . did he . . . impose himself on you?"

Her daughter straightened. "No, Mother." Her tone was defiant. "No, he did not." She shook her head. "Nor was I besotted. It was just . . . it . . . it just happened, I guess."

Helena turned back to the window. Nothing but trouble ahead. The manor didn't tolerate unwed pregnant girls. When her daughter began to show, Anna would lose her job. And when the lord found out, anything could happen. Her thoughts began to race. She'd lose her position as the village midwife as well as the cottage and then have a new baby to care for.

A light flickered at the church; Reverend Ottosson must be up. What is the time? She looked to the mantle; the clock had stopped. If the reverend was at the church, it must be time for bells. "Anna. It's going on six."

She turned and faced her daughter. "Do you love him? Albrecht?"

"Love?" Anna fell against the chair back and stared into the fire. "Love? Oh lord, Mother, I don't know. I guess so, at the time." She propped her elbows on the table, face in hands. Regret seemed more apparent than love.

Anna glanced sideway at the window then struggled to her feet; she held her daughter's arm. "Anna. Does the master know you're pregnant? Have you told him?"

Her eyes dropped.

"Anna!" She banged her palm on the countertop, her face tight, eyes riveted. "Does the master *know*!"

Her daughter steadied against the table. "Does he know? I guess not. I haven't seen him." She put the cloth on the counter and went to the loft ladder. "I've got chambers waiting, Mother; I don't dare be late." Outside, the cockerel crowed; a sliver of sun edged over figurines on the window sill, shadows fell across pink roses.

Helena didn't dare loll around either. The cottage had to be readied for inspection, and then there was Mrs. Olsson and her new baby that afternoon. She put tea leaves in the pot then ducked into her cubby. Quilts smoothed, she picked up her chamber pot and started for the door with a building sense of guilt.

Had she been a bad mother? It was so difficult being alone. Certainly, if Anders were alive, things would be different. Almost five years without a man in her life. Not that she didn't have opportunities, though. A few men showed more than a little interest, but not one of them could hold a candle to Anders. It was a sad chaste fact she tried to ignore, but the only men in her life were Reverend Ottosson, Herr Jonsson the butcher, and Herr Bejorkman, the chemist where she bought her ether and opium.

She set the chamber pot atop the woodpile then carried an armload of split spruce inside. The figurines on the window sill watched in silence while she filled the wood bin then went to the pantry for her duster.

Anna came down the ladder, underskirts swishing around stockinged feet and padded across the rug to her boots. Helena jiggled the feather-duster as she began hooking her laces.

"Anna, just when *do* you plan on telling the master?" Her daughter appeared unconcerned.

Anna stood and smoothed her apron. "Tell him, Mother?" In front of the mirror at the door, she tucked wayward strands of blond hair under her mop cap. "It hadn't occurred to me to tell him." Face to the mirror, she gave each cheek a hard pinch. "Anyway, he'd just complicate things."

"Anna!" She struggled to keep her voice level. "Could you at least tell me when you're due?" Such an obstinate child.

Anna took her cloak from the peg and held it at arm's length. Frowning, she brushed the shoulders. "Due, Mother? I don't really know. I've got to go; I'm sorry." Drawing herself up, she sighed. "August maybe." The latch leather snapped. "Bye bye, Mother. See you tonight. Oh, could you go by Herr Jonsson's and pick up a *Herald*?" She stepped into sunshine; bells began to toll.

Helena eased the window curtain aside and watched the cockerel fly at her daughter. Anna kicked hard, and the bird flapped away. Even angry, her daughter was a lovely woman. Thick long hair, lithe, with delicate features. Some said she was the spitting image of herself. Anna swung the gate open and, with skirts pulled tight, stepped from wood plank to thatch and joined a ragged queue of gray-coated workers trudging toward the manor.

So Anna was due in August. Helena sat at the table and ticked off months on her fingers. December? Where could Anna have been with the lord's son in December? Certainly not in the manor with the girls working in pairs. And with the hovering head housekeeper? Hmm, not likely. She stroked her chin. A square of sunshine crept slowly down the wall.

The lord's Christmas party maybe. With guests coming and going and bands and people dancing, who would notice a little tête-à-tête? The lord's party *was* grand. All of Sicksjo turned out to see the swells. Beautiful women in fine robes and gowns stepped from lacquered sleighs pulled by steam-snorting Clydesdales. Regents in great coats and fur hats arrived atop prancing Arabians and joined a line of guests strutting past the somber crèche of life-size figures hovering over baby Jesus and into a manor adorned in red bows, and pinecone wreaths.

Helena remembered Anna was assigned to the ladies' cloakroom that night. She said it was like a perfumed birdcage with all the ruffles and feathers and the ladies chirping about sore feet and roving hands. The décolletage alone was worthy of a Stockholm music hall.

Yes, it was easy to imagine what a fine time it was—especially for the young people. Once the fogies were in their cups and the music loud, why not steal away to a cozy place? Maybe with some delicacies and a flask or two of grog or mead. No doubt, Anna and Albrecht saluted the holidays, toasted to good times and got cozy. Then a tie was loosened, a button undone and suddenly—a horse whinnied outside. Helena edged the window curtain back; it was the overseer: officer's hat, jodhpurs, leather boots. Where had the morning gone?

In a panic, she swept the mug and bowl to the kindling bin then tossed her wrap from chair to cubby, yelling, "Coming!" She wasn't dressed! She couldn't let him in. She threw her wrap back on and with a hand on the latch, paused for breath. Cautiously, she cracked the door open, grasping for an excuse.

The overseer bent briefly at the waist. "Good morning, Mrs. Andersson," he said glancing at the chamber pot atop the woodpile. The faint stain of mustache on his upper lip curled to a smile. "I trust you were expecting me. I have a copy of our covenant for your review and a quick—"

A flurry of screeching feathers crashed against his leg. He jerked back, kicking, slipped off the planks, and fell against the gate. The cockerel flapped away shrieking.

"Oh, Herr Overseer! I'm so sorry." Helena opened the door a half-inch and coughed, then coughed again, hand to mouth. The overseer stepped back. "I'm afraid I've come down with something, sir." She coughed again for good measure. "Please, would it be possible for you to leave the papers?"

The overseer looked relieved. "Certainly, Mrs. Andersson." He unbuckled the strap on his bag. "Yes. And we should inspect the lord's cottage once you're feeling better." He rummaged through papers then extracted a sheaf. "You'll find it's much the same as our previous agreement—other than a slight increase in the tithing. Unfortunately, the manor has yet to recover from our devastating plague." He stretched forward and thrust the papers at her. "I trust you will not find this burdensome."

The Lord's crest in red wax showed on the top sheet and above multiple scrawled signatures, *Midwife* of *Sicksjo, Covenants and Duties*. A red ribbon laced through a corner and was tied in a bow. "Thank you, kind sir." Her voice was a croak. "I will tend to this promptly."

She watched the overseer go through the gate and then dropped at the table, her hands trembling. She had lied; what was wrong with her? The cottage closed in like a web. Her eyes fell on the Bible on the top shelf. Yes, read the Holy Book, it always calmed her.

She stretched for the Bible; a drop of water sprayed her cheek. A leak? She ran her hand along the shelf. Yes, water! Another drip splattered on her hand. Her Bible was sodden, pages stuck together. Her stomach plunged. Another disaster. Such a poor Lutheran; she couldn't even care for God's Book. She sagged into the chair. Fortunately, the church had a Bible; she could read there.

She put on her underskirts and second-best overdress then ran a brush through her snarl of gray hair wondering if she should wear her bonnet with the big blue ribbon. She hesitated with her hand on the door latch. The overseer? Was he still around? She went to the window and fingered the curtain aside. There he was, just up Low Road, with . . . Mrs. Wikborg and her daughter-in-law? Yes, it was them, nodding and holding their skirts tight. They shouldn't be out there too long. She dropped on the chest, eyed the clock and then went for the key.

The cockerel crowed; she peeped through the kitchen window. Mrs. Wikborg and Freja were at the gate scowling at the bird. "Coming." She threw her wrap around her shoulders. "Coming."

"Well, gracious sakes," She opened the door and shooed the bird. "What a pleasant surprise."

Mrs. Wikborg stepped back. "We heard you were feeling poorly, Mrs. Andersson." Slight empathy showed from under a burgundy shell laced in black ribbon and ties. "We shan't come in, but Freja and I are on our way to market. We thought you might be in need of something." Freja was a bland girl married to Mrs. Wikborg's son, Ingvar.

Freja stood silently behind her mother-in-law, gloved hands clasped over a worsted navy skirt trimmed in pale blue lace with a matching wrap. A feathery turquoise plume rose from her navy bonnet. The Wikborgs had a penchant for fashion, and with Herr Wikborg a solicitor for the lord, the family could well indulge themselves.

Helena covered her mouth and coughed into her hand. "How kind of you. Anna was just there, but thank you so much for thinking of me."

"Well then, you're taken care of." Mrs. Wikborg brushed a velveteen hand at the hem of her overdress, then groaning, picked a speck from the embroidery. "Mud. Why the manor doesn't put in a boardwalk is beyond me."

Freja nodded agreement. "Truly, Mother Wikborg—but remember the plague." The plume on her bonnet bobbed caution.

"Yes, the plague." Helena tried not to roll her eyes; the plague was six years ago and the manor's excuses had worn thin. She croaked agreement. "Yes, seems like just yesterday."

"Well, we're off then, Mrs. Andersson. Come Freja." Mrs. Wikborg turned to her daughter-in-law.

"But Mother Wikborg." Freja held up a finger. "Our invitation. Don't forget our invitation."

"Ah, yes." Mrs. Wikborg flicked away her lapse with a gloved hand. "Yes, Mrs. Andersson, the committee. We're forming a mother's committee. It's Reverend Ottosson's idea. We do hope you will join us."

"A committee?" She leaned forward. Mrs. Wikborg's eyes widened as the door opened; she stepped back into Freja; Freja stumbled from wood plank to wet sod.

Helena had been on enough committees to know they were not her cup of tea. Too often meetings dissolved into grandstanding or the airing of petty grievances. But she kept an open mind. "A committee for what?"

Freja raised a gloved finger. "A committee to stem the tide of illegitimate babies, Mrs. Andersson. Having the village midwife on our committee would so strengthen our message." Her plume did an enthusiastic jig.

"How relevant." Helena coughed into her hand. "May I give you an answer at Sunday service? I'm feeling a bit woozy at the moment."

Chastity before marriage *was* one of Reverend Ottosson's recurring themes. He found endless metaphors to espouse celibacy before matrimony, as well as impending doom that would inevitably befall upon those who failed to heed his words. She agreed with him about chastity but was skeptical that God levied retribution. Her observation was that humans were no more significant in God's eyes than any other of His earthly creatures. But she did know about girls getting pregnant. Whatever their circumstances, she didn't ask. It was never any of her business—until the morning bells.

"Why certainly." Mrs. Wikborg tootled goodbye. "Come, Freja; I'm sure you'll feel better, Mrs. Andersson. It's probably nothing more than a touch of ptomaine."

Freja waved. "Until Sunday, Mrs. Andersson." She clutched her skirt and minced from plank to thatch. "See you then."

She eased the door closed and collapsed in the armchair. The square of sunshine had disappeared—the figurines on the window sill brooded in shadow. What a disastrous day. A bad mother, a bad Lutheran, and now the whole village will think she's a dangerous cook. Bells sounded midday; time to get ready for Mrs. Olsson. Just as well she didn't get to church with everything so out of kilter; not a good day to be asking God for anything.

∞

2 April 1874

Daylight crept in. Her eyes were sand-filled; she hadn't slept well, did nothing but toss and turn. She tried to reason with Anna after dinner last night but to no avail. They were so at loggerheads. Her daughter was far too cocksure for a girl barely twenty-one years old. She would *not* understand she would lose her job when the manor found out she was pregnant. Not only that, but she'd be branded a scarlet woman as well. And that would be the least of it.

Sliding the chamber pot back under her bed, she shuffled to the fireplace. The hearth was cold; an empty mug and a crust of bread sat next to the basin. If the clock was right, Anna had left early. As the fire caught, she dragged a chair close and sat with feet tucked under. What to do, what to do? First, clear her head, get a hold of herself. Her eyes fell on her Bible sitting on a folded towel. She sagged.

Her daughter's predicament stalked her like a wild animal. She needed to sit quietly and read the Good Book. Talking with God always set her head straight. If she hurried, she could go to church before making her rounds. The weather wasn't great, but at least it wasn't raining. She wouldn't dare going into God's house looking like a gypsy from some dank encampment. After filling a pitcher with warm water, she took a tin of soap into the pantry and stepped into the washtub with her hair up. Now, what to wear?

At the boardwalk, she stopped and scanned the commons; not a soul in sight; she didn't have to be pleasant to anyone. No one at the gazebo or the village well either. Mrs. Bejorkman waved from her sitting room window above the apothecary. She wiggled her fingers good morning and stepped under the portico, closing her umbrella.

Herr Jonsson, the butcher, spotted her when she scurried past his window. He started from behind the meat counter with his finger raised; she returned his wave and mouthed *later*. She didn't dare stop; Herr Jonsson always had some story to share. She could apologize later.

At the end of the boardwalk, she stopped and eyed the best way; nothing but puddles and mud. But the cooper's shed was open; she could cut through there. Herr Lindberg was at the furnace with his back to her, and his apprentice—what was his name?—was pumping the bellows. She had to be quick though; Herr Lindberg was every bit as talkative as Herr Jonsson. She darted.

Stomping hard on the church walk with skirts pulled aside, she scraped her boots on the iron bar; her second-best overdress was a prudent choice. But the sun was breaking through, a much better day to talk with God. She gave her boots a final stomp and heaved the church door open.

In the narthex, she listened; nothing, only the sound of her breathing. The church felt empty, hollow, the nave a dim cavern, pews undisturbed in cold light; she had God to herself.

Down the aisle she reconsidered. People of her ilk didn't go on altars or read gilt-bound Bibles or for that matter, even sat in front pews. She retreated to a middling pew and after folding her cloak atop her umbrella, eased down trying to keep weight off her hip. Rheumatism made it so difficult to pray properly. She cleared her throat and closed her eyes. "Dear Father, Merciful God in Heaven, please hear my—"

"Why Mrs. Andersson! How nice to see you." *The pastor*! She almost swooned.

Reverend Ottosson gazed serenely down upon her, his thin white fingers intertwined across a black waistcoat. His face showed concern. "Are you well, Mrs. Andersson? I heard you were feeling poorly." A pectoral cross dangled from a soiled collaret.

Reverend was a diminutive man of uncertain years. Sunday mornings, he moved between altar and pulpit in a tired gray alb, as he espoused conservative Lutheran orthodoxy. He bobbed and nodded his head emphasizing proclamations as if God above were pulling strings attached directly to his ears. But when a stillborn baby came into her hands, she was always grateful for his presence.

"Reverend! My goodness, you about scared the life right out of me." She strained upward and eased into the pew. "I am feeling fine today, thank you for asking. Just a bit of ptomaine, I guess." There. She admitted it.

"Ah, good." The pastor relaxed. He was cautious approaching a woman praying by herself in the early morning. Too often it was a sign of family difficulty. "And everything is well with you?"

"Oh, Reverend, don't ask." She deflected his question with a feeble wave.

"I hope there is not a problem, Mrs. Andersson." His benign expression showed concern. "Perhaps I can be of assistance."

"Oh, Reverend." She clenched hard against the truth. She *did* want his advice, but how could she? She dare not say a word about Anna being pregnant—or about the father. Her eyes fell. "It's . . . it's just that . . . everything has . . . has—oh, I don't know." She fought back a sob. "It's . . . it's my Bible, Reverend, the roof . . . it leaked . . . my Bible is ruined."

"Your Bible, ruined? A tragedy, Mrs. Andersson." He suppressed a smile. "But perhaps not one of insurmountable magnitude. I believe I have a Bible you may have. And if you have a moment when you finish your prayers, perhaps you would come to my study. I'd like to ask your advice on a matter."

"My advice, Reverend?" She was flattered; it was rare to be asked for advice. Most often, she was on the receiving end. "Oh, thank you, Reverend. I had just finished."

He helped her to her feet. "I understand the Olssons have a new child. It's so nice to see the parish grow."

He took her things and handed her into his study "Would you take a cup of tea, Mrs. Andersson? I have water on." He moved a pile of papers from the side chair to the floor and motioned for her to sit.

"Tea?" She was doubly flattered. "How nice."

Reverend's study was a dim retreat of undusted books and yellowed manuscripts, smelling faintly of stale pipe smoke. His desk held a dog-eared volume entitled, *Inevitable Death: Redemption and Futility of the Human Condition*; a slew of scribbled notes surrounded a brass lamp with a soot-stained chimney.

Reverend Ottosson returned with two steaming mugs and a deep scowl. "I'm afraid the milk has soured." He elbowed a clear spot on the desk. "And your daughter, Anna, Mrs. Andersson, I trust she is well? We don't see much of her."

"I know, I've tried everything." Anna was skeptical of theological dogma and was more prone to reason and rationale than belief. She didn't believe a church, or a congregation or approbation from the self-righteous was necessary to adhere to the Golden Rule. She had warned her daughter time and time again, that not attending service would have people suspecting she was either a pagan or a disciple of the Devil, or both.

"Anna is just fine. Thank you for asking." She took a careful sip of tea. Off to a bad start, lying to a man of God.

"I'm pleased to hear that." The pastor blew across the lip of his mug. "Peter is well too? He's been gone how long now?"

"Six years, but it seems like a lifetime. He is well though, thank you. And still the consummate bachelor." That was as far as she knew; he hadn't answered her last letter yet.

He frowned. "Why so many people abandoned our beautiful Sweden for a country as raw and barbaric as America is beyond me." Reverend leaned forward, his chin unusually firm. "The promises that were made were criminal." He nodded twice to establish certainty.

She remembered the recruiters. They came in throngs with foreign accents promising top-dollar jobs and all expenses paid. But Peter was happy. He seemed pleased to be in America and never mentioned being cheated. He was someplace called Muskegon; the name had something to do with Indians. The *Stockholm Herald* recently ran an article about Indian wars in America but Peter never mentioned anything about Indians or fighting. She thought it best not to mention he made twenty-five dollars a month—ten times what he made in the village.

The pastor raised a finger. "I'm working on a sermon at this very moment to address the many opportunities that exist right here. There is no need for anyone to leave the village for some god-forsaken country." He nestled his mug into the scatter of notes. "Now, Mrs. Andersson, I'd to talk to you about something else; a committee the village desperately needs; a mothers' committee devoted to morality." His tenor notched higher—his expression hardened. "Illegitimacy is a problem sweeping the country. Unfortunately, we have the failing right here in Sicksjo as well." He jabbed a finger at an imaginary congregation in the rafters. "Intimacy among our young people is far too prevalent. It's a problem that must be corrected." He paused and measured her expression. "I hope you'll be a voice on that committee, Mrs. Andersson."

Heat rose in her cheeks. "Well, I'm . . . I'm most honored, Reverend, but. . . ."

He smiled. "You're a respected voice in this community, Mrs. Andersson. And you do know about the . . . er . . . consequences of these situations. I do hope you have the time." He nodded encouragement. "Mrs. Wikborg and her daughter-in-law have agreed to serve."

"Still, Reverend . . ."

"I know, I know, Mrs. Andersson. Finding time is difficult; everyone is so busy these days. But think of the benefit to the young people."

"It's not just the time, Reverend Ottosson. It's just that . . . that. . . ."

"Yes?"

What could she say? She couldn't keep lying. "Oh, Reverend. It's not the time, it's—I'm so embarrassed—it's Anna. She's pregnant—I'm so sorry."

The pastor's eyes froze. "Anna is with child?" His brows pulled together; he leaned back. "Well, now." His face relaxed. "Anna is certainly not the first to err. God is forgiving of His children."

He was right about Anna not being the first to err, and hopefully, about God's forgiveness too. Freja's baby was far from being premature. But more importantly, Freja and the other girls in the village who sinned, sinned with men they *could* marry.

The pastor leaned over the desk and laid his hand on hers. "You are blessed to have a grandchild on the way, Mrs. Andersson." He beamed. "The parish has many fine young men. Who is the fortunate one?"

She pursed her lips; risky territory. A direct answer was not wise; she didn't dare say it was the lord's son. "But there is a small problem."

"A problem?" The pastor stopped nodding. A look of concentration replaced serenity. He squinted as if eyeing prey. "A small problem?"

"Well, yes." Her eyes dropped. "Anna has doubts about the father." The pastor's eyebrows rose. "Yes," she repeated, "Anna's gotten herself in quite a fix."

Reverend Ottosson seemed puzzled. His brows knitted, he stared into his hands as if they contained a snarl of riddles. "She doesn't want to marry the young man?"

She shook her head, eyes filling. "It's so hard being a single mother." She fingered a handkerchief from her sleeve and wiped a tear. "I feel terrible, I should have done better with Anna." There, she took the blame.

Reverend Ottosson shrugged. "Well, I guess Anna is not the first girl to make a poor decision." He squinted one eye in deep concentration. "That's why the committee is so important, Mrs. Andersson. We need to celebrate the Good Book and to bring propriety and celibacy to the village. And, of course, we need to counter that Ellen Key person. She does women no service."

Ellen Key's free-love scandal was sweeping Sweden. Miss. Key believed women were sexual creatures and, just like men, wanted and enjoyed physical love. Sex was not a sin, nor was nudity, or coupling for pleasure immoral. She actually accused King Oskar of being two-faced about coitus—in an open letter to the *Stockholm Herald*, no less. Of course, the king was outraged and branded Ellen Key the Phallus of Sweden.

Reverend jabbed his finger on the desk top. "The time to strike illegitimacy is now, Mrs. Andersson. King Oskar, by the Grace of God, has finally acted: Unwed mothers will be sent to the prison in Landskordia."

She blanched. "Prison?"

"I'm afraid so, Mrs. Andersson." He leaned forward, elbows on the desk; notes fluttered to the floor. "Anna should marry her young man or she will have to give the baby to a farm." His chair creaked threateningly.

"A baby farm?" She could hardly utter the words. Baby farms took the money and let the babies starve. "Oh, how horrible." She shook her head. "I'm sure Anna would never let her baby go to a farm."

She fingered her mug. "Perhaps there is some other contingency." Her voice rang hollow. "Maybe there's a shelter or a home, someplace Anna could go for a few months?"

"I think not." The pastor took a sip of tea and shrugged. "The king's edict is quite clear. The Lord is obligated to send the constable." He set his mug down and leaned closer. "Mrs. Andersson, if Anna doesn't marry, the constable will haul her off to Landskordia, and the baby will end up at a farm anyway." He leaned back in the chair, his head bobbing slowly. "Yes, Anna would be well advised to reconsider her young man."

She sat stunned, dumbly twisting and untwisting her handkerchief. This was all unexpected.

"So." Reverend Ottosson fumbled with his watch fob. "I understand your concern about the committee, Mrs. Andersson. I hope both you and Anna will reconsider. Marriage is her best—" His face hardened. "Marriage is by *far* her best option."

She fought to understand what she heard. "Reverend, my mind is awhirl. This is all so sudden." She tucked her handkerchief in her sleeve and stood, hand braced against the desk. "Thank you for the tea." Her voice was weak and uncertain. "And I am so very sorry about the committee."

The pastor nodded forgiveness. "And we need a Bible, don't we?" He went to the books lining the wall and pulled a volume from the bottom shelf. "Mm, yes, here we are." He blew dust. "This Bible belonged to. . . ." He opened the cover. ". . . the Ljunggren family. Did you know them?" He put a finger on a page. "The family history is right here. Terrible tragedy, the plague." He snapped the Bible shut.

In the narthex the pastor helped her with her cloak then took her hand in his. "You will find your answer in God, Mrs. Andersson." He called Anna a poor child and said he would pray for her salvation. He pushed the door open and handed her the umbrella. "Don't forget this."

∞

That evening, she stood at the basin swirling her hand in dishwater searching for an errant knife. Her tired reflection in the window stared back; her daughter waited behind her, dish towel in hand.

Anna was nattering about the head housekeeper and a coachman as if she didn't have a care in the world. A pretty penny her daughter had no idea of the king's decree—or the prison in Landskordia. She did not want another evening of argument, but Anna had to know what Reverend said. The situation would not simply resolve itself. Certainly, no good would come if reality were ignored. She handed the knife to her daughter.

"I saw Reverend Ottosson today." She squeezed water from the dish-rag and wiped the table watching her daughter from the corner of her eye. "He asked about you."

"Oh? And what did our man of God have to say?" Anna flipped the knife into the tray. "Pray tell."

She sighed. This was no time to be flippant. If her daughter preferred to be glib, she might as well get right to the point. "Reverend said you'd better get married."

Anna blinked. Her face turned hard, eyes narrowed. "Married?" She wrapped the word in suspicion. "Why would he want me to get married?"

Helena's heart beat in her ears, she continued wiping; embers on the hearth snapped and popped.

"Mother, what did you tell him?"

She turned back to the basin, her stomach knotted.

"Mother, did you tell him I'm pregnant?"

Anna's reflection stared at her, arms on hips. She turned. "Yes, I did." The words were flat, final. "And it's a good thing I did."

Anna went stiff, her face red. She clenched the towel, knuckles white. "You told him I'm pregnant? I can't believe you told that man anything about me, Mother—especially that!" She threw the dish towel on the table. "What I do is none of his business." She paced to the floor, her eyes fierce. "Did you tell him it was the master?"

She shook her head. "No, I didn't. It doesn't make any difference."

She leaned against the counter and folded her arms. "King Oscar has decreed that any unmarried, pregnant girl is to be sent to the prison in Landskordia. If anyone finds out you're pregnant, the lord will send the constable." She untied her apron with shaking hands. "Don't you understand, Anna? The baby will go to a *farm*. Don't you understand that?"

Anna spun away, fists clenched, shoulders heaving. Lowing in the yard across the way rippled the silence.

"Anna, we mustn't be at cross purposes. We've got to put our heads together and decide what to do—what we *can* do." She was begging.

"Do? Do?" The words snapped out. "I know what *I'm* going to do." She banged a chair back under the table. "I'm leaving. I've had enough of this village, enough of the manor, enough of the lord and his . . . his whatever. It's my problem anyway, Mother. I'll deal with it myself, thank you."

"Leave?" The word stuck in her throat. "But where would you go?"

"Stockholm." Her head flipped defiantly.

"Stockholm? Who do you know in Stockholm?" There was no family in Stockholm, not even a friend.

"At the moment no one. I posted a letter to Mrs. Key's organization." Anna snatched her cloak from the peg. "I expect she'll have me." She tossed her cloak around her shoulders and banged the latch open. "Don't wait up, Mother."

Helena collapsed at the table. Her daughter always cut things loose and just let chips scatter. She never had regrets; she just moved on. There was no use waiting up; the discussion, if it could be called that, was over. She banked the fire and turned down the lamp. Maybe Anna would be more rational now that she knew about Landskordia.

She climbed into her cubby and pulled the quilt up tight. Visions of her daughter behind prison walls racked her mind, the baby starving at a farm, her twilight years as a lonely old woman haunted by memories. She watched reflections dance across *fleur-de-lis*, her thoughts roiling. She rolled over and closed her eyes; prison bars appeared. She squeezed back the image; the pastor appeared: *You will find your answer in God.* Yes, she needed Him more than ever.

∞

In the morning, she knelt in a back pew searching for the right words. Did He need to know that Anna sinned on His Son's birthday? Would

He understand why Anna couldn't marry the Master, and about the decree, and Landskordia? It was hard enough to think clearly, and the birds twittering in the arches were of no help.

The boom of the church door echoed through the narthex. Moments later, Reverend Ottosson appeared from the chancel, crossed the altar waving to her, and disappeared. Bells rang; sparrows darted and dived; twigs and feathers fell.

The pastor reappeared and came up the aisle wiping his hands on a towel. "Ah, good morning, Mrs. Andersson. I trust you are well this fine day. Things are working out at home, I hope?"

"Good morning, Rev—" She labored to the seat. "Good morning, Reverend, thank you for asking. I wish I could say that they were." His waistcoat was missing a button.

The pastor showed concern. "Perhaps a confession would ease the turmoil, Mrs. Andersson." He tucked the towel under his arm and offered an open hand. "I would be pleased to take your confession. We can pray for Anna together."

"Thank you, Reverend. Please forgive me, I was just praying for Anna. Praying that God in His goodness will not send her and her baby to Landskordia."

"Anna has not reconsidered her young man?" His eyebrows furrowed. "How unfortunate. Love can blossom within a family relationship."

"Yes, I suppose." She motioned for him to sit. "Everything is so difficult right now."

The pastor lowered into the pew, his voice soft. "Our Savior acts in many ways, Mrs. Andersson." He swept a vague arm toward the altar. "He delivers His riches to the poor and comforts the infirmed." His voice rose. "And He levies retribution to those who know Him not." His head bobbed confidently with each assertion. "Anna's imprudence will not please our Master." He looked to the arches as if expecting to see the Almighty frowning down upon them. "For Anna's sake and the baby's sake, she should marry, and marry within the church."

She did not disagree with marrying within the church. But it was all so unfair. It was not just Anna's doing. After all, being personal did take two. Her daughter wasn't a strumpet or a tart. She was a bright, responsible young woman, although perhaps a bit overconfident. A sparrow fluttered to the pew backrest and cocked its head at her.

And why should Anna alone bear God's retribution? Or the king's, for that matter? Why was it men, Reverend Ottosson included, always believed indiscretions were a woman's making? The sparrow shot upward, leaving a splat of white. She glared at the dropping. Women always took the blame. How unfair. What rot! "Reverend." Her cheeks were flushed. "It's the master. The master is the father. That's why Anna can't marry." There, it was out. Now God *and* Reverend Ottosson both knew.

His eyes opened in astonishment. Reverend Ottosson leaned back in the pew speechless, face ashen, hands fingering the towel. A sparrow dove from above, another chased. The master was the oldest son of the lord appointed by King Oskar II and held great power. He was the arbiter of laws and local disputes, and surely, his eldest son could not be publicly shamed.

Helena watched his eyes; he was never at a loss for words. "Reverend." She took his arm. "I want an audience with His Lordship." The pastor's eyes grew large. "And I would like you to accompany me. I need your help; Anna needs your help." Reverend looked ill. She shook his arm. "Please. We cannot allow this unfairness to stand."

"The lord?" Apprehension had his eyes. "Mm." His head slowly see-sawed as if some complicated twist had jammed his mind. He turned and wiped the bird dropping with his towel. "Mm . . . the lord?"

"Yes, the lord. He deserves to know he has a grandchild on the way."

The pastor nodded slowly as if experiencing a vision. His eyes narrowed. "Going to the lord is not the best of ideas, Mrs. Andersson. Asking for an audience will bring confrontation." He gestured to her. "A confrontation that *everyone* will ultimately regret. The lord will not be pleased."

She met his eye. "Nor the king."

"Nor the king, Mrs. Andersson, nor the king." His face sagged. "But." He paused for affect. "But an accusation against the lordship's son is entirely another matter. The lord will say the baby is not the master's and that Anna is a. . . ." His voice trailed off. "It is a delicate situation, Mrs. Andersson—a most delicate situation."

"Good grief! Who in the village does not know of the young man's proclivities?" The pastor knew; it showed in his eyes. "The master is every bit as accountable as Anna. Privilege should not be a means to escape responsibility."

"Escape what?" He wagged a dismissive hand. "Escape gossip? How does one prove the allegations of . . . of . . . of what? Isn't it just her word against his?" He nodded twice to validate the point.

"Well, then, Anna can accompany us. Perhaps the master himself would like to tell his father what he gave Anna for Christmas."

Reverend Ottosson looked as if armed Vikings were charging from the altar. "But . . . but . . . ." He gestured hopelessly.

"Reverend, the king's decree; is not sauce for the goose, sauce for the gander?" She took a deep breath. "By all rights, the lord should insist the master marry Anna."

The pastor's eyes went wide. "Now, now, Mrs. Andersson." She did not realize how angry she had become.

Tears welled; she blinked. She was a good Lutheran and tithed every bit she could afford and she worked church receptions and was a reliable volunteer at village fairs and festivals. That deserved some consideration. "I only want just due for my daughter. Please help me, Reverend Ottosson. Help Anna." Her voice was a plaintive bleat.

The pastor sighed. "Perhaps, Mrs. Andersson, perhaps. If there is a will, there must be a way. Let us pray to the Almighty for guidance. Possibly something can be done; give me some time."

She was not to say a word to anyone, not a word. "If confidence can be guaranteed, it would be much easier to reason with the lord. Secrecy is paramount." And he cautioned to keep Anna covered. "If anyone at the manor finds she is in the family way, it will be the lord's desk where that gossip will stop." He shuddered.

Reverend took her arm and walked her to the door, saying patience was needed. "And," he warned, "you have no promises, only my prayers."

She walked home feeling immensely better. A miracle was needed and the right man was on the job. Secrecy was paramount. Did she dare tell her daughter?

∞

3 June 1874

Foreboding slowed time to a crawl. Days inched by, each night more intolerable than the last. The clop of a passing cart sent her heart racing;

the relentless ticking of the clock stoked her all-consuming fear for her daughter. She redoubled her prayers, and showed contrition by joining Reverend's Mother's Committee.

Finally, after what seemed eons, he approached her after Sunday service and said he had an audience with the lord the following afternoon. He would come by the cottage immediately after.

Morning crept slowly to afternoon; the interval between tick and tock interminable. She held vigil praying and avoided the window. Water for tea she started far too early; the cottage was overheated, the soot vexing.

Crowing in the yard was followed by a knock on the door. She slammed Ljunggren's Bible shut and ran to the door, flinging it open. Her knees went weak; Reverend was alone. She motioned him to the table, choked with relief. "Tea?"

The pastor demurred. "Thank you, no, Mrs. Andersson. I must get straight to the point. I only have a moment—committees, trustees, paperwork, you know, the usual." He nodded twice to affirm his haste. "But I do have excellent news. The lord is disposed to see to our matter."

Relief overwhelmed her; she dropped in a chair. "The lord's not sending the constable? Anna won't have to go to prison?" God *did* answer her prayers. She dabbed tears from the corner of an eye.

Reverend sat across from her quietly smiling until she steadied herself. "Yes, Mrs. Andersson, God has blessed you and your daughter." He studied her hard. "But please understand, there are conditions."

"Conditions?" Of course, conditions. She should have expected them. "What kind of conditions, Reverend?"

"Just two. First, you must swear to tell absolutely no one of the arrangement—under penalty." He waited until she acknowledged consent. When she happily nodded, he leaned forward, elbows on the table. "And you and your daughter must leave the village."

Her stomach knotted. "Leave the village, Reverend? Our home? Where would we go? We have no money, no family."

"The lord will provide what is necessary."

"Money to leave?" She swallowed hard and tried to clear the swelling in her throat. "A bitter condition, Reverend. This is our village. It's the only thing we know. Certainly there is an alternative."

"I'm afraid there is no alternative, Mrs. Andersson." The pastor leaned back and crossed his arms. "No, the lord was firm. There is no other choice." His faced hardened to a frown. "You would be wise not to decline this accommodation."

"But where will we go?" She shivered. "Please, not someplace far. Stockholm? Malmo, maybe?"

"Hamburg."

"Hamburg? Where is Hamburg? It must be a very small village."

"Hamburg is in Germany.

"Germany? That Hamburg?" The revelation took her breath away. Germany wasn't a *terrible* place. She had read it was quite advanced and led the world in chemicals and medicine, and mass producing steel and iron. But still.

"My stars, Reverend, we know no one there. We don't speak the language. We wouldn't survive."

"The manor has its ways; arrangements will be made." The pastor's face brightened. "And Germany is Lutheran. You will be among our kind."

Her mind raced. "Reverend, could we go to America instead? Peter is there. We'd have a place."

"The Lord was quite specific; Hamburg." The pastor folded his hands on the table. "Hamburg or—"

She blanched. "Or—" The word stuck in her throat. "Or Landskordia?"

The pastor shrugged.

"This is terribly unfair, Reverend. It is hardly a just bargain." A strand of soot floated between them.

"Well, it is a choice, Mrs. Andersson, and I appreciate it is not a good one." He pushed up from the chair. "But it is a resolution short of prison and a baby farm. And you will be met in Germany." His tone was confident, reassuring. "Money and the necessary papers will await you in Gőteborg along with the name of the person who will assist you in Hamburg. "

"Gőteborg?"

"Yes, Sweden's port of entry. Customs is there. Everything comes and goes through Gőteborg." He offered his hand. "Do we have a bargain, Mrs. Andersson?"

Her mind reeled; words wouldn't form. What choice was there? Germany or Landskordia. She nodded hopelessly and took his hand.

"Good." Reverend looked relieved. He put his hand over hers and pumped. "Good. Good, Mrs. Andersson. Our Father in Heaven *is* a much better choice than the constable." His head bobbed reassurance.

∞

THAT NIGHT, AFTER dishes were put away, she pulled two mugs from the shelf and turned to her daughter. "How about some tea?" She set the mugs on the table and moved the kettle from the trammel to the counter. "Have you heard from Stockholm yet?"

Anna glanced briefly over the top of the *Herald* and went back to reading.

"Anna?" Her daughter's attitude was so annoying. This whole business was her doing, and she was behaving like a mistreated child. She could at least be civil.

"Anna! Enough!" She banged her mug on the table and snatched the paper from her daughter. "I asked you a question, young lady. Have you heard from Mrs. Key?"

Anna scowled. "Yes."

"Well?"

"She doesn't take pregnant girls." Anna flipped her chin as if it was Mrs. Key's loss. "Apparently, pregnant girls give a bad image." She shrugged. "Free love and all that."

She poured tea. "Well, now what?" The gall of that child was simply amazing.

"I don't know yet." Her daughter's tone was nonchalant, as if she had an abundance of opportunities. "I'll probably go to Stockholm anyway."

"And do what?"

"I'll find something."

"What about the baby?"

"Mother, I said I'd find something."

"I don't think so."

Her daughter's surprise turned to suspicion. "What?"

"Reverend Ottosson was here today."

"Reverend Ottosson?" Anna's face went dark.

"The lord knows about you and the master."

Amazement spread across her daughter's face. "You told the lord? About me . . . and the master?" She stiffened.

"I told Reverend Ottosson, he told the lord."

Anna looked dumbstruck; a split collapsed in the hearth, embers flew, the clock relentlessly pounded the silence.

"Why do you think the constable hasn't come for you?" She watched her daughter's face go blank. "I asked Reverend to speak on our behalf with the lord. He did, and I agreed to an arrangement that keeps you out of prison and the baby from a farm." She took a cautious sip of tea. "Fortunately for you and the baby, the lord decided to keep this whole business quiet." Her daughter sat rigid, as if struck from stone.

"You and I are out. Out of the cottage, out of the village, out of Sweden." Her eyes bored into Anna's. "The manor is engaging another midwife, and you, my dear, will be out of a job by week's end."

Her daughter rocked with disbelief, mouth working soundlessly. She gathered herself and set her chin. "Tell the preacher, never mind. I'm going to Stockholm—by myself."

"No, you're not. You're going to Germany with me."

"Germany?" Anna eyes widened in disbelief.

She nodded. "That's what I agreed to. Germany."

"Well, then go. I'm not going to Germany under any conditions. Germans are horrible—they're all a bunch of stiff-back braggarts."

She shrugged. "Germany is Lutheran."

"Good. You go to Germany. The lord doesn't have to know I'm going to Stockholm."

"I agreed to go to Germany. You're going with me."

"Mother, I'm twenty-one years old, a grown woman. I'll make my own decisions."

"Let me give you a choice then. Germany or Landskordia."

Her daughter's eyebrows went up. "You'd tell the lord?"

"It's your decision."

"Can't we go to America instead? Uncle Pete will take us in."

"Anna, use your head." She got up and emptied her mug in the slop bucket. "Even if we could fool the manor, how could you and I, two women without a man, possibly get to America by ourselves, even if you *weren't* pregnant?"

Her daughter sagged in the chair, sullen and resentful. "And one last thing." She leveled a finger. "If either of us breathes a word to anyone about this, you're off to prison. Do you understand?"

∞

Weeks passed and both Anna and the iris along the fence bloomed. She had conquered her morning sickness and entered strict confinement, which like her girth, grew to hostile resentment. When the ferry to Gőteborg finally arrived, her demeanor was that of a wounded she-bear.

Helena managed their exodus from the village quite well—considering. She spoke in confidence with Mrs. Wikborg after Sunday service and confided that Anna had accepted a position with Ellen Key's organization in Stockholm. She would be following her daughter once the details were finalized. It was an outright lie, of course, although so satisfying that she could not resist mentioning a mythical and recently refurbished *pied*-à-*terre* and promised Mrs. Wikborg a visit. They had oodles of room and she would post a note once they settled in.

Word of her leaving spread quickly. She received many expressions of good luck, some of envy, and most accompanied by subtle inquiries as to her belongings. The steamer trunk she got in exchange for Anders' old musket, the four lamps, the chest, and the chickens. The rug brought three öre, another öre for the kettle and Dutch oven, and generous Mrs. Gunvoldsson from church, gave her two full kroners for the table and all the chairs, no matter the loose bindings.

Finally, bags packed, she waited by the door for Reverend; thank God he volunteered to take them to the wharf; it was pouring rain. The trunk was packed with china bowls and a tea set wrapped in the curtains. The wraps and overskirts were followed by the tea kettle and mugs for easy access. Cloaks and tarred hats waited atop the trunk.

Reverend warned there would be no markets until Gőteborg, which with luck, was three days away. So as not to be beholden to strangers, she packed cheese, bread, and sausage in Anders' old rucksack. Toothbrushes, clean underskirts, stockings, and privy-paper were in the two canvas bags, and she had the manor's voucher plus her kroners sewn in her underskirt pocket.

Eyes cupped against window she looked into the downpour; a wagon was coming down Low Road. "Anna, it's time; Reverend Ottosson is here." Or he would be shortly. "Check and make sure we've got everything before you come down." She looked in the pantry one last time and ran her hand along the shelf over the hearth. A drip splattered; she shrugged.

Reverend's buckboard was the one he used to take coffins to the burying grounds. Rivulets of water ran from his hat to his shoulders; the mule pumped clouds of steam into the deluge.

With his offered arm, she struggled to the seat and opened her umbrella. Anna sat alongside and she pulled her daughter close; Anna shrugged away wallowing in resentment. Her life had cracked like ice on a pond and she plunged into the cold, bitter depths of reality.

At the wharf, Reverend reined the mule alongside a warren of stacked crates and baled sorghum backed against towering mounds of cordwood.

A boat was moored at the dock, held by lines thick as a man's wrist. A chipped and blistered hulk roughly a hundred feet long held a pock-marked wheelhouse topped by a stubby guy-wired smokestack; two wood benches leaned against the wheelhouse. Above the benches, in faded black letters, was the name *Elaina*. Reverend sent her to look for the captain while he unloaded the bags.

Dodging puddles, she stopped at the gangway and scanned the deck. Several crates of chickens were stacked in the stern; maybe the *Elaina* wasn't the ferry to Gőteborg.

A man in yellow oilskins emerged from a deck hatch. His hat swept down his back like a broad yellow tongue. She waved. "Captain, sir! Captain!"

"No Ma'am. I ain't the cap'n." The man pointed to another yellow slicker coming around the wheelhouse. "That'd be him."

"Captain! Captain!" She scurried back to the gangway, waving. "Sir, are you expecting passengers to Gőteborg?"

The captain touched the brim of his sou'wester. "No, ma'am. This barge don't go to Gőteborg."

"Oh dear." A trickle of water drizzled down her neck. "I understood the manor had arranged passage for two to Gőteborg." She pulled her collar tighter.

"Sorry, ma'am. Don't know nothing about that." He wiped water from his face. "I can take you to Orebro for twenty-five őre. There's another barge from there to—"

"Gőteborg?"

"No ma'am." The captain dug in his slicker and pulled out his watch. "To Thollattan, the other side of Lake Vanern. There's a canal packet to Gőteborg from there." He waved to his crew and pointed to a piling. "Sven, the lines."

She held up a finger. "Please, one moment, kind sir. I'll be back immediately." She ran for the wagon, pain shooting from hip to back.

Anna was on the wagon seat, a sodden lump of gray huddled under the umbrella; the pastor stood with the trunk and bags, his head bowed, back to the rain. "Something is wrong, Reverend. The boat doesn't go to Gőteborg."

"Well." He looked mystified. "You have to change ferries at Orebro and Thollattan, but the captain should have been expecting you. The manor assured me all arrangements were made."

"Apparently that is not the case."

"The lord must have directed everything to Gőteborg—no doubt it is my misunderstanding." He wiped a drip from his nose. "Do you have money?"

"A bit." A cold trickle ran down her back. "Maybe we should wait until things are straightened out." She shivered and hunched into her cloak.

Reverend squinted an eye then shook his head; water sloshed from his hat. "No, definitely not. Best go on to Gőteborg." He wiped his cheek. "Put your trust in God, Mrs. Andersson, not the manor—remember the constable." The *Elaina's* engine banged, banged again, coughed, and then settled in to an irregular thumpa-ka-thump.

She turned and looked at the barge and to rain-shrouded Lake Hjalmapen. What choice did she have? She was helplessly a-swirl, caught in strong currents, and nothing, no one, to cling to. "Oh, Reverend."

"God is your shepherd, Mrs. Anderson. Believe in Him." He reached in his pocket. "I have something for you." He handed her a small package wrapped in oilskin. "It's not much, but I'd like you to have it."

"Oh Reverend." She fingered the package; a small book. A pocket Bible, no doubt. "Thank you so much, Reverend; now I'll be able to keep your prayers with me always." The gift was touching; he was such a thoughtful man.

"You may find it more practical, Mrs. Andersson." He took her hand and smiled. "But it *is* a book, beware water." It was so like him to show a smile under the worst of circumstances. He shook water from his hat and went to help Anna from the wagon.

Her daughter snorted as the wagon disappeared up Low Road. "Put your trust in God! That's a good one. God hasn't done us any favors." She slung a bag over each shoulder and waddled toward the *Elaina*. "Better we put trust in ourselves."

She went up the gangway to the nearest bench and swept away puddles then plopped down. A ripe odor of engine oil, dead fish, and fresh-cut pine enveloped her. She motioned for her daughter to sit.

After checking hatches, the captain approached her with a smile. "Decided to go to Orebro, after all, eh, Ladies? Happy to have you aboard." He opened the wheelhouse door and retrieved a dented bucket with a rope lanyard. "For the ladies; when nature calls, just empty over the side. But mind you, hold the rope." He motioned for Sven to get the trunk.

The whistle blasted; the stack rattled and spewed smoke and cinders. Sven spun mooring lines from bollards and whipped them over crates of squawking chickens. A second blast of the whistle, and the *Elaina* shuddered forward, cinders bouncing along the deck. Pilings retreated and oil-filmed water appeared between dock and rail. The wharf faded away in rain as the opening grew, and the village, the manor, and all that she knew, slowly fell astern in a boil of foam and trepidation.

∞

FOUR DAYS LATER, the Gőta opened to wide channels marked by guano-covered buoys leaning in a muddy current. Ahead, rising above a mélange of low islands, white chimneys, steeply pitched red roofs, and tall masts glimmered in morning sunshine. Gőteborg, at long last, was finally in sight.

She stood at the rail of the *Juno,* a spanking new canal packet making tight circles waiting for room at the pier. Anchored schooners, colliers and coasters, fishing trawlers, and sleek private yachts, bobbed in the packet's impatient wake. On the wharf, longshoremen and stevedores piled crates and kegs into wagons and drays; people with baggage and boxes hurried between massive piles of cordwood. Red-faced constables in blue uniforms tried to control the uncontrollable under the constant blare of whistles, sirens, and horns. The bustle of Gőteborg sent a shiver down her spine; it was too exciting to read. She returned Reverend's Swedish-German pocket dictionary to her bag; he was such a practical man.

Ashore, she left her daughter with the bags and went to the line of jitneys and drays for hire. The constable at the head of the line signaled a wagon for the customs house. After a short ride, the driver stopped in front of a low-slung, soot-covered building surrounded by a concrete plaza. The plaza teemed with people and piles of luggage; a forest of masts, cross arms, and snapping burgees rose above a rusting tin roof.

She gave the driver two őre, and when the wagon pulled away, turned her back and slipped the manor's voucher from her underskirt. "Anna. Mind our things. I'm going to see to our arrangements."

The lobby reeked of sour clothing and unwashed bodies. Listless travelers sprawled on benches under a grimy ceiling of crumbling plaster; along the far wall, a restless line of people inched past grimy windows toward a *Passports/Visas* sign affixed to a wire cage. Past the cage, the wall gave way to a tunnel-like archway with a sign that directed travelers, *To All Boats.* It appeared as if all of Sweden was leaving.

She found the end of the queue and glanced at the clock above a sooty portrait of King Oscar II; the clock was missing a hand. Finally, at the cage with her hip throbbing, she unfolded the voucher and pushed it through the opening along with her best smile. She was tired but thankful.

The agent, a gangly, pimple-pocked young man about Anna's age and wearing an ill-fitting uniform, studied her. He gave the voucher a careful read, consulted his clip board, and nodded to himself. He scribbled something across the voucher and pushed it back across the counter. Andersson/Carlsson was scrawled above RM#14/1000. "Your papers . . ." He checked his clipboard. "Your papers, tickets, exit visa and . . . er . . . your other documents will be ready for you in Room 14 tomorrow morning a*fter* ten o'clock." He pointed to a hallway. "Room fourteen, down that hall." He offered her a brief, insincere smile. "Next!"

Anna appeared and elbowed her aside. "I'll handle this, Mother." She took the voucher and pushed it back at the agent, her belly pressed to the counter. "Sir, I would like our papers, please. I'm not of a mind to take a room tonight."

The man behind Helena said, "Ten o'clock is quite enviable. It usually takes days for papers to clear."

The agent pushed the voucher back to Anna. "I'm sorry, Madam. I don't have your papers. Your papers are in Room 14. Next!"

"Anna," She shook her daughter's arm. "Our belong—"

"This is poppycock." Anna was beet-red angry. She put her face to the cage. "I demand you give us our papers immediately." She pushed the voucher back through the slot.

The agent eyed the voucher as if it were vermin from some crevice. He glared at Anna then shifted his disdain to her distended midsection. He flicked the voucher back through the slot with his index finger. "Next!"

She pushed past her daughter and snatched the voucher. "I am *so* sorry sir." After apologizing to the gentleman behind her, she herded her daughter outside. She didn't have the strength to berate her, not that one more chastising would have any impact. She thanked the woman who watched their things and with her daughter, dragged the trunk and bags to a clear spot on the plaza.

She folded her cloak on the pavement. "Anna, I need to stretch out; I'm exhausted." The days of eating on the run, sleeping in snatches, bathing with wipes had her whipped. She laid down with a canvas bag under her head and closed her eyes. The familiar scent of earth and animals wafted in on a soft shore breeze; tension melted; voices and carts rumbling beyond her eyelids faded into the steady beat of her heart. Breaths deepened.

She was atop the trunk soaring high over the customs office. Anna was flogging the mule and screaming silently; the animal's mouth foamed, its eyes wide, ears flat. On the plaza below, a writhing mass of ragged bodies surrounded the constable atop a pile of bags, his legs spread, fist in the air. The wagon shuddered uncontrollably. She fell from the trunk, plummeting. . . . She screamed. Anna shook her; it was morning.

After freshening up in the facilities, she waited for her daughter in the archway to the boarding area. She was in no better mood than Anna. That unfortunate business in Room 14 with that horrible inspector was so unnecessary. He had no right to mock Anna's condition or be so crude. Her daughter was of no help either, getting so angry when they discovered the voucher didn't include meals. It was irksome enough having to run and shop with the prices what they were, no time to cash the manor's draft.

Besides a 600 kronor check drawn on the Royal Bank of Sweden, the voucher contained two exit visas, a pair of tickets on the *Rhenania*, a *Hamburg-Amerika Linie* coaster, and a business card boldly embossed with the name, *Herr Klaus E. Muhlback, Rechtsanwalt*. Underneath the name in smaller letters was the address: *17 Pasmanstrafse, Hamburg, Germany*.

When her daughter appeared, she picked up her end of the trunk and labored along behind her daughter, her hip afire. The wharf was a madhouse. So many people, so many boats and everyone in a rush, bumping, pushing, elbowing. The whole country was emptying out.

Anna set her end of the trunk down and pointed. "That might be the boat, Mother."

She dropped on the trunk and tried to catch her breath. "Anna, are you sure?" The craft was unlike anything she had ever seen. Not huge, a bit bigger than the *Elaina*, but without masts and rigging, or multiple smokestacks, or pristine decks like the other boats. The *Rhenania* was draped stem-to-stern in patched canvas and resembled a sea-going circus tent. Above a massive sidewheel, a tiny wheelhouse with two spindly smokestacks poked through the canvas.

Anna went to a bare-headed crewman at the bottom of the gangway wearing a short-sleeve striped shirt and soiled dungarees; a red bandana circled his neck. Anna nodded to the man then motioned her to the gangway. Helena gave the man their papers; he returned a half-salute and welcomed them aboard. His accent? Prussian maybe.

He motioned up the gangway. "Room on the forward deck, madams. I'll see to your trunk." He signaled to a crewmember at the rail above also wearing a striped shirt and dungarees. *"Hermann! Kommen Sei."*

At the top of the gangway, Helena hesitated. There was no clear direction. Every way was blocked by small encampments of baggage. She stepped aside. "Anna! Ask the man where the cabins are." The noise was ungodly.

The crewman bumped past with the trunk on his shoulder. *"Nein . . . ah . . .* none." He shook his head and motioned toward the bow. An elderly man guarding a corral of bags and holding a potted plant signaled a finger. "Ain't no cabins, ladies. This here's a cargo coaster."

She followed Anna following the trunk until the crewman stopped at a forward deck hatch. He set the trunk on the edge of the hatch and pushed several bags clear, oblivious to the glares of the owners. He dropped the trunk and pointed aft, his mouth searching for words. *"Kuche: dieser weg—un—*galley. *Kopfe auch so*—head." He briefly put a finger to his forehead and then disappeared.

She settled into the canvas bags; barely enough room to stretch out, but at least the trunk and the hatch afforded some privacy. Her stomach rumbling, she pointed to the rucksack. "Anna, I'm starving; what shall we have to eat?"

"We only have sausage and cheese, Mother. We have sausage and cheese for tonight, sausage and cheese for tomorrow night and the night after. And when we get to Germany, we can put kraut with our sausage and cheese."

"Stop complaining. We have bread too." She opened the trunk and rummaged. "Things could be worse, you know." She pulled out mugs and the teapot. "We're free of the constable, you're not in prison, we've got six hundred kronor, and the day after tomorrow, we'll be met by a respectable businessman." She pushed the rucksack at Anna. "Cut some sausage; I'm going for water."

She stopped at the doors along the wheelhouse. *Kuche*? Was that galley, or was it *Kopfe*? She eased open a door labeled *Die Kuche;* a penetrating shriek filled the air. People screamed; she jumped. The *Rhenania*'s whistle sounded a second time; they were leaving. She rushed to the rail, her heart pounding.

The sailor from the gangway was bent over the rail shouting through a megaphone and waving an arm. Two crewmen clattered the gangway up; people hurrying on the dock below stopped and looked. The sailor turned to the wheelhouse and hoisted a thumb. The whistle blasted again; the deck vibrated; one sidewheel groaned forward, the other backward. The *Rhenania* inched away from the dock; the bow slowly swung toward the Kattegat.

She went back to the *Die Kuche* and stepped into a smoke-filled compartment. A large steel barrel marked *Trinkwasser* sat in a puddle under a hand-lettered sign that in four languages said the *Rhenania* did not provide or sell food. Several women tended pots propped over small fires in a sand-filled tub. One lady gestured that she could share her fire. The lady and her family were from Jonkoping, and had tickets to the United States on an ocean liner out of Hamburg.

The *Rhenania*'s running lights blinked on as Helena was returning the sausage and cheese to the rucksack. After visiting *Die Kopfe* and laying out the cloaks, she took the last of her tea to the rail and stood next to her daughter in the darkness. Gőteborg was a glow in the distance. She sipped and listened to the soft throsh-throsh of the wheel and the hiss of the bow cutting black water. The Kattegat was indigo silk, sequined by the phosphorescent wake of the *Rhenania*. A hunched shape at the rail pointed toward the faint sky glow off the bow. "That's Denmark there, it tis."

"Yeah," a voice agreed, "must be Skagen."

A plaintive cry from a harmonica came from under the canvas. A man in a leather flat cap sat atop a crate playing, "Far Away Is My Love." The song was an old favorite, and she began to hum then put her arm around Anna's waist. Her daughter picked up the words, and they swayed with the music. Voices came out of the darkness. At the end, people applauded and Anna smiled.

Next to a dim lantern at the bow, two blond-haired fiddlers, roughly Anna's age, bobbed and weaved, their bows and elbows flying. A grandfatherly man squeezed a shiny black concertina, his fingers flying over the keys, while dipping and quick-stepping with three women who were whirling a skirt-flying polka. A small circle of bystanders clapped and stomped with the beat. On Anna's dare, Helena put her mug and decorum aside and danced a breathless chorus with a barefoot little girl with long braids.

Aft, past the *Die Kuche*, a scraggly, white-haired woman with a porcelain pipe sat atop a crate. Her eyes were dark and burning, and she punctuated a story with quick thrusts of the stem. A small crowd surrounded her, some standing, others on haunches, all hanging on her every word. "Laplanders," she offered when Anna said she couldn't understand. "Samis are more Russian than Swedish."

Helena rested against the rail and watched phosphorous twinkle in the wake. It was impossible not to be awed by the immensity of blackness surrounding her. Anna touched her arm. "Do you feel it, Mother?"

"Feel what?"

"Freedom. The mood, the optimism. We're all kindred spirits here, all self-reliant, confident, in search of something new. The old days are *kaput*."

"*Kaput*?" Yes, her daughter was right. The village, Sweden, all they knew was behind them. Ahead was Hamburg, Herr Klaus E. Muhlback, the attorney, and a new life. Freedom *was* an invigorating idea. She was up for another song.

∞

4 July 1874

"GERMANY AT LAST . . . thank God." A wave of relief swept over Helena. The cluster of roofs and chimneys floating in morning mist was Cuxhaven. In the distance, past Neuwerk Island, the muddy Elbe cut a welcoming swath through the lazy green hills of Lower Saxony. Another seventy-five miles to Hamburg, solid ground and stability.

And seventy-five miles to this Herr Muhlback—whoever he was. His card smacked of elegance. Anna fancied him as a well-connected solicitor for some official organization. But what if he wasn't there waiting? They were seven hundred miles from home in a foreign country and didn't speak the language. What would they do? The 600 kroners afforded little comfort.

She ducked back under the canvas. "We're on the river now. They say we'll be in Hamburg by evening."

Anna was curled against the hatch, her head on a bag. The *Rhenania* had been good for her. Maybe it was the freedom, being out of confinement, and in public again. Or perhaps it was those two blond-headed fiddler boys who showed her attention.

As day slowly gave way to dusk, indistinct shapes in a haze burned red by a setting sun coalesced to spires and chimneys. Wharfs and gantries appeared; massive brick buildings laced with iron balconies towered behind dark warehouses. Sidewheels slowed and a muscular tug bristling with hemp fenders and thick ropes appeared alongside. After much shouting and scrambling, lines were secured, and the tug guided the *Rhenania* into a narrow channel. The channel meandered past rows of tarred pilings hung with dim lanterns. Water taxis darted in and out of walled passages draped with laundry. The *Rhenania* ghosted to a stop at a landing occupied by a large building with glowing windows, colonnades. Leering gargoyles watched from ornate pediments.

People and luggage flowed down the gangway to the customs building. Uniformed men below on the dock shouted into megaphones. "*Bitte alle Passsagiere und Gepacy zum Zoll*; all passengers and luggage to customs, please."

The two blond fiddle players emerged from the queue and motioned to her daughter. Helena could not hear a word over the din, but the taller of the two tipped his cap and after a brief exchange, Anna hugged them both and beckoned to her mother. "This way," she called. The boys picked up the trunk and bags and eased back into the queue.

The flow of people coalesced in a grand lobby with multiple balconies, marble columns, and glittering chandeliers. Ahead was a barrier of turnstiles crowded with bags, boxes and impatient travelers. Beyond the turnstiles, people and porters pushed luggage carts toward exits. The fiddle players dropped the trunk at the end of a ragged line and exchanged hugs with Anna, then melted into the crowd. She dropped on the trunk and waited for the line to move.

The clock above the booths showed midnight when the inspector nodded and motioned them forward. He was a rather tall man in a crisp blue uniform with striped epaulets. A bronze tag on his shirt identified him as *L. Müller, Inspector.*

His eyes studied Helena then went to her daughter. He leafed through their documents while unconsciously fingering a mole alongside the sharp prow of his nose. *"Bitte öffnen Sie Ihren Kofferraum."*

She stepped back her face blank and held a finger in the air. After extracting the dictionary, she thrust it at her daughter.

"Bitte—Bitte öffnen Sie?" Anna mumbled to herself turning pages. "Kofferraum?"

The inspector said, "*Ja*," and pointed to the trunk and bags. "*Ja. Bitte öffnen*." Anna pointed to the trunk and then to herself. "*Ja*?" The inspector at the next counter said, "He vants you to open your trunk."

Anna undid the straps and lifted the lid. A rank odor of dank clothing and hoary cheese wafted out. The inspector wrinkled his nose then waved a hand as if shooing a gnat. *"Ja, danke, ja—das est gut."* He put a neatly folded white handkerchief to his nose and quickly closed the trunk; perhaps he was embarrassed to go through a lady's things.

Herr Müller drew a fresh breath. *"Danke, frauleins. Willkommen in Deutschland."* He pushed the papers back at Anna and scanned a mostly empty lobby. *"Nachster, bitte."*

Anna touched his arm, "*Bitte,* sir—" She fumbled through the booklet, "*Bitte,* sir, where—*woist*—how—17 Pasmanstrafse? Herr Muhlback? Herr Klaus E. Muhlback, Rechtsanwalt?" She sounded as if she was choking.

The inspector shook his head and pointed to the exit. *"Sie konnen jetzt gehen."* Anna shrugged, confused. "*Ja, ja.*" He made a motion like shooing a cat, "Okay, okay, go, go, *conge, allez, vamos, vamos.*"

Anna shook her head and rifled through the booklet. *"Bitte, ich suche sir. Geldwechse*?" Recognition appeared on Herr Müller's face. *"Ha, Geldwechsel, ja."* He pointed to a kiosk with *Devisenwechsel* on a sign above the window.

Her daughter nodded, relieved. "*Danke,* Herr Inspector. "The exchange is over there, Mother. Stay with our things, I'll be right back."

She eased down on the trunk. The clock on the wall showed half past three, and the building was empty except for stragglers. Two men strolled past then stopped, blocking her view of the kiosk. Both men were in suits with puff ties and coachman hats. One had burly muttonchops, the other was clean-shaven. They nodded and shook hands then turned to different exits. Her daughter was pressed against the kiosk window, her face livid. Helena scurried over.

"Mother!" Anna was furious. "We're being cheated." She pointed to the clerk and then to the Deutschmarks on the counter. "*Nein*! *Das ist*—is not—*nicht richtig.*"

The clerk frowned and recounted the bills, carefully placing one atop another. *"Ja, ja, ist es."* He looked confused.

The clean-shaven gentleman appeared and touched the brim of his coachman. "May I be of service, *Frauleins*?" He spoke Swedish with a distinct accent but not German. English perhaps.

Anna spun around and pulled her cloak tight. "Oh, yes, thank you, kind sir." She handed him the voucher.

The gentleman and the clerk spoke in short guttural phrases, the clerk tapping his finger on the counter, the gentleman nodding. The gentleman gave a final nod and turned to Anna. "I'm sorry, *Fraulein*; the amount is correct. Kroners hold a lower value than Deutschmarks."

Anna's face went blank, then incredulous. "Lower value?"

"Yes, I'm afraid so. The exchange rate is 5.2 to 1."

Anna picked up the money and moaned. "Mother, it's barely a hundred and fifteen marks." She looked like she was about to collapse.

The gentleman touched his hat again. "You are not in need of further assistance?"

"Just one more thing, please." Anna pulled the card from their papers. "Would you know a Herr Klaus E. Muhlback? Herr Muhlback, the attorney? He was supposed to meet us here."

The gentleman examined the card then looked at Anna as if seeing her anew. "No, I'm sorry. I don't know Herr Muhlback, but the name is familiar." Sadness flashed in his eyes. "Seventeen Pasmanstrafse is not far." He pointed to a pair of doors across the lobby. "A dray or a water taxi is available just outside. The fare is modest." He tipped his hat and wished them good luck.

The dray turned from the boulevard and clopped into a narrow cavern of sooty walls and blank windows, dark in first light. The street was deserted except for a single lamplighter snuffing wicks with a long pole. The driver reined the horse at a nondescript stoop holding the numeral *17* in a square of peeling wood. *"17 Pasmanstrafse."* The dray rocked to an uneven stop on cobblestones.

Anna pulled her close and whispered. "Mother. I'm telling the driver to wait—just in case."

The driver swung down and raised a hand for Anna. *"Bitte, funf pfennig."* He turned a palm upward.

Anna held up a finger. "I want you to wait." She thumbed the dictionary.

The driver pushed his hat back and watched Anna turn pages, skepticism showing on his face. He cleared his throat and again offered an upturned palm. *"Das wird funf pfennig, bitte."*

Anna mumbled as she flipped past pages shaking her head. *"Bitte—bitte warten."* She fingered down a page; the driver's expression turned dark. He held out his hand again. *"Madam, ich mochte jetzt Zahlung."* Anna turned to another page, confounded.

The driver snatched the dictionary and put it behind his back. Anna reached around him; he parried with an elbow. *"Frau Abgeordnete, ich muss darauf bestehen."*

Anna flashed anger then her shoulders drooped. She doled out coins, fuming, until the driver said, "*Ja, danke.*" He returned the dictionary and pulled the trunk and bags from the dray. After tipping his hat, he rumbled away, shaking his head.

Faces pressed against the upper windows of *17 Pasmanstraße.* Anna gave the nearest a curt nod and her skirt a violent shake then marched up the stoop. "At least the neighbors will know we're not simpletons." She gave the bell a vicious twist then rocked impatiently. She gave it another twist and then another. She waited then after putting her ear to the panel and knocked firmly.

The door swung back and a large man wearing a sleeveless undershirt and stern expression filled the opening. Suspenders dangled from wrinkled tweed trousers, twisted strands of black hair sprouted from huge ears. A morsel of food clung to the side of an unshaven chin.

Her daughter jumped back unsure, eyes wide. "*Guten . . . guten tag, ich suche Herr Klaus E. Muhlback, Rechtsanwalt?*"

"Was haben Sie gesagt?" The man was glowering, his words angry.

Helena tensed. Should they run? But the trunk, their things? The street was empty, not a soul about. She gripped her bag tighter.

"Herr Muhlback, bitte beachten Sie?" Her daughter stood firm, wary, but not retreating.

The man squinted. "*Ja*?" He grunted and snapped his suspenders over wooly shoulders. Crumbs fell to the stoop.

"Ich suche Herr Klaus E. Muhlback, Rechtsanwalt?" Anna was not backing down.

The man laughed, revealing uneven yellow teeth. "I am Herr Muhlback. How may I help you, young lady?"

Anna's eyebrows went up. He spoke Swedish? "Herr Muhlback, the attorney?"

"That would be me. What do you want?"

Anna handed him his business card. Herr Muhlback chuckled. He tucked the card in a fold of tweed. "Ah, yes, my fine lord friend." He leered at Anna's belly. "When are you due, *Fraulein?*"

Anna's mouth opened then closed. Her back stiffened. Before she could answer, Helena stepped past her. "Soon, Herr Muhlback, very soon. I am Mrs. Anders Andersson. I trust you were expecting us."

"Ah, the Andersson *Frauleins.*" He looked as if he had cornered prey.

"Yes, I am always expecting someone." He allowed he did much business with his lords; he was in the service of many important people.

Herr Muhlback looked at the luggage scattered on the cobbles. "*Sind ihre sachen*—ah, your things." He shouldered the trunk and bags as if they were toys. "Up the stairway, ladies."

She followed her daughter up one flight, then a second. The steps were worn and bare, the walls pockmarked, the air reeking of cabbage. A woman peered from the fourth-floor landing; she looked pregnant. At the third floor, Herr Muhlback turned and kicked open a door in need of paint. "My best accommodations for my Swedish friends." He dropped the trunk on a threadbare rug and put the bags atop a small table.

The door latch was missing; Helena pointed. "Does the door lock?"

"A lock is not necessary, madam." He grinned, his eyes dark slits. "You are in an exceptionally fine establishment." He swept his arm proudly around the room. "All the modern conveniences: appliances, running water, central heat." He pointed to an opening in the floor. "And mind; don't place anything over the registers."

An antique steel bedframe holding a rolled mattress and folded blankets sat against one wall. Opposite was a linoleum counter with a porcelain sink and a knob-handled spout. Several plates and mugs lined a shelf above the counter. The single window looked to a wall of rusted balconies and drooping clotheslines. A narrow canal separated buildings.

Herr Muhlback pointed to a small chest with a metal clasp. "Ice box." He lifted a plate on the stove and acknowledged a small bin of kindling. "Wood goes in the top, ashes out the bottom, and be sure the flue is open." He ran his hand along the shelf. "Ah, the handle for the other plate seems to have disappeared. The tin is lamp oil." He contemplated Anna as if considering a purchase. "Now, ladies, if you will allow me, I'll show you your toilette."

At the end of the hall a floor down, he opened a door to a closet with a varnished bench with a circle cut out and a small window that overlooked the canal. "The shitter." He pointed under the bench to a small pail alongside a pipe that disappeared in the floor and touched a spout on a pipe running up the wall. "Rinse water. The water comes from—"

The door swung open. A woman appeared, surprise on her face. "Oh, excuse me." An infant was in her arms.

"A moment, please." Herr Muhlback pushed the door shut. "The water may be used for washing but sparingly. It is not for drinking. Any questions?"

"The rent, Herr Muhlback. What is the rent?"

"A pittance. Just three marks a fortnight, one fortnight in advance." He opened the door. "I know such a trifling sum does me no justice." He admired Anna's bulge and sighed. "But I am compelled to be generous."

"That would be satisfactory." Anna thrust three bills at him then pushed past him to the stairway.

He called after her. "The milkman comes at six."

"Ice?" Helena asked.

"Midday." Herr Muhlback pocketed the marks. "Any further questions, madam, I'm in suite 100."

Helena walked back to the room and found her daughter moping at the table, chin in hand. Anna snorted. "Well, isn't this a fine fix we're in." Her anger wouldn't last. Helena knew she'd be scheming before long.

Helena checked the mattress for vermin before making up the bed. Yes, they were in a tight spot. But at least they had each other, and there would be work in Hamburg. Babies needed to be delivered, there'd be mothers to council, and once Anna was back on her feet, Hamburg would discover how chambers were cleaned royally.

It was on them to sink or swim. In the village, if work was unappealing, or unworthy of effort, reassignment was punishment. Anyone who didn't mind dung didn't have to do much. Hamburg was unlike the village—or Sweden, for that matter. She and her daughter were two of almost 300,000 people in a city filled with good jobs. Opportunities abounded; they just had to put their mind to it.

She just had to sit down with pencil and paper and get organized. But first, a good night's sleep for a fresh start in the morning. She put her arm around Anna and gave her a hug. "Where's Reverend Ottosson's dictionary, sweetie?"

∞

AT TEN O'CLOCK the next morning, the room was stifling. She had the floor scrubbed, the table and shelf cleaned, utensils and plates washed. The curtains were up with snippets of yarn and she put *her* linens on the bed and started a list. Anna was out scouting the neighborhood, looking for a grocer and chemist.

The trunk was in the middle of the room and when emptied, could go in the basement. But what about the clothes? She wrote hooks on her list. She'd also need a rubber sheet. What an oversight not to pack a rubber sheet. They'd need a crib soon too. Church ladies would know who might have a crib; they'd probably know who else was going to need one, which would mean a job for her. She wrote "church" on the list, paused, and bit on the pencil. She'd be smart to make the list in German; might as well start learning. She turned the paper over and opened the dictionary to the R's: Rout, rowdy, royal, ah, rubber. Concentration was difficult; someone upstairs had been carrying on all morning. Was the word s*pritze* or *spritzen,* or *gummi blatt*? Maybe she should try linoleum or oilcloth; Someone pounded on the door.

Herr Muhlback was there and definitely looked put out. Two young women peered over his shoulder, both wide-eyed, one rocking foot to foot. The dark haired one was obviously pregnant. Someone upstairs screamed.

"Please forgive the interruption." Herr Muhlback's manner did not suggest an apology. "Perhaps madam would be so disposed as to attend a young girl enjoying childbirth. I understand you have experience with such matters."

"Why, yes, certainly." How did he know she was a midwife? The manor? "Yes, just give me a moment." She went to the trunk and dug for her birthing bag. So that's what the commotion was about.

The foot-rocker nodded frantically. "Oh, yes, yes, please hurry." Apparently, there were other Swedes in the building.

Herr Muhlback's eyes rolled, his frown deepened. "Excuse, please!" He elbowed the girls back. "Don't crowd."

She scrubbed her hands, put on a clean apron, and dropped her vial of ether, scissors, and spool of cord in the pocket. "Herr Muhlback, if you would please, a large basin would be most helpful. And towels, Herr Muhlback, many clean towels."

He nodded darkly and herded the girls down the hall.

The wailing came from the floor above. Several women crowded the door, one fingering rosary beads, her mouth working silently. The room was an image of theirs, but the clothes—skirts, shifts, drawers, stockings—hung from clothesline.

An older woman, most likely the girl's mother, knelt at the bed with an open Bible, her eyes closed, hands clasped. The girl arched her back and screamed. One of the women around the doorway began to wail, no doubt guilty over that retribution nonsense. Childbirth was *not* God's revenge for Eve taking the fruit. She bent over the girl and gave her a reassuring pat.

"You'll be just fine, young lady. Everything will be just fine. Just do as I say." The girl emitted a wall-rattling shriek.

She folded a cloth and uncorked the ether, carefully counting drops—the amount had to be just right. When the girl arched her back and her lungs began to fill, she slapped the handkerchief over the girl's face and counted one thousand one, one thousand two, while watching the girl's pupils. On four, she removed the handkerchief; the girl sagged into the mattress, eyes fluttering. A voice at the door said, "Thank you, God, thank you."

Herr Muhlback burst in with a stack of towels and a basin, his eyes sparking annoyance. She took the towels then backed him into the women in the hall. "Thank you, Herr Muhlback, you may go now. In fact, you all may go now." She grabbed the foot-rocker by the arm. "Hot water." She spun the girl around. "Do you hear me? I want you to fetch hot water. Now!" She pulled the door shut and went to the lady kneeling at the bed. "Mother?" She put a soft hand on the woman's shoulder. "You'd be much more comfortable in a chair."

In the morning, she added bank to her list with great satisfaction. Yesterday had been unexpectedly fortuitous; Anna found a grocer and chemist within walking distance and the baby's arrival upstairs was providential. The girl's mother called her a saint, and her grandma was so grateful—she was more than generous. It seemed people everywhere appreciated a midwife; Herr Muhlback even put up a clothesline in their room.

She pulled a shift from the mostly empty trunk and handed it to Anna. Unpacking would go much faster if her daughter stopped nattering about the new baby upstairs.

"But think about it, Mother." Her daughter took the shift and draped it over the clothesline. "Herr Muhlback would benefit from a resident midwife. Look at all the pregnant women here. Doesn't that smack of opportunity?"

Helena pulled a mantle from the trunk. "I expect I'll get a call or two."

"No, not you, Mother, *him*." Anna draped the mantle on the line and straightened a sleeve. A voice rang in the hall. "Ice wagon!"

"We have ice," Helena confirmed. "Do you mean go into business with Herr Muhlback, Anna?" Was her daughter possessed? The prospect sounded terrible.

Anna hunched over startled, her eyes wide, and groaned. "Shit, that hurt." She leaned against the wall, holding her wet skirt at her crotch. "Oh, oh, Mother, I guess it's time."

And it was. Mother Nature, reliably oblivious to place, circumstance, weather, or wealth, put forth, with the grace of God, aided by Helena's steady hands, a wholesome, chubby-cheeked, black-haired baby girl in the early morning of August 8, 1874. She was named Anna.

∞

5 February 1882

HELENA SAT WITH her granddaughter on the sofa reminiscing through her ledger feeling rather proud of the number of babies she had delivered in the last eight years. Anna wasn't home yet; she was stopping by the bakery after work to pick up a treat; a friend coming over. But she had dinner ready and the flat fit for visitors.

Her daughter could not have been more right about Herr Muhlback; he did see the benefit in having a resident midwife. It gave him credibility with his lords, a service his competition didn't have, and a reason to raise rates. He was not as pleasant to deal with as the village overseer, but he was an inexhaustible source of pregnant girls.

Her contribution to his well-being did not lessen his complaining when she asked to move from above that fetid canal. To his credit, he realized her request made good business sense; Helena only had to infer competition. The room was hardly a flat, but it fronted on *Pasmanstraße*, the street below. Somewhat bigger than the room upstairs with two windows and a curtained alcove, but she got it as part of the arrangement. And besides the free rent, two beds meant she had to struggle for covers with only her granddaughter.

Anna did well too. She had a loyal following of housewives as well as a waiting list. By working hard and counting *pfennige*, they slowly built a home. The second-hand dresser was followed by the wardrobe. A year later, they bought a like-new sofa and end table. But they had little of any consequence other than a modest bank account and the heady satisfaction of accomplishment.

Her daughter's friend, Herr Stark—she was supposed to call him Edward—was calling. He spoke no Swedish, and when he started coming by, he didn't stay long, just a few awkward smiles, some foot shuffling before he and Anna went out. More recently, though, he was a regular caller which raised her suspicions that he and her daughter had become personal.

At dinner time, she asked her granddaughter to set the table. Anna expected to be late and said not to wait dinner. Helena spooned biscuits and stew on three plates and covered one with a pie tin. "Come on, sweetie, let's eat."

Feet stomped outside the door; Anna came in with a grocery bag in each arm and a white box tied with string dangling from a finger. *"Mutter, Edward kommt um etwa sieben."* She pushed the door shut with her foot and hoisted the box. "*Strudel!*" It was well past sunset.

Little Anna closed her book and groaned. *"Hat er?"*

Helena looked and frowned at her daughter. "What?" Anna's mind was elsewhere. She nudged her granddaughter. "What did Mommy say?"

"Sorry, Mother." Anna hung her coat and hat on the tree. "Edward is coming at seven." She lifted her daughter's chin. *"Und sie hatten,"* she warned, touching her daughter's nose with a fingertip. "And you had better be civil." She kissed Little Anna on the forehead, then went to the sofa and dropped.

"We'll be civil, won't we, sweetie," Helena assured.

Her granddaughter was such a dear, bright and dependable, with an unruly mop of curls and perhaps a bit chubby. Like every fourth grader, she was acutely self-conscious of her body. Helena was not concerned, though. When her granddaughter got older, she'd thin out and look like the rest of her schoolmates.

Two soft knocks on the door and Anna jumped from the sofa; a male voice whispered, *"Hallo, ich bin es."* It was precisely seven o'clock; Little Anna got up and went behind the curtain.

Her daughter went to the mirror. *"Anna! Ich mochte, Sie sich jetzt benehmen."* Little Anna came from behind the curtain, scowling, her lower lip sticking out. She plopped down at the table.

Anna took a quick look in the mirror, hitched her stays, and opened the door. *"Ah, Edward liebe."* Edward came in, blue eyes sparkling, bowler in hand and smelling faintly of aftershave. She stretched on tiptoes for a kiss. *"Ich habe sie verpasst."* Little Anna stuck a finger in her mouth and made a gagging motion.

Her granddaughter didn't take to Edward; he was competition for her mother. Anna was home little enough as it was, and the only man of interest to Little Anna was her own father. And just like every eight-year-old girl, she asked a thousand questions about him. Questions Helena was forbidden to answer. Her daughter demanded secrecy. The village, the manor, and especially that business with the master were all *pedantisch verboten*. Anna's message was clear: "Don't ask, don't offer. The whole world doesn't need to know everything." She was even concerned something might be blabbed to Edward, who didn't speak Swedish nor she German.

Edward smiled and bowed slightly with his bowler in the crook of his arm. *"Guten abend, Frau Andersson. Ich hoffe sie sind gut."*

She looked to her granddaughter. "He hopes you are well."

"Ich ben—ich ben—good." She hesitated, flustered. "Uhh, *danke—danke—und*—and you?"

He grinned. *"Ja, exzellent, danke."* Edward ran a hand over his blond pompadour and patted Little Anna on the shoulder. *"Und du, kleines Anna?"*

Little Anna shook off his gesture and opened her coloring book. Frustration flashed across his face. He gave Little Anna a wan smile and shrugged his shoulders. Anna glared at her daughter, frowning, eyes narrow.

Helena went for plates; her daughter set out strudel. Edward waited until they were both seated then he nodded at Little Anna, sat down, and picked up his fork. His hands befitted a man his size: strong, absent callouses, and nails clean and trimmed. He ate meticulously and chewed carefully, and when he used his napkin, he rested his knife on the edge of his plate. He was a model of proper table manners.

She had no idea of his age and knew very little about him. He was a bit haughty in a way common to Hamburg, and Anna had never mentioned his parents or if he had siblings. He seemed a man of slender means, although he dressed stylishly. A good wager would put him a bit older than Anna, maybe in his thirties.

Her daughter revealed little more than they met through one of her houses. A man of his age probably had skeletons of his own, so both he and Anna were well served by secrecy and ambiguity. Secrecy demanded strict attention, however; secrets constantly teetered on revelation and gossip.

"Kleines Anna?" Edward dabbed at the corners of his mouth. *"Darf ichmir ihre zeichnung?"*

Little Anna continued coloring as if she didn't hear. Her daughter raised an eyebrow. "Anna, Herr Edward asked to see your picture."

Little Anna closed her book, face sullen.

"Anna? Hast du mich nicht gehort?" Little Anna sat motionless; her mother glared.

Helena looked from her daughter to her granddaughter to Edward, not understanding. The smiles were gone, inflections steely, Little Anna scowling.

"Anna!" Anna said firmly. *"Mussen verstand Herr Edward!"*

Little Anna threw the book on the floor and pouted. *"Er ist nicht mein vater. Ich habe nicht zu tun, was er sagt."*

Anna went rigid, face flushed red. *"Anna!"* She banged her palm on the table; plates jumped. "I don't care if he's not your father; you apologize this instant."

Her granddaughter glared at the floor, jaw set. Anna sprung from the table and grabbed Little Anna by the arm and dragged her to the alcove. The curtain snapped shut.

Helena put hand to mouth embarrassed. "Oh, the water's boiling, Herr Star. . . er . . . Herr Edward, please excuse me." She went to the counter; Edward stared at the curtain, confused.

She could not make sense of the hissing behind the curtain. Edward winced at one outburst, and his eyes widened at the sound of flesh smacking flesh.

Her daughter emerged and apologized. "*Es tut mir leid, Edward,*" she said, giving him a peck on the forehead.

He shrugged and showed a wounded smile.

Anna slid the last bite of her strudel on Edward's plate, set her fork down, and picked up his hand. "Mother," she said, her eyes sparkling. She pressed Edward's fingers to her lips. "Mother, let's practice your German. *Herr Edward und Ich habenein baby.*"

Edward winced, then grinned comically.

Helena started. Baby? That can't mean baby. She cleared her throat. "Mr. Edward and . . ." Her granddaughter always said hear the words, make the sounds. She could hear the words all right; they were all grunts. "*Und Ich* . . . and . . . *und I haben* . . . *haben ein* what?" She smiled weakly; she was hopeless without her granddaughter.

Edward held up a finger. *"Lassen sie mich versuchen* . . . I try . . . please." Edward pursed his brows and mouthed a phrase. His face brightened. "I am . . . having . . . a baby mit . . . Herr Stark?"

Anna clapped. "*Das ist perfekt.*" She squeezed Edward's arm. "Isn't he good, Mother? We're both so excited." She gave Edward a kiss on his clean-shaven cheek. He nodded, *ja, ja,* shrugging his shoulders as if there was nothing to it.

Helena bit her lip. "Uhh . . ." It *was* baby. Initial shock turned to despair; wouldn't Anna ever learn? She got up. "Let me take care of the dishes."

She watched the table from the corner of her eye. He had his arm around her; she cuddled into him, nose under his ear. Both of them were smiling so hard their cheeks had to ache. She couldn't decide whether to be embarrassed or offended. Either way, she didn't need to suffer bad manners.

"Anna. I need to stretch my hip. If you two don't mind, I'm going say goodnight and lay down." Neither seem to notice; had she become a family accessory, a tag-along? Her depression deepened; she went behind the curtain.

Her granddaughter was sobbing, face buried in the pillow. She sat on the edge of the bed and rubbing Little Anna's back and whispered, "What's wrong, sweetie?"

Little Anna could hardly speak for blubbering. "I don't want to go to America. I want to stay here with my friends. And I don't want a baby and I don't want Mommy's boyfriend; why can't we. . . ."

Going to America? Was that what they were babbling about? Good lord, her daughter could have at least had the courtesy to say something to her own mother. And pregnant? Going to America was insane with her pregnant. Headstrong didn't do her daughter justice. "Don't cry, sweetie." She kissed the back of Little Anna's head. "It's all just talk. Dry your eyes. Everything will feel better in the morning."

Anna was the only one who felt better in the morning. Helena's despair deepened as details emerged. Anna and Edward were not going to betroth; the trip was going to take every *pfennig* they had, so to save money, he was moving in; they were leaving in time for the baby to be born in America. Thank God Anna had the good sense to have Edward sleep on the sofa.

Yes, for sure, they were leaving Hamburg for America but the decision lacked the when or where. The question of when evolved from discussion to argument. Edward didn't want to leave until November when the hurricane season ended. Anna argued November was cutting things too close; the baby was due in November. The crossing took almost two weeks, so they compromised on late October and began the argument of *where* to go in America with renewed relish.

Edward craved New York, especially Manhattan. The city had big businesses that paid big wages, and in New York he could make big money.

New York was too big for her daughter. Anna pressed for Chicago. Big opportunities existed there too. And besides, Chicago was closer to Muskegon where Peter lived—she and mother could visit occasionally.

As the day of departure approached, the flat devolved into a parochial squabble over what to pack and what to leave. Anna and Edward parried over the final word. He believed the man was the natural head of the household. Her daughter argued the family was hers as were final decisions. Necessities were weighed, concessions tallied, and eventually compromise, although often bitter, was reached. Little Anna was a thundercloud of resentment, and after she took Edward to the basement for the trunk, did her best to stay out of sight.

At last, the day arrived. Helena stood on the gangway of the *SS Borussia* with Ander's rucksack over her shoulder, waiting on the people and luggage ahead. Looming over her was the liner—massive and black, gleaming ports and pristine decks with a German tricolor snapping atop an enormous smokestack emblazoned with the gold crest of the *Hamburg-Amerika Linie.* On the dock below, upturned faces mouthed unheard bon voyages and good wishes into an incessant din of horns and whistles and wind-whipped confetti.

Little Anna tugged her sleeve and pointed to a uniformed man shouting through a megaphone. "First class goes forward," she translated. "Third class goes aft, and we're supposed to watch our step." Ahead, a queue of men in long coats and fedoras helped fur-clad women ascend a pipe-railed stairway to the upper deck.

Anna yelled, waving an arm. "This way, Mother." Little Anna pulled her into a tide of gray-clad men burdened with luggage. Following behind were women, weeping and dragging reluctant children. A man next to her had a bird in a cage on his shoulder.

She tightened her grip on her granddaughter's sleeve and kept her eye on Edward. He was carrying the two big bags; the trunk was checked through.

Carried aft by the crowd, she shuffled slowly past polished wood deck chairs, glistening ports, and pristine life rings stenciled with *SS Borussia* in precise black letters. Her daughter waited in a mass of impatient people eddying around a doorway. "Mother, this is the companionway." Her daughter jabbed her finger at an opening in the deck. "We're on the tween-deck. *Edward geht zuerst.*"

Little Anna poked her. "Herr Edward is going first, Grammie. Then you're next."

"Mother, give your bag to Edward and watch how he does this." She handed her bag to Edward; he dropped it down the opening, then spun around and, with a railing in each hand, clambered below, feet dancing down an iron ladder. "See, Mother, nothing to it."

She hesitated at the top of the companionway, her stomach churning. "Anna. Isn't there another way?"

Her daughter's head shook impatiently. "Mother, you've got to do this. Now go."

Helena backed to the railings and lowered a tentative foot. Edward and two white-capped crewmen at the bottom stared up at her. Edward waved her to go on. My god, they would see everything.

"Mo-ther." Anna gave her a gentle push, "You're holding everyone up."

With a hand locked on a rail, she pulled her skirt tight and sent a foot in search of the grating—then nearly toppled sideways.

Anna screamed. "Mother! For heaven's sake, use both hands." She released her skirt and felt her face get hot. Didn't the *Hamburg-Amerika Linie* have any sense of modesty?

She finally reached the bottom at the end of a narrow passageway, strung with overhead pipes and wires. Thick steel doors with massive hinges hung from blistered bulkheads. A sailor ahead directed single men forward, another culled single women and sent them aft.

Her daughter's hand held her back. "This must be ours." Anna pointed through a door opening that stopped short of the deck. "We're in the family compartment."

The bay appeared large enough to hold all of Hamburg, but the headroom was barely sufficient to stand erect. A long dining table separated banks of double-high wood berths. Grimy orange life preservers drooped from overhead pipes, and yellow bulbs cast a dim light through rusted wire cages. Bolts held tables and berths to the floor; an odor reminiscent of vinegar hung in the air.

Edward waited while the steward at the door consulted a clipboard then pointed across the center table. *"Liegeplatze 353 und 354."* Edward pointed to a tier of berths; the steward nodded and motioned him past.

Her granddaughter gave her a little push, "Follow Herr Edward, Grammie. We've got numbers 353 and 354."

Anna squeezed between berths, looking at numbers stenciled on corner posts. At 353, she sat on the mattress, groaning at the stems poking through the ticking. "Twenty-five marks for a cowshed; I hope at least the straw is fresh." A large woman pulling two children crowded past. *"Guten tag, guten tag."* The woman pushed the boy into 352. The man following her shouted, *"Nein, nien, nummer 361, 361!"*

Little Anna climbed in the berth. "Which way is starboard, Mommy? A thing on the wall says if the ship sinks we're supposed to go to the starboard side of the main deck. Which side is that?"

"Right side." Anna struggled from the berth. "And there is nothing that says we can't go on deck anytime we want." She pulled Edward's sleeve. "*Komm, Edward, lass uns das Schiff erkunden.* Mother, put your bag in here and let's go exploring."

"You go on. I want to catch my breath." Waiting in lines, fighting crowds, and hauling luggage had her exhausted—and she wanted nothing to do with that dreadful companionway.

"We'll be on deck, Mother. Now remember, our facilities are at the bottom of the companionway. Men use different accommodations, so pay attention to the signs."

Helena unrolled one of the two blankets stored at the foot of the berth; a tin plate, pannikin, knife, fork, and spoon bounced on the oilskin. The bags fit between the mattress and side rail, but there was virtually no privacy. Coats tucked under the mattress above she put her toothbrush and tissues in a pocket. The berth shuddered; the *Borussia* was leaving. She should go on deck . . . but the infernal ladder in the companionway. She'd have to master it or spend her voyage to America stuck below. But before the companionway, she had better put on pantaloons.

After conquering the ladder, she worked her way along the deck until she spotted Edward next to a steel stairway with a "First Class Only" sign dangling between railings. *"Wedel."* He pointed to the roofs appearing off the starboard bow. *"Dann Cuxhaven, dann das Meer."* His dream was being realized.

Her daughter was equally agog. "Yes. Just think, Mother. In another few hours we'll be in the North Sea. Won't that be exciting?"

"*Ja.*" Edward speared a finger in the air. "*Und leitet nach, Manhattan! Amerika!*" Behind the *Borussia,* Hamburg faded away in a red haze; the Elbe River glimmered in the low sun.

Helena leaned on the rail and watched the sky glow give way to shore lights. Beacons in the distance blinked white; channel markers glided silently past to the easy throb of powerful engines. Passengers lounging on the deck above faded into darkness. Her anxieties dissolved in thoughts of sleep. She covered a yawn and stretched then whispered to her daughter. "Anna, I'm going to turn in. Please say good night for me."

An indifferent spar buoy, red in the glow of the ship's light, accompanied her aft, a bell clanging leisurely. A clock somewhere chimed syncopated dings. A crewman rushed past, his heels ringing on steel. In the stern, a knot of people listened to music coming from the upper deck, their faces yellow in the ship's light. One couple danced slowly, the man holding his partner close.

Helena slipped into 353 and tucked in her blanket, careful to leave room for her granddaughter. She closed her eyes and nestled her head on her handbag. A crescendo of metallic throbbing and groaning pulsed through the berth. The sound was relentless, urgent. She sat up; was something amiss? Which way was starboard?

She peeked through the coats. People were at the table talking and playing cards. No one was running. If there was any danger, she couldn't see it. Was the noise normal? She put her head back down; the rhythmic clangor returned. She closed her eyes and tried to force scenes of placid Lake Hjalmapen and the quiet meadows behind the manor into her mind. The din was incessant. She extracted her ticket stub and chewed it soft then stuffed her ears. The clamor would not be denied; it reverberated her very being.

She awoke to her daughter's gentle shaking. "Good morning, Mother. I'm going up on deck. It's beginning to get to me down here."

"I'm awake. Even the dead couldn't sleep through that infernal racket." She had counted every clank and throb, groan, bang, and whir all night long. But how did her coat get over her? A man in the next bunk nodded and exhaled a vortex of pipe smoke. *"Guten tag, Frau."* He smiled, and she rolled over—into Edward. He was curled under his coat, an arm wrapped around a bucket.

"Mind Edward, Mother. He has a contrary stomach." Anna saw her confusion. "I moved him down. I thought we'd all do better if he was in the bottom berth."

She sat up and swung a leg over Edward. A groan came from under his coat and the rail plunged from under her. She fell into Anna's arms.

"Mother, good lord, be careful."

Had the *Borussia* taken flight? A pannikin slid from under the berth, the metal cup rattling across the aisle.

Anna steadied her. "We've left the channel, but you can still see England if you hurry."

She fought back a belch. "I need to use the privy." Something pressed on the back of her head—like a headache coming on.

"Head, Mother. A privy on a boat is called a head. I'm going up on deck. This is too close down here."

Helena started toward the passageway, disoriented, lurching bunk to bunk. People were sprawled everywhere. Some faced head down at the table; others curled against bulkheads or stretched out on the floor. The compartment reeked of rancid bodies, voided stomachs, and incontinence. The floor pitched; she hugged a post. When the compartment righted, she leapt for the passageway. Another belch pressed up.

She stumbled into the women's compartment and into several ladies clinging to a steel support. The room was alive, pitching and rolling. A tin of soap slid from under a stall, stopped, reversed direction, and disappeared. One of the women motioned her past.

The commode was an unbroken stallion, bucking and rolling, bent on shaking her off. Braced against the partition, her eyes closed, she concentrated, trying to relax. My god, how did sailors ever unclutch their innards?

Exhausted, she struggled back to 353 and climbed in, mindful of Edward. She had no interest in a last look at England or a first look at the Atlantic or anything else. Her vitals were awash, her head in a vise. She needed sleep. The mattress dropped from under her, and she slid against the side rail. The berth rose. She rolled into Edward; he twitched. She swallowed hard and fought rising spasms. The yellow light mocked her from its cage. She would never make it to America alive. If God were truly merciful, seasickness would quickly be fatal.

∞

6 November 1882

HELENA AND NINE hundred or so tween-deck passengers cheered with overwhelming relief as the anchor rattled into the muddy waters of the Hudson River. They had made it. The ordeal was over; dry land was within reach.

Under a bright sun, scores of anchored vessels clogged the river. Ocean liners, multi-masted schooners, coasters, and side-wheelers waited for one of the many hemp-nosed, smoke-belching tugs to deliver them to the Battery and Castle Garden immigration centers. Across the bay to the west, construction cranes rose above Ellis Island.

Castle Garden, née Fort Clinton, was the nation's first immigration center. The fort was built in 1808 to replace Fort Amsterdam in anticipation of the War of 1812. The army deeded the fortification to the city in 1821, and in 1824, the stronghold was refashioned as an entertainment center with landscaped promenades, elaborate gardens and fine restaurants. In 1855, it was acquired by the city and turned into an immigration center.

"My god, Mother, look." Anna stared open-mouthed at the skyline. Warehouses, wharfs, tall grimy buildings, smoke-belching stacks, and intricate iron spires rose in an all-encompassing gray haze. "Over a million people, and we don't know a single one. We don't even speak the language." She pulled at Edward's sleeve. "*Bitte Liebling, konnen wie nicht stattdessen nach Chicago gehen?* Somewhere not so huge and closer to Uncle Peter."

Edward stared at the skyline and then swallowed, astonishment on his face. There was his dream, the big opportunities . . . yet, the breadth of it all. Admiration turned to indecision. But after almost four thousand miles—he was *there*. He shook his head no and motioned to the gangway.

Helena teetered gratefully down the ramp and stepped to terra firma for the first time in two weeks. The sidewalk pitched and heaved, and she nearly staggered into the man next to her. Little Anna steadied her into a line of stooped travelers trundling along a tree-lined walk toward Castle Garden. Maple trees blazed red in sunshine. Ahead, flags and banners snapped in a crisp breeze atop a circular clerestory watching over the fort's red sandstone embattlements.

The flow of people wound past abandoned cannon ways, ramparts, and gun ports, and into a sally port with a sign proclaiming, "Emigration Depot for the Commission of Emigration of the Committee of Public Health, for the City of New York, NY. —William Russell Grace, Mayor."

The original parade ground was a warren of whitewashed brick sheds with four different signs for registration, showers, examination, and language. After going through delousing, taking a hot shower and having their privates examined, women were offered a bowl of hot soup and a biscuit before being taken to a sunlit rotunda of marble arches and columns, to await the men. Goldfish swam in granite pools below a circular clerestory.

Gas lights were burning when uniformed agents ushered in the last of the men and escorted everyone down a broad corridor of arched windows, and carved wainscots to a second rotunda. Wood benches faced an arc of uniformed men standing behind counters; gas sconces casted reflections against a glass dome.

Helena had nodded off for the umpteenth time when her granddaughter elbowed her and said it was their turn. Edward ushered them to the counter then stood at attention, his chest thrust out, as he presented their papers with a curt bow. "Herr Edward Stark *von* Hamburg, *Deutschland*." The tag identified the agent as R. Emerson, NYCE.

Anna leaned around Edward. "*Und* Anna Andersson *und Frau* Helena Andersson *von* Sicksjo—"

Edward grimaced and elbowed her back; R. Emerson, took the cards and papers with a raised eyebrow. He pondered the quarantine cards, health reports, reread the language report, and shook his head. His face hardened; he frowned at Edward. "Says you're a merchant, right? *Handler, ja?*"

"*Ja*, yes, yes." He nodded uncertainly.

"Relatives in the U.S.?"

His shoulders sagged. "Nein . . . no."

Anna stood on tiptoes. "*Ja, mein onkle*, Peter Carlsson, *ist da* Michigan."

Edward brightened. "Ja, ja, yes, *ein onkel* . . . er, uncle."

R. Emerson rolled his eyes. "And your destination is?

Edward's eyes darted uncertainly; he pursed his lips. "Manhattan."

Anna pulled his arm. *"So viele Leute, Edward, bitte Chicago."*

Edward looked confused; R. Emerson looked troubled. "Your destination is where?" He signaled to a uniformed guard at the door. Edward's eyes grew large; his shoulders slumped. "Chicago." The agent waved them past. "Next!"

Edward stared at R. Emerson. "*Das* is all?" He looked taken aback. The agent glared at him and hooked a thumb toward the exit. They were brand new Americans.

Helena sat in the lobby alongside her granddaughter and watched Anna and Edward ponder a display case on the far wall. A large map of the United States showed roads, rivers, rail lines, and ferry routes; next to it hung a battered wood rack bristling with multi-colored flyers and pamphlets. Her daughter and Edward appeared to be arguing. His finger traced the glass in one direction; hers in another. They were finding that, unlike Germany, America had no system of passenger railroads. Travel by rail required a sharp knowledge of what routes interconnected and the purchase of multiple tickets all with independent schedules.

Edward had his finger on the glass, shaking his head; Anna handed him a brochure. He shook his head no; she shrugged and held her hands out, palms up. His shoulders dropped. She put her arms around him. He pushed her away and stomped off.

Anna came back to the bench, forcing a smile. "Mother, you'll have to sleep on your coat tonight. We're staying here. In the morning we're taking a ferry to Albany. Edward's gone to buy tickets."

Her stomach fell. Hadn't she suffered sickness enough? "We're taking a boat, Anna? Must we? A train would be much faster."

"That's what Edward said, Mother. But there's no direct route to Chicago. We'd be changing trains forever. Besides, a ferry would be far more comfortable."

"Not another boat, please."

"Mother, it's just a *ferry*. We go up the Hudson River, through a canal, and then across a couple of lakes. You didn't get sick going to Gőteborg or going to Hamburg, did you? We'll all be much more comfortable being able to move around and stretch out. The trip will be pleasant. You'll see!" She motioned to the restrooms. "We should get cleaned up; the ferry leaves early."

The Hudson River Day Line dock was next to customs, and even better, Edward was able to purchase tickets all the way to Chicago thorough the North-West Transportation Company—and they handled the luggage.

The 300-foot paddle-wheeler, *Chauncey Vibbard,* virtually flew up the Hudson with a manifest of 2,000 passengers. Helena flashed past Fort Montgomery, sped below the cliffs of West Point, and enjoyed banking through tight bends with farms and villages flashing by. The 175 miles to Albany took just over eight smooth hours. She admitted to thoroughly enjoying the trip.

The canal packet was even more pleasant; only eighty passengers, and they could lounge on the cabin top or walk with the horse. The packet was narrow with barely standing headroom in the cabin, but it had curtained-off areas for men and women. At night, the table and benches flipped to berths, and Helena nodded off to a syncopated clip-clop and clean fresh air. The boat was no *Chauncey Vibbard*, however: The 363 miles to Buffalo took five days.

Attitudes became languid. Her daughter and Edward were more forgiving as wounds from previous skirmishes healed. They were in America and off to Chicago and a new life as a new family. Venting at perceived indignities ended at last—until Medina.

It was the fourth day, overcast and drizzly; everyone was tired of sitting and anxious to just *get there*. Medina was the fifty-eighth lock with twenty-nine more to go. Edward consulted his watch and made a remark about Medina, something about the puny three-foot lift. He allowed a lift like that would be laughable in Germany. Germans had the best lock system in the world; Americans should have consulted them.

Her daughter took exception. Anna lowered her knitting and cocked an eyebrow at him. "Well, you've not been to Trollhattan then." She sniffed ungraciously. "The locks there have a hundred-foot lift. Where do you find such a lock in Germany?"

And at it they went. Edward jabbed forefingers, Anna snickered, he raised his voice, she laughed. When Anna threw her knitting at him, Helena pulled her granddaughter behind the ladies' curtain. Passengers sat wide-eyed as Edward stomped stone-faced to the afterdeck and stood in the rain.

More likely, the real trouble started on Lake Erie, the third day out of Buffalo, aboard the *Peerless,* a little square-bow cargo steamer with a trio of rakish smokestacks. The coaster left Ashtabula early, its fifth stop, with boxes and barrels, nervous horses, stubborn mules, drays and buckboards and an enormous quantity of cordwood. Anna was in the salon resting; Lake Erie was a mirror turned crimson by a fierce arc of sun rising against low clouds. Silence ruled the morning save the hiss of the *Peerless* cutting still water and the cry of an occasional gull.

"Grammie, this is a really big lake." Little Anna stood on tiptoes at the rail next to Edward. "I can't see land anywhere." She turned to Edward. *"Herr Edward, konnen sie land sehen?"*

He shook his head looking apprehensive. It did seem the *Peerless* was in the middle of nowhere, as if suspended in space. In every direction, there was nothing but the sharp, flat juncture of sky and water.

Clouds thickened; the water darkened to oil. "Look, Grammie." Little Anna pointed to a murky wall in the distance. "Is that rain?" Fleeting catspaws rippled the sheen.

The clouds gathered, shedding puffs of cold air. Catspaws grew to waves, rain came in stinging sheets, streaks of spume tumbled down angry rollers. Mountainous crests flew at the *Peerless*, attacking, collapsing, and reforming. The lake boiled green and white foam.

Edward had the rail in a death-grip, fiercely squinting into the rain, jaw clenched, blond hair flying. The bow plunged, and water exploded over the deck. He reeled and wiped his face then hung over the rail, his chest heaving.

Little Anna darted for the salon. "Run, Grammie! Inside!"

She shook her head. She didn't dare go in the salon. Hunched against the wind, Helena clung to a stanchion and tried not to watch Edward. Eyes on the horizon, she commanded herself. Don't even think of getting sick. Concentrate, concentrate. Bile rose in her throat. She couldn't swallow.

Edward's head reappeared. He inhaled several deep breaths and lurched to the salon. She watched him through the port, clinging to a post, legs spread, and shouting at her daughter. Passengers looked aghast; another roller buried the bow and *Peerless* shuddered to a crawl. Edward toppled over a bench, got up, and rushed back to the rail, eyes bulging.

She fought a losing battle; her stomach was hopeless. She needed a bucket and a private corner. Why did her daughter tinker so with the truth? She had been dreadfully misled: Erie was not a lake, it was an ensnaring maelstrom.

∞

Four tense days later, the *Peerless* arrived in Detroit and disembarked passengers at the Michigan Central wharf on Towbridge. Edward stood on the dock, red-faced and arm-waving. He made a vow to whatever God Anna believed in, never ever again to board a boat. If they *had* taken the train, as he wanted in the first place, they'd *be* in Chicago. He stopped and glared at gawkers. Throwing his hands up, he stalked off in the direction of the ticket office. Other than his tone of voice, Helena could find no disagreement with his assertions.

Edward reappeared from behind a mound of cordwood holding four tickets aloft and a look of triumph on his face. The Detroit, Grand Haven and Milwaukee Railway had a train for Chicago that afternoon. He sniffed disdainfully at Anna and proudly announced there was only one transfer—at Grand Haven.

North-West Transportation moved the bags, and short hours later, Helena boarded Detroit-Chicago Number 23. A grease-blackened aisle ran between wooden benches holding bent women, weary children, and men in tired work clothes. The ones lucky enough to be close to a window held their heads near the open air, trying to escape the earthy odor of toiled bodies.

She and her granddaughter slid on the bench behind Edward and Anna. Edward moved close to Anna and offered an arm; she elbowed him away. In the seat ahead of them, a man and a woman dropped sandwich crusts on the floor. Across the aisle, a sandy-haired Norwegian removed his boots and eased his feet into the aisle; a toe poked through wool socks. A whistle shrieked, the car lurched forward with iron screeching on iron, and No. 23 clanked toward Grand Haven in a cloud of steam, indignation and resentment.

Thirty minutes out of Michigan Central, Edward opened the North-West pamphlet and consulted his pocket watch and then held it up; Little Anna peered over the back of the bench.

"Herr Edward says we're making almost twenty-five miles an hour—five times the speed of that stupid boat." His expression radiated superiority; they would be in Chicago in short order. Anna stared out the window.

His grin faded less than an hour later when No. 23 slowed and swayed to a stop at the Pontiac station. Farther out, at the Holly stop, the sandwich eaters pulled canvas bags from under the bench and exited over the legs of the sprawled Norwegian. A pucker-faced man dropped on the bench opposite her and extracted a wad of papers from his pocket. A spare woman with dull flaxen hair sat next to him and nodded to Helena. A news hawk came through the car with papers, chocolate bars, and lemon drops. Edward checked his watch and wound the stem.

West of Holly, the fields turned barren. Charred remnants of elm and oak replaced dry cornstalks and baled hay. Grass along the tracks became smudged and prickly and beset with blackened fragments. In the distance, beyond patches of milkweed and sedge, a scattering of hollow shells stood against the juncture of sky and earth: the remnants of a barn, a roofless house, a lonesome windmill.

The flaxen-haired woman leaned to her and jerked her chin at the window. "Fire. Yellow Tuesday it was, September fifth, last year—never will forget it." The man looked up from his counting and shrugged disinterest. The woman coughed into a threadbare sleeve of a frayed coat. Her face was lined and worn—her age impossible to determine. She might be twenty or fifty.

The woman looked lost in thought. "Burned a million acres, it did. Sky was yellow with smoke for a week. Nearly 300 burned alive, ones who couldn't make it to water. Even those who jumped down wells perished." The man looked from his papers and dug an elbow into her side. The woman sat back and brushed an eye. "Lost my sister and her family—up in Caseville. Never will forget it."

No. 23 sat on a siding in Durrand almost an hour waiting for a freight train to pass before continuing to stops at Corunna and Owosso. The stations were similar: red clapboard and generous eaves shading men in coarse coats and women with shawls draped over scrub-worn dresses. And every one with a water tower, lumber yard, livery, and watering pond.

At Ovid, Edward bought sandwiches from a vendor while Anna waddled across the platform. Helena and her granddaughter quietly tried to guess which men had holes in their socks. The Norwegian left at St. Johns, and a young man in a dark suit and lavender tie boarded. His case was too big to go under the bench, so he stood it on end in the aisle. The stop to take on water in the town of Shepard added to Edward's funk. Helena stretched out on an empty bench; she dozed with her granddaughter's head in her lap.

More stops at Pewamo, Muir, and Ionia, where the pucker-face man shook the woman awake. As the car emptied, the woman who had gone on about the fire nudged her and nodded at the man in the lavender tie. "Casket salesman."

Three passengers boarded at Ionia: a man and woman with a young girl wearing a dress that hung to her boot tops. A stub of a cigar protruded from the man's bushy red beard. By the time they stopped at Coopersville and Dennisons, low black clouds spit rain against glass. At Nunica, the clouds parted, and flakes of snow flashed by the window. And then, finally Grand Haven, where the Milwaukee Railroad took over.

No. 23 slowed hissing steam; silenced descended. The red-bearded man ushered the woman and girl to a horse and buckboard then disappeared into the night. The platform was deserted save for the trunk and bags sitting in the glow from the station window; dry leaves skittered past on a harsh north wind. The waiting room was empty; the ticket clerk behind the counter slept with an open book in his lap. Edward went to the counter, while Anna rushed to the facilities.

Edward returned shaking his head. He looked defeated, like a boxer too spent to meet the bell. He sagged on the bench. The Chicago train had left.

"What!" Anna was incredulous. "We missed it?"

Edward's hands dropped hopelessly, his mouth unable to form words. Wind rattled the window; a log in the fireplace settled to ash.

Anna snuffed and wiped her nose. "Well, I'm not of a mind to wait and the baby won't." She took Little Anna's sleeve. "*Kommen, Anna.* Mother, you wait here." Her granddaughter groaned and followed her mother to the ticket counter. The clerk laid a ledger in front of Anna; she pushed it to her daughter. Anna followed the clerk's finger along the ledger and eventually nodded. He closed the book and looked at his watch then nodded again. Anna returned his nod.

Her daughter lowered herself next to Edward. "*Edward, Ich warte nicht . . .*" The words were impossible to understand, but it was obvious Anna was aggravated.

Edward's eyes sprung wide, face flushed.

Little Anna, who was quietly watching, narrated: "Mommy said she's not waiting until tomorrow afternoon just to spend another day on a train with no place to go in Chicago; she's going to Uncle Peter's. There's a ferry to Muskegon in the morning—they could go to Chicago after the baby is born."

Edward leapt to his feet, face twisted in anger. He kicked the bench; the clerk looked up from his book. "Herr Edward said a bad word, Grammie."

He paced in a tight circle, seething; her daughter watched quietly.

Edward leaned back on a nearby bench, feet stretched in front of him, hands hanging limply at his side. They could have found accommodations in Chicago; Anna *always* had to have it her way. He shrugged utter defeat.

Her daughter turned to her. "Mother. There's a jitney to the ferry dock first thing in the morning. We should try to get some sleep."

Helena went to a bench in the back of the waiting room and stretched out trying to think of Peter, not the dread of another boat ride.

∞

7 November 1882

After a short jitney ride to a café on the dock for breakfast, Helena boarded the *Lara*, a squat-nosed coastal ferry. Huddled at the lee rail with Little Anna, she watched the Michigan shore dissolve in another squall of swirling white flakes. Anna sat on a crate next to a bulkhead, her back to a bitter northwest wind. Edward stood rigidly alongside with his arms crossed and studiously ignored her as she ignored him.

The *Lara* plunged into a roller. Helena squinted through the swirl, looking for trees or a shoreline, anything not pitching and heaving. The emptiness was vast, like an ocean, overwhelming, alien. She took a deep breath and chinned her muffler down; the salt pork and eggs were not sitting well.

A man next to her, the one with the collar of his greatcoat turned up and gray fedora pulled low, interrupted the battle with her stomach. She heard his question, but he may as well have been speaking Greek. She smiled at him and tugged her granddaughter closer. "What did the man say, sweetie?" In these few short weeks of travel, Little Anna had already picked up a bit of English. She pulled her muffler down, her cheeks afire. "He said . . . ah . . . is it always . . . this cold here? It's . . . it's . . . only November?"

"Tell him we're new here too. Say we don't know the weather." The man's coat looked expensive, as did his hat with the silk band and a bit of feather.

A deckhand poked his nose above the collar of his peacoat and answered the question. "Nay, mate. Not usually this cold." The sailor snuffed and ran the back of his hand under his nose. "Had a bum summer too—got a half-foot of snow in August. Some places it's still underfoot." Helena elbowed her granddaughter.

Little Anna faced the man in the greatcoat. "We are just arriving, sir, and . . . we do not understand your . . . ah. . . ." She called to her mother. "*Mutter, was ist das wort das fur wetter—ah—ja*—wea-ther . . . weather, sir." She sniffed into her coat sleeve.

"Bravo!" The man pounded gloved hands together. "You certainly are a pretty bilingual little lady for not knowing the weather."

She pulled her granddaughter tight, brow clenched, eyes sharp on the man. "What did he say? What did he say?" His comment had made her granddaughter's cheeks turn an even deeper red.

"I'm not sure, Grammie, something about a pretty lady." Little Anna bounced on her toes, a smile spreading across her face.

Helena relaxed. The man's tone was pleasant enough. "Thank you, sir." She did a half-curtsy like she used for the lord but kept a tight hand on the rail. "You most are welcome." English was no less perplexing than German.

The gray smudge of shore coalesced to a wave-whipped beach overhung by yellow bluffs and white pines dappled with birch. The *Lara* closed, engine pounding full-ahead. Blue water turned sapphire, and long breakers washed up snow-flecked sand before retreating into necklaces of foam. The *Lara* charged on. The captain seemed bent on running aground. She gripped the rail tighter.

As if by magic, an infinitesimal gap appeared in the trees, marked by a slender white beacon. The coaster slowed and glided through a narrow cut into Muskegon Lake. Wind and water quieted as if by God's hand. Large feathers of snow drift down; sawmills on the far shore screeched across calm water; beyond the sawmills, widow-walks, chimneys, and church spires faded in and out of flurries. Thank the Lord, they had arrived!

Edward dragged the trunk down the gangway and piled the bags on top. With a glare at Anna, he squared his flat cap and set off in the direction of a sprawling gray building with tin buckets lining the roof and "Ice" painted on the side in large white letters. Beneath the sign, a broad opening emitted jets of steam and the shriek of angry saws. Men with long pikes danced atop a floating morass of pine logs; wagons and carts moved between mountains of spanking white lumber and mounds of yellow sawdust.

Edward returned, clomping across the dock, shoes and trousers mud-covered. His expression needed no translation. Her daughter got up from the trunk. "Uh-oh, Mother, maybe you and Anna should look for a cart."

There was a cart in plain view, but her daughter's message was clear. Helena tickled her Little Anna's cheek. "Come on, sweetie, let's explore."

She led her granddaughter around mounds of cordwood, burlap bags of salt, kegs of brine, coiled rope, snarled fish nets, rusted anchors, and twisted piles of unidentifiable broken machinery parts. At a stack of fragrant, fresh-cut lumber, she peered around the corner and watched her daughter. Anna was atop the trunk, her face buried in her hands. Edward was ranting, his face red and twisted. "Best we wait a moment, sweetie. Can you hear what they're saying?"

Little Anna squinted, listening. "Uncle Peter doesn't live in Muskegon?"

"What?" Her granddaughter must have misunderstood. "Of course, Peter lives in Muskegon."

Edward exhausted his anger as if surrendering to some cosmic unfairness, loaded the trunk and bags into a cart and disappeared behind a mountain of snow-capped sawdust.

She put an arm around her daughter. "Anna? Are you all right?"

"Oh, it's nothing, Mother." She dabbed at the corner of an eye. "Uncle Pete lives in Holton. It's only fifteen miles from here, but the train already left. We'll spend the night in the boarding house down the road, and Edward is going to hire a wagon for the morning."

She followed her daughter to the end of the platform. The boardwalk was slick with a thick layer of mud and reeked of animal dung. Anna hiked her skirt. "Watch your step, Mother. Planks might be missing." Pellets of snow swirled past on a rush of wind and speckled the boardwalk. With a hand on Little Anna's shoulder, Helena hiked her skirt and stepped into the slime.

∞

In the morning, she awoke to her granddaughter's gentle shaking.

"Grammie, it's time, the wagon's here." She set a crust of bread and a bit of paper-wrapped cheese on the cot. "No tea, Grammie. Mommy said to hurry. She and Herr Edward are outside."

Through the window, she could see a mud-splattered buckboard; her daughter was passing bags to Edward. A skinny boy wearing a tattered canvas jacket and an indifferent expression sat on the seat fingering the reins. The snow had stopped, and the sky showed small patches of blue. It looked cold—maybe the mud had frozen. Helena hurried down.

"Mother, sit here." Anna scooched over and patted the seat. Edward and Little Anna climbed in the back with their bags. Her granddaughter propped herself against the trunk and opened her English dictionary. The boy said, "Git-up," and snapped the reins. The buckboard bumped forward; Anna grunted.

"Holton Road," said the boy to no one in particular. "Follows the Muskegon and Big Rapids tracks all the way up to Morgan." To Anna's question, he allowed he was sixteen. His freckles were the same color as the orange hair escaping his flat cap.

A mile or so out of Muskegon the sun broke through, and the buckboard clopped free of overhanging pines. The terrain ahead was raw, desolate, an alien graveyard of chest-high stumps rising from bull thistle and wilted Queen Ann's lace. Little Anna tapped the boy's shoulder. "Why trees cut like that?"

The boy twisted around. "Can't cut 'em any lower. Snow gets too deep." He clucked at the horse and began to hum quietly.

Two hours later the buckboard thumped over a wooden bridge. "Cedar Creek," the boy announced. The creek meandered around a gathering of log cabins scattered under bare cottonwoods.

Her daughter pointed. "Is that it? Holton?"

"Nope." The boy jerked his thumb at the cabins. "That's Finn Town. Nothing but Indians and foreigners. Holton's up around the bend."

"Indians?" Little Anna hung over the seat back. "Indians? Will they scalp us?" She acted more excited than afraid.

The boy laughed. "Don't worry. Them Indians are all too old."

The settlement was all that remained of the Ottawa Nation Reservation, abandoned in 1870 when Blodget & Byrne bought 4,500 acres of virgin white pine for $15,000. Ten years later, the Indians and white pine were gone, replaced by a dam, a sawmill and a general store. Swedes, Germans, and Finns flocked to Holton to claim open land.

A bit more than a mile up the road, a small weathered building came into view. The boy pointed his chin. "That there's Holton Station." A faded sign read, Holton, Mich. Pop. 500, and underneath in smaller letters, Est. 1871. A rusty iron scaffold held several barrels above a small platform. On a siding, a boxcar with the word "Jail" painted on the side sat amid shriveled milkweed and sawgrass.

The freckle-faced boy hawed the horse at a wood bridge, and the wagon bumped past the remnants of what appeared to be a burned-out mill. Ahead, a cluster of weathered clapboard buildings with false storefronts contemplated one another across a rutted swath of hard clay: general store, chemist, cobbler, smithy, two taverns, a U.S. Marshal's office, and livery. At the end of the street a lonely yellow-brick church with a white steeple sat next to a stubby water tank aloft on rusted iron pipes.

The boy reined the horse at a sun-faded awning and hopped to the boardwalk. "General store. Mr. Glade'll know where Mr. Carlsson lives."

A small sign on the wall pointing to the rear announced "Post Office." Across the road was Keifers Saloon with a row of windows along a second story, suggesting rooms for hire. The sound of a piano floated through an open door.

The boy climbed back up on the wagon and grabbed the reins. "Mr. Glade said Mr. Carlsson lives in Finn Town—the camp we passed a while back."

Her daughter's eyebrows went up. "That Indian camp?"

"A-yup." The boy snapped the reins. "Around here it's called Finn Town." He climbed back on the buckboard, geed the horse around and a short mile later, the wagon bumped into the grove of cottonwoods. The boy reined horse. "Which one is Mr. Carlsson's?" The cluster of thirty or so, snow-dusted cabins showed scant difference: Chinked walls, cedar roofs, stoops, lean-tos, privies and enormous stacks of firewood—and could it be? *Yes!* A sauna. And there, another one. It had been nine long years since she had even seen a sauna, let alone been in one.

Edward pointed to a cabin at the bend in the creek half hidden by cordwood. *"Anna, was sagt das zeichen auf eigentlich, Valkommen Min Syster?"*

"Valkommen Min Syster?" Helena's eyes went wide. The words

whitewashed on the board were for her: Welcome my sister. It was Peter's cabin!

She clambered down from the wagon and pounded on the door. The cabin was still. Was he home? She lifted the latch and eased the door open. "Peter! Peter! It's me, Lena!"

The cabin was much like the old cottage but bigger. Peter had a sofa and easy chairs and an eating area. The loft looked big enough to hold an army, and it had a stair rather than a ladder. The fireplace was cold, the hearth black, and an encrusted Dutch oven, half-buried in ashes, sat below a soot-covered kettle hanging from a rusty trammel. She tapped on the door under the stair and peeked in: a disheveled bed, scattered clothes, and a rickety chest of drawers—his room apparently. The whole place reeked of stale smoke.

The front door banged open and a familiar voice boomed away her apprehension. "Lena! Lena, you're here!" Peter spun her around. "Good news does travel fast." He pulled her into his arms; Anna hugged him from behind. Her granddaughter and Edward stood at the door, eyes wide, wondering at the joy of family.

Peter was no longer the lithe young man she remembered, but still straight and rugged, though his beard was flecked with gray. He had filled out too, but hadn't lost that wonderful twinkle in his blue eyes. She threw her arms around him and buried her head against his chest and hugged as hard as she could. She had made it—at last. It felt so good to cry with joy for a change.

∞

In the morning she blinked awake trying to remember where she was; the loft slowly came into focus. She turned over; a light flickered against the wood overhead. Silence pounded in her ears. Her granddaughter's snarl of black hair covered the pillow on the bed against the wall; the other bed was empty, covers thrown back. She pulled on her wrap and slippers and tiptoed downstairs.

Peter had his feet up on a chair, cradling a mug. A fire snapped in the hearth; steam rose from a lidless coffee pot on a grate. He shot her a broad grin, put a finger to his lips, and pointed to the closed door under the stair.

"Privy." She mouthed the word to Peter.

He hooked a thumb past the fireplace. Confronting two doors, she pulled the nearest open. A can of Dill's Balms for Bowel Pain sat on a dust-covered shelf. An oval washtub on the floor held a clothes wringer, a paddle, and carpet sweeper. A tin of Hires Root Beer Extract and a bottle of pine oil salve were next to the Dill's. Peter shook his head, and pointed to the other door.

The stoop was an unkempt repository of neglect. An old Spencer carbine leaned against the wall under a warped wood shelf holding several dusty jars, an oilskin-wrapped package and a box of Spencer Rimfires. Several paper bags and a stack of torn newsprint occupied the top of a cistern. Two baskets of dirt-crusted vegetables and a barrel of flour sat on the floor.

She peeked in a bag—eggs. They must be from the general store. She didn't remember seeing a coop. Sniffing, she poked the oilcloth. Salt pork? She snugged her wrap and grabbed a sheet of newsprint.

The path to the privy was white with fresh snow, the door cocked half-open. She cautiously peeked in and saw the seat covered with leaves and pine needles. The remnants of what appeared to be a book was on the seat alongside the opening. She wedged the door shut, thinking how disgracefully bachelors lived.

When she returned, Peter picked up a rag and reached for the pot on the grate. "You've come at a busy time, Lena." He poured a dark stream into a mug and slid it to her, then settled back with his feet on the hearth. "Finn Town's just coming into season. Things'll quiet down pretty quick, but don't feel ignored—folks are just plain busy right now."

"Season?" Peter looked so good, so healthy and confident. Of course, he *was* younger.

"Season, Lena? You bet. When the snow falls, the big wheels roll." His eyes sparkled. "That's what they say around here anyway."

"Really?" She wondered if her brother had someone special. The cabin certainly showed no evidence of a woman.

"Yeah. Most here signed on with Charles Hackley's crew. Hackley's paying a dollar and a half a day on a tract up near Pentwater. Dollar and a half's real good money for these parts." He took a sip from his mug. "Funny thing is—" He chuckled, "Funny thing is folks around here spend all summer fishing and fiddling and leave everything to the last minute. Right now, everybody's in a panic fixing harnesses, sharpening tools, getting things fixed they shoulda fixed months ago."

She took a cautious sip from her mug. "I don't see you're all that anxious to get going." Was that coffee? Surely those were grounds floating on top.

"Quick of you to notice, Sis." He grinned. "Not at the mill anymore. Place burned down last summer. No big loss though. Timbering's about shot around these parts anyway." He leaned on the table, hands clasped, index fingers pointing. "But I'm still with Blodgett & Byrne. Mr. Byrne's made me the supply man, you know, stuff coming in, stuff going out. Spending a lot of time in Muskegon now, sortin' out snarls."

"Muskegon, Peter?" She leaned back; the chair didn't squeak. The bindings were tight. Peter was so much like Anders.

"Yep. In fact, Lena, I got me a room there. Not here much anymore." He swept his arm around the room, confession on his face. "Pretty obvious, isn't it?" He grabbed the rag and reached for the pot. "How about a warm-up?"

She shook her head no. "I want to hear about you, Peter. Are you doing well? Is your health good? Do you have a lady friend? You're not getting any younger, you know."

Peter laughed. The bedroom door opened, and Anna came out.

"Uncle Pete! Mother! Good morning!" She was in an unusually good mood. Tightening the robe around her girth, she called to the loft. "Anna, Anna. Time to get up."

Joy and elation swept over her. The struggle and uncertainty of travel was behind them, and she was with her brother again after four long years. No more trains or ships or ferries or constant turmoil. Her daughter had a man, and the baby would be born an American. But poor Edward. He did not share the pride—understandably. He was a stranger in a strange land—she knew the feeling.

Over fried eggs and salt pork, Peter and her daughter got into a genteel disagreement over who should have his room. Edward's head swiveled with the conversation, but he didn't grasp a word. When Anna finally conceded and accepted the bedroom, she gave her uncle a big hug and called him generous.

Peter just said, "It's your cabin, ladies." If Edward understood, he got the first hint that he was not the head of any household when Anna declared the first chore, even before unpacking, was to clean the cabin. He chose not to do woman's work, but eventually relented to hike into Holton for cleaning supplies. He returned in a far better mood with vinegar, Monkey Brand soap, and a bottle of liquid bluing. He discovered Mr. Glade had more than a passing acquaintance with German.

Helena rested her scraper on the oilcloth and contemplated the Dutch oven on the table in front of her. The blackened crust was near hopeless, every bit as bad as the fireplace grate. She reached for the bar of Monkey Brand. Something dropped behind her and a can of Dill's Balm rolled from the pantry. Peter backed slowly out the pantry door on his hands and knees.

"Peter. Have you been feeling well?" She waved at the can of Dill's Balm.

When his head appeared, he tossed a rag at the bucket. "Oh, that stuff, Sis? Trash it. Might as well have been snake oil for all the good it did."

"Anna said the carpet sweeper didn't work, Peter."

"Yeah, I know, Lena—one thing at a time." He massaged a knee. "When's this cleaning gonna end? We've been at it seems forever."

"Peter, did I see a coffee grinder in here?"

"Ye-sss, Lena."

"Does it work?"

"Of course, Lena." He got to his feet and wiped his hands down the front of his overalls. "You know, Sis, as far as timing goes, yours might be pretty good."

"Oh, how's that?"

"Well, Thanksgiving's the last day of the month this year." He eyed the clean grate in the fireplace and nudged it straight. "If you're cooking, I'm thinking I might bring a friend to dinner—if that'd be okay."

"Why, certainly, Peter." Well, Peter had a lady friend after all. He probably had many lovely women to choose from. No doubt his friend was a striking woman. Hopefully she was Lutheran.

"A lady friend, Peter?"

"Le-Na! Whataya think?" He rolled his eyes and gave her a little squeeze. "Of course, it's a lady friend." He lowered an eye. "Now don't you go getten' the cart ahead of the horse. This is just a friend."

When Peter left for Muskegon that afternoon saying he would see her on the thirtieth, she was disappointed he couldn't stay longer. She tried not to think he left because of cleaning the cabin.

The following day came raw on a bitter wind. Cottonwoods twisted and swirled, dark clouds threatening snow raced overhead. At the woodpile, she watched a straggle of geese honk their way forlornly south with Thanksgiving on her mind. Had she been too glib with Peter? She knew nothing about Thanksgiving dinner, and she'd never even seen a turkey, let alone cook one. But there was time to find out. A place to start would be at the creek. All the ladies went there for water, and she could ask if one of them had a recipe.

When she dropped wood in the bin, the cabin was quiet. She expected to see her daughter and Little Anna filling the tub for wash. Maybe they were still up in the loft. "Anna! Are you two up there?" She waited, listening. "What? I didn't hear you. What are you doing?"

Anna clumped down the stairs one step at a time, wincing. She had her overdress clutched to her privates. "It's time, Mother. I said it's time." Little Anna hung on the stair railing behind her mother, eyes wide.

Helena was not unprepared. She had no birthing chair or rubber sheets, but being at Peter's simplified things; he had a sauna. She'd deliver the baby the old way, Mother Carlsson's way, in the sauna. A sauna was sanitary, private, and eminently cleanable.

She beckoned to her granddaughter. "Sweetie, would you please, real quick for me, start a fire in Uncle Peter's sauna." She filled a kettle with water and tossed two split logs in the hearth. Now where was Edward? Probably at Glade's jawing with the Germans.

In the sauna, she wrapped her daughter in a blanket and after bundling up Anna's clothes, she gave them to her granddaughter. "Please take these to the cabin for me, then run and see if Edward is at Glade's. If he isn't, ask Mr. Glade if he knows where Herr Edward is."

She set her bag on the bench and throttled back the stove. Ether at the ready, she settled back and watched her daughter's jaws clench.

Hours later, she had her new granddaughter cleaned up and in bed with Anna when Edward and Little Anna materialized. She found him a Keefer's, drinking beer.

Helena beamed at Edward. "Congratulations, Edward. You're a father of a perfect, eight-pound baby girl—with pretty blue eyes just like yours."

"Ein madche, huh, das ist gut." He seemed rather calm. *"Ja, ja, gut."* He knocked on the bedroom door and went in. Helena closed the door behind him and took the bucket and brush from the pantry. She started for the sauna with a change of clothes.

Cleaning revitalized her; everything was good, even Finn Town. Finished, she stripped and sat until the heat melted her worries away. Rinsing with the last of the clean water, she dressed and started for the cabin. The wind had died, and the air smelled fresh and clean. Clouds chased moon shadows over fresh snow.

She went in through the stoop and found Little Anna and a casserole and a jar of preserves on the table. "What's this?"

Her granddaughter closed her book. "Stew. A neighbor lady brought it—a Mrs. Koronrn or something like that. She came by to see the new baby; said she'd come by again."

She lifted the cover. Yum! Rabbit stew—and still hot. How nice. And how timely. Her stomach was rumbling. Curious how fast word spread about a new baby.

She pulled plates from the shelf. "Is Herr Edward still with Mommy?" He would want to eat with Anna and the baby.

Her granddaughter shrugged. "Herr Edward left; he didn't say anything to me."

"Well, I'll save him a plate." She cut bread and ladled three plates of stew. "Go ahead and start, sweetie. I'll take this one in to Mommy."

Her daughter was staring at the ceiling with the baby in the crook of her arm. "Still snowing, Mother?"

She shook her head no and put the plate on the chest. Her daughter looked more sad than tired, almost depressed. But that was not unusual; new mothers were often melancholy. She plumped Anna's pillow and kissed the top of her head. "What a beautiful baby."

"Eat," she said, handing the plate to her daughter. "Rabbit stew from a neighbor—I'm keeping Edward's warm. What did you decide to name her?"

Anna picked up the fork and sighed at the window. "Don't bother saving Edward a plate, Mother. He's gone." She stroked the baby's head. "I've decided to call her Helena."

∞

8 December 1882

Any feelings Anna had about Edward leaving she kept to herself. The few times she broached the topic with her daughter, Anna was stoic. "Edward was what he was, Mother. But think; we have Lena and we're all here together in America with Uncle Pete. How can that not be good?" She and Peter were so much alike. They didn't look back, just kept moving ahead.

Peter came for Thanksgiving with his lady-friend Karolina. He brought a bassinette for Lena, three chickens, a nanny goat, and good news: Mr. Byrne had asked him to take charge of receiving. He wasn't sure about the offer. It entailed a lot more figuring, and he'd have to move to Muskegon. But it did include a hefty raise. He figured he couldn't say no to a raise, so he'd give it a try.

Karolina clerked for a Mr. Charles Houseman at a different mill in Muskegon—the gray building on the wharf with the ice sign. She had a round honest face and a thick braid down her back. She looked younger than Peter and with black hair and eyes, definitely not Swedish. But appearances were of no matter; she was easy to like.

"Congratulations on your new job, Peter." Helena held her glass of cider over the table until everyone clinked. "Muskegon must be exciting. I'm happy for both you and Karolina."

The two made a fine-looking couple, chatting and laughing, she supplying a word when he searched, he occasionally finishing her sentence.

"Mighty fine meal, Sis." Easing his plate aside, Peter leaned back, thumbs hooked in his belt. "Best turkey ever—and that apple pie. Delicious!" Her granddaughter's head bobbed in agreement.

Nodding modestly, she quietly gave thanks to Mrs. Koronrn's recipe: Rub the bird with sage, roast it in a Dutch oven with a bit of water, turning occasionally—done when the leg felt loose.

Anna motioned for Little Anna to clear the table then turned to Peter. "Uncle Pete, what will you do with the cabin when you move to Muske—"

"Anna!" The nerve of her daughter. "Peter will tell us in good time what he wants to do with the cabin." The cabin was none of their business.

Peter laughed and winked at his niece. "Well, little lady, I do have a thought, and with luck, it might just turn a buck or two."

Helena was confused. "Peter, you're going deer hunting?"

He guffawed. "No, Sis. Hunting for money, not deer." He pulled out his pipe and turned to Anna. "Here's what I'm thinking: You and your mother here take in a boarder—a woman, of course." He tamped tobacco in the pipe with a finger and snapped a match. "Having a boarder would take care of the costs here, plus you and your mom might get some help with the chores." He drew on the pipe and blew a plume of smoke upward and jabbed the stem at his sister. "Okay, Sis, I know: Another mouth to feed. But other than that, what do you think?" He leaned back and contemplated her. "We split the take. I take half, you take half."

"That's very generous, Peter. But not very fair." Stay in Finn Town without Peter? They were a family; they should be together. "Someone would buy this cabin; you should sell it."

Her brother was certainly very giving, but take in a boarder? Cooking and clean-up was easy enough, but still, did she want to live with a stranger? And what did she and her daughter know about inn keeping? Moving to Muskegon with Peter offered opportunities. There would be plenty of pregnant women, and Anna would have houses to clean. She took a sip of cider and and assessed his reaction. Peter's face was blank; Karolina's impassive.

But he did not sound disappointed. "Well, think about it anyway, Sis." He gave her a brotherly pat. "You know I'd love you to come to Muskegon too." He went to the stoop for his coat. "I'm going to see to the chickens—back in a couple of minutes."

After dishes were washed and put away, she sat with her daughter and Karolina and played with Lena while Peter and Little Anna cleaned out the shed. After moving in the chickens and goat, he hauled water from the creek for the cistern. Neither he nor Karolina seemed in a hurry to get back to Muskegon.

Dusk had closed in when her brother and Karolina drove away. She let the window curtain fall back and turned to her daughter. "Best we move to Muskegon with Peter. There's nothing to do here. Muskegon will have plenty of work for both of us and a real school for Little Anna." Nothing was wrong with home schooling, but a real school with a real teacher and classmates would provide a better education.

Anna untied her apron and cocked her head. "Mother, moving in with Peter is *not* a good idea."

"Anna, Peter can't afford two places. He'll want us with him in Muskegon."

"Mother." Her daughter's shoulders sagged with frustration. "Didn't you see the way she looked at him?"

"Who? Karolina? Well—"

"Mother! I can't believe you didn't notice." She took a lamp to the fireplace and rummaged in the bin for a match. "I'll wager that Uncle Pete betroths Karolina." She put a match to wick then replaced the glass. "If you were a new bride, would you want a bunch of family moving in?"

"That's the way. Karolina will understand."

Her daughter went for another lamp. "Well, Uncle Pete's going to have two places until someone wants this one. And more than likely, that won't happen in the dead of winter, if ever. We shouldn't just live off Uncle Pete; a boarder would help us all."

She nodded to the loft and put a finger to her lips. "Shhh . . . arguing will only upset Little Anna. She's already moved more than any nine-year-old should."

"Moving in with Uncle Pete is so *old country*, Mother." She started for the bedroom. "I need to check on the baby."

Good lord, she didn't want a boarder; she'd love to live with her brother. Although Anna could be right. Perhaps times *had* changed—but she hadn't and neither had Peter. The whole business was irking; every time she just got settled, some cockamamie change popped up. She had to find out more about Muskegon.

In the morning while dusting soot, she paused at the window and scratched rime from the pane. Still snowing. Cottonwoods were shouldered in white and Cedar Creek was hidden by drifts. Only mid-winter and the day was already so bleak, it felt like dusk rather than mid-morning. "My stars, Anna, light a lamp." Her daughter was at the table nursing Lena in the gloom.

The cabin may as well have been on the moon. Finn Town was all but empty. The flurries after Thanksgiving turned thick, and as soon as family could be sent to stay with kin, men headed north like an army called to battle. The cabin was windowsill-deep in snow, the drifts in Holton Road shoulder high, and her granddaughter hadn't been to the school in Holton for better than a week. Silence pressed in like a head cold.

Anna pulled Lena from under her shirt. "When this snow disappears,

Mother, we should be looking for a boarder. We'll get notices up in the general store and maybe the post office." Lena hiccupped and squirmed.

She reached across the table with a spit-up cloth. Her daughter wouldn't let go of this boarder idea. "Anna, we've discussed all of this. Look out the window. How are we going to do anything with snow up to our hips?"

"I agree, Mother—for now." She stood Lena up. "But even when the snow is gone, the chance of finding a single schoolmarm or a seamstress or a milliner in Holton is probably nil. And even if we did find someone. . . ." Anna grabbed the cloth and wiped drool from Lena's face. ". . . how happy would we be with a woman bent on finding a man rather than filling the cistern or splitting wood?" She felt her shoulder for spit-up. "We should take in a man, Mother. Men can afford more."

She sagged. "A man? Where would he sleep? And what will we do if he's liquorish or snores or curses or runs off in the fall timbering? A body can't be too careful." Her daughter was not thinking clearly.

"Oh, Mother, don't be so closed-minded." Anna put Lena on her shoulder and stood. "I'm going to change her."

Helena went to the window and scratched more rime; not a track or footprint in sight. Even Mrs. Koronrn gave up her daily constitutional. And she was *always* out, bundled up, wading through drifts, knocking icicles loose, making snow angels. It probably made the woman feel like she was back in Lapland.

Being trapped in the cabin made Helena desperate for conversation. Except for the coldest days, Mrs. Koronrn was a willing neighbor, but unfortunately spoke almost no Swedish. Conversing with her made for few words and many gestures, but nevertheless, better than nothing.

Mrs. Koronrn and her family came to Finn Town three years earlier. Her husband was killed the first winter they arrived when a trip bunk broke and he was crushed by a log. Last winter, a son who worked as a raft driver slipped between logs in the Pere Marquette River and perished. They never found him, not even the next summer. Winter had her petrified; the poor woman had no girls. Her other two boys were timbering near Ludington. But if it weren't for Mrs. Koronrn, she would have gone half mad, beating a pot for civil conversation.

Unremarkable days slid to frozen weeks; a month passed and then another. Daily flurries were joined by rain with the silence broken by rumbles of thunder. The brief moments when blue sky appeared gave her hope.

April arrived anew, the air fresh and smelling of promise. Jumbles of crocuses dappled the ground and Holton Road turned to a river of muck. Snow retreated and men swaggered back to Finn Town flush with winter wages and a reckless thirst. The doors at Keifer's remained open until sunrise, and the syncopated rhythm of the "Maple Street Rag" echoed through night air. Mrs. Koronrn warned that a respectable woman wouldn't be caught dead in Holton until the sheriff had every one of them locked up.

With planting season looming, Helena went outside and scrutinized what once was a vegetable garden: Limp Baltic ivy entwined in crumpled chicken wire, fence posts askew and thickets of dead milkweed. More chores, it seemed, every time she turned around there was more to do. The day was gorgeous, but the amount of neglect put her out of sorts. She went back inside for work gloves.

Anna looked up from her mending. Lena was on the rug sputtering, her arms and legs flailing. "Mother, everything doesn't need to be done today. It's beautiful outside. Enjoy the sunshine."

"Well, the garden won't plant itself." She did feel irritable. "We *do* have to eat, you know."

"We're not going to starve, Mother. Take a break. Go window shopping in Holton or something. The road's dry enough if you walk to the side." Lena gurgled and tried to roll on her stomach. "I'll be just fine with Lena, and Sister will be home from school shortly."

Lena rolled over and started to cry; her daughter felt Lena's diaper. "See what Glade's has for fresh vegetables."

Perhaps she should walk into town. She'd been cooped up in the cabin for months and the day was so nice. Her hip felt up to it, and she could even treat herself to an ice to chase away the blues. There was still better than a dollar left from her last delivery. And with the men back in Finn Town, the end of the year portended a rash of new babies.

On Holton Road, she stopped and watched a work crew shoveling stone from a lorry. The foreman said the road was going to be graveled all the way in to Muskegon. A crew was repainting the railroad station. There was even a new schedule board: trains stopped thrice weekly, and there was a new route all the way to Big Rapids.

The remnants of Byrne's mill were gone except for some cement slabs. Main Street was graveled and buggies were everywhere. People crowded the boardwalk, a gentleman hawking a shiny two-bladed plow was surrounded by several men in bib overalls.

The barbershop next to the livery was crowded. The boots and shoes in Thompson Bros. window looked expensive—especially the pair of ladies' brown lace-ups. The post office moved to a storefront across from Glade's. Keifers' door was wide open, with loud voices, piano music, and the heavy odor of stale beer spilling to the boardwalk.

Helena stopped and glanced at the upstairs windows at Keifer's and flushed red. Mrs. Koronrn told her in strictest confidence that Keifer's sold naughty pictures. And worse, in the upstairs rooms, men and women got personal and didn't even know one another. She had no idea how Mrs. Koronrn knew all of that; apparently she was not as dowdy as she seemed.

Glade's screen door tinkled when she pulled it open. The store was dim and quiet, downright sleepy. A woman and young girl sorted through buttons and snaps. The bonnets on the rack were all too feathery for her taste. The fabrics looked stylish; maybe she might sew a new uniform for Anna. Her daughter needed to make a good impression when she started looking for work in Muskegon. The cabin was up for sale, but so far there was no interest.

The onions and potatoes were no better than the ones at home. And the prices. Good lord! Thirty cents for a half-peck of potatoes, forty cents for onions! Beets were even more expensive. And the peas and beans. She definitely needed to rethink her garden.

No interest in hardware or cement, paint, cartridges, fishing tackle, nets, or beaver traps. And considering the prices, it was not worth going to the meat counter. But the beets and carrots did look especially good. After picking out a dozen carrots and half as many beets, she carried them to the counter, the wood floor creaking accusations of extravagance.

An elderly man stooped with rheumatism and wearing red suspenders over a too-large flannel shirt took her beets and carrots. He quickly counted with bent fingers and delivered a lightning strike to two keys of an ancient cash register. The tray sprang open with a loud *ka-ching*.

"That'd be sixty-four cents, Mrs. . . . ah . . ." He reached for a bag and after fumbling with an edge, snapped it open. "Yes, please; sixty-four cents."

"Andersson, Mrs. Anders Andersson." She did a slight curtsy. "I'm pleased to acquaintance you." The man was probably John Glade himself. He certainly worked the register as if he owned it. She handed him a silver dollar and motioned to the window. "Where everyone are?" People hurried past, bumping, stepping aside, tipping hats.

Mr. Glade raised an eyebrow and frowned. "Whazsthat?" He dropped the coin in the register. His fingers fluttered uncertainly over the till.

The poor man must have misunderstood. He was probably hard of hearing. "Where from?" She nodded to the window.

His face flashed recognition. Mr. Glade pointed to the bag on the counter. "From Ed, that's where. He grew 'em." He handed her change, jerking his chin toward the back of the store.

"In fact, there's Ed right now." A man wearing a black porkpie was bent over a box of asparagus.

Was her English that bad? She started to repeat her question then thought to leave well enough alone. The man in the porkpie saw her looking at him and touched the brim of his cap. Something was unusual about him. Maybe it was the nose. He smiled. She looked at Mr. Glade and back toward the window, confused.

Mr. Glade chuckled. "Oh, you meant the people outside." He braced both arms against the counter and straightened his back. "Mostly immigrants, Swedes, Finns, Norwegians, Germans—you name it. They're coming by the trainload." He spoke slowly, hoping she'd understand. Farms had sprung up north of town with hundreds of cows and acres of sorghum, but best to keep it simple.

"More cows than you can count." The word around Holton was that the Germans were riding the boom in condensed milk. Condensed, or evaporated, milk was a big industry. Gail Borden commercialized the process before the Civil War and the product became widely popular as it could be safely stored unopened for months. Refrigeration ended the boom. He left that conversation for another day.

She thanked Mr. Glade then made her way across to Rhodes Drug Store, which was also empty, except for a man talking to a clerk at the soda counter. The man seemed agitated. He wanted something, but she couldn't discern what it was. But Rhodes had ice. A poster behind the counter showed a lithograph of a red ice in a wafer cone.

The clerk stepped back from the counter and spread his palms questioning. The man raised his voice. She didn't recognize the language, but it seemed prudent to wait by the magazines.

She scanned. *Life, Look, Peterson's Ladies National, Harper's Bazaar.* Thumbing through *Peterson's Ladies National,* she thought Anna would enjoy the latest fashions—but three whole cents? She returned *Peterson's* to the rack. The man at the counter slammed his hand down and stomped to the door. The screen slammed behind him.

She went to the counter and eased on a stool. When the clerk came, she pointed over his shoulder to the ice poster. "Strawberry?" The clerk nodded then smiled when she said, "*Danke* very much." If language was any indication, Mr. Glade was right. Holton was a muddle of immigrants.

Despite the throb in her hip, she returned home with a feeling of satisfaction. A pleasant afternoon browsing around chased her blues away, *plus* she had a strawberry ice.

Her daughter was in the easy chair with Lena. Helena held up the bag. "I only bought carrots and beets. I can't imagine how Glade's can get away with charging those prices."

"I know," Anna agreed. "When I was in there to see if Mr. Glade knew of a woman looking for a room, I had a look. Mr. Glade knew of several people who were looking, but they were all men."

Anna held out Lena. "Here, take her for a minute. She's hungry." Her daughter unbuttoned her overdress. "But Mr. Glade did introduce me to a nice man who supplies vegetables for him—he's looking for a room." Anna pulled Lena close and winced as she latched on. "He lives in Muskegon with his brother right now." Lena belched. "Good one," Anna said.

"By chance is his name Ed? There was an Ed in Glade's today: medium height, gray eyes, big nose. These are his beets and carrots."

"His name is Ed Anderson, Mother—he's Norwegian. Mr. Glade says he's very responsible. And his nose isn't big."

She studied her daughter. Her reaction sounded suspicious. "How is it you know this normal-nose Mr. Anderson?"

"Oh, I don't *know* him, Mother. I've just seen him around." She held Lena at arm's length and made a clown face. "We should consider him though. I think he'd be a good boarder."

Lena voided her bowels and started to cry. "Sister! Sister!" Anna called to the loft. "Please come take Lena. She needs changing."

"Well, nice or not, I still don't think so, Anna." Men were difficult creatures, and her daughter was a poor judge of the species. This Ed popped up too quickly and sounded too good.

∞

By week's end, Helena had the garden cleared of weeds and the posts mostly erect. She was ready to go to Glade's for chicken wire. Thank goodness Glade's delivered because they were the only cabin in Finn Town without a man or a wagon.

On the boardwalk, she stomped and shook dust from her skirts. Her hip felt pretty good—must be the weather. She reached for Glade's screen door. The door abruptly opened and swung into her face, followed by that Ed fellow who about knocked her over.

She gasped and grabbed her bonnet. Her handbag thumped to the boardwalk.

"Holy gol-drottin, ma'am! I am *so* sorry!" Ed steadied her arm and stooped for her bag. "Musta been day dreamin'—you okay?"

"Why, yes, I think so." She gathered herself and straightened her bonnet in the window reflection.

"Ed Anderson, ma'am." He tipped his cap, red-faced. "And please excuse my language." He stepped aside and held the door open. "Smock looks right pretty, Mrs. Andersson."

Well now. He knew her name—and noticed her smock?

"Why, thank you, Mr. Anderson. Have we met?" She snuck a glance at the window and adjusted her bonnet.

He stammered and cleared his throat. "Ah . . . well, kinda. When you were in here the other day, old John Glade let it slip you were Anna's mother." A twinkle started in his eyes and blossomed to a friendly grin. He had good teeth—and he was taller than she remembered.

"Ah, I see, Mr. Anderson. We had your carrots and beets the other night. They were delicious." She nodded for emphasis. "Today, I'm here for chicken wire."

"Well, you've come to the right place." He ushered her through the door. "Can I give you a hand getting it in your wagon?"

"Why, thank you, Mr. Anderson, but I'm afraid I'm afoot. I'll have it delivered."

"Well now. I'm going right past Finn Town on my way back to Muskegon. I'd be pleased to drop you and your wire off."

Her mind was on a strawberry ice, but meeting this Ed Anderson out of the blue was *quite* a coincidence.

And he knew her name and where she lived. Interesting. "Why, thank you, Mr. Anderson. I'd be honored to accept your generous offer."

She settled with Mr. Glade and found Ed and a roll of wire waiting atop what appeared to be a huge wooden bin on four wood-spoke wheels. An ox waited in the traces.

"Ain't the most comfortable wagon." He boosted her up to the wood-plank seat. Then with a foot on a spoke, he hoisted himself and snapped the reins. "Git, Oskar." The wagon clunked forward; she grabbed the plank.

"Have you been in Holton long, Mr. Anderson?"

"Little better'n a year now, ma'am. Came from Norway in '81." He rested his elbows on his knees, fingering the reins. "Came over steerage from Christina. Seasickness 'bout did me in."

"I sympathize, Mr. Anderson." The wagon lurched—she tightened her grip on the plank. "Do you have family in Norway?"

"Nope. Nobody left. Just me and my brother, Benjamin, in Muskegon. He talked me into coming over." He looked older than Anna. Maybe three or four years. Thirty-four would be a good guess. "Yeah, been by myself since I was fourteen. I was a drummer boy in the army. Then after jackin' lumber for a while, I got smart and quit. Jackin's too dangerous, a man can get himself killed even being careful."

"It's an arduous trip from New York, isn't it, Mr. Anderson? Did you come by boat or train?"

Ed flipped a rein at the ox. "Me'n Oskar here walked."

"Walked? Really! From New York. That's a considerable distance."

"Eight, maybe nine hundred miles, give or take. It took the better of three months. I was pretty well tapped out back then." He leaned sideways and pulled out a pouch. "Mind if I smoke, Mrs. Andersson?"

She watched him with his pipe: Confident, his hands calloused but with clean nails and strong fingers. And what an adventure, walking all the way from New York. Ed saw her looking and winked. Yes, confident. That was probably a good word for Ed Anderson. And Mr. Glade might be right about him being honest and reliable. "Smoke? Please do. You farm, do you?"

"Yes'm, timbering's pretty well shot around these parts. Most everything from Ludington to the Indiana line's been clear-cut." He bit on his pipe and snapped a match with a thumbnail. "Farming's the future: sorghum, hay, mostly feed, although I do a few vegetables—just things that winter well."

Ed cupped the match and pulled. "Been renting some acreage just north of here, up with all those Germans and cows." He expelled a stream of blue smoke. "Can't believe the goings-on about condensed milk." At the bridge, he geed the ox into the cottonwoods. "But I'm able to put a little away. Want to have a place of my own someday."

He reined the ox in front of the cabin. "This one, right?"

After jumping down, he offered a hand. "Careful there, Mrs. Andersson; it's a long step."

Down, she shook her skirts loose. "Thank you, Mr. Anderson. And if you're in Holton regularly, perhaps you'd like to come to Sunday service. We're Lutheran, of course, and the church is Methodist-Episcopal, but the Good Lord hears all voices."

"Well, thank you kindly, ma'am. I do appreciate it. But I'm afraid I'm not much on church-going." His eyes canvassed Finn Town. "Nice little spot. A lot like the old country, only flat."

So, he didn't go to church. Was he an atheist or agonistic? "Oh, are you not Lutheran, Mr. Anderson?"

Ed swallowed and shifted foot to foot. "Well mostly, ma'am. But I'm pretty much backslid, I'm afraid."

"A few Sunday mornings would remedy that." Thinking of Reverend Ottosson, she nodded twice. "It's a lonesome life without the Almighty."

"Yes'm; the Good Lord and me talk every now and then." He shrugged apologetically. "It's just I figure He's got better things to do than have me pulling at Him." He pointed to the wagon. "Lemme get that wire."

So he's backslid, just like her daughter. Ed stood the wire on end next to the fence posts and returned, dusting his hands.

"Well, Mr. Anderson, I surely do thank you. For your help with the wire, but especially for the ride home. It's been a pleasure talking to you."

"Likewise, ma'am." He touched the brim of his porkpie and with a foot on a spoke, hoisted himself up, and nodded good bye; Oskar lumbered forward.

She stood watching the wagon turn on to Holton Road. There was something about him—but she couldn't quite put her finger on it. Ah, yes . . . they had been speaking *Swedish.*

∞

9 April 1884

ED'S BACK AND forth to Muskegon put him past Finn Town almost daily. Occasionally, he dropped off a half-peck of carrots or beets, saying he just happened to be in the neighborhood. It was no more than good manners that Anna returned the courtesy by inviting him to dinner. And as the dinners grew more frequent, she eventually decided to agree with her daughter and take him in; people could think what they may.

The day he came to discuss terms, she made a chicken stew with dumplings and rhubarb pie for dessert. Privacy was her only concern, so she decided to hang curtains across the loft and assign Ed the bedroom. His caveat was knocking before coming in the cabin or out of his room. Ed said there was no hurry to rearrange things as he was wintering in Muskegon with his brother. He planned to move in next spring when the weather turned decent, and one blustery day with a biting north wind, Ed showed up.

She let the window curtain fall back. "Anna, Ed's here." Her daughter ran to the wagon with a shawl thrown over her head. Ed tipped his hat then swung Oskar to the shed and dropped the tailgate. The plow to one side, he unloaded several bags of seed, a mechanical planter, assorted rakes, hoes, shovels, a toolbox, and an old valise with a knotted rope handle. After moving the coop aside, he racked his tools along the wall of the shed and stacked his seed bags. After tethering Oskar, he headed to the cabin with his valise, and Helena became an inn keeper.

Ed was mostly gone except for supper. When Helena came down from the loft in the morning, a fire was usually going and a full kettle steamed on the trammel. The wood bin and cistern were reliably full, and once Ed got his planting in, he finished up her garden, put a new seat on the privy and a latch on the door.

After dinner one night, while her daughter and Little Anna were cleaning up, he brought up the aggravation of hauling water from the creek and thought he'd dig a well—if that was okay with her.

Her daughter and Lena were outside when he arrived some afternoons later with the back of the wagon half full. Ed dropped the tailgate grinning. "Leftovers from a barn raising; traded a bushel of beets for everything." He shook his head. "Them Germans got more cows than they can shake a stick at."

Anna put Lena on her hip, and watched him pull planks, an iron pipe, a bag of cement and an old steel-handled pump from the back of the wagon followed by a pile of cobbles. "Startin' the well?" Her daughter always seemed to know what Ed was up to.

Ed nodded and made big eyes at Lena, then brushed a finger under her ear. She gurgled and kicked. "Getting cuter by the day, isn't she?" The plan was to dig on the weekend with his brother coming to help.

Benjamin showed early, and he and Ed started digging and hauling. Sandy spoils came up by bucket; shoring driven by sledge. When the water was knee-deep, they lowered cobbles, followed by buckets of cement. By nightfall, the shoring was trimmed and the hole covered.

The following day, Helena was at the counter when the bit of an auger popped through the wall just above the floor. Ed came in with a wrench in one hand and a pump in the other then eyed the hole. "Close enough." When he finished, he pumped and primed and pumped and primed until water gushed. She decided taking Ed in was an excellent decision.

For Anna's thirty-second birthday in July, he bought home a stove—in pieces. Ed didn't tell Anna anything, but after singing happy birthday, he said he had something for her outside in the wagon.

Her daughter hitched up on a spoke and stretched over the side rail. "Good lord, Ed, what is it?" A helter-skelter pile of odd-sized iron doors, wire handles, barrel-shaped drums, along with a bent piece of soot-covered chimney pipe surrounded a squat, dirt encrusted iron chest with animal-like feet.

"It's a stove. Place up in Hesperia burned and I got it for almost nothing." Ed lowered the tailgate. "Don't look like much right now; just needs a little elbow grease." Once he got the stove together and the flue in, the cabin went from smelling like an old smokehouse to Lorillard Red Cross pipe tobacco.

∞

Autumn retreated, leaves fell, and the pace of Finn Town accelerated toward a winter of timbering. Inside the cabin, activity slowed to the satisfaction of accomplishment. Ed was pleased with his season. The weather was cooperative, and people with a taste for fresh vegetables continued to come to Holton. He added to his savings and was quietly proud of what he got for the last of his tomatoes: a gallon of maple syrup and two jugs of apple cider.

Anna decided a little celebration for a successful year was in order. She baked a cake to have with the cider. It wasn't really a cake and barely sweet. Just lard, sugar, egg, and flour mixed with a bit of cinnamon, sour milk and baking powder baked in a greased pan.

Her daughter set the cake on the counter and pointed to the dining table. "Isn't that something, Mother?" Lena was in Ed's lap squealing and pushing an old rubber tennis ball in his face. He was chewing at the ball and growling ferociously. Sister held him captive from behind.

"They just can't get enough of him, can they?"

"And he, them." Helena lined up four glasses. "Can Lena have some?"

"She can have some of mine." Anna motioned her close. "Just so you know, Mother," she whispered, "Ed and I are having a baby." She put her hand on Helena's arm. "Now don't make a fuss. I'd like to keep this to ourselves. And yes, I did tell Anna—she's excited."

Resignation washed over her. Wouldn't her daughter ever learn? "I can't say I'm surprised, Anna." She suspected her daughter and Ed were up to no good the day she saw Anna jiggle her behind at him. "I just hope you will marry this time."

"Oh, Mother, don't be that way." Her daughter sliced through the cake, rotated the pan and sliced again. "Church weddings are for the privileged."

She sighed to herself and shook her head. Her daughter was thirty-two. Why couldn't she be more prudent? She was setting a bad example for her girls. What will they think of their mother when they get older? Marriage brings respectability and substance to a family. It was just not right to make babies absent of holy wedlock. If she was old fashioned, so be it. She followed her daughter to the table.

∞

Red and wrinkled Norman Anderson slid into her hands in the early morning of June 24, 1886. At Norman's first cry, Ed was in the sauna like a cat on a mouse. He couldn't have been prouder. His new son, naked, cuddled on Anna's breast. He rode straight to Muskegon and came back with a rocking chair.

A year and a half later, when Laura came, he built rooms in the loft. Carl followed two years later just in time to disrupt Anna's thirty-seventh birthday party; Ed went out and bought a buggy and a saddle-tan Morgan named Buck. But when Benhart arrived in 1892, when Anna was thirty-nine, her daughter confessed she'd had enough. "Mother," she panted. "This one's it. No more kids; I'm getting too old."

Mrs. Koronrn came to see the new baby and sat with Helena for a cup of tea. She ticked her fingers. "So that be five now?"

"Six if you count Little Anna." She had a hard time believing it herself. "But Anna said Benhart's the last; she's nursing him until he's thirty."

Mrs. Koronrn's expression didn't change. "She say now."

Mrs. Koronrn had a point: Her daughter could be red-faced hot, stirring a tub of laundry, Sister and Lena pushing and pulling at each other, Carl and Benhart howling to be fed, and when Ed walked in the door, her eyes would sparkle.

She poured two glasses of hard cider and with Mrs. Koronrn, toasted Benhart's arrival. They both agreed that Ed needed to find something else to do.

∞

The cabin settled into a circannual rhythm of planting, nurturing, reaping, and rest. The seasons rolled reliably by. With Norman working with Ed, the vegetable bins in Glade's General Store were always full and the cabin never for want. The garden flourished under Sister's direction. Laura willingly learned the finer points of weeding and watering, Lena more reluctantly. But when Finn Town emptied to the call of virgin pines, the season of rest inevitably moldered and silence festered. Only Norman and Laura, with their books, seemed comfortable locked in solitude.

Helena watched the children from her easy chair with heavy eyes. The cabin was stuffy, and she was drowsy. Benhart's shirt was so tight, he looked like pork sausage. Carl's hand-me-downs would fit him better, but Carl was so hard on his clothes. Benhart was about to start kindergarten, and he shouldn't go to school looking like a rag-a-muffin.

Benhart was on the rug playing with the toy horse he got for Christmas. Lena crept up behind him and snatched the horse. Benhart screamed, "Mine! Mine! Mine!" Lena held the horse over her head. He lunged for the toy and fell back wailing.

Sister screamed and grabbed the horse from Lena. "Stop it, you snot! That's *Benhart's!*" Sister pushed Lena away; Lena fell against the counter. The horse bounced under Norman's chair; Norman tossed it to Carl.

Her daughter didn't look up from her mending. "Children, children. Whoever has the horse, please give it back to Ben." Benhart jerked the horse away from Carl, and Carl began howling; Lena pushed Sister. Sister grabbed a fold of Lena's arm and pinched. Lena screamed.

Ed looked over the top of the *Muskegon Chronicle.* "Girls, girls, please!" Lena held her arm and ran to him sobbing. She dropped at his feet and snuffed the back of her hand across her nose.

Anna screamed, "Out! All of you! This minute! Out!" She threw her mending in the basket. "Out! I mean out!"

Ed lowered the paper. "Boys, did you hear your mother?" Lena snuffed and glared triumphantly at Sister. He pushed Lena off his leg. "You, too. All you kids git." Sister pulled Benhart to his feet and dragged him to the stoop, her face hard with anger. The stoop door slammed; silence settled in.

Helena closed her eyes. January was a difficult month—all the snow, all the quiet, all the idle time. But winter was good for her hip. She nestled into the chair.

Ed muttered about something in the *Chronicle.* He must be out of sorts again. She opened an eye. He was worked up about an article the other day too.

"Gol-drottin Democrats." Ed rattled a page at Anna. "That bonehead in Lansing will have all our money if we're not careful."

Anna pulled a sock from the basket. "I believe Governor Pingree is a Republican, Father." She ran a hand inside the sock then sighed at her finger poking through a hole.

Ed wouldn't be dismissed. "I meant those galoots in Washington." He jabbed the page with a finger. "Ever since that Cleveland and his fast-talkin' bankers took over, the bottom fell out of everything. Money's not worth a plugged nickel anymore."

"Father, do you like Harrison because of being a Republican or because of tariffs?" Anna stretched the sock over a darning egg. "Turn the lamp up a bit, would you please."

"Huh?" Ed slid the lamp closer to Anna. "Well, Harrison's a pretty smart cookie, and he knows a bit of inflation is good for farmers. Good for us too. I borrow money every spring, you know."

"If you say so, Father." She threaded a needle.

Ed had a full head of steam. "Here's an example for you. I gotta follow rules that were made for big outfits, like have a license and keep *official* records—whatever that means." He shook the paper. "Every time I turn around there's some smart-alecky know-it-all from the county telling me what I can and can't do." He threw the paper in the kindling bin. "Government's enough to drive a man to drink." He pulled the paper from the bin and smoothed it.

Ed was peeved about change. But what hadn't changed in fourteen years? Holton had electric lights, telephones, steam heat, and indoor commodes. Main Street was paved in red brick and concrete replaced boardwalks. Fancy Victorian homes lined Church Street—Ed called them picket-fence mansions. The Muskegon & Big Rapids laid a second track, and the new Apel Hotel served afternoon tea on the balcony under a snarl of overhead electric wires. Progress, however, was slow to find Finn Town.

Ed got to his feet. "'For you know it, the government'll be telling us how to use the privy." He dropped the paper in Anna's lap. "If you ask me, Mother, it's gotten too crowded around these here parts."

"Mmm, I guess so," Anna replied vaguely. "Mother and I don't get out much." She wove her needle through the sock and snugged the thread. "Maybe you should holler for the children, Father, it's getting late."

Ed pulled out his pouch and fumbled for his pipe. "Way too crowded to suit me." He started for the stoop, shaking his head.

"Well, complaining won't help." She parted threads with the needle. "Maybe you should do something about it."

"Well, maybe I will. Maybe I just will." The stoop door slammed.

The next day Ed was still at loose ends. He wandered the cabin, looked out windows, assessed snow drifts all the while muttering to himself. His to-do list was done, and there was no sense going to Holton to jaw with cronies as they were off clear-cutting up near Ludington. He needed to get out of the cabin for a while and get his mind on something other than spring. Anna wanted him out from underfoot too. She suggested he ride in to Muskegon and spend a day or two with Benjamin so she could start a new overskirt. And he did.

The overskirt was for Sister; she had her first job. Mr. Rhodes heard she was good with languages and hired her for the store. But even with Ed gone, just getting the linen cut was a struggle. Lena and Sister would not leave each other alone. Lena sulked around complaining about never having anything new; Sister gloated. Lena complained that Sister's hand-me-downs didn't fit; Sister called her scrawny. When Anna finally got the dress pinned together, Lena called it a tent. And the following day, while she was struggling to get the hem straight, she banished Lena to upstairs when she called Sister fat.

When Helena returned from the privy, sobs were coming from the loft and her daughter was on her knees basting Sister's overskirt, obviously irritated. "Mother, are Laura and the boys still down at the creek—Sister, hold still." Sister was on a stool holding the waistband, a triumphant smile on her face.

Helena pushed the curtain aside. "Don't see them, but here comes Ed." Having all that time to herself didn't seem to help her daughter's mood.

Anna took pins from her mouth. "They're probably out there throwing snowballs at each other. Lord knows, someone will come in crying—Sister, for the last time, stand up straight."

The stoop door opened and Ed appeared, stomping his feet. "That coffee, Grammie?" He rubbed his arms. "Phew, cold out there."

Her daughter didn't look up. "You see the kids, Father?"

He took the mug of coffee she poured. "I did, Anna-Banana. They're out sliding on the creek. I warned them about the thin ice around the big willow." He took a sip from the mug and leaned against the counter squinting at Anna serious like. "Anna-Banana, what would you say to owning eighty acres?" His arms were crossed. A smug look suggested he had swallowed the proverbial canary.

"Eddy acers uff wut?" Anna took the pins from her mouth. "We'll finish this later, Sister. Go do your studies."

"Eighty acres of our own." His eyes looked watery, like he was holding back a sneeze.

Anna's eyes narrowed. "You don't say."

"I do say. Benjamin found out from Karolina that the National Bank of Illinois crashed to the tune of $22 million dollars. Her outfit was a big depositor. Nearly wiped'em out."

"You mean Charles Houseman's company?" Anna's eyebrows went up.

"Yep, one and the same." His smirk broke loose. "Ben says old man Houseman's strapped for cash. He's looking to sell."

"So what's that got to do with you?"

His grin spread. "Ben figures him and me can go in and buy a quarter-section dirt cheap. We split it fifty-fifty; he takes eighty acres, I take eighty; we each get our own piece."

Sister ran to Ed. "We gonna buy a farm, Poppa?"

"Could be, little lady." He draped his arm around her. "Not a farm, though, an old lumber camp."

Anna raised an eyebrow. "You been there?"

"Yep. Me and Benjamin rode up for a look. It's not the easiest place to find, but the trees are cleared, soil looks good, and there's a creek."

"Ed Anderson! You're off buying property and didn't tell me?" She glared at him. "You certainly could be more forthright!" She threw the pin cushion in her sewing bag. "Eighty acres. Now where you going to get that kind of money?"

"I got some put aside, and I know you've squirreled away some of what I've been giving you." He set the mug down and wiped his mouth. "And then there's the bank—my credit's good."

He stretched back and pulled Sister with him. "Piece is in Branch, about fifteen miles east a Ludington, right on the county line. There an old bunkhouse and cookhouse, a couple of sheds, and stumps galore, but the soil looks just right." He straightened up and gave Sister a pat. "It'll be a rough deal for a while. More work than you can shake a stick at, but we got ourselves a pretty good crew here."

"Sister, let's finish up." Anna patted the stool. "Well, Father, you think you can make a deal with Mr. Houseman?" She held the skirt around Little Anna's waist. "I guess that looks about right—Mother, what do you think?"

"About the skirt or the eighty acres?"

"Mother, the skirt. And stop wiping the counter, you're going to wear right through the linoleum."

Ed allowed he and Benjamin had their numbers all worked out. The going rate for clear-cut was $2.75 to $3 an acre, but Houseman needed money so there was room to haggle. Ed wasn't about to pay three bucks an acre, although he saw the danger of offending Mr. Houseman with an offer too low. He and Benjamin figured a $1.75 was a good place to start.

He went to the Grange then over to the Farmers' Cooperative and asked around about land purchases and filing papers and picked up pamphlets on stumping and seeds and fertilizers. When Anna asked what he was up to, he replied, "Just doing my homework."

Benjamin set up a meeting with Mr. Houseman, and Ed was off early to Muskegon. He took $10 from Anna for earnest money along with her basket of fried chicken and bread ends. Helena thought her daughter was acting as if buying property was nothing to speak of. But it was on *her* mind. Property owners! Who would have thought?

Ed got home late with a long face. "Old Houseman's one tough customer—surprised Benjamin, too." He dropped at the table.

"That so?" Anna looked up from her sewing. "There's a plate in the oven, Father—Mother, you sit still. I'll get it."

"Not very hungry, but thanks." Ed propped his chin on a palm. Anna slid a plate in front of him. "Meeting didn't go well." He picked up a fork. "Houseman'll only sell a whole section—640 acres. And he wants three bucks an acre. No way we got that kind of money."

Anna looked disappointed. "Did you tell him no?"

"Didn't have to." He poked at a chicken breast and diddled wistfully in the beans. "Guess I'll turn in." He stood and tossed his pamphlets in with the kindling.

In the morning, Helena came downstairs and found Anna in her best dress. "Mother, we may be going to Muskegon." It took her daughter awhile to convince Ed that walking away from the 640 acres at three dollars was just plain smart. Three dollars was just the first shot; Mr. Houseman wanted a deal and wouldn't let one slip away so quickly. "Ed's in Holton calling Mr. Houseman to see if there's any flexibility in his position." She pulled Ed's pamphlets from the kindling and dropped them on the table.

Ed came back saying Mr. Houseman was willing to talk again and that he called Karolina so she could get word to Benjamin. He went for blankets and told her they'd get something to eat in Muskegon. "Let's get a move on, Anna-Banana. You need to use the privy?"

"Just did. Mother, we'll be late." Anna grabbed Ed's arm and rushed him out the door.

Helena spent the day cooking and cleaning and nagging about schoolwork and keeping Sister and Lena separated with Anna on her mind. The vision of her daughter in a meeting with Muskegon bigwigs had her preoccupied. A wood-paneled room with portraits of gentlemen with stern expressions hung in her mind. There was her daughter at a glass-topped conference table negotiating with successful businessmen; an overseer taking copious notes; and rows of desks in the outer office with women hunched over typing machines.

The vision became less consuming when the task of getting the children to bed sapped the last of her energy and exhaustion overcame fantasy. With everyone upstairs and the cabin still, she picked up the *Chronical* and collapsed in the easy chair.

She woke to Anna shaking her shoulder. She sat up; the *Chronical* slid to the floor. Her daughter was mouthing, "We got it. We got it." Ed stood behind her wearing a foolish grin and holding a pail of beer.

Anna pulled her arm. "Come on, Mother. We're celebrating! We got the property!" Ed offered her a mug and hoisted the pail. She shook her head; judging from the amount of remaining beer, they must have started celebrating in Muskegon.

Ed and her daughter were in their cups, and she was not in a mood to endure liquorish shenanigans. "Congratulations," she said, patting Anna's arm. "I'm going to bed."

In the morning the cabin smelled of cold ashes and stale beer. She started a fire and set the pail outside. The bedroom door was closed, so she decided to hold off on breakfast.

Her second mug of coffee was about gone when Ed padded out of the bedroom looking rough around the edges. "Good morning," she smiled, "how about some eggs?"

Ed shook his head. "Feeling a bit indisposed this morning, Grammie." He steadied uncertainly against the counter.

"Coffee?" She set a mug on the table in front of him. "You got the property? That's wonderful. Congratulations again."

He put a fist to his mouth and belched. "Unnn, holy gol-drottin—yeah, we shook hands at $2.50." Ed belched again and rummaged on a shelf. "Bromo–Seltzer up here?" He pulled out a blue vile and levered the pump handle. "Me'n Ben didn't—" He poured white powder in his mug. "Me'n Ben didn't want to go that high, but Houseman agreed to sell us 240 acres instead of the 640. Me'n Ben each took 120, but we had to sign an indenture for $300 dollars. Could tell the old man needed money. His building was vacant, no desks, no machines, only a small table in an empty office. And I gotta say, Grammie, that Anna-Banana of yours is really somethin'."

"No need to tell me. She does have a way."

"Yup, that she does." Ed leaned back against the counter and watched bubbles dance in his mug. "Houseman took a real shine to her." He took a pull on the mug. "Said he'd put Swedish Settlement on the deed just for her." Ed put a fist to his mouth and belched magnificently. "But we got it. Houseman could have called it Rutabaga for all I cared." He chuckled and pulled a forearm across his chin.

Anna came out of the bedroom, bare feet showing below her nightshirt. "Father, that Bromo?" It was not like Anna to be seen without first pulling a comb though her hair. "Let me have a swig." She took Ed's mug and disappeared into the bedroom.

That night she snuffed her lamp, feeling particularly good. For the first time ever they owned land—what an achievement. And her daughter, running a household with a passel of kids, putting good food on the table, keeping everyone decently clothed, and still able to tuck a little away. Anders would be so proud. She drifted off to sleep thinking Ed would want to get going as soon as the mud dried up, and she should get that gol-drottin steamer trunk cleaned up. Good lord, she was beginning to sound like him.

∞

10 May 1897

Spring had never come slower. Ed had hoped to be on the road the week after Easter, but it started to snow again. He planned a route through Hesperia and up to Island Lake where they'd stop for the night.

In the morning, just north of Allen Creek, they'd turn west to the road to Walhalla. Fifty miles all totaled, he figured—two, two and a half days tops.

He rode Buck up Holton Road almost every day trying to wish away the mud. Both the wagon and buggy were greased and ready, tools stowed in the back next to the bags of seed, the camp gear cleaned and aired. The steamer trunk was packed and her daughter nattered constantly about weather. Helena kept her patience; Mother Nature could not be hurried. Gabbing with Mrs. Koronrn and teaching Benhart to tie his shoes kept her mind occupied.

The weather and Ed remained forlorn until early May when he announced that he had ridden as far as Hesperia and the road was pretty well dried out. "Might as well finish packing and get this show on the road," he announced.

Sister was excited to be on the way. She had her replacement at Rhode's trained and had been studying Ed's pamphlets from the Co-op and Grange.

Lena was thoroughly depressed and complained incessantly. She was in the tenth grade and had a had a crush on a classmate; leaving Holton would end her life. Who in their right mind would give up shops and friends and go live in the wild? Anna just ignored her.

The day of the move came wrapped in a thin mist smelling of wood smoke and animal dung. Ed had the top up on the buggy, the camp gear in the boot, and Buck in the traces. He and Norman circled the wagon for a final check. Ed rearranged the kettles and skillets in the washtub and gave the rope holding the table another tug. Satisfied, he threw a handful of corn in with the chickens. Finally, he and Norman lashed the tent atop the pile and tethered the cow behind.

Helena hugged Mrs. Koronrn; they both promised to write. One of Mrs. Koronrn's boys was taking the cabin. Her son was recently betrothed, and there wasn't room in her cabin for the bride's parents. She was most grateful for her help working things out with Peter.

She thanked Mrs. Koronrn again for the bag of hard-cooked eggs and heaved up on the buggy alongside her daughter.

"Twenty miles to Island Lake," Ed shouted. "Let's get to it." He slapped the reins on Oskar's rump. Norman said, "Git-up," and Buck fell in behind the cow.

At the bridge to downtown, Helena craned for a last look at Holton. Roofs and storefronts floated dreamlike in a wispy haze under the watch of a legless water tower. Norman looked, her daughter looked, Laura, Lena and Benhart in the back of the buggy looked. In the wagon up ahead, Ed and Sister and Carl looked. Even the cow looked.

Holton Road was passable to Hesperia, but further north, the swollen White River had the bridge awash. Ed waded across probing planks, jumped up and down a couple times then shrugged. He led Buck across but was fearful for the wagon. To lighten the load, he and Norman carried the plow, the seed, and feed bags across. Anna and the girls dragged the tub with the skillets and pans. Helena took Carl and Benhart looking for morels.

Dusk had surrendered to dark when the wagon was back together. "Best we camp here for the night." Ed pulled two axes from the wagon and handed one to Norman. "Let's get a fire started—Anna-Banana, you and the kids could get out the fish poles and see if anything's biting." If Ed was disappointed in barely making twelve miles that day, it didn't show.

By late morning the next day, they were through Allen Creek and headed west on Jackson Road. Sister and Lena walked behind the wagon holding Benhart atop the cow. Anna and the boys followed in the buggy; she rode next to Ed in the wagon.

The throb in her hip had her attention when Ed reined Oskar at a pair of tracks emerging from a field pink with milkweed blossom. He unfolded a paper and squinted north. "Looks about right." He geed Oskar into the milkweeds.

As shadows lengthened and the air cooled, milkweed gave way to pockets of trillium poking from under swamp oak and maple. She nudged Ed. "Children should eat soon, Ed. You plan on stopping for a bite or do you want to set up for the night?"

"Getting hungry myself." He dug for his watch. "Yup, near dinner time, isn't it? If I figured right, Pere Marquette River's just up ahead. We'll camp there."

A bridge appeared. Ed took no notice and bumped straight across. "Old John Glade sure knows these here parts; the Pere Marquette apparently runs right to Ludington." He pointed to what looked like an old mill. "Suppose that belongs to Butters. John said when old Horace

Butters passed, his son took over the business." He held his hand against the sun. "Supposed to be a sluice somewhere here, but I don't see it—probably overgrown."

Helena squinted. So this is where Mrs. Koronrn lost her boy. Overhanging branches cast a deep shadow over a narrow river laced with fallen trees. It seemed no more than a creek. She shuddered and looked away.

The track smoothed and bits of gravel appeared through the weeds. "Telegraph Road," Ed said, shooing a horsefly. "Back in '83, Butters' Mill used to be a head camp. John said there's an old telegraph line somewhere along here." He pointed with his chin. "Looks like a good spot just afore those maples. Once we get to Manistee Junction, we got smooth sailing all the way to Branch Township." He snapped the reins and started to hum.

The following day was pleasantly warm under a cloudless sky when the wagon bumped over the Pere Marquette & Flint railroad tracks and on to the smooth gravel of Route 20. Ed geed Oskar and gave Helena a reassuring wink. "Four more miles and we're there."

An inn appeared ahead opposite the tracks and a small railroad platform. Anna wanted to stop and ask about shopping and markets. Ed hawed Oskar and turned in to Nichols Inn.

Nellie Nichols greeted them on an expansive front porch. "Welcome to Manistee Junction! I'm Nellie." Furniture piled atop the wagon and a cow tethered behind screamed newcomers.

Nellie and her husband, Frank, were one of the first settlers in Mason County. They built the inn in 1880 and added the store and livery after the Pere Marquette & Flint railroad laid tracks. Room and board was 50 cents a night.

Nellie invited everyone to relax in the wicker chairs and brought out a pitcher of ice water and glasses. She was thrilled to be getting new neighbors. Yes, she had heard the National Bank of Illinois crashed, and everyone knew of the lumber camp because Houseman left it such a mess. "Corner of Tyndall and Decker, isn't it?" Nellie smiled and nodded to Ed's question. "Tyndall *is* the county line, Mr. Anderson." And she told Anna that Tallman would have everything she needed. "Yes, good shopping and quite convenient, Mrs. Anderson. Just take Decker Road west around the lake and you're there."

Route 20 remained smooth, as well as deserted. Ed figured the road was in good shape because the railroad kept after it. He never did put much stock in government. Helena sat alongside him, trying to ignore her throbbing hip.

The sun was overhead when Ed spotted a two-track emerging from a jumble of swamp oak and pine saplings. The trail continued across Route 20 and ended at a railroad siding knee-deep in switchgrass. He reined Oskar and hopped down. "Got a bite for us, Mother?" Thank God, it was her turn to ride in the buggy.

Anna collected sandwich wrappings and held up the last bite of cheese. Ed shook his head, finished his water, and pointed to the trail coming from the swamp oak. "Camp's up the county line . . . uh . . . Tyndall, maybe three, three and a half miles. If we get a move on, we could be there in maybe another hour."

Optimism ended a hundred yards into the swamp oak at a fallen tree. "Uh-oh." Ed hopped down and disappeared into the undergrowth. He returned swiping burrs off his pants. "Brush is too thick. Guess we'll have to clear our way." He dropped the tailgate and pulled out axes and gave one to Sister, Lena, and Norman, and they all started chopping. Carl watched his brother hack at a tree and howled for an axe of his own, but he was only seven. Laura and her daughter pulled limbs aside; Helena kept Carl and Ben out from underfoot.

As dusk gathered, fallen trees continued to materialize, and Ed decided to set up camp. He sent Sister and Norman back to the Pere Marquette River with the animals and fishing poles; Anna and Lena set up the tent while Ed sharpened axes and Helena started a fire. Between mouthfuls of fried trout, Ed estimated they had cleared a good half mile.

Clearing started anew at first light and by mid-afternoon the thicket opened and the sky reappeared. Ahead, a barren landscape of shoulder-high stumps and brush stretched from where the vine-twisted growth ended at the county line and to the west as far as the eye could see.

Ed pointed his ax at the stumps. "The clear-cut is Houseman's. The thicket is Lake County. We're just up a bit."

Helena sat next to Ed, amazed at what Houseman had wrought. The earth had been shaved to a stubble of stumps and a tangle of discarded limbs and brush. She turned to the east and looked to the undergrowth; a glint of light in the scrub elms caught her eye. She squinted. Vine and sumac climbed around hewn logs and wound through moss-covered shingles and rusted tin. A wagon wheel with broken spokes leaned under a hole that might have been a window. A shard of glass blinked at her.

"That a cabin, Ed?" To her, it looked more like debris than a building.

Ed jabbed his chin at the woods. "Probably an old hideout. Union government paid a bounty for men to join the army and fight the Rebs. Some deserted before their hitch was up so I'm guessin' there's all kinds of bounty-jumpers hanging low in these parts."

Stumps gave way to a pocket of grassland guarded by a rusty iron gate absent of fencing. Ed hawed Oskar into the switchgrass and jumped down. "We're here!" he shouted.

The gate hung between two vine entangled posts; a padlock dangled from a rusty chain. A faded sign nailed to one post read, "No Trespassing Keep Out."

Ed smacked the lock with an ax and pushed the gate open. "This here's it, Anna-Banana." He swept an arm at a tree line in the distance. "All the way back, 120 beautiful acres."

Her daughter snorted. "Good lord, Father. Couldn't you have just driven around the gate?"

"Pa?" Norman looked confused. "There's nothing here." The slope of grassland ended at a swath of cattails swaying in the light breeze.

"Camp's down by that oak, Son." He handed Norman the ax. "How about getting rid of that sign for us."

A rutted trail led to a pair of buildings hunched under a canopy of scrub elm. A battered oak stood apart like a wounded soldier; cattails meandered behind the two buildings and disappeared among stumps. Ed pointed. "That would be Weldon Creek."

He clucked Oskar between the buildings and nodded at the larger one. "An old bunkhouse." Holes gapped between warped boards; tatters of tarpaper draped from roof battens. A rusty washtub laid atop a broken peavey; two steps led to an empty door opening draped with webs and dead flies.

Anna sat in the buggy unblinking. She considered the two sheds crumpled at the side of the bunkhouse. "Well." Her eyes went to the door opening and a pyre of collapsed bunk racks inside. "Well." Sawgrass shimmered in low light; a critter moved under a pile of debris.

Ed nodded optimistically at the smaller building. "Cookhouse's in better shape—got rooms with doors."

Anna climbed down and signaled her mother that she should hold the kids. Her daughter stepped gingerly through the cookhouse door and surveyed, hands on hips. "What's that thing?" A large iron box, half-buried in leaves and bird droppings, sat against the opposite wall.

"Cook stove." Ed pushed back his porkpie. "Big one too: Probably fed seventy-five, a hundred jacks."

"Suppose that hole in the roof is for the flue."

"Suppose so. Flue's probably still around somewhere."

"Windows missing, walls full of holes, place full of trash and critters." Anna stepped back and looked up. "No roof either." She scowled at Ed.

"Anna-Banana, now look at our blessings." He swept his arm in a broad circle. "Besides a hundred-twenty prime acres, we got an okay cookhouse here, a ready-made barn—so maybe it needs some work—and we got a good . . . a . . . mm . . . a good . . ." Ed dropped his arm.

"A good gate, Father?"

He banged the cookhouse wall with his hand. "This here's probably been put together so tight it couldn't be tore apart." Something inside clattered.

"What?" He avoided her stare. "We'll cover the holes with the tarp. It's better than livin' in the tent, isn't it?"

Her daughter sighed and looked at the children, her face long.

"This here floor's decent, too." He nodded confidence. "Don't worry about the raccoon poop; it don't hurt nothin'." A puff of breeze sent dry leaves scurrying; a crow cawed.

Anna turned slowly. "Well." Her shoulders sagged for a moment then straightened up. She put her shoulders back and took a deep breath. "Well, don't we have our work cut out for us. Guess we'd better get started."

∞

Day started before dawn with fried fish and potatoes. Time ruled, and if not satisfied, failure would befall them. Ed and crew had, at best, seven months to plant and reap what would bear them through the winter. He and Oskar tipped stumps and started a burn pile. Sister and Buck plowed uneven furrows around stumps and planted sorghum. Norman scavenged lumber from the bunkhouse and patched holes in the cookhouse. Carl and Benhart pulled countless brook trout from Weldon Creek. Anna and Lena put in a garden, while Helena and Laura cleaned and cleaned and cleaned.

Nellie Nichols proved right about Tallman—it did have decent shops. Especially Buckout's, the general store, with those new-fangled arc lights and steam radiators, plus a moving stairway to the mezzanine. Steam and electricity came underground from a generator in the mill on Tallman Lake.

But did Tallman have everything? Helena thought not. Granted, Tallman was only a six-mile ride around the lake, but the only church was Congregational. Tallman had room for improvement.

Days sped by, shoots appeared and blossomed; buds became peas and beans. Game was plentiful and Lena became an expert shot with the .22, and many critters trying to snitch garden greens ended up in a pot. Leaves eventually reddened and dropped, snow fell, the temperature plunged, and when the ground froze, Ed and crew sheltered the animals in the bunkhouse. After putting runners on the buggy, they retreated to the cookhouse.

By his compliments, she knew Ed was pleased with what they had all accomplished. He figured they got enough sorghum to feed Buck, Oskar, and the cow for the winter despite him gabbing with every curious soul who rode over from Tallman to see where the smoke was coming from. The cookhouse was livable, although the huge stove kept the big room an oven while the bedrooms stayed like ice. And Norman, not even thirteen, patched the roof and siding and put in a window. The window was just a piece of glass in wood stops, but it did make the big room livable.

Swedish Settlement, as Anna deemed the camp, slowly settled into deepening snow and falling temperatures. Between snowfalls, tracks occasionally appeared in Tyndall Road. A white blanket buried the burn pit and reduced the stumps to stools topped by white cushions.

Ed and Norman came in from tending the animals and stomping their feet. "Freezing out there." Ed blew on his hands and brushed icicles from his beard. "Coffee, Grammie, coffee! Who's got coffee?" Her daughter was at the table sorting through the wash and checking for mending. The girls and Benhart were playing Alouette on the floor.

Ed took a mug from Helena and after a swallow, turned to Sister. "You're right again, little lady. It is a lot colder today."

Sister's eyes narrowed and she fingered a card. "Gonna be even colder tomorrow, Poppa." Benhart put a card down, Sister laid hers on top and picked up both. Benhart scowled.

Anna looked up. "You two going to start that woolly bear foolishness again?" Ed and Sister had been teasing her, saying wooly bears predicted cold weather.

Ed grinned and blew his nose. "Anna-Banana, you don't believe in wooly bears?" He gave her his Oh-My look and winked at Benhart. "Those bears tell you everything you need to know about the weather—right Sister?"

Anna groaned. "The worst part about winter is listening to the two of you."

Norman scowled at the wall. "What was that? Ma, you hear that?"

"Only thing I hear is your father bedeviling everyone."

Sister laid her cards down. "Sounded like a train."

"Did, didn't it?" Ed scratched a hole in the hoarfrost and put his nose to the glass. His shoulders shrugged. "Gotta be down by the siding. Maybe I'll go have a look-see." He set his mug down and pulled on his jacket.

Sister got up. "I'll go with you Poppa." A chorus of me-too preceded scrambling for coats. Norman threw on his jacket and went for the buggy. Not one to miss the excitement, she heaved from the easy chair.

A train *was* at Branch siding. Men were unloading wooden panels and bundles of rope and giant wheels from almost a dozen flatcars. A line of boxcars held horses.

"Logging crew." Ed looped the reins around the dash and poked Carl with his elbow. "Boys, whadaya say we take a closer look." He swung down on the bow socket and reached up for Benhart.

"Don't be gone long, Father." Her daughter tucked the lap robe tighter. "Too cold for us just to be sitting here."

Ed and the boys came back with their shoulders hunched, hands in pockets, and puffing bursts of white. Ed snuffed and called to Anna. "Remember Justus Stearns, Mother? That's his crew—boys, hop in, let's go." Carl threw a snowball at Norman; Norman fired one back at Carl.

"Stearns, the big gun?" Her daughter showed surprise. "The one who stumped for President Harrison last time?"

"One in the same. Operates outta Baldwin now. Boys! It's time. Let's go." He climbed into the seat. "They're gonna cut 160 acres right behind us; all the way over to Tallman."

"Snow deep enough, Father?"

"Don't matter no more, Anna-Banana. See those big wheel things with the spokes coming off the flatbed?" The wheels were twice as tall as the men. "Logs hang underneath off the axle. They haul'm right across bare ground these days. And those panels? Ready-made walls for the cookhouse and bunkhouse. He picked up the reins. "Everything's different now—Carl, Norman. I mean now!"

A snowball flew through the buggy and smacked Laura on the shoulder. Anna yelled. "One more, Carl Anderson, and you'll go hungry tonight!"

"Make'em walk back," Sister said.

∞

The gray days of winter passed slowly; the cookhouse fell into a restless stupor of inactivity other than schooling the children and Ed, who went daily to watch Stearns' logging crew under the guise of exercising Buck. Helena coveted the thought of spring, when she could at last *do something* and the gol-drottin logging would end. Every waking hour, horses—led by cursing men—dragged massive logs down Tyndall, followed by the clamor of engines and metallic clanking.

Flurries finally turned to drizzle and the earth to mud and Stern and his crew disappeared. With the mud came peace and quiet. Once Tyndall was passable, Ed took everyone over to Decker Road to see what Stearns had done. The section appeared as if a cosmic hand had swiped the earth away and left stubble, limbs and brush—massive piles and piles of brush. If it weren't for the rise, the bunkhouse would have been visible.

The year leaped toward summer, and the garden bloomed. Ed and Carl planted more sorghum, and Norman put in the new double-hung windows Ed got on terms from Butters and fixed leaks in the roof—other than the one at the flue. With Anna, the girls, and Benhart, Helena helped expand the garden and put up more wire.

The Fourth of July came and went, and hot weather settled in with a vengeance. Helena was on her knees weeding the garden and trying to remember the last time it rained. The ground was like hard tack, grasshoppers snapping about, lettuce and beans stunted, Weldon Creek shimmering in the heat. Not even hornworms in the tomatoes. She couldn't imagine anything ripening even with Ed watering from the barrels he rigged on the wagon. She pulled erect on her hoe and wiped her forehead.

A plume of yellow dust chased a lorry up Tyndall. The area was growing. A parcel across Tyndall had sold, but Ed couldn't remember the name of the buyer. The Pere Marquette & Flint ran three trains a day, and Mason County put down gravel between Branch and Tallman, although the county didn't touch the Lake County side of the road. He figured that was about all you could expect from government.

The lorry stopped at the gate and a woman hopped down. It was Sister. She had a new job and must have hitched a ride from the siding. Her experience at Rhodes landed her a position at Pomeroy's Ice Cream Parlor in Scottville. Anna was ecstatic that her daughter took the job; Sister was twenty-four and couldn't depend on Ed forever. Back and forth to Scottville cost sixteen cents, but Anna took no mind. She wanted Sister out meeting people and even let her keep a bit of money for herself.

Sister waved and went around the side of the cookhouse. Helena heard her call, "Hi, Poppa, hi Carl." If the two of them were still stumping in all this heat, they must be burning up.

She lifted a limp leaf of lettuce with her hoe. Dry. The whole garden needed watering, but she hated to interrupt Ed if he was stumping. But still, they had to eat and the plants needed water.

She mopped her face and looked at the cloudless sky. A little dark over toward Tallman—maybe rain. Better wait before bothering Ed.

She could hear voices around the corner of the cookhouse. Visitors—or something going on at Butters? Visitors would definitely slow Ed down. But it was getting darker—must be rain. Not voices though. Not thunder either. It sounded more like a crowd cheering. Maybe a game somewhere.

Ed came around the corner of the cookhouse pulling Oskar by the lead. The animal jerked and snorted, its eyes wide and rolling.

"Fire!" he yelled, "Mother! Mother! Fire!" He backed the ox to the water wagon and fumbled with the traces. "Fire! Fire over by Tallman, Mother! Get the kids!"

Helena wheeled around. Smoke! Dark tongues swirled skyward over the back forty. A flame licked up and then another.

Anna burst through the cookhouse door, her face dissolved in terror.

Ed set his heels and pulled hard on Oskar's lead. The barrels rocked, the wagon bumped forward.

"The kids, Mother! The kids!" Ed was screaming. "Get the kids!"

"My God!" Anna shrieked. "Sister! Lena! Fire! Get Benhart and Laura!" Norman and Carl came tearing around the corner. Sister charged out the door with Benhart by the arm, Laura and Lena close on her heels.

"Out in the road!" Ed dropped the reins in Tyndall and set the brake. "Everything out in the road!" He ran for the bunkhouse with Norman and Carl close behind. "Cut 'em loose: Buck, cow, chickens! Cut 'em all loose! Get everything out front!"

Carl tore wire off the chicken coop and screamed. The coop exploded in a burst of feathers. Buck galloped past.

A window opened in the cookhouse; clothes and bedding and drawers flew out. Helana grabbed an armful of coats and dresses and ran to the wagon. Anna ran past dragging two chairs. Norman flew by with axes, tools, and seed bouncing in the wheelbarrow. Sister and Lena wedged the table through the door and dragged it to Tyndall.

Anna pitched blankets and linen under the table and screamed. "Where is it, Ed? Where is it?"

Ed clambered up on the wagon seat. "Looks like it's headed this way! But can't tell for sure!" A trio of deer bounded past. Rabbits and squirrels darted from switchgrass. "If it jumps the creek we're in a heap a trouble!"

Helena stumbled back to the cookhouse, panting, her heart pounding, one leg like rubber. She yelled at Anna. "The trunk! Did you get the trunk!" Weldon Creek burst into a wall of red. Her daughter pushed her back.

"Too late, Mother! Run, just run!"

Sister and Lena had Laura and Benhart backed up against the wagon holding hands. Benhart was bawling. Ed threw the tarp over the pile of clothing and furniture. "The tent!" Ed yelled at Norman. "The tent! Spread it out, soak it down. Soak everything down! Empty all the barrels!" Searing air gusted past, embers soared overhead. The privy burst into flames.

"It jumped! Quick! Everybody run for the creek!" Ed grabbed Benhart and pushed him at Sister. "Git goin'! Don't you dare let him loose!"

Ed undid the traces and slapped Oskar on the rump. "Git!" he screamed. "Git!" Anna grabbed Laura and ran headlong after Sister and Lena.

Helena ran, but switchgrass grabbed at her—her leg wouldn't work. Stumbling, stumbling. Please Lord, don't fall. The bunkhouse roof erupted in flame; burning tarpaper shot skyward.

Sister waded into the cattails, Benhart in her arms. Ribbons of flame came from the coop.

Helena staggered, her lungs on fire. The wind blistered, roared. She couldn't breathe. Something crashed into her. She pitched forward gasping, braced for pain. Please Lord!

It was Ed. He had her around the bosom, half-dragging, half-carrying her. Windows in the cookhouse exploded; she choked water from her lungs; the cattails went black.

∞

Light gradually seeped into her consciousness. Helena jerked awake. Overhead, a sliver of sunshine gleamed through vine-tangled boards and rusted tin. A thicket of swamp oak watched through a doorless opening. Somewhere, something lowed. She was on a tarp under a blanket in her shift. Every bone in her body ached, the smell of burn overpowering. Where were her people? She struggled to her feet and hobbled through the opening.

They were at the wagon watching smoke rise from hot ash. She limped from the swamp oak and followed her family through burnt switchgrass.

Ed shook his head. "Really somethin'." The bunkhouse was a smoldering pile of cinders. The cookhouse roof had collapsed along with most of one wall, and there was no trace of the privy or coop. Shards littered the ashes: A splinter of glass, a blackened spoon, Ed's mug, the basin, soot-covered and warped, china calcified to white dust, the trunk a skeleton of blackened metal bands, the air foul with the rancid stench of burnt pine and utter defeat.

Ed pulled in a long breath. "Coulda been worse. Everyone's safe, and we still got furniture."

Anna stood mute hugging herself. Sister, Lena, Laura and the boys stared wide-eyed. The silence was a shroud, Laura's sniffling the only sound.

Ed reached for her daughter. "Now look-it here, Anna-Banana, we're gonna be all right." He pulled her head to his shoulder. "I'm gonna build you a real house—promise." He rocked her gently. "This here fire just saved me the aggravation of tearing this old camp down." Anna's shoulders heaved. She couldn't remember ever seeing her daughter cry.

ANNA

11 November 1907

"*H*APPY BIRTHDAY TO *you, happy birthday to you . . .*" Anna sat at the dining room end of the table listening to the voices, her heart bursting with gratitude at the bounty surrounding her: The house Ed promised, the barn, the abundance of sorghum, her healthy family, and of course, her mother. Seven years ago when the fire came through, no one would have thought it possible. The grass fire that caught hold of Stearns' brush burned everything to the ground between Decker Road and Route 20, including the Grange office and the Farm Bureau.

"*. . . Happy Birthday . . .*" Helena gazed upon her daughter, standing at the center of the table, marking the beat with a finger. The table was just some planks Ed rigged up, but the tablecloths covered the sawhorses so it looked just fine. Mother sat to the right of Lena and her friend David. Sister and her husband, Willis Pomeroy, sat opposite to keep the boys and girls separated.

"*. . . dear Le-Na . . .*" Ed and the men at the front-room end of the table bellowed out words. Truth told, there was more harmony in a train wreck, but the neighbor ladies at her end—Fredericka holding Anna Marie on one side, Astrid and Gerda on the other—all sang beautifully.

"*. . . Happy Birthday to Youuuu.*" Her daughter bowed. Sister marched in from the kitchen carrying a brown-frosted pan cake with five rows of flickering pink candles. She bent stiffly at the table with a triumphant smile on her crease-lined face and presented the pan like a royal tribute. The children whooped and clapped.

The fire had ignited new life in Swedish Settlement. Fred and Fredericka Zweigle came from Germany in 1903 after a stop in Philadelphia, where Fred worked a year at his father's bakery while he and Fredericka studied English. Fredericka had dark bushy eyebrows and a long braid down her back; both spoke English very well.

It was odd, though, that they still lived in that old cabin across Tyndall. Ed and the boys made it livable for the year it took to build the house and Fred fixed it up too. But why he didn't put in a real floor was a mystery. Fred was a fine husband and father, although he always had something more important grabbing at him than building a regular place for Fredericka. He just was steady and sure, always careful to see that things turned out as he planned.

They had six kids: Helen, Amelia, Hank, Bill, Fred Jr., and baby Anna Marie. She and Fredericka were best of friends, close enough that Anna delivered Anna Marie a few months ago.

Fredericka had asked Mother to midwife, but she said she was past delivering babies. So Fredericka suggested Anna and Mother team up. It was a hot night with the stove roaring, but as it was Fredericka's sixth, the delivery went fine. Fredericka was so grateful, she named the baby after Anna and Marie, her mother.

Following the Zweigles were the Thorsons: John and Astrid and their boys, Seymour and Andrew. Matt and Gerda Stevenson arrived not long after, with their four kids. John and Matt built houses opposite one another on the other side of the county line at the corner of Tyndall and Decker.

Benhart's voice rose above the clapping. "Blow, Lena! Come on, blow!" Hank Zweigle agreed. "Blow, Lena, blow!" The two boys were the same age and inseparable.

Lena pulled her hair back and leaned forward; flames flickered on her face. A shiver swept up Anna's back. She shuddered, then looked to see if anyone noticed.

Her daughter took a deep, closed-eye breath and blew. Amelia and Fredericka clapped.

Willis yelled, "Bravo!" and elbowed Norman. Lena curtsied to Willis.

"Lena," John Thorson called from the end of the table, "How does it feel to be twenty-five?" John, Matt, and Ed were sitting together and had a pail of beer under the table.

Lena grimaced and waved as if swatting a gnat. "Old." She grinned and sat back down between Mother and her friend.

Astrid yelled at her husband. "John Thorson! You mind your manners. It's not polite to ask a lady her age." Astrid poked her. "Well, I guess it ain't much of a secret, is it?" Astrid and Gerda were enough younger than her to make her feel ancient, but John, Matt, and Ed hung together like the Three Musketeers.

Ed yelled back. "You callin' my daughter a lady?" He was bouncing Sister's daughter, Gladys, on his knee. He laughed and slapped John on the back. Little Gladys said, "Gitty-up, Grandpa." She was going on four.

Mother patted Lena on the arm and slid a knife and the stack of plates closer. She wagged a warning finger at Benhart and Hank Zweigle.

Willis held up an ice cream scoop. "Who wants ice cream?" He pulled the top off a brown tub labeled "Pomeroy's Ice Cream Parlor."

"All you kids get in line now—no pushing. That means you too Norman."

Norman laughed; he was twenty-one.

Sister had a real find in Willis Pomeroy. He was a gentleman, polite, well-mannered, and soft spoken. They married in the Methodist Church over in Scottville a year after the fire. The church was filled with flowers for the ceremony, and ice cream and soda pop was served at the reception afterward. That Sister said vows in a church was an eye-raiser considering she never had much in the way of religion. A church wedding was probably Willis's mother's doing—mothers are like that. Of course, Mr. Pomeroy paid for the whole affair. His place in Scottville had him pretty comfortable; enough so, he opened another one in Freemont for Willis.

Anna leaned against Astrid for a better look at her daughter's friend, a David Houston. He was dressed to the nines in a red bow tie, plaid wool suit, a stiff-white collar, and had a solid build. Clean shaven he was, and his nails were neatly trimmed. Possibly he was three or four years older than her daughter, but maybe not.

He was a guest at the Stearns Hotel in Ludington where Lena worked the front desk. Some thought Mr. Stearns hired her because of the fire, but Ed snorted that was too farfetched. Justus Stearns was not the kind of man who'd find guilt in burning down a settlement. He figured Lena was smart and responsible and putting a good-looker at front desk was just shrewd business.

Lena started at the hotel cleaning rooms and commodes and had to quit high school to get the desk job. But she quickly worked her way up to day manager. She invited David to her birthday party because he was a nice man and all alone.

Anna leaned forward and cleared her throat. "Mr. Houston, you're from Boston I understand."

"Yes'm." He met her eye. His teeth were white and even. "Salem, actually, Mrs. Anderson, just outside Boston." He speared a bite of cake. "Mmm, delicious." He wiggled his fork at Sister. "Never had better."

Sister grinned awkwardly, heat rising in her cheeks. She rapped on the table. "You kids clear your own dishes when you're done now."

Gerda whispered. "He *is* a looker, isn't he?" Astrid and Fredericka leaned in, their ears cocked.

Fredericka agreed, "An Adonis. Look at those blue eyes. Lucky Lena." Gerda nodded.

What was it about appearance, Anna wondered. Why would Mother Nature make some as striking as her daughter and this David Houston? Such beauty only drew attention to everyone else's ordinariness.

"What brings you to Ludington, Mr. Houston?" She ignored Lena's frown. If her daughter was going to bring a man home, she could expect questions.

Ed answered. "Cement. What's that company again, David?"

"Carolina-Clinchfield, sir." David touched his napkin to the corner of his mouth. "We're out of Charleston—Charleston, South Carolina, that is."

"It's an enormous company." Her daughter practically gushed.

David's laugh was deep and resonate. "Well, we do have a pretty good railroad and a few coal mines."

She spoke louder. "And Mr. Houston, what do you do for a—"

John Thorson cut her off. "Yeah, I heard of your outfit. Got an operation over in Union City—right?"

"Yes, sir, we do, just south of Battle Creek." David pushed his plate back. "We sell Portland cement in Ludington and Muskegon, Grand Bend and—"

Her daughter interrupted. "David's the sales manager." She looked proud enough to burst.

"Whoa, hang on there, Lena," David laughed. "I only have ten states."

"Interesting, Mr. Houston. Do you have family in—"

"That Portland cement's pretty good stuff." Matt Stevenson this time. "Limestone, shale, gypsum and plenty a heat, ain't it?"

"Yes, sir, that's right." David ran a hand through his blond pompadour and put both elbows on the table. "Right now most Portland cement comes from Europe. But we're about to change that. We've got plans for seventeen new plants."

Anna sat back in the chair. Men! What frustrating creatures. No one ever thinks to ask an important question. Good lord, who cares about cement or gypsum or Europe? What about David Houston, his family, his siblings? How is a body supposed to learn a thing?

Laura pushed back from the table trying not to be seen. She dropped her napkin on the chair and tiptoed upstairs. Gerda looked at Anna, a question on her face.

"Menses. She'll be back down."

"Laura's such a lovely child," Gerda offered. "Like a delicate flower, every bit as pretty as Lena and yet so helpful."

"Anna?" Fredericka tapped her arm and nodded to the baby buried in her ample bosom. "I should go. It's time to feed Anna Marie."

"Leave?" Anna frowned, disappointed. "So soon?" If Fredericka left, other people would follow, and the party would break up before she knew a thing about this David Houston. "Let's you and I sneak into the kitchen. Nobody'll miss us."

She stood and wiggled a finger. "Everybody just sit still now. We're just going to feed the baby." She picked up her teacup and motioned to Fredericka, who stood up with Anna Marie in her arm while bending for her cake plate. She was a graceful woman for her size.

Sure as shooting, as soon as she and Fredericka stood, Astrid and Gerda called to John and Matt for coats. Astrid tapped her arm. "Boys got chores to do, Anna. I'll send them for the chairs in the morning."

"That was one fine meal, Mrs. Anderson." David flashed a wide smile. "I really do appreciate you having me."

Lena had David's coat over her arm, running her fingers through the fur collar. "I'm just going to say goodbye." She opened the door for David and followed him out.

Just like that, the party ended. Sister got the girls hauling plates and glasses to the kitchen, the boys disappeared outside, and the men went to the stoop for an after-dinner smoke. The din coming from the kitchen reminded her of the old days at the manor.

Anna sat alongside Fredericka on the front room sofa feeling miffed. She didn't learn a thing about this stranger from Boston. Mother hobbled past with an apron of crumbs.

"Mother, let that be. Come sit. The girls can clean up."

Lena came in from the porch and stood at the front window, rocking foot to foot, her arms wrapped around herself. She had to be half-frozen; she'd been outside long enough to benumb the devil himself.

Fredericka nodded at Lena. "Someone looks smitten." Her daughter had the curtain hooked back, forehead to glass, trying to follow David's sleigh as it disappeared down Tyndall.

"Oh, I hope not." The manor's long-forgotten Christmas party burst alive and sent a tremor through her. Still, she had to trust her daughter; Lena knew better than to . . . to. . . . She set her cup on the end table. "Lena, Willis and Sister are here. You could be more sociable; go play with Gladys."

Her daughter let the curtain fall back and sighed like Kitty O'Neil in the talkie *Kathleen Mavourneen*. "He is so cute." Lena so resembled Edward, every bit his height, his coloring, carriage, and most certainly his disposition, always quick with a complaint. Lena would be surprised how much she resembled him.

Her daughter fingered the locket around her neck. "Aunt Ricka, thank you so much for the necklace. It's beautiful." She hung over Fredericka, trying to see Anna Marie under Fredericka's blouse.

Anna frowned. "Lena, don't be a pest. Go get the teapot for us, please." She pointed to Mother asleep in the easy chair, her head back and mouth open. "And wake Grammie. She's drooling."

Fredericka beamed at Lena. "Oh, she's no pest. Would you like to burp her when she's finished?"

"Oh, yes—please!" Lena's face radiated. "And maybe I could take her picture." She picked a camera up from the end table. A gift from her friend David—one of those new Pocket Kodak cameras that Butters had in the display case. Considering her daughter barely knew this Mr. Houston, the camera was, indeed, an extravagant gift.

Her daughter came back with the teapot and took Anna Marie, and squeezed in the easy chair alongside Mother. "Oh Lena." Mother blinked awake and dabbed her chin with a hankie. "My stars, I must have eaten too much." She scooched sideways and hooked her cane over the arm. "The cake was sumptuous, wasn't it, Lena?"

Lena's nose twitched. "Mmm, guess so." She put Anna Marie over her shoulder with a kiss and started patting.

When Sister and Willis married and moved to Freemont, Lena acted as if she had been bested by a long-time foe. Sister had a man; Sister had a baby; Sister always got new clothes. The moping was endless. Ed figured giving Sister money was part of the resentment. It wasn't a lot of money, just a bit to help Sister set up housekeeping. She deserved something. She put up with more than any child should suffer: eight years in a tenement, Edward Stark, immigrating to America, Finn Town, a logging camp, and then the fire. And she was always a help, never a hindrance. No one was supposed to know about the money, but secrets have a way of escaping.

Fredericka warmed her tea and watched Lena burp Anna Marie. "Mighty fine-looking daughter you've got there, Anna. A real beauty, just like your house."

Anna hid a smile. Praise was welcome, and she had no reason to disagree. Ed did build a fine house. Pragmatic, like himself, absent of ornamentation, with pious white clapboards under a tin roof and a generous front porch. Just four rooms up and four rooms down, each with a window smack-dab in the middle. Symmetrical was a good description.

The kitchen was big just as she hoped with the pump right at the basin, plenty of cupboards, *and* a new Clapp stove with an attached boiler. When the house was finished, Norman surprised her with a porch swing, and Ed carried her up the two plank steps and across the threshold. The children and Mother cheered and clapped; she felt like a new bride. But Mother said it best: "If only the Lord of the manor could see you now." What Ed didn't get around to was an indoor privy, but he promised he would. And until then, she had her own room for the Singer.

Sister burst in from the kitchen with Gladys at her heels and began folding tablecloths. Gladys spun in a circle calling for grandpa. Not seeing him, she wheeled around and ran back to the kitchen yelling, "Grandpa! Grandpa!"

"WILLIS!" Sister roared in the direction of the kitchen. "Willis

Pomeroy! You mind your daughter now!" She picked up Mother's piece of cake, smiled at Lena holding Anna Marie, and went to the kitchen. Lena rolled her eyes.

"I got her." It was Ed's voice.

The stoop door banged opened and voices rushed in. Carl yelled, "Out of my way, bonehead!"

"Stop shoving!" Benhart hollered back.

Sister's baritone rose above all voices. "CARL! YOU LEAVE THAT CAKE ALONE! THAT'S GRAMMIE'S!"

"Boys! Boys!" It was Ed. "Save the roughhouse for outside."

"Is what's-his-name gone?" Carl wondered aloud.

Benhart's voice broke to a squeak. "Who?"

"The guy from Boston, Mr. Beautiful."

Her daughter scowled, eyes dark. Mother patted her knee. "Just pay no attention, Lena."

"Hey, did you hear the one about the traveling salesman and the farmer's daughter?" That was Carl.

Sister's snorting rose above the laughter.

"Boys!" Ed's voice. "That's enough now." Lena handed Anna Marie to Fredericka and started toward the kitchen, blood in her eye.

Another brouhaha. Anna pushed up from the sofa and grabbed her daughter by the arm. "That's enough! All of you! That's enough! Do you hear me!"

∞

Holidays came and went; contentment drifted to boredom in deepening snow. Ed read bulletins from the Grange and the Farmers' cooperative, tinkered with the hot water boiler or went over to Buckout's to jaw with the men. The children studied lessons, Norman got a job working at Butters' Mill in Tallman, and Anna and Mother worked on, oblivious to any change in daily routine other than the weather got warmer and the days longer.

After picking a bouquet of daffodils for the table, Anna poured a pail of water from the boiler and set it atop the Clapp. She planned fried chicken for dinner and went outside to the run to set a bird. After setting the streaming pail alongside the stump, she cornered a brown, and administered a deft *thwack* with the hatchet. The brown sprinted headless across the pen, red pumping skyward.

"Hi, Ma. Chicken tonight, huh?" She jumped. It was Norman.

Her son swung down from Sally and ran his hand down the horse's nose. The brown and white Appaloosa nibbled and nosed his glove. He pulled Sally's face to his.

"Good lord, Norman! You scared me half to death. Home early, aren't you?" He had a new job. Mr. Butters promoted him to finish carpenter when he saw the knack Norman had for woodworking. He gave his pay envelope to her but kept enough out to take in an occasional movie when a good one came to Ludington.

"Finished up. But I got another job. One of them spiral stairs." He unbuckled Sally's saddle and swung it over the fence rail. "Ma, did you know Mr. Fuller's got his mill up for sale?"

"Really? The one on Gooseneck Lake?" She handed the hatchet to Norman. "Get me another brown would you please, Norman. Pluck this one too; water by the block."

"Sure, Ma." He opened the pen gate.

"Norman."

"Huh?"

"Sally first?"

"Oh, yeah. Thanks, Ma." He started to the shed with the hatchet in hand and Sally nosing his back. "Ok, girl, ok."

"Norman?"

"Yeah, Ma."

"The saddle."

"Oh yeah, right. Thanks again, Ma."

∞

After a supper of fried chicken with potatoes and onions, Ed stretched back in the chair while Grammie cleared the table. "Mighty fine meal, ladies, mighty fine." He tucked fingers in his waistband. "Leghorn, wasn't it, Mother? Thought you kept leghorns for eggs." Ed worried a tooth with a toothpick.

"I know." She scowled at her son. "Told Norman to set a brown." Laura looked at Norman, her fingers masking a grin.

"Sorry, Ma. Couldn't catch a brown." He jumped up and started for the kitchen. "Come on, Sis, let's give Grammie a hand."

Grammie came back in untying her apron. "Isn't Norman something? Such a considerate boy." She spotted a crumb and brushed it into a napkin. "Where is Lena tonight?"

"She's in Ludington, Mother." Anna raised her eyebrows at Ed. "Something about a banquet, Father. The hotel needed extra help. That's what I was told anyway."

Benhart held up a fist. "Ready, Carl?"

Carl shook his head. They were playing Morra for the last piece of chicken. Ben's legs sprawled from the chair with a casual elbow on the table smiling at the deep concentration on his brother's face. "Betcha Mr. Wonderful is in town—come on, Carl, count."

The furrows rutting Carl's forehead relaxed, and he snickered. "You mean the traveling salesman?" The furrows returned, his eyes narrowed. "One, two, three, shoot." he thrust two fingers at his brother. Seeing Benhart's forefinger, he shrugged. "Two out of three?" Ben snorted and reached for the chicken.

"Boys, take that sarcasm somewhere else." Caution was in Ed's voice; he thumbed at the stoop door. "Git the .22 and git after that critter that's been chewing on the cellar door." He raised his eyebrow at Anna.

"Don't look at me, Father. Lena said she had to work."

"Oh?" Worry showed on Grammie's face. "Work all night? Is there a chaperone?"

"Mother, you know Lena." She shrugged at Ed. "I did say something, and she accused me of being an old fuddy-duddy. I'm told times have changed." She eyed the mending basket. Do the mending or start a shirt for Carl? He had grown so. She had the pattern and there was enough cambric.

"Mother, I don't think we have to worry about Lena. She's a responsible young lady." Start the shirt. The sewing room afforded peace and quiet.

Norman appeared in the doorway, Laura behind him, her hand on his back. He elbowed her hand away and straightened his suspenders. "Just wait, okay, Sis.

"Finished up, Ma. Mind if we use the buggy tonight?"

"The buggy?" Her face was blank; what in the world would the two of them want the buggy for? "Well, if your father says so."

"Where you planning on going, son?" Ed looked him in the eye.

"Scottville, Pa. Won't be but a couple of hours. Right, Sis?"

Laura peered around Norman and nodded. Curls the color of honey framed a serious face and wire-rimmed spectacles. "It's a meeting, Poppa," She pushed her glasses up with a finger. "A study meeting."

Ed looked unusually stern. "A study meeting now. Hmm, about what?" He paid little attention to the children's whereabouts when they were young; kids needed to learn to take care of themselves. But now that Lena and Laura were young ladies, he'd gotten decidedly more cautious. Ed didn't need to worry about Laura, though; she had a steady head on her shoulders and wasn't prone to gadding. Besides, Norman was going with her; that study meeting must be something special.

"It's about science, Poppa." Laura jiggled on her toes. "Won't last but an hour and we'll be home straight away—promise."

Ed relaxed "No stopping at Pomeroy's for a soda?" The twinkle in his eye returned. "Well, that'd be a first." Laura gave him a hug, then pulled Norman for the stoop.

"Hitch up Buck Norman, he could use the exercise." Anna glanced at the clock on the end table. "Father, pass me the lamp, would you please. I'm going to start a shirt for Carl."

Grammie was astonished. "Laura's going out . . . and to a meeting? Well, isn't that something." Laura usually spent her leisure time reading and Grammie worried that she had turned into a bookworm and would ruin her eyes.

Anna tapped the table with a firm finger. "Laura *should* be out meeting people. She'll never find a man reading a book. And it's not that kind of meeting, Mother." She picked up the lamp. "I think it's a get-together about some religion Laura read about."

"Lutheran?" Grammie's eyes lit up; she clumped her cane on the floor. "Wouldn't that be nice? If you ask me, that's exactly what Tallman needs: a good Lutheran church. Those Congregationalists have such an ordinary service."

"You'll have to ask Laura about that." Anna rummaged in the mending basket for pins.

Ed cleared his throat. "Heard something interesting the other day." He rested his elbows on the table and examined his toothpick.

"What's that, Father?"

Ed acted like he had some big secret. "Old man Fuller's selling the mill."

"Must be so. I heard that myself." She relished the surprise on Ed's face. "The mill over on Gooseneck Lake, right, Father?"

"Right." Ed sounded disappointed. "But it ain't no rumor, Anna-Banana. Fuller might have a buyer too." He sat back and rolled the toothpick to the side of his mouth.

"Is that right? You know who, Father?"

"Sure do." Ed looked mighty smug. "Know 'em all." He leaned back in the chair and put his hands behind his head.

"Well now." She eyed the Singer in her sewing room. Was there no escaping? "And who would that be, Father?"

"Me'n Matt, and John, that's who. We're thinking of going in together."

She put the lamp back on the table and sat down. "You and Matt and John? Buy Fuller's mill?" He sounded serious. "What on earth do the three of you know about running a shingle mill?"

That was just like Ed, finding something new to chew on when he already had a mouthful. He, Carl and Ben had their hands full just working a quarter section, and now he wants to run a shingle mill?

Apparently, Ed and company didn't learn from that school house fiasco four years ago. Whatever possessed them to go in on a deal like that was beyond comprehension. The three of them decided eight miles to Route 20 and Benson was too far for the young ones to walk to school even when the weather was decent. They agreed their kids deserved better so they built a schoolhouse on John's corner at Tyndall and Decker.

A fine schoolhouse it was. But the three musketeers didn't foresee schools were going up everywhere, and schoolmarms were as scarce as an honest politician. They finally found Miss Stevenson in Muskegon and agreed to pay her thirty dollars a month, plus give her room and board. Matt and Girda took her in. They thought they might be related but it turned out Miss Stevenson wasn't even Swedish. A year later, the folks over in Green Lake built a school of their own and hired Miss Stevenson away. The three of them were real put out; they didn't seem to care about saving thirty-dollars a month.

"What do the three of you know about runnin' a shingle mill?"

"Not much to know. Place pretty much runs itself. Got two steam-powered Hanson Uprights, both are old, but in good condition. Marshall Butters sends over his pine trunks—they're called bolts—and we run 'em through the Hansons, and shingles drop out the other side. No shaving, no drawing, no nothing, just good solid shakes."

Wood shakes were clean and gave a house stature. Better than tin, that rusts, the rust dripping and staining whatever was below. And besides, the mill was awash in bolts and he could get them for almost nothing.

"Well, isn't that something. The Hansons do everything." A shingle mill sounded worse than the schoolhouse debacle.

"Yup, sure do. Modern manufacturing is really something." He looked pleased with himself. "Wish I'd used shingles on this place instead of tin—we got rust everywhere."

She had a sinking feeling. "Ed, can't you just buy shingles? Why buy a mill?"

"Diversification, Anna-Banana, diversification." He agreed with himself. "Right now we got all our sorghum in one basket."

"Don't you mean eggs, Father?" Ed never was a fancy talker.

"Now don't you go confusing me. You know what I mean." He sat up and put the toothpick in his pocket. "Sorghum's about run out around these parts. Germans back in Holton got all the cattle and there's not much call for feed around here. Everyone's diversifying."

"Is that so?" Fredericka did say Fred was talking about opening up another quarter-section of fruit trees. "Guess I'm a bit surprised, Father. You ever think about fruit trees?"

"Hey!" Ed jumped up. "Was that a shot?" He headed for his coat. "Sounds like the boys got something."

"It's always something, isn't it?" Grammie folded her napkin and reached for her cane.

Anna found the pins in the mending basket and finally went to her sewing room. It was too late to start a shirt, and she didn't feel like it anyway. But she could sit by herself in peace and quiet and worry about Lena spending the night in Ludington.

∞

12 December 1907

HER ANXIETY ABOUT Lena was prescient. Her daughter was leaving, and leaving with a man she scarcely knew on a train to Jacksonville, Florida. Good lord, the first time she laid eyes on David Houston was barely a month ago and she hadn't seen him since.

But he was a letter writer. Lena had a stack of them, and they all made her behave like a lovesick teenager. She about wore out the curtain standing at the front window looking for Mr. Bergez, the postman. And now she knew the reason: Lena's knight had come to carry her away.

And carry her away from what? From the privy and the cook stove and the iron hand of the seasons? There were no rings or promises exchanged, or plans made. Her daughter was off with a man who she knew nothing about. And Lena could not have been more inconsiderate, leaving just before the holidays. David had to stay on schedule. He had an important job, had to be in Jacksonville by the first of the year. Well, la de da!

"I'll send presents from Florida," Lena decreed. As if that was what Christmas was all about. Carl called her snooty; it was hard to disagree.

Anna stood at the kitchen window, staring blindly at snowflakes drifting from a vanilla sky. The commotion above moved from the girl's room to the hallway and down the stairs. It was all so wrong; Lena would simply not listen to reason.

Admittedly, this David Houston was a compelling opportunity. A woman needed a man to escape home and spinsterhood. He was a rare prospect in a hinterland such as Branch. David could open the world for Lena. She could experience what she had only read about: big cities, high fashion, indoor plumbing, waiters, doormen, chambermaids. And with children inevitable, she would at last overtake Sister and wipe the smugness from her face.

"Anna?" Grammie called from the doorway. "Anna, come. Lena wants to take a picture."

Anna threw her apron across a chair and went to the front room. Lena's bags that had been waiting at the door were gone; someone was making a racket in the yard. "What is that god-awful noise?" Mother and Laura had the curtain pulled back looking out the window.

Laura pointed. "Car horn, Mother. Come look."

David was parked out front, one foot on the running board of a shiny black Reo motor car with red spoke wheels. Benhart was alongside fingering the large brass horn. Ed, Norman and Carl had their heads under the black canvas top. Benhart crushed the horn bulb—the horn blared. Carl banged his head against the top. Hank Zweigle came running across Tyndall with Fred Jr. and Bill close behind.

Anna pulled on her winter coat and stepped to the porch. "Benhart! Enough! You'll wake the dead!" Not more than thirty minutes ago, this highfalutin' David Houston from Boston pulled right up to the front step and tooted for her daughter. It was bad enough he didn't come to the door, but worse, Ed and the boys bolted outside as if the house was about to explode.

Lena pulled her arm. "Mother, you and Dad stand on the bottom step with Grammie. The rest of you line up behind." She handed the camera to David then squeezed in between her and Ed. "Everybody smile now."

David stood with his heels together and bent over the camera. "Ready? Say cheese everyone." Anna did her best to look happy as the box uttered a *schwick*. David checked the film window and held up a finger. "One more." After winding the knob, he squinted again. "Ben, please look at the camera . . . one, two, three—good one!"

Lena cheered and gave each of the boys a squeeze and kiss on the cheek. She hugged Laura, who thanked her for the clothes. Lena was buying all new outfits in Jacksonville. The two of them whispered and hugged again. She put her arms around Ed. He looked like he was in pain, had trouble getting words out. "Write your mother, now," was all he could manage.

David put Lena's valise in the back box and eased her into the passenger seat. He and Ed pumped hands. "I'll take good care of your daughter, sir. Promise."

He gave each of the boys a mock punch on the arm and hopped on the running board. "Florida here we come." With a sweeping wave, he ducked into the car. The magneto clicked; the engine sputtered, then roared. He lifted the windshield and squeezed off two loud honks. The chain clanked into gear and the Reo jumped forward.

The car dissolved to a grainy image in a flurry of snow. Ed turned to her and Grammie. "Can you imagine? That Reo Runabout cost over $600."

Grammie was not impressed. "I just hope they don't get stuck in the snow."

Norman snorted. "In that car? With eight horsepower? That baby can do twenty miles an hour on the straightaway. They'll be in Florida in no time."

"Norman," Laura snickered. "They're taking the train—remember?"

He blushed. "Oh yeah, right, Sis."

She turned to Ed, questioning. "The train, Father? What about the Reo?"

He put his arm around her. "Anna-Banana, what difference does it make? You're all bound up. She loves him. He loves her. Stop worrying." He put his arm around her, and his eyes twinkled. "At least, he didn't ask for my ladder."

She shook him free. Ed could be so dense. She was fighting back tears, and he's cracking jokes. It didn't look like love to her. It looked more like urges.

∞

The void left by Lena's absence was filled by tranquility. As winter passed to spring, Ed, Carl, and Ben heeled to the pace of Mother Nature while Norman battled the realities of customer satisfaction. The women continued to worry over the weather and Lena's whereabouts.

Spring had finally arrived, and Anna was making dinner. She moved the Dutch oven from the Clapp to the kitchen table. "Laura, are the men ready to sit?" The oven held the three mallards Carl bagged. Two were for supper and the third for tomorrow's lunch.

Laura glanced through the doorway. "Looks like it. Even Norman."

She handed the bowl of turnips and beets to her daughter and followed her to the dining room with the ducks. She set the platter and knife in front of Ed. "Careful, everyone; there may be shot."

"Smells wonderful, Anna." Grammie passed a serving to Ben.

Ed took a bite of duck and chewed carefully. "Anything new from Lena, Mother?"

She shook her head. The first letter came just after New Year's on watermarked stationery with "The Seminole Hotel" embossed across the top and "For Discerning Travelers" below. An upper corner held a chromolithograph of a ten-story, red brick hotel. The second letter was on rich beige stationery with "Helena A. Houston" in gold scrolled at the top. Both were from Jacksonville and if exclamation marks were a judge, her daughter was having a wonderful time. "Just the two letters so far, Father."

Ed speared a piece of duck then pointed his fork at Laura. "How about you, young lady? You hear anything new from Lena?" Clever of him to ask Laura. She was always at the window when Mr. Bergez came with the mail. All eyes went to Laura; the boys leaned in. Laura shook her head. "Nothing, Poppa."

Ed niggled a tooth. "Sounds like Lena's having the time of her life."

The letters spoke of indoor commodes and tuxedoed waiters and rooms set with white tablecloths and silver and china, seeing football games, marching bands, shopping in the best stores, and coming home to nary a chore. He forked a chunk of turnip and winked at Grammie. "I'll bet Lena's even got a chambermaid." Grammie covered a laugh.

Ed considered. "I wonder if maybe Lena's living a little too high—affluence is a bad thing to get used to."

"Oh Poppa." Laura snorted and fingered her glasses up. "Who wouldn't love living high off the hog—except possibly you?"

She watched Ed enjoy the laughter. Her daughter was dead-on; his idea of fancy living was little more than three squares a day, a warm bed, and his family's comfort.

When the teasing ended, Laura asked for the buggy. "The road's dry, Mother. Can we go to Scottville tonight?"

Ed's grin faded. "Who's we?"

"All of us." Laura pointed a finger at the boys, and they nodded. "Norman and I have our meeting; Carl and Ben want to go to *Pomeroy's*."

"Anna." Grammie's brows pulled together. "Don't you think Ben is a little young to be—"

She interrupted. "He's sixteen, Mother. He's got to learn." She nodded at Laura. "But help Grammie in the kitchen first." She turned to Carl. "And you keep an eye on Ben, you hear?"

∞

The letter she anticipated arrived early May; her daughter was expecting. Lena wrote they had rented a house in downtown Jacksonville at 1543 Laura Street, and she had a housekeeper and a nanny to help when the baby came. The house sounded quite grand: two verandas, one off the front room and the other off the upstairs bedrooms, plus a commode on each floor.

In September, a letter announced the arrival of Stanley Houston on the seventh and included photographs: Lena holding the baby on a shady veranda, wicker rocking chairs in the background; Lena and Stanley on a sidewalk in front of a house shadowed by thick cypress trees; David holding the baby with two black women in housekeeping dresses, standing alongside.

Grammie passed back the photos. "It's too bad Lena didn't name him Peter or Anders or Ed." She shrugged. "Stanley must be a Houston name, but it does have a nice ring to it. I just hope everyone's doing well."

Ed folded the letter muttering to himself. "I guess I'd better get back out there before Carl and Ben come after me."

He was anxious to finish cutting the sorghum so he could schedule the thresher crew with the McCormick. He took a final sip of coffee and stood. "By the way, Anna-Banana, John and I'll be closing on the mill next couple days. Scottville Bank approved the loan."

"You and John?" She pushed table crumbs into a pile. "What happened to Matt? I thought he was part of it."

"Nah, Matt said he couldn't." Ed started for the stoop for his boots. "Said Gerda was still peeved about the schoolhouse thing. No matter. Just leaves more for me and John."

"Well, working a mill sounds iffy to me, Father." It was too late to argue; what's done is done. "But if that's what you want, I just hope you'll be careful."

Gerda was smart to keep a tight rein on Matt; people who worked at Fuller's lost fingers.

∞

Grammie's hope that everyone was well was for naught. Wasn't four months later her brother, Peter, died. It was sudden, Karolina said. He was just sitting in his chair talking to her, when his eyes went blank and he flopped over. She was right there, but he had no breath or pulse. The coroner had no idea of what killed him. Grammie was hysteric; her younger brother gone and not knowing why. And as Karolina and Peter never wed, the cabin went to her. Thank goodness Karolina had family and she had Mrs. Koronrn in Finn Town.

Before the pain of Peter's death receded, Ed's brother fell ill. The doctors first thought Benjamin had typhoid with the fever but later decided it was cholera because of the cramps and diarrhea. When the coroner opened him up, though, they found it was pneumonia that did him in.

Ed had a hard time between making wood shakes and running back and forth to Muskegon to watch his brother die. Benjamin just wasted away, not able to take a decent breath, drowning in his own juices. It took all of his worth to pay the doctors, but with Ed the only kin, he wound up with Benjamin's 120 acres—and the note to the bank.

Peter's death followed so soon by Benjamin's clung to Grammie like nettles. She was preoccupied, looked over her shoulder as if expecting something to befall her at any moment. In the grip of the threes; one more death was inevitable. Whose would it be?

Anna rolled her eyes. "Oh, Mother, don't start that again. You're going to worry yourself sick over an old wives' tale." But the passing of Uncle Peter and Benjamin so close together did bring threes to mind.

"We should just count our blessings, Mother. We're all healthy, the mill's doing fine, and there's no reason for that to change. Besides, Lena just gave you a brand-new great-grandson." She opened the oven door and tapped the crust rising above the bread pan. "Five more minutes."

Laura called from the front room. "Moth-her, Aunt Ricka's here."

Fredericka clumped into the kitchen in her stocking feet with Anna Marie bundled in her arms. "Hope I'm not interrupting anything, Anna, but I need a breath. Fred's driving me crazy. Doesn't know what to do with himself when he can't get out and about. This mud can't dry up soon enough to suit me."

She agreed. "And everyone else."

But unlike Fredericka, she didn't have men underfoot. Ed, Carl, and Ben were at the mill every day and Norman had his own work. But poor Fredericka, she was stuck with Fred and three boys.

She filled the teapot. "Laura, why don't you unbundle that poor baby for Aunt Ricka." Sitting and having a cup of tea with Fredericka, Mother and Laura made a day special.

Fredericka plopped down and shrugged her coat to the chair back. "Well, what do you hear from Lena? Bread smells wonderful, Anna."

"Well, let's have a slice." She moved the butter tub to the table. "Lena didn't say too much in her last letter. Sounded like she still has a case of the blues."

Grammie snorted. "Makes you think, doesn't it? Lena alone in a strange town with a new baby, David gallivanting to Atlanta and Tallahassee and Savanna and who knows where else?"

She couldn't disagree. "Well, the two of them certainly are a modern couple."

"Need the privy; tea's going right through me." Grammie pulled her cane from the chair back. "Don't say anything important till I get back."

Laura held out both hands for Anna Marie. "Lena is living the life of Riley *and* seeing the country, Aunt Ricka." Anna Marie squirmed and tried to slide from Fredericka's lap.

Fredericka pulled a lace-trimmed hankie from her sleeve and blotted her nose. "Life of Riley?" She raised her eyebrows at Anna.

"High off the hog." She nodded at a magazine on the table. A woman in a Gibson-girl cut wearing an elegant strapless gown smiled from a deep red cover. "Some guy named Riley travels with wealthy people then writes about them. Laura's taste in magazines is getting real high-falutin'."

Fredericka picked up the magazine. "*McClure's*? That Riley guy must be *real* high-falutin'. This magazine costs a whole dollar."

Laura objected. "That's for an entire *year*, Aunt Ricka." She snuggled Anna Marie. "It's a literary magazine. Mother and Poppa gave me a subscription for Christmas. They want me to get me some manners—like Lena." Laura pulled her glasses down and crossed her eyes at her mother.

Anna ignored her. "It's hard not to be envious."

Fredericka's face beamed. "Anna, you must be so proud of Lena."

She nodded. She was proud enough to burst. "Who'd ever thought one of my girls would do so well?" She leaned toward Fredericka and covered her mouth. "Must be Edward's doing."

"Oh, really!" Laura stuck out her tongue. "But we're all just tickled pink for Lena, Aunt Ricka. And I love the magazine. There's some wonderful verse, and they've been running Willa Cather's biography of Mary Baker Eddy—Mrs. Eddy is such an amazing woman."

The *McClure's* series portrayed Mrs. Eddy as one of the country's most prominent women. Thrice-married—divorced, abandoned and widowed, she was a deeply religious woman who overcame seemingly impossible health and personal difficulties. Besides founding a religion that drew over 250,000 followers who built better than a thousand churches, she authored fifteen books, multiple journals, and started a daily newspaper that achieved international respect. Mrs. Eddy believed that disease was a mental error, not a physical affliction, and that the science of prayer, rather than medicine, was the path to healing.

"Anna!" Grammie burst through the stoop door. "Anna, quick, get Ed's gun."

"Gun, Mother? What on earth do you want a gun for?"

"You see the size of that buck down by the privy?" She went to the counter and leaned to the window. "It's at the creek now. Why aren't there any men around when you need one?"

"Mother." She stuffed back a laugh. "What would we do with 150 pounds of venison?" Mother must be losing her mind.

"Do? My stars, Anna—"

"Mother, it's been ages since Ed shot a deer, let alone dressed one." She snorted. "Probably forgot how by now." It was that mill. Life was all shingles, shingles, shingles. There was no time for plowing or planting or growing or even milking a cow. They reaped in a Tallman store now: milk, meat, supplies, and everything else. Even the cellar was about empty.

Ten years ago, working 120 acres of your own was the dream of a lifetime. Now, 240 sat fallow, other than the garden and chickens. Ed and crew had definitely become citified. Curious how progress pulled people off-track bit by bit and made changes without being noticed. She wasn't sure what progress was anymore.

In April, the myth of threes reappeared. Mr. Bergez banged on the door in the wee hours and Ed read the telegram aloud with everyone standing around the dining room table in nightshirts. STANLEY PASSSED 4 17 09 STOP NOT WELL STOP COMING HOME 04 27 09 ON GRAND RAPIDS INDIANA NO 213 STOP LENA.

Anna pulled on boots and ran across Tyndall to use the Zweigles' telephone. The call must have cost a fortune with operators switching back and forth and multiple connections. And then she could hardly hear her daughter with all the buzzing and static. She had to get the charges from Fredericka.

Lena sounded weak, even bitter. The delivery went well enough, but she came down with something in the hospital then passed it to Stanley. The poor little fella never did get well. He was in and out of the hospital the entire seven and a half months of his life. He was buried in Woodland Cemetery just outside Jacksonville. She said nothing about David and didn't know what was ailing her, but if she was to die, she wanted to die at home.

Tuesday, April 27, arrived to hurried preparations. She waited for Ed at the stoop door tapping her foot. The Grand Rapids-Indiana No. 213 was due that afternoon.

"Father, should we take the wagon? Lord knows how many bags Lena'll have."

Ed consulted his watch then shook his head. "If we're gonna beat Lena to Ludington, we need the buggy—the wagon's too slow."

Grammie held out a blanket. "Anna, here, take this. Lena might not remember how cold it is in April." She leaned close and hissed. "See? I told you I had a premonition."

"Mother, just stop it." She turned to Laura. "We should be back before dark, but don't you and Laura wait supper on us. Feed the men."

When Lena's telegram arrived, Laura began praying for her sister. She kept a Bible and Mrs. Eddy's *Science & Health with Key to the Scriptures* on the stand next to her bed along with a pencil and notepad. She said it was just things she had learned at the Society in Scottsville. She hoped to help Lena.

Buck showed white lather cantering into Ludington, but at Sherman Road, the traffic slowed then came to a stop. When the buggy ahead moved, Ed jiggled the reins—Buck pulled a few paces forward then stopped. Ed suspected some wagon up ahead was too wide to pass the trolley when it stopped. The buggy just ahead clopped forward, then stopped.

Anna was as tight as a banjo string. "Gol-drotten traffic's slow as molasses, Ed. What time is it?"

"Five minutes later than you asked last time, Anna-Banana. Git!" Buck pulled forward. She rued not leaving earlier. The Flint & Pere Marquette ferry docks, Stern's mill, and the shuttle to Epworth were all at the end of James Street. People and rigs were coming and going every which way and the line waiting to turn onto James appeared endless.

"Ed. What time—"

"Enough, Anna-Banana. When was the Grand Rapids-Indiana ever on time?" The wagon ahead of Buck moved. Ed hawed the buggy around to James Street.

Grand Rapids & Indiana No. 213 arrived dependably late and clanked to a halt in a cloud of steam alongside the Epworth shuttle. The donkey engine at Stern's mill emitted earsplitting whistles, followed by the deep blasts of the incoming F&PM ferry No. 21. The wood-hulled Ann Arbor No. 2 and side-wheeler *John Sherman* were outbound to Manitowoc. Anna stood on tiptoes looking for Lena across a sea of people.

Ed pointed. "That her?" A tall woman in a slim, ankle-length black dress with puffy sleeves and a fur wrap stepped from the Pullman. Her black bonnet was cocked fashionably over one ear. She waved a gloved hand at him.

Anna dodged through the crowd pulling Ed behind her and put her arms around her daughter. There was nothing there. She was all skin and bones—good lord, how much weight had she lost? Lena wheeled around to Ed and fell against his shoulder. "Oh Poppa, I thought I'd never make it. Please take me home."

Ed ran Buck right up to the porch steps and carried Lena in the house. Grammie and the boys stood quietly while he got Lena up the stairs to Laura. The covers on Lena's old bed were turned back and an afghan ran across the foot of the bed. A vase on the window sill held stems of daffodils.

Norman puffed into the room with a pair of bags. "That's all four of 'em." He dropped two matching leather valises alongside a small leather trunk with brass trim. "Branch air'll fix you up quick as a wink, Sis. Good to have you home."

Laura picked up Lena's hand and caressed it. "And in your own bed again,"

She did not resemble the vibrant twenty-five-year-old that barely a year earlier puttered down Tyndall waving goodbye from a shiny black motorcar. Her cheekbones were stark again her pale skin, waxen and sallow. Eyes peered from dark recesses.

Ed started for the door. "Mother, I'm going over to Zweigles to call a doc."

"Don't call the old guy," Carl said. "He uses leeches."

Lena raised a tentative hand. "No doctors, Poppa, please, no doctors." Her head rocked on the pillow with closed eyes. "No more doctors."

"Huh?" He scowled at her looking confused.

"Poppa." Laura took his arm. "She's exhausted, Poppa. Let her rest." She spread the afghan across her sister. "What she needs more than anything right now is sleep."

Medical treatment came with hazards; remedies could kill, and regularly did. Some treatments—from drinking radium water or mercury to sitting in hydro-electric baths—promised a wide range of benefits. Many people saw the preferable path to recovery as prayer and belief, instead of being bled to death, poisoned, or electrocuted.

Laura took Carl and Ben by the arm and marched them to the door.

"Lena needs rest. I'll be down in a while." She patted Norman on the arm. "Would you mind bringing me that soup that's on the stove, please?"

Ed looked at her wide-eyed. "Well, holy gol-drotten." He looked baffled. "How in the world . . ."

She gave Ed a gentle push. "Not now, Father. Let's eat. Grammie's got our dinner ready." Ed went downstairs, shaking his head.

In the morning, Anna was in the kitchen with Grammie when Ed came in. "Carl and Ben gone already?"

She stood and nodded yes. "Want eggs, Father?" Grammie set a mug of coffee on the table and pushed it at Ed.

He jerked his thumb at the ceiling. "How's she doin'? What's going on up there?"

"Laura says she's much better, Father," Anna said, looking to her mother for confirmation. "You might hold off on calling someone."

Grammie agreed. "Laura and Norman have been upstairs praying for her, Ed. Must be working if what she ate for breakfast is any measure."

Norman came into the kitchen carrying dirty plates. "Lena's doing great, Pa, no need for doctors."

The forkful of egg bound for Ed's mouth halted. "Is that so?" He set the fork down and cocked an eye at Norman. "Thought you were a carpenter, Son. When did you learn doctoring?"

"Didn't, Pa." Norman shook his head. "I don't know a thing about medicine, but I learned at Society in Scottville that healing comes from God, not medicine."

Grammie agreed. "Could be true, Ed. One thing for sure, doctors didn't help a single soul back in 1868 during the plague or your poor brother a year ago, either—God rest his soul." She warmed his coffee. "People should give prayer a chance. The Good Lord is far better than anything comes out of a bottle."

Norman nodded. "Grammie's right. Mrs. Eddy says that illness is caused by false belief. Medicine doesn't work; healing comes from God."

"Mrs. who?" Ed squinted at Norman.

"Mary Baker Eddy. She founded Christian Science."

Grammie nodded. "Faith in God is what it is, Ed. The Good Lord hears our prayers, heals the sick, feeds the needy—every Lutheran knows that." She thumped her cane to validate the certainty.

Ed tossed his napkin on the table. "You're telling me it's all in Lena's head?" He gave Norman his don't-fool-with-me look.

"Not exactly, Pa." Norman put the plates in the sink. "Mrs. Eddy teaches that sickness isn't real; it's an illusion. We can help Lena by knowing the illusion is false—help her know the Truth."

"Now wait just a minute." Ed looked incredulous. "You're telling me there's no such thing as sickness?" Norman nodded.

"Then why in the world does anybody need healing? If you ask—"

"Prayer, Ed." Grammie interrupted. "Them Scientists call praying a lesson."

Norman's grin widened. "Not really, Grammie." His face went serious. "We don't ask God to hear our prayers. Mrs. Eddy wants us to see that illusions are false and not just pray for help." Norm explained he learned Mrs. Eddy's interpretation of the Bible by reading *Science & Health*. Lessons were published in the *Christian Science Quarterly* and often read aloud during Sunday services.

So that was what Laura had been talking about. Anna's eyes widened. "You got a *woman* pastor, Norman?"

Grammie snorted. "Lutherans have men for pastors—not that your mother ever knew."

"No, not a pastor, Ma. Mrs. Eddy doesn't want anyone to stand between us and God."

Ed rolled his eyes. "Suppose that does cut down on the politicking some."

Norman didn't hear. "Mrs. Eddy has us read parts of the Bible, and then she explains what each passage means."

Ed raised a finger. "She tells you what the Bible means? How is it this Mrs.—" He stood and fumbled with his suspenders. "How is it this Mrs. Eddy gets to decide what the Bible means?" He shook his head. "I ain't got time for crazy talk." He snapped a suspender over his shoulder and ran a thumb up and back.

Anna tucked in his shirttail. "Her color is back, Father. Lena does look a lot better."

Ed was justifiably skeptical. Norman was the quintessential optimist, and sometimes he had trouble sorting hope from fact. "Got to get a move on." He drained his mug and pulled on his jacket. "But if you ask me, this healing business is pie-in-the-sky. A doc makes more sense than trying to wish away whatever ails you. Anna-Banana, try to talk some sense into those girls." He put on his porkpie and turned for the stoop.

"Prayer is a powerful force, Ed," Grammie said, wagging a finger at him. "The Good Lord hears all voices."

"Well, Mother Andersson." His face broke into a grin. "If *you* say so. But what I'm hearin' is doctors and religion cancel one another out." He pulled the stoop door open. "Seems like they oughta work together, help one another." The stoop door closed.

Through the balance of the week, the girl's room door remained closed and Norman bussed food and dishes up and down the stairway. After ironing the last of the bed sheets, Anna folded them and dropped them on the hall table, then went on the porch for a breath of air. RFD No. 2 was leaving Zweigles' mailbox and skittered across muddy Tyndall, stopped and tooted twice. Mr. Bergez waved out the window and she waved back. The truck pulled away, shimmying sideways and spewing syrupy clouds. Surprising how well those Walkers managed in mud. The government must know something about electrics that Mr. Ford didn't.

A pair of robins sidled past, their heads cocked. One took flight and landed on the porch railing, its beak dripping mud and root. She shooed the bird and went down the planks to the box. The robin flew to the far railing and glared at her.

The *Ludington Daily News* was wrapped around three postcards all addressed to Lena. The top card had a picture of David and two friends in bathing suits and "Isle of Rose, S.C" scrawled across the bottom. She contemplated turning the card over, but, no, she wouldn't feel right. But she could look at the pictures. Another was David sitting on a fake alligator wearing a bowtie, bowler, and a silly grin; the third showed better than a dozen men in tuxedos sitting around a banquet table littered with beer bottles.

She dropped the mail atop the linens and started up the stairs. Ed was going to be late again. That mill had become a handful.

She tapped on the girls' door and went in. Laura was propped up in bed reading to her sister, her finger tracing a line in Grammie's old Bible. Lena was lying alongside in a plum-colored robe with floppy sleeves and a book in her lap. The daffodils on the windowsill radiated sunshine.

"Just doing our lesson, Mother," Laura said. "Come on in."

"Mail." She dropped the cards in Lena's lap; her daughter's eyes lit up. Lena pushed her book aside and read the cards over and over like an infatuated schoolgirl. Strange a few scrawled words and a picture would have that kind of effect. "You girls want a plate brought up tonight?" Both shook their heads and chimed, "We're ready to come down."

Ed was home early. He said the problem with the Hansons wasn't near as bad as he expected. She gave him a kiss. With a mug of coffee from Grammie, he went into the dining room. Moments later, the kitchen door reopened. "Seen the paper, Anna-Banana?"

"No, Father, but one did come." She went to the bottom of the stair. "Laura! Norman! One of you got the *News* up there?"

"I got it." Norman clumped down the stairs and dropped the paper in Ed's lap. "Pa. *Dr. Jekyll and Mr. Hyde* is playing at the Lyric—want to go to Ludington tonight? That Betty Harte is a real dish."

"That'd be a waste of a perfectly good nickel, Son." He leaned back and jerked his chin at the stairs. "Now how's Lena doing? She still feeling better?"

"Sure is, Pa, couldn't be better."

He considered Norman with a skeptical eye then pushed up from the table.

"That right? Maybe I'll judge that for myself." Ed started for the stairway; Lena swung around the newel post, her arms spread.

"And here I am, Poppa! How do I look?"

Laura was on the step behind her. "Doesn't she look fabulous, Poppa?" Lena had on a velvet housecoat with an embroidered collar. Her hair was brushed out and her cheeks tinged with a trace of blush.

"Holy gol-drotten." Ed's mouth hung open; Lena did look radiant. Not half-dead when he'd carried her upstairs four days earlier.

Anna peered from the kitchen. "Well, look at *that*; hard to believe even with my own eyes."

Grammie peered over her shoulder. "Power of prayer, Anna." She tapped an accusing forefinger on the door frame. "You should be more grateful yourself and thank the Good Lord for all he has done for us, for all of the times He came to our rescue." She looked at Lena with wonderment. "But, goodness gracious, that *is* a sight to behold. Them Scientists must have some direct line to the Almighty."

∞

13 September 1909

When the roads became passable, the recipient of Lena's infatuation arrived in a mud-covered Pierce Arrow and spirited her daughter away. David apologized for not being able to stay; people were waiting on him in Union City. Lena left looking not only radiant, but relieved.

Skunk cabbage and blood root bloomed where sorghum once grew; the mill produced pine shakes despite the ancient Hansons. And as the last of the baby robins fluttered from the nest on the porch, Laura came down with a cough she couldn't shake. The cough deepened, and her stamina faded along with her appetite. Nevertheless, she insisted she was just fine; there was no cause for concern.

Beeps signaled the mailman; Norman was at the mailbox and RFD No. 2 bumping away. Her son dropped a magazine and several envelopes on the side table. He put one envelope aside and stacked the others.

"We got a present from Lena." He waved a copy of the *Christian Science Journal*. "She got us a subscription."

He folded the journal around the stack of envelopes and gave the top one to her. "This one's for you, Ma. Everything else is for Laura."

Ed snorted from the easy chair when Norman went up the stairs. "Seems like most of what we hear from Lena comes from up there."

"It's what sisters do, Father." Anna picked up the envelope and squinted at the return address then opened the envelope. "Birmingham, Alabama. . . . Well, Lena's pregnant."

"Huh?" Grammie's mouth pursed. "And Stanley not gone a year yet? A little soon if you ask me."

Ed chuckled behind the paper and folded back a page. "Well, there ya are." He pointed to a headline. "Guess I was right for once: Free silver's dead as a doornail and the gol-drotten bankers got all the money. Farmers are gonna die." He shook his head. "Thank God, I'm out."

Ed wasn't one to gloat, but the mill *was* doing well. Well enough to put in electricity, a tub, and a commode. Carl had reason to gloat, too, but like his father, he savored success privately. The Flint & Pere Marquette railroad offered him a job in the machine shop, and Ed urged him to take it. F&PM was a big step up from the mill, and while he didn't mention it, Ed thought it would do his son good to be on his own.

Ben came in and eased on the sofa alongside Grammie. "Hey, Pa?"

Anna waved the letter at her son. "Ben . . . Lena's pregnant."

"I know. Isn't it great?" He looked at his father. "Pa, you see that bit in the paper about them new shingles? Figure it'll affect us?" Ed's head appeared from behind the *News*, his eyebrows up.

"I did see. That guy in Grand Rapids—Henry Reynolds right—cuttin' shingles from tarpaper. Can you imagine anything uglier? Naw, Son, forget it, it ain't gonna affect us. Cockamamie schemes are a dime a dozen."

Anna frowned; what is it with men, more interested in tarpaper than babies.

"Ben. Does Laura know when Lena's due?"

"I think she said September."

She ticked her fingers. "Six. David picked her up not six months ago." She turned to Mother and laughed. "Seems she and David are keeping busy."

∞

Weeks slipped by unnoticed in daily routines; Laura's appetite continued to wane. Her bones showed, pressing against translucent skin. Lena wrote regularly. A *Christian Science Sentinel* appeared in the mailbox every month along with the *Journal.* Norman read nightly to Laura and helped her reply to her sister. Both insisted there was nothing to worry about; they were just working through a little something.

The maples were red when Lena's letter announced the arrival of little Laura on September second; everyone was doing well. Her daughter enclosed a photograph of she and the baby both dressed in white, Lena looking like a stunning Gibson Girl posing outside a large brick building with massive Doric columns. Another showed her holding baby Laura with a tall Negro woman standing alongside against a background of manicured lawns and mounds of hostas.

She waved the pictures. "Photographs from Lena, Father. Come look." Ed was at the dining room table with his ledger open, head in hands. Several piles of paper scraps surrounded the ledger.

He didn't look up. "Later, okay?"

"They left Jacksonville, Father, and bought a house in Birmingham, Alabama. She's got a maid and everything. Lena's living high."

He fingered a scrap of paper. "High time for me would be figuring out who owes us what." He pushed the paper aside and jotted in his ledger. "Between getting bolts in the door and shingles out, then gettin' our money, plus keeping those gol-drottin Hansons running, has me and Matt goin' crazy. I got no time for pictures."

Ed's satisfaction with the mill had turned to stubborn determination. Pulp mills paid top-dollar for bolts, and costs had gone out of sight. At the same time tar-paper shingles became popular, and when lumber yards started carrying them, the price of pine shakes plummeted.

"Well, I'll leave you be, Father. I'll be out on the porch." Anna rocked in the swing and waved to Fredericka at her mailbox. Fredericka waved back and started across Tyndall.

Fredericka clumped up the planks, mopping her face. "Phew, can't cool down fast enough to suit me."

"And everyone else." Anna patted the swing and held up the photographs. "Sit a minute; got pictures from Lena."

Fredericka squinted and smiled, sighing at each image. "Living the life of Riley, isn't she?" She handed the photos back. "How's Laura doing?"

"Not well, I'm afraid . . . and I'm at a loss for what to do." She pushed gently and set the swing squeaking. "Laura's not a child anymore, and she won't listen to me or Ed. She can hardly walk, and both of them—Norman as well—swear she's getting better." The swing stopped. "And I haven't told Ed, but I found blood on a wad of Albany tissue in her room."

Fredericka sat silent then patted her on the knee. "Why don't I look in on Laura? I'll pretend I'm just saying hello." The swing bounced; Fredericka got up. "Wait here."

Anna rocked gently wondering what Fredericka would think. It seemed obvious that Laura was failing. Would Fredericka see something that she didn't—or didn't want to? A crow landed, and strutted along Tyndall. Grammie came out with two glasses of water and set them on the porch rail, then disappeared back inside without a word.

Fredericka let the screen close quietly. "One sick little girl you got up there, Anna." She took the water from the rail and handed a glass to Anna, easing alongside her on the swing. "She couldn't say much because of the coughing, but you're right; she does believe she's getting better." She took a sip of water and swiped her upper lip. "My sister, when she was sick back in Philadelphia, looked the same as Laura: bright eyes, waxy skin—and the shivering."

"What did your sister have?"

Fredericka set her glass down and took her hand. "Consumption."

She rocked the swing gently and stared with blank eyes at the empty bird nest. The swing moaned woefully; a second crow joined the first.

"Anna," Fredericka squeezed her hand, "I'm so sorry."

She shook her head, her eyes on the birds.

"Anna, you need help. Laura needs help. See someone." Condensation ran down Fredericka's glass and spotted her apron. "A health department office just opened in Ludington. Talk to them; they'll know what to do." She put her arm around Anna and hugged. The crows took flight.

In the morning, stacking dishes on the shelf, Fredericka's advice twisted in her head. She had to do something, but what? Did she dare go to the health department? Laura would resent it. She banged the silverware door shut; Laura was her daughter, she *had* to help. But how?

"Mother, would you mind starting dinner today? I'd like to run in to Scottville for some fabric. Ed needs a new shirt."

"Scottville?" Her mother looked surprised. "Doesn't Buckout's carry material?"

"I'm thinking about buying ready-made." She started for the stoop to hook up Buck then change into her dark underskirt, with a short linen overskirt and three-quarter sleeve blouse. She took her bonnet with the long ties and headed out.

At Manistee Junction, she turned into Nichols' yard, and after giving the stable boy twenty-five cents to watch and water Buck, she walked across Route 20 to the train station. Now, what to tell the health department?

∞

That night, Anna lay awake, staring into the darkness. A cool breeze swayed moonlit curtains—tree frogs pulsed. "Father? You asleep?" She leaned close and listened to soft breathing. "Ed, you sleeping?" She touched his shoulder.

"Wazthat?" Ed jerked; covers slid sideways, the bedsprings creaked. "Huh?"

"I asked if you were asleep?"

"Well holy gol-drottin, Anna-Banana, wadya expect?"

"Ed, I got something weighing on me." The mattress jostled and his shape rose against the headboard.

"Well, let's hear it." He did not sound put out.

"Went to Ludington today, to that new health department."

"Health department?" The mattress bounced; Ed propped on an elbow. "About Laura?"

"Yes." She raised against her pillow. "She's really sick, Ed. She's got TB—tuberculosis."

"Huh?"

"Consumption, Ed. Fredericka's sister died of it. There's no cure."

Silence; his shape stared into the darkness.

"The doctor at the health department said Laura should get to a hospital in Battle Creek. See a doctor by the name of Kellogg, John Kellogg."

"Well, you know she ain't gonna do that."

"TB's contagious, Ed. It can't be prayed away."

"What about Lena? She and Laura prayed away whatever she had."

"Ed, it's been months."

"Well, we should think on it. Let's not jump too fast."

"Best think quick, Father. Cat's out of the bag."

"How's that?"

"They told me they're obliged to come for a look."

∞

Unannounced, the health department came and examined Laura. When they left, all of what Anna knew and believed was stripped away by edict and law. Chaos now reigned. The yellow quarantine sign on the porch warned all to take heed, to visit at one's own peril. Masks were mandatory, expectoration held death, a Mason jar was the grail, carbolic acid and water the savior. Albany paper must be burned and linens boiled. Absolutely no touching or comforting allowed; only fresh air was permitted. The litany pounded on her consciousness every waking hour.

Norman clumped down the stairs carrying Laura wrapped in a blanket. His sister was like a child in his arms, little more than skin and bones.

"Here she is, Ma." The bathwater was ready and the soap and towel on the commode; Anna slid her face mask in place.

Norman set Laura on the commode seat. "Want me to scrub your back, Sis?"

Laura's lips moved; he cocked his head close. "What's that?" Norman blinked and laughed. "Well, I don't see that's such a big deal."

"Norman. Stop teasing your poor sister." She tried not to notice her son's lack of a mask. He was every bit as stubborn as Laura. She pushed him through the door. "Out."

She eased her daughter out of her shift and into the tub. "Call when you're ready to come out." Laura slid into the water with her eyes closed and nodded.

Anna pocketed her mask and went to the porch and stood, her arms crossed against a chilly breeze. Spent corn stalks swayed under a leaden sky. Pods split open on the dry milkweed along the road. The words from the health department nurse still thudded in her head: "No question,

Mrs. Anderson, your daughter has tuberculosis." If only Laura had gone to Battle Creek. Maybe Dr. Kellogg would have or could have helped. She rubbed goose bumps on her arms feeling old, helpless. Yes, everything has its time, but her daughter? At twenty-two?

"Anna?" Grammie held the door ajar. "Maybe you'd better come in. Ed's getting a little hot."

Ed and Norman were in the dining room, Ed stiff in the chair with his arms crossed. "Now lemme tell *you* a couple a-things, Son." He jabbed a finger. "First, there's no cure for what your sister's got, so stop worrying someone might make her take something." He jabbed again. "And second, what the health department *wants*, is for your sister to have lots of fresh air. Christian Science ain't against fresh air, is it?"

"No, Pa." Norman shifted to the other foot. "But Pa, the masks, the medicine, the sign on the front porch, they're all symbols of error." He raised both arms, palms outward. "We've got to help Laura know the illusion is false."

"Well, Son, I don't see where any of that rubs with fresh air." He leaned forward on his elbows. "The best thing for Laura is for us to do what the health department says."

"But Pa—"

She interrupted. "It's a good time to talk, seeing we're all here. You want the first shift with Laura tonight, Father?" Norman turned and started up the stairs, disgusted.

"Fine." Ed shrugged and called after his son. "The health department is the best chance Laura's got." A door upstairs slammed.

"We can pray, Ed." Grammie slid into a chair. "That's what we can do. Pray."

"Huh?" He squinted as if he didn't understand.

"The Good Lord healed Lena, didn't He?" She shook a finger at him. "That's proof that prayer works. Norman's right. We all need to have faith."

"I don't see where God's done us any favors." Anna crossed her arms. "Stanley, Uncle Pete, Uncle Ben. And that plague you're always talking about, Mother. How many died? I'll bet they died praying, too. We need to get Laura to Battle Creek."

Ed shook his head. "She ain't gonna go, you know that."

Grammie rapped a finger on the table. "And what difference would

Battle Creek make? We've got more than enough fresh air right outside." She held up her mask. "And doctors. Lena learned all about doctors, hospitals, elixirs; they didn't do her any good. They likely would have killed her—like they did Stanley. If you ask me, Norman's got the right idea."

Ed sagged at the table. "Guess prayer's the only thing we got to work with, Grammie."

He was as deep in the dumps as she had ever seen him. This thing with Laura was a terrible weight, and, on top of that, the bank sent a foreclosure notice on the mill.

Ed grabbed his coat and followed her upstairs. At Laura's door, he waited for her to tie on his mask. "Laura says I need to know the truth, Anna-banana. How do I go about doing that?"

"It's called praying, Father."

"Do I pray for Laura or pray against consumption?" He adjusted his mask. "Been a long time since I asked the Almighty for anything. How do I start?"

Anna knocked on the door and pushed him into the chilly bedroom. Norman was in his coat with a blanket over his lap reading to Laura. Her daughter was buried under a mound of quilts, her hair an ashen halo around a pallid, but determined face. She reached for the door knob. "I'll ask Grammie for you, Father."

Then Laura was gone. She drifted slowly away like white silk of milkweed on a warm fall zephyr. Ed bought a plot at the new cemetery out on Bachelor Lake, and then the fuss of what to do with Laura's remains began.

Everyone but Norman wanted a proper ceremony. Ed got a casket catalogue, and Anna talked about having a wake in the front room. Grammie wanted to invite the pastor from the Congregational Church in Tallman to say a few words.

Norman would not hear of it. Death was not to be celebrated or mourned. The Society taught that Laura simply rose to the next level and left her mortal being behind. He knew what she wanted. He heard it directly from her. She wanted nothing. No announcement, no grieving, no wake, no luncheon, no anything else. The discussion ended when Norman relented to Willis reading the Lord's Prayer at the grave site.

Bachelor Cemetery was a mile or so northwest of Tallman on Bachelor Lake. Being new, the cemetery couldn't speak to attributes other than a lake view and a couple of headstones in an open area where the switch-grass had been mowed. A shed off to the side had a grave plan wrapped in celluloid nailed to the wall. Across the lake, a steam shovel worked noiselessly in a gravel pit.

Ed took Anna out to place the grave blanket just before the holidays. They found the cemetery snow-covered and the surrounds quiet and peaceful. The lake was a saucer of white held by low hills, the only sign of civilization, a roof here or a silo there. Silence reigned supreme.

Buck's tracks were not the first. Someone had visited a stone up near the shed, but there were no other grave blankets. Anna had fashioned one from fresh pine and adorned it with a floppy red bow. She laid the blanket and stared across the lake, adrift in memories. Ed went back to the buggy and waited quietly.

"Sorry, Father," she said climbing on the buggy. "Got lost in my thoughts."

Ed gave the reins a flick; the sleigh glided to Sugar Grove Road. "Do some Christmas shopping at Buckout's, Anna-banana?"

"No, not today, Father, let's just head home. I'm not ready for Christmas." She was out of kilter; her daughter was gone, Sister had her own life with Willis, and Lena would rather be with David than family. She didn't come home for Laura and the photographs she sent from Charlotte were an affront: Lena and baby Laura, both dressed in white. Lena, lounging on a sumptuous veranda; people in white wicker chairs wearing big grins; a long valley and lazy mountains fading off in the background. Lena could have at least worn black.

Ed patted her knee. "Not like you to miss a shot at Buckout's." He slid his hand under the lap robe and took hers. "Been a tough year, hasn't it?" She nodded.

Ed geed Buck around on Morse Road. "Yep, tough year for everybody, including them Christian Scientists."

"Scientists? How so, Father?"

"Saw in the paper that Mrs. Eddy died. The caption under photograph said there were better than a thousand people at her funeral. I wonder if this religion thing is really what Norman makes it to be."

"Just leave it be, Father."

∞

14 September 1912

The letter from Lena pronounced a move to Ludington, Michigan. She read the letter aloud at supper; the expressions at the table showed disbelief: Mr. Beautiful, corporate mogul, holder of her daughter's infatuation, and absentee son-in-law, was moving to Ludington, Michigan? He was forsaking elegance and opulence for a remote lumbering town of barely nine thousand? The skepticism was palpable.

Ludington's wide sandy beaches did entice the well-to-do from Chicago. Grand summer homes abounded in nearby Epworth with the owners delivered from Ludington by private railroad. And David could reach all of his territory from Ludington, so perhaps moving was a way to avoid the home office. Yet, his being on the road meant Lena and her daughter would be alone more often. Initial surprise turned to suspicion.

Lena went on to write that she wanted to put down roots. She was pregnant again and tired of stuffy waiters and finding her way around strange cities and dealing with indifferent housekeepers. She wanted a real home, a place of her own to raise her family. Anxiety at the table softened.

David had already purchased a house just two blocks from the Stearns Hotel; the yellow Victorian at the corner of Ludington Avenue and Lavinia. Lena apologized for him not visiting, but plans changed at the last minute and he had to go to Atlanta.

Anna begged off on midwifing. Ed was going crazy trying to keep the mill afloat and she and her mother were left to pick the garden and get everything to the cellar for winter, so little time was left to help Lena move in.

On October 13, little Virginia was born. Not long after, Lena sent an invitation to come see the baby. Ed begged off saying he couldn't spare the time, but offered to drive them to Manistee Junction.

At Nichol's Inn, Ed slowed Buck. "Thought Grammie and Norman were coming, Anna-Banana, what happened?" He thumbed at the inn. "Want a soda? You've got time."

"Oh, Mother said she didn't feel up to it today, but I thought Norman was coming."

Nichol's veranda was busy and a number of men and women sunned themselves on the steps; the yard was full of buggies plus a motorcar or two. She shook her head.

"It's a beautiful day, Father. Let's just wait over at the station; the Pere Marquette & Flint'll be along shortly." Ed snapped the reins and hawed Buck around.

"I don't know what happened to Norman. I was surprised he changed his mind."

Ed stopped Buck alongside the platform; a smell of fall was in the air, trees along Emerson Lake starting to show color.

Ed knotted the reins and niggled a callous on his thumb. He seemed a thousand miles away. He and Matt were at the bank earlier, but he had yet to say anything.

"How'd the meeting with the bank go, Father?" She watched his eyes.

Ed shrugged disinterestedly. "They called our note. It's over. Bank's got the mill and wants what we owe 'em, plus interest."

Anna's stomach churned; the bank held the mortgage on the house too.

She rubbed the back of his neck. "I'm sorry to hear that, Father." Poor Ed, he must be devastated. The mill was his whole life.

"It was that circular, wasn't it?" Lumberyards posted a report from the Board of Fire Underwriters warning that pine shingles were a fire hazard. Insurance companies got wise and stopped covering buildings with wood shakes. Once word got around, fire departments set up a howl and business at the mill wasn't worth a fire under the coffee pot.

"What'll you do now, Father?" Ed wasn't someone who was going to hire on somewhere.

"Do?" A whistle sounded from Emerson Lake. "Do what I did—I suppose."

He considered his thumb. "I used to grow a pretty good beet or two. People are still eating vegetables." A smoke-snorting black engine with three cars and a tender chugged around the curve; Ed sat up and freed the reins. "Give Lena a hug and a kiss for me."

"Thank you, Father. I'll be back on the 5:40 remember."

She ran for the middle car and dropped in an empty row. Crumbs were on the maroon plush of the seat and not a porter in sight. People were behind her; she brushed them off and sat down.

The car jerked forward, and Anna watched Ed and Buck disappear in a cloud of steam. She felt alone. She had counted on Norman and

Mother for company, especially Norman on the ride to Lena's. The jitney was infamous for its brazen riders, and Norman would have been a buffer. Of course, Lena wouldn't think of learning to drive, let alone hitching up a buggy.

Norman must be feeling more poorly than he let on. He knew Carl was stopping by Lena's after work and had looked forward to seeing him.

Carl was doing well at the machine shop. Working for the railroad was a big change from working with Ed, but Carl liked the freedom of living in the city. Last she heard, he was still seeing Elsie. She and Elsie got to know each other when Laura passed. They were perfect together; Elsie was a substantial woman with an honest face and a fine cook to boot.

Norman's absence nagged her. He said he was feeling fine, but maybe he was hiding the truth. Of course, he was like Laura; he'd be on his last breath and not admit it. Lena would ask why he didn't come, and she had to be careful even discussing sniffles around her. She'd just say Norman missed the train—*that* would be believable. But no matter, she had to keep an eye on him. Something was going on.

The train slowed and stopped at a small red shelter with bilious yellow trim. The sign of the wall announced, Custer, Michigan, Pop. 1,200. She looked out the window onto a small brick shop next to a weathered barn with a saggy roof, a miry cattle pen, and a listing silo, guyed by rusty wire.

No sooner was the train back up to speed when the brakes screeched again and the Scottville station appeared. Another dreary stop: piles of rusty iron, unidentifiable machine parts, and the backside of tar paper-roofed buildings strung together by drooping wires. She nestled her head against the seatback; a good time to enjoy a quick nap.

∞

At dinner that night, she had Ed, Mother and the boys laughing about her visit. "Lena deserves a lot of credit moving halfway across the country to an empty house and then having a baby. But Grammie, you would have died; the place was out of control. Lena had two housekeepers trying to clean around half-empty boxes while the nanny frantically chased Laura from room to room."

Norman laughed, but he didn't look good. He definitely looked like he was coming down with something. When Ben asked about Carl, he excused himself and went upstairs.

Norman stopped going to Scottville on Wednesday nights and she started to worry: He was not just working through a little something. Norman took a vacation from work saying that a bit of rest would put him back on his feet and promised Mr. Butters he'd be back in a week. But like his sister, he wasted away. Old fears reignited; would this end like Laura? She had to do something, but what? Make him well? She moved him into the girl's old room.

A few days later she found Grammie at the window with the curtain hooked back. "Anna. Come look."

She set her knitting basket on the floor and peered over her mother's shoulder. A shiny black Ford motor car was out front. A woman about Norman's age got out of the driver's side and went around and opened the passenger door. The woman was dressed stylishly in a dark tailored tunic with an ankle-length skirt, heels, and a wide-brimmed hat. But only a city girl would wear fancy shoes like that to a farm.

An elderly lady in a black jacket with a high collar and prominent shoulder pads emerged from the passenger side. She pulled herself erect and surveyed the house, then said something to her younger companion and adjusted her plume-feathered bonnet. After pulling her skirt tight over high button boots, she took the younger woman's arm and started for the porch steps.

"We would have called, Mrs. Anderson," the older of the two said when she opened the door, "but we couldn't find a number." A large goiter pressed against the woman's collar. She offered a hand. "I'm Mrs. Snyder and this is—"

"Ma, I'm sorry. I forgot." Norman was at the bottom of the stairs. "This is Mrs. Snyder and Amy Pentworth. They're from the Society over in Scottville." Her son looked like he had on hand-me-downs from a larger man. A dangling belt tongue hung from trousers, his pants bunched up at the waist. "I asked them to come over and help with my lessons." He motioned the ladies upstairs.

Anna welcomed and when they went upstairs sat with her knitting. The clicking of needles filled the room; she caught snatches of conversation that drifted from above.

Grammie pushed out of the easy chair and reached for her cane. "Hip's nagging me, Anna. Think maybe I'll stretch out a bit."

She raised an eyebrow. "Sofa's free, Mother. It'll save you a climb."

"I think I prefer my bed."

"Better take a glass with you anyway. Your hearing isn't what it used to be."

"Anna! How unkind. I'd just like to know what those Scientists pray about." She started for the kitchen.

Knitting in silence, she harbored the same thought. How does this religion work? What do they talk about? It can't be as simple as just praying.

An hour later, Norman waited at the top of the stairs while the ladies came down. At the front door, Mrs. Snyder held out her hand and took Anna's. Condolences appeared to be coming.

"Mrs. Anderson." Mrs. Snyder pressed her hand. "We want to thank you so much for the generous donation to the Society on Norman's behalf. We were not aware that Mrs. Helena Houston was your daughter." She continued to hold her hand and reached for her companion's. Mrs. Snyder closed her eyes. "Divine Love always has and always will meet every human need." She opened her eyes and leveled her belief at Anna. "Prayer is the affirmation of Truth despite the illusion of error, Mrs. Anderson. Norman will find Truth. God is All-in-All."

The following weeks Mrs. Snyder and Miss Pentworth were reliably punctual and persuasively optimistic. Norman was determined and committed to Science. They emphasized that besides their visits, they devoted an hour each day to working on Norman's behalf.

That night, Anna sat on the edge of the bed in her nightgown watching Ed unbutton his shirt. "So that's what I'm told, Father. But Norman's doing no better than Laura did. Ed, we gotta do something. We can't just let him die without doing something."

Ed twisted the light switch, and the room fell to darkness. "I don't see those ladies from his Society have done him much good either." Ed sat down; the mattress bounced, springs groaned.

"We sure did raise some stubborn kids Anna-banana—lay back and relax, wouldya, please. There's nothing we can do tonight."

"Ed, we're putting people at risk. You know he's contagious. David won't let Lena come anywhere near here; we haven't seen Carl and Elise in ages." She slipped under the sheet. "We need to start thinking of Ben and Mother and everyone else who comes on the porch."

"Don't disagree." Ed rolled on his back. "And I can't fault David or Carl either." He sent an arm searching and found her shoulder. "I still got that quarantine sign. Maybe I'll just stick that back up. You still got face masks, ain't you?" He pulled her close. "I'm going over to Freesoil in the morning to see where they get their vegetables and hopefully land a customer. Maybe I'll swing by Scottville on the way home. I heard there's a new TB clinic there."

∞

Regular as clockwork and just as snow started to fall, the black Model T showed up out front. "They're here." Mother let the curtain fall back and reached for her cane. "Think maybe I'll start supper early today." She clumped to the kitchen and pulled the door closed.

Through the curtain, she watched Miss Pentworth steady Mrs. Snyder up the porch steps. Feet stomped, followed by silence. Anna stood by the door waiting, her heart pounding. When the knock finally came, she waited a moment then opened the door. "Mrs. Snyder, Amy, how nice to see you again." She motioned them in. "You are always so prompt."

The ladies hesitated as if suspecting a trap. Cautiously, they stepped inside, faces hard and rigid.

"Oh the sign." Anna waved dismissively. "Please ignore it; we're only trying to be good neighbors. The yellow is ugly, isn't it?"

"I must say, Mrs. Anderson, I'm a bit surprised."

She invited them in; Mrs. Snyder declined. Her eyes fell on the box of face masks on the table then the jar of carbolic acid on a stair step. "Apparently Norman has a doctor."

Anna shook her head. "No, not at all, Mrs. Snyder. We don't . . ." She shook her head again. "No, no, we don't have a doctor. Norman doesn't even know about the sign. The masks, they are just things we had. We're just trying to be good people, Mrs. Snyder, do the right thing, not harm anyone. Norman knows nothing about any of it."

A look of resignation appeared on Mrs. Snyder's face; her head swayed imperceptibly. "Mrs. Anderson, medical paraphernalia give credence to the illusion. Clinging to corporeal sense and the false trappings of error prevent healing. Nothing but God's likeness must abide in our vision and thoughts."

"I agree, Mrs. Snyder. We're all trying to pray . . . ah . . . *work* for Norman." She kept her expression agreeable. "Norman appreciates your help and your guidance very much, just as I do, Mrs. Snyder. We count on your visits. Please, let me show you up." She was pleading.

"No, Mrs. Anderson, I'm afraid not." Mrs. Snyder fingered her collar free of her goiter. "Under the circumstances, there is nothing we can do." She looked to Amy, who nodded in agreement.

"Mrs. Snyder—Amy—Norman's pain is real. His shortness of breath is real. He coughs blood. I live with those things every day—they're not illusions." She spread her arms. "But, believe me, Mrs. Snyder, Norman has had no medicine or doctors. He just believes. He just wants help believing. Can't you help him?"

"I'm sorry, Mrs. Anderson." Mrs. Snyder took Amy's arm. "Come, dear."

She stood, watching them leave, her heart sinking. What could she tell her son? She had severed his lifeline.

That night, after everyone had gone upstairs, she went to say goodnight to Norman. She had told him earlier about Mrs. Snyder and Amy and how sorry she was for the quarantine sign and that she was just trying to do the right thing. He seemed not to care; only pain showed.

The clock showed nearly midnight when she put on a mask and eased into his room. Little clouds of vapor accompanied her breath. She lowered the sash halfway and pulled the chair close to his bed.

Norman's eyes opened and the mound of quilts shifted. "Just lying here in the dark, Ma, waiting for death." His voice was a croak, eyes a pair of blazing topazes.

She found his hand under the quilts. It was large and knotted, his fingers grotesquely swollen. She rubbed his hand between hers.

"Pa went to the health department in Scottville. They said there's a new treatment for what you got." She looked at him hard, seeing pain in his face. "Norman, it's something new. Maybe you should give it a try."

He turned his head and took a labored breath. "Maybe I should, Ma." He coughed. "Maybe I should."

The next afternoon, a handsome Dr. Brockstanz came to the door, stomping his boots and smelling faintly of disinfectant. She showed him up, deciding he was German; the coloring, the stature, although maybe not the demeanor or accent. Grammie guessed he was thirtyish, and it was probably his parents who came over.

Thirty minutes later, Dr. Brockstanz came down the stairs with his mask and stethoscope in hand and perched on the corner of the sofa with his arms crossed.

"I'm afraid I don't have good news. The tuberculosis is quite advanced. And . . ." He hesitated. "And considering the amount of fluid in Norman's lungs, it's rather remarkable that . . . that . . ." He looked at his hands as if he had lost something. "It's such a shame we didn't catch it earlier."

The doctor brightened. "Fortunately, Norman is strong and determined, so there's hope." He reached for his bag. "He allowed me to give him an injection of tuberculin—"

Ed shot his hand in the air.

"Tuberculin," the doctor explained, "is an extract of the tubercle bacilli." He held up a vile. "We think tuberculin may cure tuberculosis."

Tuberculin was discovered in 1890 by Robert Koch, a German scientist, and won worldwide acclaim fame for what was believed to be a cure for tuberculous. But autopsies eventually revealed that tuberculin did not kill the bacteria but activated latent bacteria. In sum, it didn't work.

The doctor held up another vial. "This is laudanum. It's a powerful pain sedative so mind the dosage. One-half teaspoon, no more." He handed the bottle to her. "I gave Norman a dose upstairs so he should be comfortable for several hours."

Laudanum brought optimism to the dinner table. Norman became serene and actually smiled once. He allowed he felt much better but was very drowsy. Despair turned to hope; medicine and belief were in accord.

That night she eased into Norman's room filled with optimism. The room glowed with moonlight, fresh snow glistened outside, the window a frame for a Currier and Ives.

Anna pulled the chair close to Norman, pulled her coat tight, then tucked her feet under his quilts. He rolled on his back, covers rising and falling in steady meter, his rattle even. It seemed a miracle that he was so peaceful for the first time in months. And Christmas was just two weeks away; maybe it was a night for miracles. She breathed in cold fresh air and watched the shaft of moonlight inch across stitched panels; her eyelids grew heavy.

Norman swung the covers back, clambered out the window and

jumped. She struggled after him screaming silently, her legs in cement, immovable. He ran to the cookhouse and disappeared inside; flames burst through the roof. Then he was at a window trying to escape. She lunged and fought for his hand—it was beyond reach. She screamed silently and jerked awake.

Her neck was frozen stiff. The room gray in in dawn's half-light, a dusting of snow on the window sill. Her son was still under the mound of quilts, one hand lying free. She reached to hold it. It was stiff and cold.

∞

15 June 1915

The Pere Marquette & Flint groaned to a stop; Anna pulled Mother into the boarding queue. Slipping into a mid-car window seat, she sat and fanned herself with a train schedule. Hot. Grammie dropped alongside and put her head back; she would be snoring before long, her mouth open.

Visiting Lena's was exhausting. Seven-year-old Laura was like a wild Indian, chasing her sister Marion around the house; the screaming and howling was deafening. Virginia—with her affection for ballet—was constantly whirling around and wanting attention. Despite the disorder, her daughter simple rose above the pandemonium with ever-changing cooks and housekeepers and nannies and again becoming pregnant. A good part of the struggle to see her grandchildren was taking the jitney; David was never home.

Rolling out of Custer, supper came to mind. There were only the three of them now. Ben moved to Ludington. He went to work for Stearn's when the bank took over the mill; Karolina had put in a good word for him. The bank was off Ed's back too. Fred Zweigle was bent on more peach trees and made Ed a generous offer on Benjamin's 120. Ed paid off the bank *and* had enough left to buy a truck. Not a new one, a 1914 Ford, but in decent shape. Like Grammie said, she had her prayers answered. Hard to believe the Good Lord stepped in on her behalf; probably had more to do with being bull-headed. Scalloped potatoes with the leftover ham would be easy enough for dinner. The train slowed, and she nudged Grammie awake. Nichol's Inn and a black truck waiting at the train platform came into view.

Ed held the truck door open and helped her and Mother up. "How are the—" A whistle-shriek and clank of iron couplers overcame his words as the PM&F pulled away for Manistee. "I asked, how are the girls doing." He pushed the starter—the engine fired. Ed waited for a passing motorcar. Once the dust settled, he released the clutch, and the Ford bumped onto Route 20.

"The girls? Growing up. Laura's going in the second grade and runs at full speed, full time. Lena thinks she'll grow out of it. Virginia's almost four and already taller than Laura."

Grammie leaned around her. "And that little Marion, Ed—what an imp and as cute as a bug's ear."

A brown motor car with two couples pulled close behind and swung out to pass. The driver beep-beeped then roared past in a cloud of dust; Ed rolled up the window. "Gol-drottin kids."

Anna shook her bonnet off. "David was in Union City, so we had to take the jitney—I sure wish Lena would learn to drive. I can't imagine how she manages with him not being there. Got more that she can handle just with that house and the girls, and she's pregnant again. Can you imagine? The baby's due in February.

"But she does look great, Father." Anna dropped the bonnet in her lap. "And she's after David to buy a new house; says she needs a bigger one. The Lavinia place is too small and too far from shopping. She's got her eye on a big one over on Court Street—place even has turrets. David is fighting her; he wants her to learn to drive."

Ed returned a wave to a passing buggy. "I'll bet Lena gets her way." Ahead, a brown motorcar was pulled to the side. "Well look at that." The motorcar was cocked on a jack and missing wheel; alongside, two men were bent over a tire. Two women watched from car windows, chins resting on crossed arms. Ed touched the brim of his porkpie as they puttered past.

The Pere Marquette & Flint from Baldwin roared past with a string of boxcars and a swaying red caboose. Grammie's eyes were closed and her head against the window. Ahead, the blue sheen of Emerson Lake spread between trees. A dozen or so motorcars were parked in front of a long, low-slung log building like grazing cattle. A hand-carved sign at the drive read, "Emerson Motor Club." Ed motioned with his chin. "Jasters look like they're doing pretty well."

Few thought Ern and Barbara Jaster would have any luck starting a motorcar club in Branch. But people became believers when the well-to-do in Epworth decided motoring out to a club was great fun. It probably helped that the Jasters had a bar.

Ed turned on Tyndall; the truck clunked into a rut. "Oof." Grammie sat up. "I sure wish somebody would fix this road."

Anna was stiff-armed against the dash. "Not much better than the day we first came through eighteen years ago." She chuckled. "Seems like just yesterday."

Progress was at it again. Stealthy and relentless, change had arrived imperceptibly. Gone were the stumps, sedge, and scruff pines that gave way to endless furrows and chest-high fields of sorghum. Ahead was a tidy plot of lettuce, beets, and sweet corn surrounded by orchards of peach and cherry trees and scores of men working on tall ladders. Above it all was the Zweigle manor, rising proudly white against a cloudless sky, and attended by barns and outbuildings.

Mother pointed to the house. "Ricka wants an addition? I can't imagine."

Ed pulled the truck alongside the tractor and stopped. "Must be a female affliction."

"Female affliction, Father?"

"Women wanting bigger houses."

∞

The holidays came with excitement known to mothers and grandmothers of young children. The following brief period of rest and resolution was overtaken by controversy about the war in Europe. President Wilson severed ties with Germany when Kaiser Wilhelm shelled the English coast and declared unrestricted submarine warfare. The president pledged neutrality—until a German sub torpedoed the Lusitania.

The *Ludington News* howled about the influenza raging in Europe, devastating troops in crowded trenches. Nevertheless, Tallman boys lined up to fight the Huns. Thank goodness Carl had a family, and Ben wasn't the brawling type.

"Well, isn't *that* something!" Anna set down her morning coffee and folded the paper back. "Look here, Mother." The headline was in black 72-point type: *Wilson Calls for Declaration of War.*

"I guess we're in for—" Someone pounded on the front door.

Anna-Marie stood on the porch hugging herself, shivering. Snow covered the top of her boots. "Aunt Anna! Momma says you need to come right over! Your granddaughter Laura is on the telephone!"

Lena's daughter calling Zweigles first thing in the morning? Was the baby coming already . . . or. . . . She yelled to Grammie. "Mother, I'm going to Fredericka's!" She ran, mindless of anything but her daughter.

Laura was bawling. Mommy was sick and daddy wasn't home. The nanny quit when mommy got sick. Voices howled in the background.

She found Ed in the barn with his head under the truck hood. "Lena's sick, Father. David's gone and so is the help. Laura's been caring for Virginia and Marion and she's scared to death. We got to go."

Ed screwed a cap back on and slammed the hood. "Get your coat. I'll be out front."

At the Manistee Junction curve, Route 20 looked slick and Ed tapped the brakes. "Dollars to doughnuts, Lena has the flu. One of the kids probably brought it home." The road straightened and he picked up speed. "That's gotta be a rough proposition for someone about to have a baby."

"Probably is the flu, Father. Laura said all Lena did was cough and throw up. I can't imagine she didn't get help."

"You know Lena wouldn't call anyone. The help probably took off for fear they'd catch what she's got."

Influenza was all the talk at Buckout's; most families had someone sick, with death often coming quickly. Unusually, it was mostly striking adults, not children.

The house was what she feared: clothes strewn about, sink piled with dirty dishes, waste bin reeking, soiled diapers in the bathtub. The girls raced to her, crying and wanting to be held. She hugged and consoled and wiped eyes and passed the girls to Ed. "Girls, girls! Look at poor Grandpa. He needs hugs." The girls ran to him; she ran to the stairs.

Knocking lightly, she cautiously opened the bedroom door; the smell was rank. Her daughter was in bed, a pitcher on the nightstand and several wadded towels on the floor next to a covered pot. Lena registered a faint smile of greeting. She stepped past the dresser and secretary and threw open the window. After feeling Lena's forehead, she picked up the pitcher and pot. "I'm going for fresh water."

Ed had the girls collecting toys and gathering dirty clothes for the laundry chute. She put a finger to her lips and motioned him to the kitchen.

"Ed, she looks terrible and she's due anytime. She can't sit up, skin's almost blue, and she could hardly talk for coughing." She opened the Kelvinator and squinted inside. "She wouldn't hear of a doctor; someone from the church was supposed to stop by—we need milk and eggs. We should get a hold of Carolina-Clinchfield and—cheese too—and ask them to find David. Tell him he's needed at home. Maybe he can talk sense to her." She started for the telephone. "But first I'm going to ask Frederick to have Fred bring Mother and the birthing bag over."

Two days later, David showed up frazzled, looking like he had been a couple of days away from a decent sleep. He went right upstairs, goggles, duster and all, and it wasn't long before she could hear him. He got louder and louder, something about not taking care of the children, why didn't she call somebody? He eventually gave up and changed into some clean clothes.

She sat with her daughter, listening to her pray between bouts of coughing. Around midnight, Lena's water broke. Everything was set: Grammie saw to the girls; she and Fredericka cleared room around the bed and spread the rubber sheet; the men heated water and paced. It was a wonder the girls could sleep through all the bustle.

Even panting and her face red with defiance, her daughter continued to pray. Slowly, her coughing eased and her color returned. She and Fredericka were amazed. Then, about the time the sun was peeking up, Lena popped out a perfect baby boy. And she never coughed again; she was back on her feet that very night. To say everyone was astonished was an understatement. David couldn't believe it, and Ed said Christian Science was the gol-durnest thing ever. Religion never was her cup of tea, but the fact of the matter was her daughter was cured and the baby was healthy. It had to be a miracle. Another wonder was the Mother Church in Boston published Lena's testimony.

∞

James Houston had arrived on February 4, 1917, well and strong. David relented and rented the big house on Court Street so her daughter could walk to shopping. Then less than two years later, everyone packed up and moved to Port Huron with Lena six months pregnant. One of David's customers—Port Huron Fuel & Supply Company—lost its general manager and the owners offered him the job. Lena was not at all excited about moving. Port Huron would be her fourth new city, and, besides, she had expected to put down roots in beautiful Ludington. But the move came with a substantial increase, and Port Huron *was* three time the size of Ludington. She could stand eating in elegant restaurants again.

David rented a place in Port Huron at Howard and Eighth, and her daughter was left to pack up the Court Street house. Upon arriving in Port Huron, Lena immediately complained the house was far too small. She did concede, though, that the neighborhood of broad-porch bungalows and hosta-encircled elms was lovely. David promised something larger once he got the lay of the land. Then, in the midst of unpacking bags and boxes, Lena delivered a baby girl. Norma took her first breath at Port Huron General on September 20, 1920.

Once Lena was situated, she wrote for her and Grammie to come and see the new baby. Two tickets on the Pere Marquette Limited accompanied the letter. The tickets showed first-class service between Ludington and Port Huron with only four stops. Grammie begged off. Spending a few days at Lena's with five children in a small house was not something she wanted to endure. Ben, though, was happy to come along. Hubbub didn't bother him—he could sleep hanging by a foot.

At the station, Anna gave Ed a goodbye hug. Taking Ben's arm for support, she smiled as the porter went up the step. Ben led her down the aisle of the Pullman then stopped mid-car and hoisted the bags to the overhead rack. "Take this one, Ma." He pointed to a pair of seats. "Fred Zweigle said the best ride was away from the wheels."

She eased into the lounge chair. The car was far above her expectations: thick carpet, comfy seats, everything clean and neat, the air fresh. A mirrored wood serviette at one end held glasses in long racks and linen napkins. The panel under her window opened to a desktop. A white-jacketed porter came down the aisle placing small round tables in front of passengers. She spotted Ed on the platform searching windows and rapped on the glass. He squinted at the car ahead.

The porter offered a table.

"Please," Ben replied nodding his head.

After spreading a white tablecloth, the porter placed two menus and set-ups on top. Anna looked around, trying not to show excitement, as if taking a Pullman Parlor Car to Port Huron was something she did routinely.

Ben ran his finger down the menu. "Club sandwich sounds good." He tossed the menu on the table. "So, Ma, David's a big shot now?"

She decided on the watercress sandwich. "Well, we'll see. That's what Lena claims. But sometimes things aren't as they seem."

She should be mindful of being accused an old fuddy-duddy. Steam clouded the window, and the car jerked gently forward. Ben found an *Argosy* in the rack and settled back.

The rhythmic rickety-click, and trees flashing by the window brought to mind that endless train ride with Edward, Mother and Sister. She never heard a word from him. For years, she thought he might at least contact his daughter. But no, never a letter or even a postcard. Grammie thought he was not the kind of man to put stock in family.

Grammie and Ed got along famously; they were buddies. She thought the world of him and he her, and they were probably already telling each other tall stories. Grammie was eighty-nine—or so she thought. Her hearing was mostly gone, eyes not much better, and arthritis had her in a firm grip. Most of the time, she slept in the easy chair or sat at the kitchen table, watching birds fluttering in and out of the old oak. Anna considered the oak an eyesore, with its dead branches and remnants of old tree houses. But Ed called it a memory tree and decided he'd just leave it alone for a while.

Squealing brakes broke her reverie; Ben looked up from his magazine.

"Reed City, Ma. Looked like you were in another world." The porter appeared, and Ben ordered their sandwiches and two Coca-Colas.

She turned to Ben. "So what do you hear from Carl?"

His face brightened. "All good. Pere Marquette & Flint moved him up to a lathe operator and gave him a raise. And somehow. . . ." He laughed. "Somehow, Elsie is still tolerating him."

"We haven't seen much of Carl since Norman passed." Her eyes turned sad. "He always says Pere Marquette's keeping him too busy."

"It's an excuse." Ben waited while the busboy poured water. "That religion business really got to him. He's still upset."

"Does he blame Ed'n me?"

"Carl believes Laura—and Lena—led Norman along. Norman

wasn't anything like those two. Laura and Lena were dedicated and single-minded. Norman believed as he did because *they* believed. Carl thinks everyone should have known that Norman never had a chance. He thinks we *all* betrayed him."

"But Norman was a grown man. How could Ed and I—"

The porter appeared with a silver tray and a generous smile. He set covered china plates on the table, and with a "Bon appétit," whisked the covers aside. Slices of orange, pear, and pineapple artfully surrounded a handsome sandwich nestled in sprigs of green. She picked up her fork and admired the Pullman Company crest cast into its handle. Were the green leaves parsley? She lifted a sprig. It was. She unfolded her linen napkin and peeked at the couple eating and chatting across the aisle.

"But, Ben, Carl knows that Ed and I are not Christian Scientists." She took a bite of sandwich. The car moved forward and water glasses jiggled. She dropped the sandwich and grabbed for her glass then realized there was no need. She looked to see if anyone noticed. The couple across the aisle were staring at her with wide eyes. Her stomach plunged. She was an interloper in a hoity-toity world she didn't understand. She shouldn't have asked about Carl, and she wasn't going to ask about Ben's job or his girlfriend, Nellie. For that matter, she didn't like watercress much either. "Ben, maybe belief is like medicine. It doesn't work the same on everyone."

Ben waved away the idea. "Don't ask me, Ma." He opened the *Argosy*. "I'm staying out of it."

She awoke when the conductor came past calling, "Port Huron, next stop, Port Huron please." The train slowed and ground to a halt. The aisle filled with travelers waiting for the conductor to place steps to the platform.

The station was enormous: two stories with a peaked roof and gables and dormers and scalloped eaves. Red brick piers and tall windows arched above a long platform awash in travelers. Ben spotted David. "There. Straw boater, striped blazer."

David looked the epitome of success in a red-and-beige blazer, white shirt, and bowtie. His sharply pleated trousers matched his cream-colored brogues. He stood on tiptoes looking to another train.

Her daughter was alongside wearing an elegant blouse and pleated navy skirt with a drop-waist tie. Her linen cloche had a row of stylish buttons above one ear. They left the children home with the housekeeper, Mrs. Myree.

A newsboy went past holding up a *Port Huron Times Herald.* "Nineteenth Amendment passes! Nineteenth Amendment passes!" The headline shouted, "Women Win!"

David led them to a shiny black sedan with side vents and spoke wheels and put the bags in the trunk. Opening a rear door, he doffed his boater and bowed.

"Ladies, allow me." He handed her and her daughter on to the running board then eased the door closed. "Ben, you ride shotgun."

Ben pointed to the chrome figurine about to soar from the hood. "Packard?"

David nodded. "Yep, Nike, the Goddess of Speed." He climbed behind the wheel and jerked his thumb toward the back seat. "Need a big car to go with a big family." He put his foot on the clutch and jiggled the shift rod then pushed the starter button. The engine purred to life. He shifted and the sedan bounced onto Twenty-Fourth Street.

Her daughter immediately started in on how small the house was. David had no idea of the room needed for five children, although he did the best he could considering the timing. Howard Street *was* close to town, and he could walk to work. Did she mention they just joined the Black River Country Club?

"David?" Lena leaned over the seatback. "Take Lapeer, would you? I want Mother and Ben to see your Tenth Street project." She sat back and moved her handbag to the jump seat. "David's a bit of a hero, Mother."

Her eyebrows went up. "Oh, how so?"

"The city's replacing Tenth Street at the bridge. But after the contractor ripped up the pavement, he found he couldn't get cement. Everyone was up in arms about it."

Ben twisted around. "Sounds like poor planning to me."

"No, not really. The contractor purchased the cement in plenty of time but couldn't get it delivered. Apparently, there weren't enough railroad cars." Lena said there was an article in the *Times Herald* about the lack of railroad cars in the country creating a transportation crisis.

"And that made David a hero?"

Lena's face radiated pride. "He found a boat." She leaned forward and patted him on the shoulder. "He drove to the Lafarge Company in Alpena and rented a freighter. The *S.S. Hazzard,* delivered all 4,000 barrels right to the Port Huron Fuel and Supply dock in the Black River. Can you imagine! His name was all over the papers, and he got elected president of the Port Huron Builders Exchange."

David pulled to the curb at Tenth Street. Across Lapeer and behind a line of barricades, men with shovels and high boots surrounded a barrel-shaped machine spilling gray concrete into a steel chute. Workers with trowels on long poles smoothed the mix level. An open bridge trestle loomed above the workmen.

David twisted around and looked over his shoulder. "Work is supposed to be finished next week." He pulled away. "And Ben, I need to apologize. Something's come up, and I have to leave first thing in the morning." Her daughter went quiet.

The Packard rumbled across red brick to Eighth Street where David slowed and signaled a right turn. He turned again at Howard and pointed up the street. "We're at 803. Lucky to have it with the housing shortage like it is."

In the morning David was gone. Lena took Anna shopping, with Norma in the buggy, while Ben, James and the girls took the bus to Lakeside Beach. The following afternoon was a picnic at Pine Grove Park and a day later an excursion to Sarnia on the ferry.

Wednesday, while they were still at the dinner table after Mrs. Myree left, her daughter suggested another outing. "There is a service tonight. Going to church would be something for us to do." Ben looked as if he had been stabbed in the stomach by a pang of gas.

The church was just two blocks away on Sixth Street, a short walk on a pleasant fall evening. Laura and Virginia were capable of watching Marion, James and Norma for an hour or so, and it would be a good night to go because the service was one of the last in the Masonic Temple. The construction of the new church at Sixth and Union was almost finished.

Ben begged off. "You know church-going's not my cup of tea, Sis." But he thought he'd walk to the Temple with them and then check out downtown.

Her daughter led them to a hulking structure of gray granite and limestone crowding the sidewalk just shy of Water Street. "Masonic Temple, " Lena announced in front of a hardly church-like entrance. She turned and aimed a finger at the Court House across the street. "Ben,

Barnett's Drug Store is just past that monument on the lawn over there. We'll meet you at the soda fountain in forty-five, fifty minutes—okay?"

The temple inside was elaborate. Ornamental chandeliers hung between high limestone walls with leaded glass inlets. A mauve carpet ran down the center of the room and up a broad set of arched steps to a dais holding a pair of lecterns, reading lamps, and upholstered high-back chairs. Lena surveyed the crowd and pointed to a pair of seats. "We should have left earlier."

The room quieted and a man in a dark suit and a woman in a floor-length gown walked out from opposite sides of the stage and sat in the high-backs. He wore a boutonniere, she a white corsage. The organ started, and people stood and sang. Lord, her daughter couldn't carry a tune. And yet, it didn't seem to bother her. After the hymn, the first reader, and the second, got into some back-and-forth about the scriptures. He read passages from the Bible and she followed with Mrs. Eddy's interpretation of the passage. After the second hymn, the auditorium went quiet. The readers sat stone-faced, the silence eerie. She could hear the man behind her breathing.

After what seemed like hours, a woman near the front stood and began speaking. "Through my testimony of healing—" She swallowed hard. "My heart goes out in gratitude to God for Christian Science. What a blessing it is." She coughed into her hand then continued, her voice barely a whisper.

She could not hear. She looked to her daughter. Lena had her eyes squeezed tight. The woman sat and after another long period of silence, a man stood and spoke. Eventually, a second woman got up. A lengthy silence followed. The first reader nodded to the organist and the final hymn began. The hymn must have been one of Lena's favorites, judging by her enthusiasm.

After the service, her daughter led her to a couple in the crowed lobby. The gentleman was rather slight and wore a dark pinstripe suit, vest, and a high-collared shirt. She recognized the woman. She was the first person who gave testimony, the one wearing the gray jacket and a rose on her cloche. Lena gave the woman a peck on the cheek. "A lovely testimony, Therese, just lovely." Her daughter pulled her close. "Mother, meet Mr. and Mrs. Ernst—Maxim and Therese. Our Uncle Max and Aunt Therese—the children just love them."

Mrs. Ernst did not look well, her face heavily powdered, her eyes bright as if prescient.

Anna stared, taken aback. Mr. Ernst stepped forward and bowed amicably. "Mrs. Anderson, what a pleasure." He moved his bowler to the crook of his arm and extended his hand. He wasn't her daughter's height but had a way about him that made his presence larger, like a genteel man comfortable with success. He and his brother, Herbert, who was a few years older and a bachelor, owned several properties in town.

Lena nattered on about the house Mr. Ernst was building a couple of blocks west of the Lauth Hotel. It was part of his new Ernst Court housing development. Lena thought Mr. Ernst's timing was perfect. The entire country was booming, and Port Huron was no exception. Putting up a half dozen nice homes in the midst of a housing shortage was smart business and no doubt would result in a lovely nest egg. She was impressed with her daughter's knowledge of real estate.

Mr. Ernst waved away the compliment. "Helena, thank you for the advertisement, but so far we've only sold two lots. Herbert bought one; I bought the other." He blinked as if remembering something and jabbed a finger at Lena.

"Helena, you got an envelope from the Mother Church today, probably about your application. It's in the desk drawer in the reading room. Would you like to have it tonight?"

Her daughter's eyes noticeably brightened. She had applied to be a reader and had been waiting to hear if the Mother Church had accepted her for classes. Lena allowed that if she had to wait to hear until tomorrow, she wouldn't be able to sleep a wink.

"Mother," she gushed, "The reading room is right across from Barnett's. I'll take you to Barnett's then dash across the street for half a second."

The Christian Science Reading Room was on the fifth floor of the People's Bank Building, formerly the Meisel Building, at the corner of Military and Water Streets. The reading room held a trove of Mrs. Eddy's writings and provided a quiet place for study and meditation.

Lena dragged her mother through the knot of people waiting at the trolley stop in front of Barnett's and through the screen door. She pointed in the direction of the magazine rack. "The soda fountain is back that way, Mother; I'll be back in a jiff."

Ben was at the counter hunched over *The Adventures of Superman*. A banana split sat alongside the comic book. Anna slid onto an adjacent stool. "Superman winning?" He smelled like beer.

"Superman always wins, Ma. Where's Lena?"

"She ran across the street to get something. She'll be back in a minute. Church was kind of boring. What did you do?"

Ben looked sheepish. "Walked around, had a beer."

"Whereabouts?"

"Other side of the bridge. Carl heard of some hot spots and said I should check 'em out." Ben spooned up a gob of strawberry ice cream and dabbed his chin. "A couple places were really something." He drew back. "Now Ma, I didn't go in any of them; you had to be a member. But what I saw through the door was really somethin'."

Port Huron was infamous for its First Ward, a stretch of derelict buildings along Quay Street between Huron Avenue and the railroad bridge at the mouth of the Black River. The anchor of the First Ward was Roche's Bar, a small brick building with shuttered windows that glowed red from the light of a neon Open sign. It was a place where certain telephone numbers were available to trusted customers. Further along Quay, shadowy figures loitered in dark doorways; cars driven by searching men cruised slowly by. For a price, it was said, the First Ward offered whatever the imagination could contrive.

Ben turned serious and leaned close. "Ma, I seen something maybe I shouldn't have." He pushed his sundae aside. "I stopped at this place just off the main street for a beer. Well, David walked in and he didn't see me sitting there at the bar."

"Really! He was out of town, wasn't he?"

"No, he was with one of those girls. They took a booth in back and acted like they knew each other pretty well. Anyway, I skedaddled." Ben's eyes went wide. "Uh-oh, here come Lena."

Her daughter came striding past the magazine rack, her dress flowing, a white envelope held high. "Hasn't *this* been a wonderful day!"

LENA

16 October 1921

WHAT HAPPENS IN the First Ward, stays in the First Ward proved to be a testosterone-fueled myth. Ben was neither the first nor last to see David in the presence of a painted lady. Philanderers who frequented Roche's Bar or stalked dance halls or slinked up Quay Street stairways relied on the secrecy of other philanderers. Inevitably, back-slapping loyalties leaked to did-you-know gossip. The knowing smile behind a gloved hand caught Lena's attention as did the growing awkwardness at bridge parties. Absurd, she thought, that David could be cheating. Although, he *was* on the road a great deal of time and temptations *were* plentiful—women smoking and drinking in public places, wearing flimsy little dresses barely covering a thing, behaving like speakeasy floozies. She was honor bound to investigate the whispers and glances and put this ugly gossip to rest.

The next time David was abruptly called away, she waited until night settled in. She put on a prim-looking Sunday dress and bonnet and marched into the First Ward with her umbrella under her arm and fire in her eye.

She started down Quay to the open door with a huge racket blaring from inside. A large doorman wearing an indifferent expression blocked her way.

"I'm here for my husband," she announced, looking the man straight in the eye.

He shrugged. How many times had he heard just that? The man told her to come back after she joined the club. But as he turned away, she could see over his shoulder and through the cigarette smoke, a straw boater amid men cheering bare breasts and David was wearing it.

∞

She thundered back to Roche's bar and stormed in. The men at the bar looked as if they'd been struck by a great light and parted before her wrath. The bartender froze in silence, his eyes big. A man holding a fedora over his face bolted from a back booth; a door opened then slammed.

Lena pulled out her pad and pencil and after scribbling a note, folded the paper then scrawled David Houston across the front. She pushed the paper at the bartender and left with her head held high. She didn't remember walking home.

Two weeks later she still hadn't seen or talked to David. He was well aware from her note that she would call the police if he showed his face on her porch. But he called and called, and Mrs. Myree continued to tell him that she was not available. She was hurt, mystified at what compelled him to go to those places. Certainly, he must have known he would be recognized and people would talk. Her reflection in the hall mirror stared back. Was it her? She *was* thirty-nine and a bit heavy, but goodness gracious, she'd given the man six children. If he preferred long-legged hussies painted with spangles and rouge, so be it. She would not be played for a fool. If it weren't for the fact her children needed a roof over their heads and food on the table, that man would be out of her life forever.

Supposedly, no one knew of her situation other than Mother, Ben and, of course, Mrs. Myree. She told Maxim a white lie, saying that David was gone on a special project. But people had to know he was not just out of town. He had to be sleeping and eating somewhere; probably too embarrassed to be at the Harrington; most likely he was at the Lauth. David *should* be embarrassed; she was certainly ashamed to be seen in public.

When anger subsided and bills accumulated, she relented to meet him at Diana's Sweet Shop on Huron Avenue—but only after lunch and before the tea-time crowd.

Diana's, depending on individual circumstances, was either a quaint tea room, a romantic hideaway, or a secure place to conduct delicate business. The small lobby was trimmed in leaded glass and a double bank of confessional-like wood booths that stretched almost to the tin ceiling. Tables in the booths were shadowed by low-hanging Tiffany lamps. So powerful was Diana's draw that the city permitted the restaurant to operate without toilets. Customers and employees in need of facilities went next door to use the toilets at Sperry's Department Store.

She looked at David through angry eyes from across the small table. "Does this woman have a name?"

He was crestfallen, on the verge of tears. David gulped, his eyes searching the narrow aisle between booths, pleading for help. "Phyllis," he choked.

"You mean the Honey Bare on the placard out front?" Diana's was a place where one could speak frankly, if quietly. She glowered. "Well?"

"Lena, for God's sake, please." His face cratered with remorse; a vein pulsed in his forehead. "Lena, I've said I'm sorry a thousand times; I want to move back home—please. I have a right to be with my children, don't I?"

He reached for her hand. She pulled away.

He opened his wallet and folded a sheaf of bills into a neat stack then pushed them across the table. "You must need money. Please, take this."

She looked away, her eyes on the Tiffany lamp, tracing its patterned intricacies in red and green and gold. She couldn't feed five children on her own. Then there was the rent and the rest of it. And she couldn't take a job with the babies. What choice did she have?

"David, I've got to go. Norma needs to be fed." She tucked the bills in her bag and adjusted her feather cloche. "I'll think about it."

He stood with her. "Lena, please, I promise I'll make this up to you." She turned and left.

His calls continued, she fretted. The facts were inescapable; she needed support. There was no imaginable way to extricate him from her life and still provide for her children.

The phone rang. Mrs. Myree looked through the archway pointing to the earpiece in her hand, her face questioning. "It's Mr. Houston again."

She laid her crocheting aside. "I'll take it, Mrs. Myree, thank you." She dropped in the chair at the hall table. "Yes, David."

She frowned. "Yes, David, I'm fine, thank you." Her eyes narrowed. "Yes, David, I have given it some thought." She sighed at the ceiling. "Yes, David, I hear what you're saying, but I don't see how you living here could possibly work."

David blathered on. "Yes, David, I know you're paying the bills. The house is too small; where would you sleep? With the furnace?"

An eyebrow went up. "Yes, I do remember." He promised a bigger house once he got to know Port Huron. "Who? Bill Willson? Who's he? A realtor?" She jotted down the name and number and sighed again, slumping in the chair. "Yes, David, I suppose so." She hung up the phone with a sinking feeling; would she trade her pride for a larger house?

Mr. Willson picked her up the following afternoon in a white Wills Sainte Claire, a roadster that smelled of new leather. He knew David through the Chamber and was glad he could be of service. Of course, the rental market was tight, but he had a few houses she might like although nothing close to downtown. She agreed; she was aware of the housing market and was resigned to taking the trolley.

The Wills Sainte Claire turned on Military Street and once past Griswold, the homes turned stately. South of the railroad tunnel to Canada, they became grand estates.

"The brown one over there is the Murphy's." Mr. Willson motioned to an ornate wrought iron fence guarding a large dark manor with turrets and a widow walk, beset by formal gardens. He nodded to the river side. "The white one is Moore's." The grounds resembled a Spanish villa with arched stucco walls and red-tiled roofs. A sweeping lawn held a large swimming pool and a white stucco cabana alongside the St. Clair River.

"Terrific neighborhood here." Mr. Willson flashed a big smile. "There's one up ahead I know you're going to love."

She appraised the lush yards going past, the number of windows and chimneys and balconies. She imagined the upkeep. The realtor had misunderstood; David would never let her buy anything so ostentatious.

"Oh, Mr. Willson, nothing on the river, please. I have babies. I'm sorry, but nothing on the river."

Mr. Willson turned back to Tunnel Street then cut over to Seventh. The Wills Sainte Claire canvased to Eighth and Ninth. The neighborhood was perfect: big trees, big yards, sidewalks. But no realtor signs. There was nothing for sale or for rent.

Mr. Willson stopped at Griswold Street. "You don't want anything around here, Mrs. Houston. Nothing but immigrants and riff-raff." He turned left for Tenth Street. "Let's give the north side of town a try." The Wills Sainte Claire sped past dreary stores with upper flats and outside stairways, yards with tall weeds and abandoned machinery. "Not a good neighborhood."

He turned north on Tenth. "I've got two listing up around Pine Grove." The rumble of rubber on brick quieted at Water Street and the car purred across the Tenth Street Bridge. He turned and grinned at her. "Mighty fine organization, that Port Huron Fuel and Supply."

A mile further, he turned on Scott Avenue and pulled over midblock then grunted at a small Victorian. "Too late, sign's gone."

A second place on Willow Street was far too small and a bit run-down. The realtor sagged in the seat, hands gripping the leather steering wheel. "Well, Mrs. Houston, let me show you something else." He turned the car around and headed south on Willow then turned on Lyon Street. "Now, please understand, Mrs. Houston, this is out-of-school—no guarantees."

He stopped in front of a large American foursquare, bristling with dormers. A porch ran the length of the front, and a paved driveway led to a garage and a fenced backyard. Generously landscaped front yards with tall elms lined the street, and at the end of Lyon, a blue slice of the St. Clair River appeared.

Mr. Willson nodded at the house. "Owner's a friend of mine." The layout was pretty standard; front room and parlor on either side of an entry hall; dining room, big kitchen, and pantry to the rear; five bedrooms and a bath up and another bath down; a dry basement and an attic perfect for a playroom. "The tenant who's in there has some kind of problem, and my friend would be a lot happier with you and Mr. Houston. If you like, I'll say something to him."

She did like the house and neighborhood and so it came to be. Given the circumstances, she could have done far worse. Yes, David was back, and she had to suffer him at the dinner table but no more than that. He paid the bills, she had the big bedroom, and he used the downstairs bath along with James. She and the girls got along just fine in the upstairs one.

Her decision was good for the children. They stopped asking where their father was, and she was tired of fabricating excuses. His absence had worn on all of them. James and Norma were too young to understand but they sensed something wasn't right.

The move to Lyon Street came together in a whirlwind. The furniture she had didn't begin to furnish the new place, and her new purchases were confined to what Howard Furniture had on the floor. But they did have a perfect secretary for her room, and Davidson's had a lovely sofa and two wing-backs that complemented what they brought from Ludington. There was a good choice of rugs at Scott-Drolett, and Port Huron Paint hung the wallpaper—a medium burgundy with a light twill—the minute the floor varnish was dry.

Bradley's, the movers, did a fine job packing and unpacking and didn't ding a thing. Mr. Bradley himself oversaw the move; said he knew David through the Chamber of Commerce.

Transferring the children from Van Buren Elementary to Garfield was a hassle. Those people who ran the schools simply refused to understand she didn't want her children vaccinated or examined or tested or subjected to any other unnecessary personal affront. But the district insisted she come in again for a second meeting with the superintendent, Mr. Packard, the district's attorney and the head nurse. The papers were idiotic; she signed them out of frustration.

But in a way, the hullabaloo in moving to Lyon was restorative; she was a proud presence out in public again with her man under control. She was a woman in charge. People respected that.

∞

Fall wore to winter, and her ire cooled to ice. Mrs. Myree's Thanksgiving turkey was superb, as were the trimmings, but neither aroma nor flavor could overcome her discomfort of being in a room with *him*. Christmas was a charade. Opening presents was as cold and unfeeling as the enameled nutcracker on the mantle. But when she watched her children fawn over his presents, it was difficult to keep satisfaction from interfering with animosity.

David devoted himself to spoiling the children. He gave the girls fine wool coats with real fur collars. James got a tweed car coat with handmade leather buttons, and Norma unwrapped a Baines-Wear knitted coat and matching pants. He even gave her an extravagant lamb's wool coat and kid gloves—not that she would ever be caught dead wearing them.

Weekends, he packed the children into his brand-new jet-black Packard sedan with tan leather seats and chromed wheels and took them ice skating at Palmer Park. He treated them to children's matinees at the

Majestic or the Huron or the Biju, buying them Jujubes and Milk Duds that ruined their dinners. When summer came, Mrs. Myree packed sandwiches, and they drove out to Lakeside Park to swim or to City Dairy for ice cream or a drive up the lake with windows down, palms out the window slicing air. Each day David's smile grew bigger, and the children loved him like life itself.

He and the children were at the beach when Mother called to say that Grammie died. Lena sat in the front room with a long face and told David the sad news when they returned. He accepted the news with mild interest and excused her melancholy by saying, after all, Grammie was almost ninety. Of course, no one knew Grammie's age for sure.

She ignored his aplomb. "David, she was like a second mom. I need to go home."

"For a funeral? I thought you didn't believe in funerals."

The man was so exasperating. She was going home for her mother and her family, not for a funeral. "The children and I will take the train. You can have the house all to yourself."

He eyed her, considering. "Why don't I drive you?" A bit of sand showed on his ankle. He saw her look and brushed it into his beach towel. "I can get away for a few days, maybe make a few calls around Ludington." He started for his room.

"I'm happy to drive you over, but I don't want to stay at the farm. Call the Stearns and book some rooms. I'll bunk with James."

An early start on a bright morning and a quick lunch in Reed City had them checked in at the Stearns in time for a quick swim at the beach before going to the farm. In the morning, she waited in the lobby for David and the children to bring the car around. The hotel seemed different than she remembered. The marble floor was worn dark, weary cushions slouched on sofas, and in the corner, an unhappy rubber tree drooped listlessly. But it *had* been twenty-five years, after all. She went through the vestibule; a stiff north wind blew under a leaden sky. Not a day to be outside.

There weren't but three cars in front of the house; probably folks just walked over. And for once, the children didn't run screaming in the front door like wild Indians. Even kids sense death demands respect.

It wasn't long before Ed went around moving people to the dining room. The table was filled with Gerda's cakes and Astrid's bread and jars of Fredericka's thick peach preserves. A stack of cups and saucers were next to the urn, and in the middle of the table, the small varnished box that Ed made for Grammie's ashes sat between vases of black-eyed Susans and yellow daylilies.

Grammie made it clear that when her time came, she wanted to be cremated. She didn't want to end up in a hole in the ground.

"Burn me," she declared. "And throw the ashes to the wind—but mind you, not the creek. I'm done with seasickness."

Ed surveyed the room. "Guess we're all set to go." He turned to the pastor from the Swedish Mission in Ludington. "We appreciate you coming, sir." The pastor touched the brim of his hat. He was in his liturgical vestments: a gray waistcoat trimmed in purple, silk sash, ruffled white shirt, and a bicorn hat.

Ed picked up the box on the table. "You ready, Grammie?" He and the pastor led the group around to the old oak. Mother had on Grammie's old sash with the beads and stood with Ben, Willis, David, Lena and the girls. She had changed into the traditional white hose and white strap shoes. Laura and Virginia passed out small stems of lilac tied with blue ribbon. Carl and Sister waited a respectable distance away, standing with their arms crossed.

The pastor read verses in Swedish from Grammie's Bible followed by English passages. Lena didn't remember the Swedish, but the pastor sounded sincere. When he finished, Ed tilted the box over his head and poured white dust to the wind. Clouds swirled, lifted and soared away. Voices from men picking peaches filled the silence.

A few days after returning home, Maxim called to say Therese had passed; he was having a small luncheon and hoped she could attend. The event was held at the Harrington Hotel. Many of the people Lena had only seen in dungarees and boots or housedresses came dressed in their finest. They shed tears when they laughed or simply wept in silence. The luncheon was for them to remember, to grieve. Therese did not need consolation—she had taken her leave.

The screen door opened; David appeared. "Nice night, isn't it?" He let the screen close quietly then propped against the porch railing with his arms crossed. "How was the luncheon?" Porch lights glowed down Lyon Street; the sound of crickets filled the darkness.

Her thoughts shifted from Therese. "Nice. The Harrington does a fine job."

"How's Max doing?"

"He's a bit adrift now. Therese was his anchor, you know." She set the glider in motion. "Fortunately he still has his brother, Herbert—and Science, of course."

David pulled in a long breath. "There's smell of fall in the air tonight; we'll have leaves to rake soon." He straightened, his arms braced on the railing. "Lena. Do you remember what you were doing twenty-two years ago today?"

"What I did twenty-two years ago, David? I barely remember what I did two weeks ago."

"You don't remember?" His smile showed surprise in the glow of the front window. "We first met twenty-two years ago today. The lobby of the Stearns—remember?"

The image flooded back. "I do remember." How could she forget the day he swept into the lobby, striding between sofas and potted palms, calfskin boots clicking on marble, doormen and bellhops trailing.

His eyes were the bluest she had ever seen; she remembered his faint scent of aftershave. And that beautiful beige suit and vest, the salmon tie that matched the band on the straw boater under his arm. He was such a rake. But time and travel left its mark on him too. He had matured; he had softened. He was no longer the impetuous boy riding the fake alligator in Charlotte.

David swung a leg up on the railing and admired her. "You looked lovely behind the desk, so professional in your high-neck lace blouse with that gold tie and your hair tousled like a Gibson Girl." A moth fluttered against the screen. "Then when I asked for a room, you replied, 'Are we expecting you, sir?'"

He studied her. "You still look lovely."

She could feel his eyes. The memory was warm, intimate, comfortable. He acted as if he truly loved her; he was contrite. He had provided five lovely children and a fine home and a bountiful table. And she had been so lonely. She patted the seat cushion.

David eased alongside. The mournful groan of a ship's horn sounded from the end of the street. "Freighter." Two faint moans in the distance answered.

She turned; he kissed her lightly. His bulk was warm, the hint of Old Spice familiar. A feeling of wholeness washed over her. She threw her arms around his neck and kissed him hard.

Stephen was born nine months later on March 17, 1925.

∞

17 May 1926

WINTER PASSED WITH everyone sledding at Palmer Park or clambering on ice floes piled along Lakeside Beach. As weather warmed, David took the family and Mrs. Myree to Detroit for Tiger games at Navin Field or on the *SS Ste. Claire* to Boblo Island. An occasional weekend was spent racing to Ludington for too-short respites at the beach and quick visits with Mother and Ed. Then without telling her, David quit Port Huron Fuel & Supply.

Perhaps a hasty decision was excusable as workplace differences often raised temperatures and produced impulsive decisions. But before David quit, he took a job in Detroit.

She couldn't move to Detroit. She had a toddler and five children in school. Laura was a girl scout, Virginia had her ballet group, and Marion had her clubs. How devastating. She and David had patched things up so nicely since that unfortunate business, and then he went and just mindlessly disrupted everything. Who was going to mow the lawn, haul the ashes, or shovel or rake? Didn't that man ever think ahead?

David had his reasons for quitting. He had been at PHF & S for better than six years and felt stuck in the same job. He was bored and wanted new opportunities; Paint Creek Coal offered them. But he wasn't going back on the road selling coal. Paint Creek wanted to expand, and his job was to build and train a sales staff. The office was not that far away; he planned on taking the Interurban for the fifty miles to Detroit. The ride was only ninety minutes and he could read the papers.

She found unexpected benefits in his new job. Other than the occasional time he drove the Packard to work, he was tied to the train schedule. He left promptly in the morning and returned home at the same time every night.

Nevertheless, that tawdry business from a while ago picked at her.

David was back on the road and beyond her guidance. But he was forty-seven. Maybe his libido had gone flaccid like his jowls and paunch.

In the morning, she held his suitcoat while he buttoned his vest. “Don’t forget we have Crystal’s party tonight. Can you take an earlier train?”

David shook his head. “Nope, can’t do. I’m going to be late. Gotta drive today. I’m taking a greenhorn to Cleveland to show him how to sell coal.”

“But what about the party?”

“Take Laura. She plays bridge better than I do. Virginia can babysit.” He gave her a kiss on the forehead. “Norma feeling any better? Seems like the hacking is getting worse.”

“She’s feeling better, David. It’s just winter weather. Half the children in Port Huron probably have a croupy cough right now.”

She got Laura and Virginia off to school then bundled up James and Marion and put Stephen in the stroller for the walk to Garfield. Norma had a runny nose and coated tongue. Keeping her out of school for a day was better than another confrontation with the school nurse.

After Mrs. Myree arrived, Lena took the trolley downtown to the *Times Herald* offices for the photographs that accompanied the article on Virginia. On the way home, snow started to fall, and the thought of David driving home from Cleveland crossed her mind.

In the morning when she went for the paper, an inch of snow covered the lawn. David did make it home last night nor did he call. She had Laura and Virginia sweep the steps before school and then made a hot mug of lemon-water laced with honey for Norma. When Mrs. Myree arrived, she dressed for the day.

As she came out of the bathroom, Mrs. Myree called up the stairs. “Mrs. Houston? Mr. Houston called. There’s some big storm in Cleveland and the roads are bad.”

Stuck in Cleveland? Seemed Cleveland always got more snow.

“Mrs. Myree, did Mr. Houston say how long he expected to be there?”

“No, ma’am. Said he’d call back.”

Poor David, how unlucky. Hopefully he got a hotel room before everything filled up. But even then, he’s still wearing the same clothes. But it won’t be the last time winter weather had snagged him. He should have stayed at his old job.

By lunchtime, sunlight streamed through windows and the lawn showed more green than white. David still had not called. What did he expect of her? She couldn't read his mind. And it would be just like him to forget to call, although the lines could be down. But why wait in suspense; she could call his office. They would know how to reach him. She went to the hall table and gave the operator the number.

"Good afternoon, Paint Creek Coal." The voice was not familiar.

"Mary?"

"No, this is Hazel. Mary's no longer with us."

"This is Mrs. Houston, Hazel. I'm trying to get in touch with Mr. Houston."

"Please hold while I ask. This is only my second day."

"Mr. Houston is in Cleveland. I'm hoping you have a phone number so I can reach him."

"Let me ask. Please hold." Lena heard a clunk and faint voices. "Mrs. Houston, I'm sorry, Mr. Houston isn't in at the moment. But I do have a phone number."

Lena gave the number to the operator and after a moment of static, a woman's voice said, "International Operator."

She hesitated. David said he was going to Cleveland. Maybe plans changed. She gave the operator the number and agreed to accept charges. The line filled with clicks and shrills and, after a long moment of silence, ringing.

A woman's voice answered, "Hello?" A dog barked in the background.

A wrong number? "I'm trying to reach a Mr. David Houston. Do I have the correct number?" A child on the other end screamed and began to cry.

"Oh, looking for Davey, eh? He's gone until this evening. Would you like to leave a message or call back in the morning?"

Her knees buckled; she collapsed on the chair.

The woman said, "Hello?"

"Message?" The word choked. "Uh . . . just tell him Lena called."

"Oh, you must be the new Mary." The dog barked; she hung up.

She staggered to the front room and fell on the sofa, hands pressed to her ears. How could that be? The realization fell with unbearable weight. She choked back a sob. She couldn't fall apart; she had children to care for. She went to the phone and thumbed for the number of Orr's Hardware. The locks needed to be changed.

That night she was tormented. How could she have been so blind? The vision of him enjoying that woman's comfort, sharing her bedroom, eating at her table, was impossible to overcome. Were the children his? And was she the only woman? Truth was relentless, pounding, insatiable. She was no different than any other unfortunate wretch deserted by her man. Mother survived it. Mrs. Eddy survived it. Scores of abandoned women in Port Huron were surviving it. Knowing the truth did not ease pain. She threw the covers back and snapped on the table lamp. She had to be strong, put this evil from her mind. She reached for her *Science & Health.*

Midmorning, David pulled in the driveway. At least he had the common sense to show up when the children were in school. She asked Mrs. Myree to take Stephen upstairs and to close Norma's door. The back door rattled; moments later David came up the porch steps and rang the bell.

She unlocked the door and cracked the storm. "David, I don't want to talk to you, listen to you, or ever see you again. Please leave."

"Lena, be sensible." He pulled the storm door open. "Let's behave like adults. We need to talk."

"David, if you set one foot in this house, I will call the police."

He stepped back, and the door swung against his foot. "Call the police?" He held his palms out looking surprised. "Whatever for?"

"I will call them, David, and I will tell them you assaulted me."

His face went dark. "Lena, I live here. You can't keep me out of my own house."

"You should have thought of that some time ago, Mister."

"Lena, I pay the bills around here."

She reached for the storm door. "And if you continue to pay the bills around here, I won't have to tell the police you abandoned your children." She kicked his foot aside. "If and when I'm ready to talk to you, I will let you know." She pushed the front door closed and set the lock.

When she got a hold of herself, she went upstairs to check on Norma; her daughter was finally asleep, fitful as it was, but the coughing had stopped. She felt tested, challenged by her faith. She had to know whatever had Norma in its grip was false and that David could not drive her to mortal error. It was so hard for a seven-year-old to understand that

God was all in all. She had to find a way for her daughter to know the Truth. But how could she help Norma when he addled her thoughts so?

After the children were off to school, she sat at the kitchen table with a cup of Sanka and the morning mail—advertisements and something from Federal & Commercial Savings Bank. And what's this? An envelope addressed in David's hand. After extracting a check, she wadded up both the envelope and the letter. He could write any preposterous thing he wanted, but she didn't have to read it.

The Federal & Commercial letter was a notice the bank had foreclosed on the house; rent checks were to be sent directly to F&C. Mr. Willson's friend must have defaulted. Would the bank sell the house at a discount? Probably. She'd have to move again. She slumped in the chair.

But maybe there was another way. A gleam of an idea was in the bank's letter. She could make some calls and do some reading; possibly she could make a clean break with David.

∞

When she had her facts together, she relented to meet David. Of course, he wanted to meet at Diana's Sweet Shop again. Appalled, she stood in the lobby until her eyes adjusted to the shadows. He had such a twisted mind; he was waiting in the same back booth. No doubt, he gave credence to those who say criminals return to the scene of their crime.

She faced him across the table, back stiff, face hard, eyes level. Her heart pounded. He realized she wasn't about to speak and cleared his throat.

"Lena." He cleared his throat again. "Lena, you're making too much of this. This is not the end of the world. I'm not going to leave you. I love you, and I love my children."

He was infuriatingly calm and logical and blindly compartmentalized; he was impossible.

"Lena, people can love more than one person. We should all try to get along, like a big family. Nothing needs to change. I won't be in Port Huron any more or any less, and you'll have the same freedom and support I've always given you." He put both palms on the table and radiated confidence. "You know that I *am* a good provider."

Her expression hardened. "Are you finished?" She opened her

handbag and took out a piece of folded stationery. "David, I've given this a great deal of thought."

She pushed the paper across the table. His eyes scanned the paper, those beautiful blue eyes, eyes no longer hers.

His eyebrows went up. "You want me to buy you the house?"

"Not for me, David, for your children. They *are* yours, you know."

"Lena, don't be ridiculous." He tossed the paper on the table. "I'm not buying you a house."

"It may be your wisest choice." Her words were calm. "It could keep you a free man."

"What?" He eyed her, suspicious, wary.

"Bigamy is illegal in this state, David." His jaws clenched. "I understand bigamists can go to prison for ten years in Michigan." She pushed the paper back at him. "And I can't imagine how Paint Creek Coal or anyone else with any sense of decency would tolerate a bigamist."

His face flushed. "Lena, that's stupid. We're not married. We never have been."

"David." She narrowed an eye. "I've lived with you for more than twenty years. I've traveled with you, slept with you, bore your children, and entertained your friends as your wife. That, Mister, is marriage according to the law in this state—common law marriage."

Color drained from his face. "That's extortion, Lena. That's illegal."

She snorted. "Well, let's call it a private settlement then." She returned his glare, her eyes flashing daggers. "Or if you prefer, we can let the sheriff decide what to call it."

His eyes narrowed—forehead furrowed. "If I don't buy the house, you'll call the sheriff?"

She studied him calmly. "All I want is a home for my children." He glared at her, stood up, then without saying a word, walked out.

The next weeks passed in a blur. She prayed for Norma, argued with David on the telephone, and worried and worried. Norma continued to languish and a feeling of inadequacy fell over her. It had to be her fault her daughter wasn't doing better. She could not bring healing thoughts to bear with such anger churning her. Thank heavens, Maxim was there to steady her and guide her through the legal intricacies of purchasing property.

David, though, outfoxed her again. He did buy the house as she demanded, but he had some big-time Detroit lawyer draw up a fancy agreement that deeded the house only to the children. The paper she reluctantly signed gave him control of the children's shares until they became of age. The arrangement rankled her to no end, but she had a place to live and support money to boot. She told the children their father had found someone he liked better.

Once the agreement was finalized, she devoted herself to working with Norma. After giving David's things to charity, she turned his bedroom to a healing room and put in a comfortable chair, reading lamp, and ottoman. Her mind was finally clear, and with redoubled efforts, her daughter would surely break free of the evil that held her.

She was reading to Norma when Mrs. Myree called up the stairway. "Mrs. Houston? Telephone. It's the school; the nurse would like to speak to you."

"Mrs. Houston? Sorry to bother you." The nurse's tone suggested she was quite happy to bother her. "James isn't feeling well. Could you come over and pick him up, please? We have him in the office."

She agreed to come right away without realizing James couldn't walk home from school if he wasn't feeling well. He was too big to carry. Call Maxim? She hated to bother him, but he would be put out if she didn't. She gave the operator his number.

Lena carried James down the school steps, his head buried in her coat collar; Maxim opened the backdoor of the Durant. "Lena, you probably ought to sit in back with him." He handed her a towel. "Just in case."

Maxim engaged the clutch and accelerated on to Garfield Street. "What did the school have to say?"

"The usual, Maxim, the usual." James shook with a spate of coughing. "They say he needs to see a doctor." She cuddled her son. "The nurse said it could be something-theria. I don't remember—it's all poppycock."

He nodded agreement over his shoulder. "Probably is diphtheria; newspaper says it's going around—supposedly a problem."

And a problem of epidemic proportions too. News articles would later report deaths of 4,000 children that year despite a proven antitoxin.

"I don't read those articles, Maxim." James gasped and began coughing again. She held his head and rocked him. "It's just so difficult with children. They're frightened. They're too young to understand."

"Well now, Lena, you've got two under the weather. That's a handful." He slowed for Lyon Street. "Maybe you should give Carrie Steffy a call—or talk to her on Sunday after church."

Carrie Steffy was a Christian Science practitioner certified by the Mother Church as a skilled and devoted professional friend and persuader. Christian Science practitioners did not pray to God on behalf of the person in need, but instead, prayed to help that individual realize the power of Christ to heal. Carrie's task was to persuade Norma of exactly that power and help her see past the evil of her illusion.

"Carrie? I don't know, Maxim. I'm on a tight budget. I don't dare say a word to David. You know how he feels about Science."

The Durant bumped into the driveway; Maxim shut off the engine and twisted around. "Lena, if you have no objection, I'd like to make arrangements with Carrie. We're *all* going to fight this thing."

And the battle was fought to the bitter end. Despite countless mugs of hot honeyed tea, Carrie Steffi's daily intercession, Maxim's constant prayers, and her full-bore willpower, Norma died in December.

"God is all in all." Maxim gently pulled the blanket over Norma's sunken face. "Spirit is the real and eternal—matter is only temporal."

Carrie put her arm around Lena and hugged; she pulled Carrie close and wiped an eye, then embraced Maxim.

"I can't thank you two enough. You've been so wonderful, my friends, my staff, my comforters."

Maxim opened the bedroom door. "Lena, I'm going to call the Smiths. They'll take care of everything for you." He found when Therese passed, not every funeral home in Port Huron wanted a Scientist's business. Arthur Smith Funeral Home was discreet. Some families preferred more privacy than others, and they handled details quietly.

Carrie jotted in her notebook.

"Lena? The usual time with James tomorrow?"

"Yes, Carrie, please. You've been so wonderful."

"Shall I stay while you tell Stephen and the girls?"

"When Smith is gone, I'll just leave the door open. They'll understand."

The children did understand with the exception of Stephen. At two, he was too young to comprehend death but sensed sorrow from his sisters. She assured the children that Norma had just gone to a place even better than home. She had risen to a higher level as they all would someday—there was no call for mourning. That night, she wept quietly in bed.

The following afternoon, Lena rested in a wingback staring mindlessly at the presents under the tree while Carrie Steffy worked with James upstairs. How was she going to tell David about Norma? She would rather hang in a gallows than talk to him. But she should at least write.

She opened her note box and her eyes fell upon the gifts for the children. Her mind filled with disgust and resentment. She shook her head; she wouldn't allow any feelings except for strength and resolve. She uncapped her Parker and wrote:

"*Dear David, Saturday night Norma's spirit passed from the turmoil of this material life to the peace and glory of eternal heaven. ~ L*"

She reread the words and nodded to herself. The envelope she addressed to Paint Creek Coal with Personal across the front.

A car motored slowly past the window, stopped, backed up, and pulled to the curb. "St. Clair County" was painted on a door below a Department of Health emblem that outlined a freighter. A man got out of the car and came up the walk. She set the card aside to give to the postman.

Mrs. Myree opened the door and when the man asked for Mrs. Houston, she stepped into the hall. "I'm Mrs. Houston."

He handed her a card. "Sorry to bother you like this, Mrs. Houston, but we haven't been able to reach you. I'm Mr. Neil Clancy, the pathologist for the St. Clare County Health Department."

"How may I help you?" She had instructed Mrs. Myree not to answer the telephone.

"I'm here to check on. . . ." He consulted his notebook. "On James Houston, if I may. I'm following up on a report from Garfield School. James may have a contagious illness."

She stood mute and measured the pathologist, her face stern. He was a big man with tired eyes, or maybe he was just resigned.

"The school advised us of your religious preferences, Mrs. Houston. I'm only going to make a cursory examination. I have nothing to administer, so please don't be alarmed." His eyes looked apologetic. "I'm only here to see if there is a danger to the community. I'm sorry. It's the law."

The man was polite, and she had enough run-ins with the school nurse to know the law. She took Dr. Clancy up the stairs and knocked on James's door.

"Carrie, may we trouble you?"

Carrie looked up from the chair beside the bed; her face flashed recognition.

"Oh dear, the health department."

"Nice to see you again, Mrs. Steffy." Dr. Clancy pulled a surgical mask from his pocket and, after snapping the band around his ears, went to James. He lifted an eyelid and put the back of his hand to his forehead. He then ran his fingers below his ear. Her son barely registered the doctor's presence, his chest heaving short breaths.

Dr. Clancy stepped back and removed his mask. "Mrs. Houston, your son is seriously ill. He has all the symptoms of diphtheria; significant weight loss, sallow skin, difficulty breathing. He should be in a hospital."

She stood mute, expressionless. Carrie put her hand on her arm.

"Mrs. Houston, there is a very effective antitoxin for diphtheria now. Surely you remember the dogsled run to Nome not long ago. That serum saved hundreds of people, if not thousands. Your son can be treated. He could survive this."

She'd heard enough about people blathering about Nome and dogsleds. It was one of those stories she could not avoid. The radio coverage was endless for better than a week; twenty mushers, 150 dogs covering 674 miles in five and one-half days to deliver serum.

Lena took Carrie's hand and faced the doctor. "Thank you for coming, Dr. Clancy. I very much appreciate your concern."

He looked drained. "Mrs. Houston, diphtheria is highly contagious. It can easily spread to others." Carrie lowered her eyes.

Lena looked at him, her face expressionless. "Thank you, Dr. Clancy."

His shoulders dropped. "As you wish, Mrs. Houston, as you wish. Please know though, the law requires me to post a quarantine sign."

She watched through the window while he retrieved a yellow quarantine sign from his car. She let the curtain fall back when the pounding started. She turned to find Mrs. Myree standing there with her coat and purse.

"Mrs. Houston," Mrs. Myree apologized, "I got family too. I can't be working where it's apt to kill me." She opened the door. "I'm so sorry, Mrs. Houston."

∞

Not a week later, while she was with James, Laura shouted up the stairway for her. She apologized to Carrie and Maxim. "I'm sorry, I'm needed downstairs."

"We'll carry on," Maxim replied. Carrie nodded.

Laura had her back to the front door, her eyes wide. "It's Poppa, Mother. And he's got people with him—one of them is a policeman!"

She asked Laura to take Stephen up to the playroom before opening the door.

"Yes?" Her eyes shot daggers at David. A slight woman in a frumpy tweed coat with a leather belt stood between David and the officer. Her cloche was equally bedraggled.

The officer tipped his cap and showed a stern expression. "Madam, we're here on a child abuse complaint." The woman stepped forward and handed her a card: Cicely Baird, Child Protective Services, St. Clair County.

"Protective services?" She caught her breath. "Did *he* tell you my children were in danger? Did he tell you that?" Anger stiffened her back.

David moved a step closer. "Lena, you're killing my children." His face was flushed and twisted. "I want my children away from you and your ungodly religion."

Miss Baird held up a finger. "Enough. Mr. Houston. Please control yourself."

David brushed her hand aside. "I'm not going to stand idly by and let—"

The officer took David by the arm. "Let's let the county do its job, sir." He turned David around and ushered him down the steps.

"Mrs. Houston. The department has a child abuse complaint and by law, we must investigate. May I come in, please?" Miss Baird's tired inflection suggested she would investigate one way or another. She stepped aside.

Miss Baird looked through the front room arch and took note of the sofa, the two wingbacks, the inlaid glass coffee table, the framed pictures on the walls and the unopened presents under the Christmas tree. In the dining room she noted the Victorian table surrounded by upholstered chairs, the Persian rug, and the painting above the glass china cabinet. "Very nice home, Mrs. Houston. Now may I see the young man, please?"

Lena eased the door open to her son's bedroom. "We have a visitor, Miss Baird. She is concerned about James's wellbeing."

Maxim stood. "Well, aren't we all." He offered his hand. "How do you do, Miss Baird, my name is Ernst. This is Mrs. Steffy."

Miss Baird looked at James and blanched.

"This boy is terribly sick. Why isn't he in the hospital?"

Lena's face turned to stone. "I am caring for my son in the way of my belief."

"Caring?" Miss Baird looked to Maxim; he met her eye. She turned to Carrie, her face showing determination.

Miss Baird's voice turned firm. "You're Christian Scientists? And how do I know? Do you have some kind of proof that you're a practicing Christian Scientist?"

"I can testify to that." Maxim extracted a card from his pocket secretary. "I'm on the board of the Port Huron First Church of Christ Scientist." He handed the card to Miss Baird and motioned to Carrie. "Mrs. Steffy here is a Christian Science practitioner registered with the Mother Church in Boston. In addition, Mrs. Houston is our church-sanctioned second reader. Let me assure you that we are doing everything in our power to heal James."

Miss Baird's lips moved wordlessly. "But, Mr. Ernst—" She looked from Maxim to Carrie and then to Lena. Their expressions were somber, unwavering. She looked at James and turned away. "Thank you, Mrs. Houston."

∞

January wore to February, the days dull and white and cold. Time was meaningless. Cook, clean, care for James, and help with schoolwork. Each day brought repetition. Arthur Smith had called again about Norma and urged Lena to get to the courthouse and buy a grave.

Leaving James with the children was not the best of ideas, but when Carrie arrived, she was able to make a quick trip downtown to visit the courthouse and buy Valentine's Day cards at Barnett's to cheer up the children. The county insisted they quarantine right along with James.

The courthouse was not a place she enjoyed; three massive stories of brick and limestone with the entrance at the top of a heart-challenging flight of concrete steps. At the landing, she leaned against the railing and caught her breath. Using both hands, she pulled the massive wood door open, then dropped on the first bench in the corridor, trying not to pant. Her head felt light.

A wide, lengthy hall lined with frosted windows and glass-paneled doors ended at a similar entrance. The sound of typewriters chattering came through open transoms; a clerk hurried by, her heels echoing on worn oak. At the far end, two policemen sat on a bench talking.

She opened the door marked Treasurer. A woman in a knee-length print dress and her hair curled in a tight bob came to the counter. The clerk nodded at her request to purchase a gravesite and disappeared into a storage room, returning with a large sheet of stiff paper.

"Cemetery map," she said, as she rotated the paper to Lena.

Looping roads wound through sections marked by rectangular grave sites, many marked with an X. She could not remember what section Therese was in, but she did recall Maxim saying Scientists were not allowed in every section. She dropped her finger in the middle of the map. "Section G?"

The woman nodded. "Lot 41 with eight graves is available." She pulled a form from under the counter. "Now let's see, Lot 41—um, eight. That will be $100."

Lena interrupted. "I just need one grave, please."

"The city sells graves by the lot, Ma'am."

"Miss, I don't have a hundred dollars, I have a child to bury."

The woman's face softened. "Oh, I'm so sorry. Let me get my supervisor."

She left the treasurer's office feeling somewhat better; she had to buy three graves, but the chore was taken care of. The clerk said internments would start as soon as the ground thawed and the sexton would contact her. Barnett's card rack was next.

After picking out three pink Happy Valentine's Day cards for the girls, a roly-poly balloon card for James, and a card with a dancing bear for Stephen, she waited for change at the counter. Usually, a dollar went in each card but things were tight; better to spend the money with Carrie. She licked the envelopes and slipped them into her purse.

Clouds soared overhead when she got off the trolley. Snow was on the way. Carrie was sitting in the living room when she came in, her face somber. Carrie stood and put her arms around her and pulled her close. "Lena, I'm so sorry. James has left us."

The cemetery called a month later and said the ground had thawed, and the sexton would like to get her on the calendar. The scheduled morning came clear and cold with a thin blanket of snow and puddles topped with ice. A stiff north wind skittered dead leaves along Lyon when the girls got off to school. Carrie came to babysit Stephen while Lena took one of the new city buses to the cemetery. She got off at Holland and walked to the drive between Sections B and C. The cemetery was a frozen crust, headstones capped in white, trees bare, the wind bitter.

The sexton and his men were waiting at the grave, leaning on their shovels. The earth had been forced open, a cruel wound in a white mantle. She stood alongside the gash, her back to the wind, and looked sightlessly at the boxes. The sexton's men watched her, their collars turned up, trousers whipping against shovels.

The sexton looked to Lena and made a questioning motion. She shook her head; she had nothing to say. Mrs. Eddy's words filled her mind. *O gentle presence, peace and joy and power.* Her babies would live forever and ever.

The sexton nodded to his men. The men lowered the boxes, James at the head, Norma at the foot. They coiled up ropes and picked up shovels. *Keep Thou my child on upward wing tonight.* The men worked silently, solemnly, clods thudding a final requiem. *His arm encircles me, and mine, and all.* The hole filled—the men stepped back at disinterested attention. The sexton nodded, and Lena nodded back to acknowledge the finality. He tipped his hat and motioned his men to the truck. The engine fired and they rumbled away. *No snare, no fowler, pestilence or pain; no night drops down upon the troubled breast.*

She pulled a hankie from her pocket and blew her nose. Finally, it was done. She turned from the mound of clay and faced the wind. Across Gratiot, the lake was a surging boil of whitecaps. *When heaven's aftersmile earth's teardrops gain.* She cut across to the bus stop. *And mother finds her home and heavenly rest.* Tree branches whipped overhead, snow crunched underfoot like broken crystal, the wind a knife. It fit her mood; it gave her strength.

∞

18 June 1931

Lena took the calendar off the kitchen wall and turned May over; half the year gone already. Rent was due, school was out the twelfth, and her reading room duty was the week of the fifteenth, and—was it? Yes. The second anniversary of Dad's death. Had it been two years? She pushed the salt and pepper shakers aside and wiped the tabletop. Poor Dad. Eighty-four hard years just wore the man out, although he was able to work—and happily worked—until his dying day. It was sudden. Mother found him in the barn all blue-like and ran for Fred Zweigle, but Dad was gone. Ben suspected it was a heart attack or stroke or some other medical poppycock she didn't care to know. Dad in all his love and goodness was not material, he was spiritual. He would live always.

And Mother was going on eighty. She was too old to be home alone so Ben and Nelly took her in. When she moved to Ludington she had Ben and Carl sell the farm. A buyer wasn't likely any time soon. Nobody had any money. President Hoover promised he'd fix things after the stock market crash, but no. Banks closed, businesses went under, and jobs all but disappeared.

Ben said Mother was getting along just fine. She was still tough as leather and just as bossy, always after someone to hook up the buggy so she could drive out to Bachelor Cemetery and sit with Ed. She hadn't seen any of them since Dad's service. She needed to call.

Rinsing the dishcloth, Lena noticed the sprig of lilac on the sill had wilted. New flowers would have to wait; she was off to the reading room and wanted to be back home before Stephen got out of school. The study syllabus to become a practitioner was far more than she even imagined, and anxiety nagged her.

But she couldn't forget about talking with Virginia and Marion about getting summer jobs. The girls needed work experience so they could take care of themselves if need be. Laura didn't gallivant around all summer when she was in high school. She found jobs, and when she graduated, her references landed her a full-time position at Sperry's Department Store.

Marion needed encouragement, and Virginia wanted to work. But Virginia was grounded. She didn't graduate despite repeated warnings about too many senior parties. Virginia was taking summer classes in English and typing.

But Marion needed encouragement. Why she was so reluctant to find something for the summer was beyond her. Marion was sixteen and certainly mature enough, but she was so obstinate; defiance showed every time she was given a chore.

Money was too tight to have anyone just sitting around. Virginia would be eighteen in October, and no doubt, David would stop sending her support payments as he did when Laura turned eighteen. Fortunately, Laura and her high school sweetheart, Donald Wismer, planned to marry, so she'd have one less mouth to feed. She dropped the sprig of lilac in the trash.

The elevator lobby in Peoples Bank was unusually quiet. Folks must be on vacation. The bus was half-empty too. The elevator door opened and she said, "Good afternoon, fifth floor, please." The pleasant young man at the control rattled the grate back, and up they went.

The corridor on the fifth floor was deserted; the clicking of typewriters echoed off gray marble walls. A scent of wharf and backwater wafted through the open window at the end of the hall.

Maxim was behind the desk when she opened the reading room door. "My stars, Maxim, I never expected to see you here." He was hunched over the Underwood, his suitcoat unbuttoned, forefingers hovering above keys. A finger stabbed; a metallic click faded in the traffic noise coming through Huron Street windows.

"Miscommunication, Lena." He looked perturbed. "Too many people away; I thought the easiest thing was to just fill in myself."

The tables and wingbacks in the reading room were empty, the reading lights dark. He ratcheted the carriage return, leaned over the machine, and slumped back. "Infernal device—what brings *you* in today?"

She emitted an audible sigh. "My application; I'm far from ready." She hung her bag on a chair-back and checked her reflection in the window glass. She pulled the hatpin from her Eugenie clutch, mindful of the artificial rose. "I'm such a slow reader and Mrs. Eddy wrote *so* many books."

He squinted one eye. "Can't imagine the Mother Church makes it easy to become a practitioner."

She laid her Eugenie on the table and patted tight curls.

"Just the *syllabus* for the primary class has me overwhelmed."

The applications were rigorous. The first application required two weeks of classroom instruction in Detroit. Then there was self-study, working as a Science healer, and earning references from those she helped with documentation, and witnesses for each healing. Three healings were required. Self-healings didn't count and two of the healings had to be of a physical nature.

Maxim eyed the Underwood. "You'll do fine, Lena. I'll wager you'll sail right through with flying colors." He rolled a fresh sheet of paper in the typewriter.

"How go Laura's wedding plans?"

"I hope well, Maxim." She pursed her lips. "But just between the two of us, I'm not sure."

He showed surprise. "How so?"

"Well, Donald's a Methodist you know. They think differently." She hesitated. She never should have brought that up. Maxim didn't want to hear about the unfortunate business with Donald's parents—nothing but grief right from the beginning. Mr. and Mrs. Wismer objected to their son marrying a Christian Scientist. It was a big stink. She gave Maxim a wan smile. "But it will work out. We just have to know it will."

"Lena, you worry too much about your children. Laura's marrying into one of Port Huron's most prominent families, Virginia's practically a professional ballerina, and Marion couldn't be more popular. Your children are good Scientists, and Stephen is only in the second grade. Lena, you've done well for your family, especially raising them by yourself."

"Oh, Maxim, stop." He did have a way of making her feel better. "How's your brother doing?"

"Herbert's trying hard, Lena. But he's not as sure on his feet anymore, having a bit of trouble getting around. No complaints though." Maxim wasn't one to discuss a challenge someone might be having, but Carrie Steffy made an offhand comment at church the other day that sounded like Herbert could be under her care.

Maxim chuckled. "I guess both Herb and I are wrestling a case of old age."

Behind his smile, his eyes showed resignation. "In fact, I'm going to move in with Herbert—he and I don't need two houses and it'll save me a lot of back and forth." He brightened. "Who was that realtor who helped you with your place? I may give him a call."

She was taken aback. "Sell? Really, Maxim? I certainly sympathize about the back and forth, but sell Therese's home?" Back and forth was a short walk past two empty lots, but pairing up made sense. Maxim was getting up there and Herbert even older. "I'm the one who should be selling, Maxim. I need something smaller and closer in."

"Selling the house bothers me too, Lena. But it's time." He hesitated and considered a thought. "Now, why don't *you* buy my place? That's a sale Therese would approve."

Carol French stuck her head through the doorway, wiggling fingers, and mouthing, "Powder room."

"Ah, my replacement." Relief hung on his words.

She turned on a desk lamp and put her binder on a table. "Maybe your house is something we could talk about later, Maxim."

"Good idea." He jabbed a finger at her. "Now get after those books."

Lena turned to the wall holding Mrs. Eddy's writings. *Science & Health,* she knew from reading in church, and she just finished *Unity of Good and Unreality of Evil.* Maxim's suggestion sniggled at her. Buy his house? It was smaller and *much* closer in. Once the girls were gone, Lyon Street would be far too big and expensive.

She took *The First Church of Christ Scientist Miscellany Writings* to the table and opened her binder. Study, she told herself. Don't daydream about Therese's house. His suggestion was simply pie-in-the-sky.

The clock on the wall was showing 3:00 when she said goodbye to Carol French and headed to the elevator. Thinking a walk home would be too hot, she crossed Military Street to wait for the bus in front of the Michigan National Building. The crowd was thin there too.

Marion wasn't home so she started Stephen on homework and took the *Times Herald* out to the porch to await her daughter. Fanning herself with the paper, she waited on the porch swing, Therese's house still on her mind. Buying it was an intriguing possibility. But as nice as the home was, Maxim had never put in gas. Did she want to go back to cooking on a wood stove? But maybe a mortgage could include gas service. Marion bounced up the steps and went for the screen door.

"Marion, dear." She patted the cushion. "Come sit a moment, please. I'd like to talk."

A difficult conversation portended, but it was high time her daughter came to grips with reality. Marion was instantly wary, barely on the swing, glaring down Lyon Street, eyes narrow, face tight.

"Marion, we need to talk about responsibility." She explained one more time how a summer job would bring benefits beyond income. She would get experience, find new friends; working would make her confident and self-sufficient. Laura was a fine example. Marion needed to change her attitude and be more positive like her sister. She'd be a senior next year, and had to prepare for her future.

"Now, Marion. I don't want you lazing around the house all summer again. I want you to find a job." Her daughter sat stone-faced, unmoving. She patted Marion on the knee and got up. "Thank you for understanding, dear, I know this will all work out for the best."

No sooner had she got to the kitchen, the front door slammed and Marion appeared in the doorway. Her eyes were flashing, face red, and tears streamed down her cheeks.

"You think you know everything, Mother! Well, you don't, Mother, you don't!" She flounced angrily and kicked the door. "You think you're so superior! I hate it! I hate this house! And I hate you!" The door wedge flew across the kitchen and caromed off a chair leg. The door whupped closed. Her daughter ran up the stairs; in the morning she was gone.

Marion's act of defiance was a body blow to her resolve. But like her mother and her grandmother, she forged ahead, deliberate and relentless to safeguard her daughter. But first, she had to find her. By the time Maxim arrived, she had grilled Laura, Virginia and Stephen. No one had a clue where she'd gone. Stephen stood by the phone while Maxim drove to her the laundromat, the Coney Island, the bus station and the train depot, while Herbert took Laura and Virginia to Marion's girlfriend's houses and around the school.

Her daughter turned up three days later in Ludington at Ben's. Ben said he answered the door and there she was, bedraggled, snot-nosed, and sullen. Marion wouldn't come to the phone though. She told Ben to say she was never going back to Port Huron, and nobody could make her. Ben's advice was measured. He said not to worry, the important thing was that she was safe. He and Nellie would keep her until things cooled down. He thought sharing a room with Mother might help Marion rethink things.

Indeed, it seemed rooming with her seventy-nine-year-old grandmother straightened Marion out. Or maybe Ben's influence or Nellie's empathy eased the way. But something did straighten her out, and she plunged directly into reality.

A month after graduating from Ludington High, she got married. Karl Hawley was seven years her senior and the son of Hawley & Son Coal & Feed. At first blush, the wedding appeared to affirm Marion's vow of never returning to Port Huron. But for reasons unknown, she decided to be married in the Lyon Street living room.

Anna came on the train with Ben and Carl and their wives; Sister and Willis drove in from Freemont. Rev. Albert Ruff from the English Lutheran Church on Sixth Street officiated. Laura stood up with Marion, and Ben, bursting with tear-stained pride, gave the bride away. David was noticeably absent, but no one gave him a second thought.

The girls decorated the house and tables in Marion's delphinium blue and hollyhock pink, and the Sunday Society Section even noted that "the nuptials were held on the bride's grandmother's eightieth birthday." The photograph of Marion was lovely.

And Karl's parents. No matter that they belonged to The Church of Christ, they charmed her to death and thought Science was as good a belief as any. Marion was unusually warm and contrite and seemed glad to be back home. Carl was over his hard feelings about Norman too. The wedding proved to be a perfect conclusion to an awkward situation. She couldn't have been more pleased—or thankful.

But Lena was not one to dwell on success. David's support had all but stopped. Marion was married, and Laura and Virginia were of age to live independently. But she couldn't make do on what she got for Stephen. The cold fact was that she needed a job as well as a less expensive place to live. Maxim's suggestion to buy his place made sense. The house was a three-bedrooms bungalow with a covered porch and the front bedroom big enough for her rolltop and reading chair. And being so close in, she wouldn't have to rely on the bus when she found a job.

Maxim offered to finance her; he was always her pillar. But there was David. The girls owned their own shares in the house, but he still controlled Stephen's. She would be wise to seek Maxim's advice after church.

If there is a will, there is a way. And when will was called for, she was first on the scene with an abundant supply.

Out of the chaos of hosting Marion's wedding in late July, she struck a deal with Maxim for his house and managed the transfer of the children's shares to her. She persuaded Peoples Bank to give her a mortgage despite being a single, fifty-three-year-old woman without a job, supporting a minor child, and who couldn't even drive a car. She moved to 933 Ernst Court just before Laura's April wedding and rented the garage to a gentleman who boarded across the alley. Having Maxim to guide her was a godsend.

In January, Franklin Delano Roosevelt was sworn in as the nation's thirty-second president, 472 electoral votes to Hoover's 59. But despite the New Deal Reconstruction Finance Commission, the CCC, the NRA and a blizzard of congressional acronyms, for sale signs and out-of-business notices continued to pop up along Huron Avenue and Military Street.

The holidays at 933 were overrun by crushed moving boxes and crates, cleaning buckets and rags, positioning and repositioning furniture, all the while her mind on Laura. Donald's parents, Fred and Blanch, were adamant about stopping the wedding. Laura, though, was undeterred and plunged ahead with arrangements, attendants and decorations, while prattling nonstop about honeymoon destinations.

Despite her discrete probing, Laura and Virginia were vague about wedding plans. The phone bill revealed that Marion was also involved, and the giggling behind the girls' door suggested her daughter was planning a big affair. Her worries abated when Laura asked if she could have a reception at the house after the ceremony; apparently, things had worked out with Fred and Blanch.

Lena shopped for a dress and accessories that befitted the mother of the bride and addressed invitations with Laura. At the last minute, the minister at Donald's church, the First Methodist over on Lapeer Avenue, decided he wouldn't marry a Christian Scientist.

After profound embarrassment, bitter disappointment and lame explanations, her daughter swung from depression to command and found the nearest clergyman, who in her opinion, harbored no such prejudices. Laura told friends and family that plans had changed, and the wedding would be a private ceremony in Mount Clemens—no guests *or* parents.

Lena was justifiably hurt and privately outraged. Her daughter probably acted as she did to spite Donald's parents. There was no reason to go forty miles out of town for the ceremony, though. Laura could have called that nice Reverend Ruff from the English Lutheran Church of Our Savoir who married Marion. Laura was so insistent, so headstrong.

Finding a job proved to be elusive and resentment had to be pushed aside. She couldn't be distracted. She opened the *Times Herald* at the table and read the headlines. The hothead in Germany was after the Jews again. Seventy-three people were killed in an airship crash in Lakehurst, New Jersey. It's illegal now to own gold. Why didn't the paper ever print something uplifting? She pulled out the classified section and turned to the Society page. Virginia said Laura's wedding announcement was in the paper.

The paper had a brief Wismer-Houston notice at the bottom of the society page but no photograph. *The marriage of Laura Houston, daughter of Mrs. D. H. Houston, 933 Ernst Court was solemnized . . .* ?" Solemnized was certainly the wrong word. Fiasco was more appropriate. ". . . *in the residence of the Rev. Jacob Wulfman . . .*" And look at who stood up! Maurice Roche—the First Ward saloon keeper. And a rabbi married her daughter? Well. At least they didn't have the affair in Roche's Bar.

What a masterpiece of invention; credit the Wismers. The whole debacle was made into a silk purse, and on top of that, they gave Laura and Donald a brand-new Model C Ford. She tossed the society page in with the kindling and opened the classified section.

∞

19 May 1935

THE GREAT DEPRESSION continued to dominate headlines. Banks failed, jobs were nonexistent and Oklahoma, Texas and Colorado almost disappeared under unrelenting dust storms. Even the gentleman who rented her garage asked for credit.

Maxim was unnaturally glum. Rumor going around was he and his brother lost several properties and others teetered on insolvency. Laura and Donald were getting help from his parents, but they were optimistic

Donald would land a job with the school district. Marion said Hawley & Son let people go, but fortunately coal was a necessity.

At the kitchen table, Lena stared bleakly, chin in hand, at the classifieds, wondering why she was even looking. There was nothing part-time, and Stephen was too young to be left alone. A few open positions—typists, clerks, secretaries—were full time, and, even then, those jobs required experience like being able to type at a certain speed, take shorthand, or operate a switchboard. Apparently, penmanship and responsibility were less valued than knowing how to operate a machine. Her skills were obsolete; it was difficult not to be discouraged.

Virginia could not find a decent job either, despite having a diploma and all those typing classes. But she was persistent, and the Works Progress Administration hired her for the sewing room that opened on Huron where L. Higer & Son used to be. She liked the sewing room and helping the less fortunate gave her a sense of purpose. Her $8.25 a week also helped with expenses.

She finally resorted to taking in laundry. Doing wash for strangers wasn't grand work, but it was something she *could* do. And she could do it on her own schedule. At fifty-one, she wasn't about to get on her hands and knees and scrub floors. Maxim built a fine basement and had put in a good hot water boiler, double laundry tubs, plenty of electrical outlets and enough headroom to hang bed sheets. The basement was another reason to be thankful.

Taking in wash proved not to be enough to pay all the bills. After painful self-reflection, she appealed to the city tax board. Groveling before strangers was a humiliating experience. They insisted on making her personal records public. Who owned what and how much and how did she come to own it? But she ate her pride and her property taxes were cut in half to $1,200. Soon afterward, David's check for Stephen stopped coming.

Nellie's phone call started her thinking. Mother had slowed down considerably and at times appeared addled. She was slow getting around, needed help with steps and stairs, and Nellie hinted that Lena might want to spend time with Mother. Her government check for thirty dollars could be the answer to her prayers.

At first, she didn't know where she could put her; Stephen and Virginia still needed bedrooms. But there *was* the cubby under the attic stairs. If she fixed it up—cleaned, painted, ran an extension cord—it would make a dandy hideaway for Stephen. He loved the idea and Mother moved to his room.

The cubby worked out well. Better than a hideaway, it became Stephen's DH-4 Liberty in Captain Midnight's Secret Squadron Flight Patrol. He decoded cryptic messages every evening except Saturday and Sunday. Between Mother's government check, Virginia's WPA wages, and taking in wash, Lena found hope, if not satisfaction.

She hung the last clean undershirt on the line and unplugged the Maytag; it was lunchtime. She stopped on the stair landing and looked out the alley door to the weather. Laura was having a backyard get-together later that afternoon to celebrate Donald's twenty-ninth birthday and his new job at the high school teaching shop. Laura was ecstatic; they wouldn't be beholden to Donald's parents anymore.

Heaving up the top six steps to the kitchen, she started a fire in the stove. The house was quiet except for the snap of kindling and the hum of the Kelvinator. Mother must still be asleep. If not, she'd be at the top of the stairs banging her cane for someone to come get her.

Mother was on the front room sofa wrapped in an afghan, thin white hair splayed around gaunt cheeks. Her boney knees protruded from a worn cotton nightdress. She looked asleep but her eyes stared out the window.

"How in the world did you get downstairs, Mother?" She had shrunk to half her size, eyes gray with cataracts, joints swollen.

"Down? Down the stairs, Lena? I walked. I ain't dead yet."

She picked up Mother's hand and squeezed the patchwork of liver spots and sat down. "A penny for your thoughts."

Mother's eyes fluttered. "Save your money, Lena. Mine ain't worth that much."

She pushed her steel-rimmed glasses up with a crooked finger and turned back to the window. "Just thinking of old times. Just old times." Across Ernst Court, a farmer planting seed pushed his planter steadfastly along, the blade spinning off small clods.

Lena knew the stories of the village in Sweden, getting to Germany, and crossing the Atlantic from Grandma Andersson. She was proud of how Grammie and Mother helped build a country and loved hearing the stories.

She rubbed Mother's hand. "What was the best time?"

"Ed." The name snapped out. Not surprisingly, Ed was the watershed. He made the family, set the standard, plotted the course, and provided them safe harbor. He left his mark on his children and stepchildren and their children.

Mother cleared her throat. "Lena, you've done well." Her words were matter-of-fact, she motioned to the wingbacks, the end tables, the burgundy wallpaper, the pictures on the walls. "You've done better than any of us."

"I am grateful, Mother. But I do wish some things had been different."

Mother withdrew her hand and held up a yellow nail. "Lena." Her voice cracked. "Regrets are shackles. Don't let other people decide what your mistakes were. That's rubbish." She jerked her afghan tighter. "Should I regret you? Sister? Should you regret Laura and Virginia and Marion and Stephen because of a shameful example of a man? No. You can't undo the past, Lena. The best you can do with history is gloss it over. But nevertheless, don't forget the blessings."

Her eyes went back to the window. "If I had been less cocksure and not so bullheaded once upon a time, I would have died scrubbing floors in Sicksjo. There would be no you, no Ed, no Norman—no anybody."

"The lord's son. What was his name?"

"The son? Albrecht?" Memory clouded Mother's face, her eyes searched as the neighboring farmer trudged back past the window. "Albrecht was a story your own girls need to know. They need to know we women are gullible, maybe even hexed. We make bad decisions about men. It's in our blood."

Lena patted her mother's hands. "Nevertheless, we've had God's blessings." She started to get up; Mother held her wrist.

"You should know this too. Your father wasn't entirely to blame for what happened. I knew it wasn't going to last." She paused, her head nodding slowly.

"Edward had a woman—children, I don't know. We were going to erase the past and start anew, no questions, no explanations."

Her eyes followed the seagulls swooping behind the farmer. "But Edward was all I had—all your grandmother and sister had. We were helpless without a man. Perhaps I used him. But I vowed to myself to stay with him no matter what. He saved me the trouble. The blessing from

Edward was that he got me and you and Sister to this country—and to Ed. Ed was worth it all."

Mother pushed forward. "So now you know, Lena." She pulled on the sofa arm and inched to the edge of the cushion. "All this gol-drottin jibber-jabber has worked me up an appetite. When's lunch?"

By the time the kitchen was cleaned up and Mother settled in her room, it was going on three o'clock. She hoped to catch the 3:10 bus to Laura's house. Virginia was there already helping set up. "Stephen," she called up the stairway, "We need to go."

Laura's was just out Lapeer between Thirteenth and Fourteenth Streets. Her neighborhood was nice, older houses with generous porches. Imitations, really, of grand old Victorians but without the turrets and ornamentation of better neighborhoods. Several had been converted to apartments.

The bus wheezed to a stop at Thirteenth Street and the door whooshed open. She held Stephen's arm crossing the street. "Now remember, this is an adult party so behave yourself." Stephen ran pell-mell up the sidewalk and disappeared between houses.

Once past the blue Ford coupe in the driveway, she spotted Laura in the backyard. After getting a peck on the cheek and glass of lemonade, she learned that Stephen was in the kitchen getting a bottle of pop. Donald's parents, Fred and Blanch, had come and gone.

Of the group of young people at the back porch, she didn't recognize anybody except Kenneth Peck from church, the girls in Virginia's ballet class, and Maurice Roche, the saloon keeper. The girls were in long crepe dresses with floppy shoulders and flowers in their hair. The boys were dressed to the nines in trim, broad-shouldered suits, straw hats, and shined shoes. They all looked gorgeous. She took a sip of lemonade and tried not to stare.

Donald was at the picnic table adding balloons to a Happy Birthday banner. She plunked down on one of the folding chairs alongside the table, a chair leg plunged into the soft dirt; her lemonade sloshed. "Good Lord!" she gasped and after hitching up her chair, looked to see if anyone noticed.

"Careful there, Mother Houston." Donald motioned to her glass swathed in wet napkin. "Freshen your drink?" He looked the model of success in his gray-plaid suit, starched white shirt, and a maroon necktie.

Donald was average in size and stature and exuded the comfortable image of a man happy with his circumstances.

She shook her head and laughed. "Please, no, Donald. Apparently, I've had one too many already."

Thirteen-month-old Donald Jr. came working his way toward her, sticky hands grasping from chair to chair. At her knee, he studiously looked for his next handhold, snot curling over his upper lip. She peeled her napkin free of the glass and swiped his nose. He took no notice, his eyes riveted on the seat of the picnic table.

Donald Jr. came along the last year about the same time as Stephanie, Marion's daughter. One was born on May 6th and the other on September 16th, but for the life of her, she couldn't remember who came first.

Laura was pointing at the apple tree in the yard and shouting. Virginia was on a branch striking a pose in her ballet slippers, a forearm draped to her forehead. Billows of crepe floated around her. On branches of their own, her cronies, Jeanne Merritt and Phillis Koreiba, also echoed great tragedy. She didn't recognize the girl with the camera standing with Laura and Stephen. Lena needed to tell Virginia she shouldn't be climbing trees in her good clothes.

Virginia dropped to the ground and led her *entourage* across the yard doing *jetes,* arms out, skirts lifting and falling. When she got to the group at the back porch she stopped and did a slow *releve*, pink slippers gracefully appearing from under pale lilac. A boy she didn't know tipped his fedora and applauded. Maurice pulled a flask from his suit coat and proffered it. Virginia did a *grande jete*, and *pirouetted* away. Maurice took a swig and handed it to boy in the fedora. The girls looped back to the tree, dipping and rising. Kenneth Peck cut across the lawn toward her.

"Love your hat, Mrs. Houston." Kenneth was a solid boy, perhaps overly so, but most pleasant. He had his shirtsleeves rolled up and a suitcoat draped over his arm. Beads of perspiration showed on his forehead. He extracted a neatly folded white handkerchief from a back pocket, blotted his face, and adjusted his bow tie.

"Why, thank you Kenneth." She had on her straw cartwheel with the mauve wrap. The hat wasn't her best or even fashionable, but on a day like this, a broad brim was essential. She motioned to the back porch.

"Now tell me, Kenneth, who is that next to Maurice Roche? The young man in the fedora?"

"Name's Gale, don't know his last name." Ambivalence showed on his face. "He's not from around here. He's a pal of Maury's."

Maurice's friend pulled a pack of cigarettes from his pocket, shook one up and offered it to Margaret Growie, who smiled a yes, thank you, as did Sandra Roche. The young man was tallish and quite fashionable in a brown pinstripe suit with narrow shoulders and outsized trousers with bold cuffs. Maurice pulled out his own brand, and heads bent toward his Zippo.

"What a show-off." Laura hung over her shoulder, and propped an arm on Kenneth. "Can you believe it?"

Virginia was laughing and tugging on Maurice Roche's arm. Virginia: never shy of attention and enjoying the limelight. Lithe and leggy, some thought of her as vivacious, far different from Laura, who was moodier, more self-conscious. Laura was not a reed like her sister either, she was . . . ah . . . more well-endowed—like the placards in the lobby of the Majestic Theater.

Kenneth stood and swung his suit coat over a shoulder. "Got to go, Mrs. Houston. I'll see you Sunday—Laura, see ya later."

Laura slipped into Kenneth's chair. "He's uncomfortable."

"Uncomfortable?" She raised an eyebrow. Kenneth wasn't uncomfortable around her. To the contrary, the two of them saw things much the same way and found plenty to talk about. "Why would Kenneth be uncomfortable?"

"Oh, Mother!" Laura rolled her eyes. "Can't you see? Look at her." Virginia was leaning against the back porch lattice, her head bent soulfully on an arm stretched along the handrail.

"See what?"

"Virginia's flirting with Gale. That's why Ken left. Don't you remember? Virginia used to date Ken. They went to our wedding together."

"Virginia's flirting with who?"

"Gale Forbes." Laura pointed. "Brown fedora, thin mustache. Ginny's gaga over him. Says he's a divine dancer." Her daughter stood. "I'm going for lemonade." She adjusted a strap under her top. "Let me know when you're ready to leave, Mother. I'll give you and Steve a ride home."

She scanned the yard. She was the only senior.

"You're right, dear, I should go. Stephen can walk home when he's ready."

Maurice Roche saw her looking and tucked the flask inside his suitcoat. "I suppose Virginia will miss dinner tonight."

Laura nodded. "Yes, Mother, but don't worry, I've made chili for later. But please take Steve with you."

"Why? Stephen can walk."

"Mother, he's twelve years old. I don't want him spoiling everything."

She should have known. The party was about to start. She didn't need to say goodbye to anyone; she just needed to disappear.

"Well, you go get him then." She started for the driveway and the blue coupe.

After a nerve-jerking three-quarter mile, Laura lurched to a stop in the alley. Lena got out of the car trying not to look shaken and moved the seat back for Stephen. Her daughter was a hazard, talking and gesturing and so oblivious to grinding gears.

She thanked her daughter and went inside to call Maxim. Virginia was gaga over some whisky-drinking stranger, and Maxim would probably know whoever this divine dancer was that made her daughter act like a teenager. He knew just about everyone in Port Huron.

Maxim answered the phone, and she did call at a good time. He and Herbert were just sitting and yacking. Did he know this Gale Forbes?

"He's about the same age as Donald Wismer, tallish, slender, natty dresser."

Maxim didn't recognize the name.

She laughed. "Maxim, I thought you knew *everyone* in town. This Gale Forbes was at Laura's party with that Maurice Roche crowd. There was some drinking going on."

"Were the girls drinking too?"

She snorted, "Of course not. And yes, I know Prohibition's been repealed. I'm just concerned about bad apples. Virginia is at such a vulnerable age."

Herbert started bellowing in the background, and she told Maxim they could talk later.

The following Sunday, Lena was in the second reader's dressing room frowning at the clock. The service had run over with an unusual number of testimonies that morning. She hung her gown in the closet and checked herself in the mirror. After a second look, she adjusted the floral band on her navy Florentine and smoothed the front of her dress. Satisfied, she went out through the church auditorium. People were still on the sidewalk chatting.

Halfway down the front steps, she stopped and looked for the girls and Stephen. Maxim and Clare Sperry, the owner of Sperry's Department Store, were off to the side, their straw bowlers bobbing casually in mutual agreement. Clare's darling wife, Florence, wasn't in sight. The girls were over at the curb, so Stephen must be close. She worked her way over, nodding and smiling thank yous to compliments on her reading. She tapped Laura's arm.

"If you and Virginia want, go find Stephen and start for home. I need to talk with Uncle Max and Mr. Sperry for a minute." There was a possibility Maxim and Clare were discussing the purchase of the house next door to the church.

Clare removed his bowler and took her hand. "A lovely reading, Helena, just lovely." He leaned forward and brushed his cheek against hers. Clare was such a gracious person. Florence too, and both of them so tall and athletic.

"Lena." Maxim pointed to the brown bungalow next to the church. "Clare and I were just talking about buying the house. We could spruce it up and move the Sunday school over there. What do you think?"

She nodded. "Oh, I'm all for it, Maxim. We need classrooms. It's like a zoo with all the children in the basement." The bungalow provided the only possibility for the church to expand. The strip of lawn between the building and Union Street was a setback, and a public alley ran behind the church.

Maxim rubbed his chin. "A shame we didn't make everything bigger when we had the chance."

Clare stood on his tiptoes and scanned Sixth Street for Florence and the car, then turned to her. "It *is* a good time to buy—if you have the money. Rates are down, but credit is tight. I think, though, Peoples will understand our need."

Peoples Bank would understand. Sperry's Department Store was one of People's biggest customers. When the bank needed assurances from the church, Clare quietly provided them.

A horn tooted. Clare turned and waved at a green convertible; Florence waved back.

"Got to go." He patted her arm and nodded to Maxim. "Let's try to finalize this at the board meeting." He dodged between parked cars.

"Lena," Maxim said, "I have a bit of information for you. The young man you asked about, Gale Forbes? His name is actually Gaylord. Lives with his mother above that party store on the corner of Griswold and Sixth."

"That place?"

"Yes—if you can believe it. His mother is a widow, father was killed in the war. They're from Detroit. The boy dresses windows at Springer & Rose, and they're apparently as poor as church mice."

"How did you find all that out?

"Therese's younger brother works at Military Street Billiards. Apparently, the young man is well known there." He touched her arm. "Come, I'll give you a lift home."

Military Street Billiards was an inscrutable storefront cloaked by a drooping awning just a few doors south of Barnett's. She had never been inside, but a glimpse through the front window curtains revealed a dimly lit pool hall with low-hanging lights and green-covered pool tables. Indistinct figures slouched on high wood stools against shadowy walls. In the summer, cellulous clicks resonated through the wood-framed screen door and patrons looked to see who was on the sidewalk before entering.

She waved goodbye as Maxim backed from the alley. Laura and Virginia were waiting for Donald on the porch glider and prattling about someone at the birthday party. She dropped in the chair next to the glider and waited until their gossip ran its course.

"Laura." The girls turned. "I heard something today about Donald's birthday party you should know."

Laura threw her hands up and slumped in the glider. "Oh, Mother, please, stop with the Maury Roche thing. He's a very nice person. He's not what you make him to be."

Virginia agreed. "He really is nice, Mother."

She held her tongue. By whose standard was Maurice Roche deemed nice? Had her daughters' values changed?

"Virginia." She spoke firmly, "I saw people drinking whisky in public. *Nice* people don't do that."

Laura jumped to her sister's defense. "Drinking is not illegal, Mother."

Yes, she was aware Prohibition had been repealed. Although, when Roosevelt signed the 21st Amendment, many people accused the Democrats of destroying the country's morality.

She shook off Laura's fact. "Well, drinking *should* be illegal. And, your friend Maurice had a pool shark with him too—*gambling* is still illegal in this state."

Laura showed disbelief. "Pool shark? Really? Who?" Virginia sat silent, stone-faced.

"Gaylord Forbes—Maurice's friend. That's who."

A blue Ford coupe pulled in the alley, a youngster waved from the backseat.

"Don and Donnie are here!" Virginia bolted from the glider and ran down the steps.

Laura sighed loudly. "Oh, Mother. You're imagining things. Nobody's a pool shark—or breaking the law." She bent for a kiss. "I'll call you tomorrow."

The phone conversation with Laura the next day did nothing to soothe her qualms. Virginia had her worried. Something wasn't right, but she just couldn't put her finger on it. Anyway, it had been a while since the talk on the porch, and Maurice Roche hadn't come up again. And that was bothersome too. Her daughters may be just ignoring her and quietly doing what they pleased. Virginia would never think of going behind her mother's back. But Laura? Laura was unpredictable.

Virginia being gone so much added to her concern. Granted, her daughter was almost twenty-five and entitled to her own comings and goings, but she *was* still living at home. She wasn't one to pry or interrogate, but she was Virginia's mother, and if only out of courtesy, her daughter could be more open.

An opportunity to gain insight was coming shortly. Laura was hosting Thanksgiving dinner but had never done a turkey so she was coming over for guidance. The Ludington kin were coming as well as Maxim and Herbert and Laura enlisted Virginia's help.

She was ready and waiting. Water was on for Sanka, her recipe box was on the table along with a pencil and notepad and. . . .

The front door banged open. "Sis, I'm here!" The door slammed shut; Laura burst into the kitchen. "Where's Steve, Mother? Let's get started, I can only stay a minute—Don goes wild watching Donnie. Oh, I forgot my pad. Do you have something I can write on, Mother?" Laura dropped at the table. "Good lord, Mother." She groaned at the stove. "Why don't you get something decent to cook on?" Steps come down the stairway. Virginia came in and quietly sat next to her sister.

Lena moved the teapot aside and closed the damper under the grate. "Stephen is raking leaves for Maxim; it will do Donald good to watch his son; a pad and pencils are in the top drawer, and I can't afford an electric range." She poured water into three mugs and stirred in Sanka.

Laura popped to her feet.

"I should call home and see how Don's doing."

Laura disappeared to the hall—Virginia followed. What was it with those two? The voices in the hall sounded like *both* of them were talking to Donald. Patience, she told herself.

"We're back." Laura flounced down on a chair and pulled Virginia next to her.

"Yes, I see." She poised pencil over notepad. "Now let's start with how many. Who's coming?"

Laura held up a thumb and two fingers. "The three of us, Steve, Don." She switched hands. "Uncle Max and Uncle Herb, Grammie, Uncle Ben, Uncle Carl, Aunt Elsie and Aunt Nellie." She squinted. "No, wait. Carl and Elsie not coming. Neither is Marion. That makes—"

Virginia interrupted. "You forgot Donnie."

Laura nodded. "Right, and Donnie makes twelve. Twelve, Mother."

Lena wrote twelve on the pad then hesitated. She touched the pencil to her lip. "Isn't that eleven?" She ticked fingers. "Yes, eleven." She looked to her daughters for confirmation. Laura was glowering, her face dark under clenched brows. Virginia stared at her sister, eyes wide.

Laura's chest heaved, and her back stiffened. "I invited Gale Forbes, Mother."

Color rose in Virginia's face, tears welled.

She slammed her pencil down. "You invited a whisky-drinking pool shark to our family Thanksgiving, Laura? How could you?" Virginia buried her head in her hands.

She turned to Virginia. "Are you still seeing that boy, Virginia?" Her voice was hard.

Laura put her hand on Virginia's arm. "Mother, just for once, won't you lighten up? Gale Forbes is not some kind of degenerate. He's a very nice person."

"He drinks in public, and it's well known around town he's a gambler." She rapped the pencil on the tabletop. "Drinking and gambling make a bad combination in a man, Virginia. I know you're an adult, but you should end this infatuation immediately. You should not see men who are imprudent."

Laura stood and put her arms around her sister.

"Mother, they're married. They've been married almost two months." The kitchen plunged in silence, broken only by Virginia's sobbing and the rumble from the Kelvinator.

Lena carefully laid the pencil down and closed her eyes. The pain was breathtaking.

Tears streamed down Virginia's cheeks. "I'm sorry, Mother. I'm terribly sorry." She ran from the kitchen. Stairs creaked, and a door slammed upstairs. Silence returned, embers snapped, and the Kelvinator clunked to a stop.

Laura put the mugs in the sink and walked to the doorway on her way to the stairs. "Mother, I'm taking Virginia home with me. We can talk later."

She sat stunned, her eyes closed as if in a trance. The aching was hers alone to bear. She sat at the table trying to understand until Stephen came in looking for dinner. She fed him in silence. After doing the dishes, she went outside to clear her mind. The aching in her heart was unbearable, her thoughts not that of a believer in Mrs. Eddy's teachings.

She walked along Ernst Court and stopped just before Herbert's house. The sky's red glow was giving way to night. A cardinal glided past, touched down on a fencepost, then flew off across the cornfield. She walked back and stopped where the street ended at Lapeer Court, her mind trying to clear turmoil. She turned and started back. Maxim appeared from the darkness and fell in alongside.

"Evening, Lena." His voice was soft and reassuring. "Fine night for a walk, isn't it?"

She took his arm and step by step the words came out, haltingly and painfully, how she had been deceived—the minister in Detroit, strangers for witnesses, and most of all, Virgina's betrayal. Maxim walked alongside, his head down, silent except for an occasional murmur of acknowledgment.

He slowed. "Lena, you got me working up a sweat. Let's take a break."

He led her across the asphalt to the cornfield fence. Maxim put both hands around a fence post and stretched back looking skyward. The night was gray; lights on Water Street glowed against a dishwater overcast.

"First, Lena." He faced her in the darkness, "I know this hurts you dreadfully, but you can't take it personally. Your children love you; you have done remarkably well with every one of them. It's just the younger set. They're all that way. They're gay and free and self-centered, not the least concerned with consequences or the damage they inflict."

He surveyed dry corn stalks. "You're stuck with what happened, Lena. You can't change it; you can't undo it; you have to make the best of it." A distant horn of a freighter bound for Muller Brass sounded.

"What other choice is there, Maxim?"

"I know this will be hard Lena, but why don't you celebrate Virginia's marriage? Think of what it would mean to her—and it could avoid awkward explanations."

"Celebrate, avoid? What do you mean, Maxim?"

"Throw a party, Lena. Throw a surprise party, invite people. In fact, invite Wilma Meedy. It'll be all over the papers." Wilma and her husband were members of the church, and Wilma had a connection to the *Times Herald.*

"A surprise party, Maxim?"

"In a way: Let people think you *wanted* Virginia's wedding to be a surprise, like you planned it all along. Make a big deal of it, have a door prize or something like that—no one need know any more."

"Well, what a thought, Maxim. Mmm—a door prize."

∞

Thanksgiving proved to be a day of healing. Laura's trimmings were delicious even with the turkey taking an extra half-hour. Maxim was an old hand at mingling, easy to engage and a good listener. He spent time talking with Gaylord and found out that the marriage in Detroit was a crazy, spur-of-the-moment lark. He also learned that Virginia had only spent one night with her sister, and the next day moved into Gaylord's flat above the party store.

The next day, Virginia called again to say how sorry she was and apologized one more time. She said they had disappointed his mother too, and what seemed like a fun idea at the time was all so stupid. Could she make amends by inviting both mothers to a shower?

The combined efforts of Maxim, Wilma Meedy, and especially Lena, put the Houston's back on the Sunday society page. Her daughter and Gaylord went to Askar-Shain for wedding photographs, and the *Times Herald* ran a lovely picture of Virginia.

The announcement accompanying the picture practically gushed. "*Mrs. David Houston entertained at a lovely party Friday evening in honor of her daughter…The news of the wedding was concealed in the door prize which went to Mrs. Robert Emery.*"

Even the *Detroit Free Press* ran the photograph and a nice but brief notice. And then, the *Times Herald* ran lovely announcements of every one of the showers and luncheons and bridge parties held in Virginia's honor including who won the door prizes. She was back. When it came to stitching a silk purse from disaster, Mrs. David H. Houston was one of the best.

Perhaps she had been unfair judging her new in-law and invited Gaylord's mother over to get to know her. The showers were too hectic to have a meaningful conversation, but now that the holidays were past, there was time to be social and learn how the new couple were doing. She only knew that her daughter and Gaylord slept on a daybed in the front room.

The tea kettle was on the stove and kindling under the grate when stomping on the porch rattled the front door. She'd start right out calling Mrs. Forbes, Clara, but she had to be conscious of her being Catholic. It would not be a good time to bring up Christian Science.

She welcomed her daughter and Clara in the hall with a smile, and after taking a kiss from Virginia, helped brush snow from their coats. Virginia handed her a bag. "Cookies, Mother. We made them this morning. Mother Forbes has an electric range."

Virginia pulled two pair of shoes from a larger bag and set one pair at the telephone stand for her mother-in-law.

Coats put away, Clara followed her to the front room with a slightly rolling gait as if the floor was unsteady. She was a sturdy woman of uncertain age with stout legs showing below a gray polka-dot dress and a deeply resigned face framed by thin, ashen hair.

"You have a lovely home, Mrs. Houston." Clara lowered herself in a wingback. A brief flash of a knee garter showed above heavy beige hose.

"Please call me Helena, Clara." She smiled permission. "I understand you have a daughter too."

"Yes, I do—Loraine. She's two years younger than Gale and married."

"And I understand you're from Detroit. What part of the city?"

"Oh no, I'm not from Detroit. Loraine and her husband, Jack, live in Detroit. I was staying with them." She crossed thick ankles. "We're originally from Cleveland. Harvey, my husband, was a ship's captain before he went into the navy. His company was based there."

She explained that freighter captains and crews enjoyed unusual marriages. Great Lakes freighters—and the thirty-five or so men who crewed them—sailed the entire shipping season, nine to ten months depending on ice. Boats spent few days in port, only to load or unload, and then they were off again.

Captains, however, had elaborate quarters, commonly a suite of ornate, wood-paneled rooms for wife and family. It could be that Virginia had a seafaring mother-in-law who had walked many a deck. But Lena was curious why her husband left the relative comfort of a laker to join the navy. Hauling taconite from mine to smelter was a priority war defense job.

"Harvey joined the navy when we went to war in 1917." Clara paused, unemotional, her face barren, accustomed to explaining misfortune. "We were going to move to Newport, Virginia, to be closer to him, but before housing could be worked out, he was killed—everyone on board his ship perished. Gale was only eight."

"Oh, how horrible. How did it happen?"

"No one knows to this day." Clara's voice was devoid of emotion. "The navy Board of Inquiry first believed the *Cyclops* was torpedoed by a German U-boat. But the German admiralty denied they had any submarines in the Bermuda sector on March 4, 1918, the day of the last contact with the *Cyclops.* And when the war ended, German admiralty records verified they did not have a submarine in the area."

"Why was the *Cyclops* going to Bermuda?"

Clara shrugged. "The *Cyclops* was a collier, it supplied coal to the Atlantic fleet. It had left Brazil bound for Baltimore, Maryland. The ship went down with the entire crew of 306 southeast of Bermuda. My husband, Harvey, was second in command. The boat was initially listed as missing which led to a big investigation. They first looked at paranormal events that you hear about around Bermuda, but the navy finally concluded the eight-year-old ship suffered a massive structural failure in high seas."

"How horrible!" She shuddered. "I can't imagine. Did you have family you could turn to?"

"Not really. My family, the Laudemans, were all gone by then. Harvey had two brothers in Algonac, but there was bad blood."

"My word! How did you survive?" The conversation had taken a dark turn. They were not talking about her daughter's new life or future.

Clara continued, matter-of-factly. "The navy gave us benefits. We stayed in a shelter for a while. Gale quit school, and Harvey's old company in Cleveland, Pickands Mathers, gave him odd jobs around the docks. When he turned sixteen, they took him on the boats as a wheelman. When Loraine got married, I moved in with her and Jack."

"Well, isn't Gaylord a fine son, taking care of his family like that! What brought you to Port Huron?"

"Gale. One day he had enough of the boats. He happened to be in Port Huron, and went out and found a job. When he rented the apartment on Griswold, he asked me to move in."

The kitchen door whumped shut, and Virginia came from the hall with a tray of cookies, cups, and saucers. "Here we are ladies—three Sankas." She edged the lamp aside and set the tray on the end table. "We have good news. Gale has a lead on a job." She pulled the second wingback closer. "Mueller Brass is supposed to get a big government contract to make bullets; they might be putting on another shift."

She frowned. "I suppose he meant munitions."

"We're going to war," Clara said flatly. "We always go to war."

She sighed. The papers and the radio *were* full of war talk. "I can't imagine what's happening in Europe is any business of ours." She passed cookies. "Those people over there have been fighting since time immemorial. We should just forget all that unfortunate business. It's not going to affect us. Now, Virginia, tell us about your plans for the weekend."

∞

20 May 1942

CLARA PROVED TO be prescient: the country did go to war. Muller Brass put on a night shift and hired Gaylord to drive a high-low on the receiving dock. Military conscription returned, local draft boards were instituted and boot camps opened. Yet the fighting in Europe seemed to exist only in the headlines.

Her attention and energies were consumed by washing and ironing, caring for Mother, and the arrival of grandchildren. Germany's annexation of Austria in 1938 was overshadowed by the birth of Gaylord Jr. The invasion of Poland a year later took a back seat to the arrival of Laura Lee Wismer, and Japan's incursion into China was lost in the coming of Laura's second girl—little Normajean. Even Germany's brutal conquest of France and the low countries in 1940 seemed more abstract to her than the reality of making the mortgage payment.

But then Japan bombed Pearl Harbor on December 7, 1941, and Congress declared war. And when Germany declared war on the United States, Stephen quit Port Huron Junior College to join the navy, and war took on new meaning.

The conflict had Port Huron booming. Mueller Brass, Acheson Oildad, and Little Brothers Foundry pulled men to the city in droves. Uncle Sam needed able-bodied men with essential skills, but those with flat feet or poor eyes or other disqualifying infirmity joined the fight by making 50-caliber machine gun casings.

Lena did not lack for people wanting laundry service; even the gentleman across the alley paid for what he owed on the garage. Despite her revulsion to fighting, she did her part. She was meticulous with ration coupons, scrimped on sugar, meat, and canned goods, and bought the blackout curtains recommended in Civil Defense bulletins.

The day Stephen left, she huddled against the bustle and noise on the railroad platform with her son and Maxim. The Chicago & Northeastern had just arrived, the Flint & Pere Marquette was still unloading, and Stephen's train, the 3:40 p.m. Grand Trunk to Detroit, was waiting on the inside track, steam leaking between gleaming iron wheels.

She held Stephen's hand and tried to hide her fears. "Now, Stephen, promise me you won't do anything foolish." A poster of a ship sinking under a cloud of black smoke was on the wall of the station. The words "Loose Lips Sink Ships" ran across a red sky and blue sea in frantic white letters. The thought made her shudder.

Stephen's hand was hard and warm, his fingernails spotless. He belonged in a Norman Rockwell painting in his white bell-bottoms, navy tie, and gob cap tipped jauntily to one side. His blond hair, blue eyes, and willing white smile were fit for the cover of *The Saturday Evening Post.*

Her spine tingled; she was so proud. She was sending her eighteen-year-old son off to war. But her stomach was clenched with fear. Stephen was assigned to a destroyer bound for Admiral Nimitz's South Pacific fleet.

Stephen squeezed her hand reassuringly. "I promise, Mother. You know I'll be just fine." Maxim nodded somber agreement.

"Are you sure you'll have enough money?" The War Department paid fifty dollars a month, an enviable wage in Port Huron. The department encouraged servicemen and women to have some of the money sent home to avoid pursers having large amounts of cash at the front lines or at sea. Stephen opted to keep twenty dollars and have the rest sent to her. The monthly check was for a bit less than thirty dollars once the life insurance was deducted.

Her son grinned. "Yes, Mother. I'm sure I'll have enough. I don't expect to need much in the middle of an ocean." Maxim showed a wan smile.

A whistle pierced the air; couplers banged and clanked.

"It's time." Stephen put his arms around her, then gave Maxim a hug.

"Thanks a million for everything, Uncle Max. I'll be back soon." The two of them thumped backs. Maxim couldn't get any words out; he just jiggled his head and snuffed.

Stephen ran, snorts of steam chasing his ankles. He cut into the line of white uniforms, grabbed the handrail, and swung up. Lena and Maxim stood mute and when the caboose rattled past, he took her arm and they walked in silence to the parking area.

He helped her into the front seat of his new black Oldsmobile 68. "I'm dropping you at Virginia's new place, right?" She nodded, and he turned on Twenty-Fourth Street.

"Let me know if the wind is too much." Maxim rolled down his window. He glanced sideways; Lena was deep in thought. "Lena?"

"Oh, sorry, Maxim, I was just thinking of Mother. I guess I got lost. No, the window isn't too much, thank you. The fresh air feels wonderful."

"Maybe feeling a bit lonely?" He was quite perceptive. She was alone for the first time in her life. Mother passed barely a month ago, and now Stephen was gone, and she was counting pennies in an empty house.

Mother was eighty-nine when Lena found her on the sofa with her eyes closed and head back. At first, she appeared to be napping, but when she shook her, nothing. It was very considerate of Mother to go so gracefully.

As was her custom, she managed her mother's disposition with steely dispatch. No announcement, no memorial service, no headstone. She called the Smiths and had them see to the paperwork and make arrangements with Lakeside Cemetery. Then on a beautiful spring afternoon, she rode with Laura and Virginia in the blue coupe and watched the sexton place Mother alongside Norma and James.

"Maxim, I haven't been alone a half a day yet." Sadness stirred, and she looked to the fields passing by. "Yes, you're right. It will be lonely." She faced him. "But I will say, I'm thinking about letting out Mother's room—to a gentleman. I'd like someone to help me with the coal and ashes." His eyebrows went up.

Mother was gone and so was her government check. With a boarder, she could pay her bills and maybe quit taking in wash. Her ad in the *Times Herald* offered, "Room to let; 2 meals, housekeeping, close to bus route."

The traffic light at Lapeer turned red. Maxim braked and signaled a right turn. 24th Street ended at the Mueller Brass plant, a massive hodgepodge of red industrial buildings and smoke stacks.

Maxim pointed to the guard shack at the plant entrance. "How's your son-in-law Gaylord doing?"

"From what I hear, well. He works a lift on the night shift, moving copper tubing from the loading dock to the manufacturing floor."

Virginia was tickled pink about the job; without it, she would still be sleeping on a daybed above the party store. They were moving into their new place that morning and had invited her to stop by. "Laura has Little Gaylord so I'll get to see all the children when Laura brings him home."

The Olds slowed. "Virginia's place is coming up, isn't it?"

She pointed. "Corner of Eleventh, driveway is in back."

Maxim pulled into a cinder driveway and stopped short of an empty two-car garage. One garage door was up, the other was open and hung askew; roof boards showed where shingles had disappeared.

He put a hand on her sleeve. "Lena, I have a little something for you." Maxim handed her a thin blue box with a gold anchor embossed on top. "I thought this would look good in your front window."

She held up a piece of white silk with an embroidered blue star surrounded by a red border. The gold lanyard had tassels on each end. She gave Maxim a bear hug of thanks then got out of the car giving quiet thanks to God. When Maxim pulled away, she went around the side of the house.

The house was an old duplex owned by the elderly couple living upstairs. She went past a door saw-cut into the siding that led to a basement apartment and a side porch that was Virginia's entrance. A pile of flattened cardboard boxes sat in front of the door. Her daughter was at the sink scrubbing and humming to the music from a Bakelite radio atop a squat white refrigerator. She knocked; Virginia jumped.

"Oh, it's *you*!" Her daughter's hand dropped from her mouth, relieved. "Come on in, Mother. Laura and the kids should be here shortly." She pulled off rubber gloves. "If you want, you could make up the bed while you're waiting."

A small, four-burner electric stove was wedged between the sink and refrigerator and looked as if it needed chipping, rather than scrubbing.

"Sheets are on the table." Virginia pointed. "The second set and extra blankets go under the bed."

Linens under her arm, she squeezed past the dining table to a nicely furnished front room. A coffee table and sofa sat under the front window with an easy chair next to a side table. A framed mirror was propped on a dresser hiding the front door, and a box of children's toys sat in a corner.

"Virginia, where's your mother-in-law?" She expected to see Clara.

The Bakelite went silent. "Detroit." Virginia craned her head through the kitchen opening. "She moved back to Loraine and Jack's. Gale took her right after the movers came."

"To Detroit? Did you get a car?"

"No, no. Maury Roche loaned us his. He's been a generous friend—we used our gas coupons, of course."

She stared at the sofa, the framed prints on the wall. All of Clara's things. The realization gave her pause. Was this how it ended? Being passed between siblings, possessions that took a lifetime to acquire, abandoned? No, that would never do.

The bedroom was small and had a high window with a torn shade; a double bed filled the entire room. She snapped a sheet open and began tucking.

With the second set of sheets under her arm, she eased behind the dining table and opened a narrow door. A rusty shower compartment, a small sink and a medicine cabinet sat opposite a lidless commode. "Virginia? Where does young Gaylord sleep?"

"With us." Her daughter came in from the kitchen pulling off rubber gloves. "I wonder where Laura is? She should have been here by now."

"Virginia. You know sleeping like that is not good for the boy." Good lord, what had her daughter gotten herself into?

"Mother, Gaylord catches the 10:30 bus to work every night and doesn't get home until we're up in the morning. It's just me and Little Gale in the bed."

She let it be. Gaylord certainly didn't work *every* night, and where he slept was none of her business. Virginia was doing the best she could with what she had; she put the second sheets back in the miniscule bedroom.

Someone knocked on the door and when Virginia returned from the kitchen, she was frowning. "That was Mrs. Landon from upstairs, Mother. Laura called and said she and the kids were running late."

"We should not be surprised." Laura was always running late. But why would she be running late; Laura only lived two blocks away. Disappointing. She wanted to see her grandchildren, but she wasn't going to sit around for who knows how long. Virginia had things to do and so did she. Laura would probably show up with a passel of excuses, and she wasn't in a humor to entertain self-serving explanations. She'd take the bus and call a few numbers in the classifieds to see what rooms were bringing.

The bus slowed in a whoosh of brakes, and when the door levered open she was still rummaging in her purse for a nickel. It aggravated her when people fumbled while she waited and here she was fumbling.

The bus driver showed surprise then smiled and nodded.

"Afternoon, Mrs. Houston." She stopped rummaging and looked. She couldn't place him. He was a lanky man in a blue cap and uniform with a coin changer on his hip. The hand-lettered placard over the side window read "Your Driver Is Stanley Szyman." Driver Szyman pulled a handle and the door elbowed shut.

"Good afternoon, Mr. Szyman. Forgive me, but have we met?" She continued to dig in her bag.

"We haven't really met." Brakes whooshed and the bus lurched forward. "I'm a friend of your daughter, Laura." He hooked a thumb at the placard. "I'm Stan Szyman, as you can see."

She steadied herself on the fare box. Mr. Szyman was Laura's friend? He looked quite a bit older, lines around his eyes, gray in his sideburns and mustache. "Mr. Szyman, I'm afraid I can't find my coin purse. May I give you a dollar?"

"Mrs. Houston, this ride's on me." He dug in his pocket for a nickel and dropped it in the box. "Now how are Donnie and those two darling girls doing?"

"Uh . . . just fine, thank you, Mr. Szyman. Oh . . . and for the ride, too." She sat in the front seat, knees together, and looked out the window. Quite curious, this Mr. Szyman.

He glanced over his shoulder. "That Donnie is what now? Ten?" The light at Tenth Street turned green. "Your stop is Ninth, isn't it?"

"Yes, Ninth Street, please." The bus shuddered to a stop. "Thank you, Mr. Szyman." He smiled and doffed his cap, revealing a receding hairline. Definitely older than Laura. She stepped down; the door whooshed closed. When the exhaust cleared, she crossed Lapeer to Lapeer Court.

Her ad in the *Times Herald* brought a deluge of queries, and the first callers sounded anxious. By midmorning she raised her rate, and by the time she stopped answering the phone, she had raised it again. She could have rented Stephen's room, too, except that it *was* Stephen's room.

She kept inquires short and pointed. First a polite exchange about the weather to glean the caller's way of speaking and his demeanor. She told the female callers she wanted a man. When the matter of meals came up, she mentioned Sunday dinner, which led to the question of the caller attending morning service. If the voice on the line sounded promising, she went genteelly to her bottom line: no smoking, no drinking, no carousing. A Mr. Fredrick met the criteria, and she gave him her address.

He was a lean and wiry man of middle age employed by Acheson Oildad in a position he wasn't allowed to discuss. Mr. Fredrick had bulging eyes and a milky face and usually wore a sweater vest over a striped shirt and bow tie. She judged him to be both conversant and a good listener. She said he could move in any time, and she offered her hand on the arrangement.

That night, she retired with a feeling of accomplishment. She was getting ahead—finally. Stephen's money was coming, the room was rented, *and* she was out of the laundry business. That GE range she coveted was almost within reach. She fell asleep full of loving thoughts to keep Stephen from harm—and to guard all the troops fighting with him on Wake Island.

∞

21 August 1945

MR. FREDRICK PROVED to be a perfect tenant and two years slipped amicably by. On trash day, ashes and bins were reliably outside the alley door. He kept the yard mowed, leaves raked, and the sidewalk and steps cleared of snow. Not unlike having an impulsive tic, Mr. Fredrick was averse to malfunction. A loose doorknob, a dripping faucet, or a squeaking hinge was quickly silenced. He was a moderate eater, didn't entertain women, came and went quietly, and paid his bill promptly. He fit nicely with her expectations and made the GE electric range affordable.

Dinner was on her mind; something to go with Swiss steak. Easing Stephen's service flag aside, she squinted across the street thinking of corn. The farmer was out there, his red cap barely visible. She grabbed her coin purse; maybe she'd buy a peck of tomatoes too. With vegetables, her steak would go far enough to invite Maxim and Herbert. It was nice to have company with Mr. Fredrick. He was so intelligent it was difficult at times to understand him.

Halfway across Ernst Court, bedlam broke out. Horns blew on Water Street and Lapeer Avenue. Bells rang at First United Methodist and Our Savior Lutheran, way over on Sixth Street. The air raid siren was screeching. She couldn't imagine what all the fuss was about.

The screen banged open. Mr. Fredrick burst out on the porch bellowing, fists clenched aloft. "We won! We won, Mrs. H., we won! The war is over!" He jerked the screen open. "The radio, Mrs. H. The radio! Come on!" The screen banged shut.

Late afternoon on August 14, 1945, Port Huron erupted in celebration. The hope promised by victory in Europe came to pass. Hydrogen bombs dropped on Nagasaki and Hiroshima had done the job. People poured from buildings, traffic stopped, radios blared, and in the streets, strangers danced with strangers. Lena gave quiet thanks the fighting was over, and her son would soon be safely home.

Soon, Stephen and all of Port Huron's servicemen and servicewomen would return to a city that was as different as they once were. Wide-eyed eighteen and nineteen-year-olds who left for war, returned as gritty, battle-tested adults, many with families. Port Huron, once a burgeoning city was unexpectedly stripped of government contracts, generous wages, and help wanted signs.

The call for 50-caliber machinegun casings came to an abrupt end, and when Mueller Brass eliminated the night shift, Virginia's husband went on unemployment. In short months, labor became a buyer's market as jobs and available housing all but disappeared. People were left wanting, and the influx of veterans boosted the premium on already expensive lodging.

Room rates went up and an underground market of who-knows-who flourished. Somehow strangers learned that Stephen's room was vacant—his military service wouldn't end until July 1949. The inquiries were incessant and irritating. The phone seemed to never stop ringing.

She heaved from the sofa and snapped at the phone. "I'm coming. I'm coming." How did people find these things out? She snatched the hand piece. "I'm sorry, you've been misinformed. I do not have—"

"Mother?" It was Virginia.

Her frown faded to pleasant surprise. "Oh, yes, I'm sorry, dear." Sobs came over the line. Her daughter was crying. Her frown returned. "Virginia. What is the matter?"

She listened. "Try to get hold of yourself, dear." Sobs turned to snuffling. "Yes, that's better. Now, tell me what's wrong." Her face clouded. "You have to move?" She squinted an eye. "Why is that?" She shook her head then shook it again. "They rented your place to someone else? That doesn't make sense. Why would they do that?" Her eyes searched the ceiling. "Yes, I understand you have to move. But I don't understand why."

Virginia may not have understood either. She only knew what Gaylord told her. Despite her own mother's prowess in business dealings, she'd come to believe that good wives didn't concern themselves with finances or leases or contracts—that's what men were for. Men worked for wages, hauled trash to the curb, killed vermin, and ate what was put in front of them.

Her daughter had to move for *some* reason. But was it any of her business? The matter was between Virginia and her husband. "I really don't know what to say, dear. Did Gaylord say why you have to move?"

"Something about a nephew just back from Germany and needing a place for his family," Virginia said.

"Well, yes, apartments are scarce." There was no sense asking Virginia about leases or written notices or causes. What was done, was done. "Yes, dear, I suppose I can ask around at church Sunday." She nodded. "Yes, Monday is a good time. We can talk then."

Monday mornings, Virginia usually brought her dirty laundry over on the bus while little Gaylord was in school. She looked forward to Mondays, having a cup of Sanka with her daughter between loads and getting caught up.

Lena ran the last pillowcase through the wringer and handed it to her daughter. "Well, that went quick." Virginia pinned the case on the line and followed her mother up to the kitchen. She spooned Sanka in two mugs, then stirred in hot water; Virginia looked miserable, eyes puffy, red.

"I asked several people about apartments after church yesterday," she said. "From what I heard, it seems only the well-connected are finding anything."

Virginia had to be out of the Lapeer apartment when school ended in June. She was worried sick. Gaylord lost his job and Clara's assistance check was going to his sister Loraine. Her daughter feared they'd be put out on the streets.

She watched Virginia morosely circle a spoon in her mug. Should she mention Stephen's room? If she did, she would be inviting a whisky-drinking, cigarette-smoking man into her house. But he *was* family.

Nevertheless, it still wouldn't work. She had one room and one bed, and there were three of them.

Virginia uttered a mournful sigh; she reached for her daughter's hand. "I can imagine how you feel, dear. I'd offer you Stephen's room, but there's no room for another bed." She patted Virginia's hand. "And I can't have anyone sleeping on the sofa with Mr. Fredrick here."

Virginia brightened. "There's Steve's old cubby under the attic stair?"

She hesitated; trepidation pounced. She loved her daughter and grandson, but that Gaylord. . . . Would he tolerate her rules—especially about smoking and drinking? And did she want a rambunctious seven-year-old tearing around the house? No, of course not. She was past that. But what could she do? She was Virginia's mother.

The arrangement provided mutual feelings of regret and resignation. A coarse individual would be living in her home. Virginia was mortified, and Gaylord, after pushing his mother back on his sister, had not only lost his livelihood, but their home. The day school let out, a red truck with Roche's Lounge painted on the door arrived with Clara's furniture. The only smile in an atmosphere of gloom was young Gaylord who was about to get his own room.

∞

Footsteps thundered up the stairs; the bathroom door banged shut. Moments later, the toilet flushed, and footsteps thundered back down the stairs. Virginia yelled something from below—the screen door slammed. Lena got up from her desk and pushed the door shut. What a ruckus. Stephen wasn't like that when he was that age. She moved the vase of iris from the window sill and lifted the sash. A warm breeze, smelling of freshly-cut grass, ruffled papers on her desk.

That the living arrangement survived two full years was due in no small part to the house Maxim built. The front bedroom was her savior, her private haven. A big double bed and bedside table, dresser, wardrobe, and vanity were at one end. At the other, her reading chair and ottoman, the roll-top desk and chair, and file cabinet. When she was not in her room, she kept the door locked, and the key in her pocket.

Circumstances carved a wary routine. Dinner and bathroom schedules were absolute and inviolate, decorum was to be maintained. Most

Saturdays, she had the house to herself. Mr. Fredrick had a bridge group, and usually, Virginia and her family went for an outing with Maurice Roche and his girlfriend. She hoped her daughter had sense enough not to take young Gaylord to a roadhouse or saloon or, for that matter, any place that served alcohol. Sunday was a quiet day. Of course, there was church, and the accolades she received on her reading were an invigorating tonic. She made the afternoon dinner special by setting out good china and having everyone dress.

Virginia's husband was quite well spoken for a young man without a high school education. He was polite and an attentive listener as well, although he carried an odor of cigarette smoke about him. To his credit, he found a job in an impossibly tight market—in Canada, though. He interviewed with CHOK-Sarnia Radio, a start-up FM station, and three months later they hired him to sell air time in Port Huron—but on commission. Virginia allowed he was doing well. He enjoyed meeting people, and people seemed to be comfortable with him. He had a difficult assignment though. Selling advertisements for a foreign radio station and going back and forth on the ferry for meetings was a trying job.

How he managed to pay the rent was a mystery. But he was as punctual as a timepiece. A folded white envelope appeared under her door, always on the first. Perhaps she had misjudged him. Time would tell.

The household routine ground steadily along until mid-April, 1949, when a letter postmarked Naval Station San Diego arrived.

She pushed the letter across the kitchen table to Virginia. "It's from Stephen. His discharge went through. He's coming home." She followed her daughter's eyes as they ran down the paper.

Virginia handed the letter back. "Steve bought a car. And he's going to drive home and see the country—how exciting." Her smile disappeared. "Oh, his room though." Stephen wrote he would be home by the Fourth of July and hoped for a picnic. Virginia sagged. "Mother, what will we do? Steve will be home in two months."

Virginia had been searching the classifieds daily and took the bus to look at different places. But the rents were so high, especially on the bus route. She would have to give up eating to pay the rent, let alone the security deposit. The places that were affordable were not on the bus route and too far out without a car. Her angst increased as the days loped across the calendar until finally, the inevitable afternoon arrived.

A dusty green Dodge pulled in the alley and stopped alongside a red, white and blue festooned "Welcome Home Stephen" sign. Laura and Virginia had hung strings of additional crepe paper around the porch and above the card tables set up in the hallway and living room. Everyone was there.

Stephen stepped out of the car wearing a white T-shirt, dungarees, and a deep tan. He had filled-out. He was no longer a lanky, uncertain teenager. He was hard and muscular, one of the millions who fought—and won.

Cheers greeted him followed by kisses and hugs and handshakes. With help from the girls, she herded everyone inside for rib roast and vegetables. After the women finished the dishes, they brought out Sanka and ice cream, and the questions began.

Yes, he was on a destroyer, a radioman, third class. No, Stephen wasn't worried about being torpedoed. His ship wasn't considered big enough to be worth sinking. But he did get the living bejeezus scared out of him. They were in a night battle off Guadalcanal. Pitch black, couldn't see a thing, huge guns flashing in every direction. Then in an instant, an enemy ship going full tilt went past in the opposite direction. So close he could see surprise on the faces of enemy sailors. But fortunately, it happened so fast that neither ship got off a shot.

With more hugging and backslapping, the party ended, and the inevitable question of who was sleeping where filled the room. Stephen offered a quick solution. "Why don't nephew here and I double up in the cubby? The bed in there is twice the size of the bunk I slept in for three years." And that night, a twenty-two-year-old hardened war veteran began sleeping with his eight-year-old nephew. It wasn't the best of arrangements, but the situation was what it was.

Gaylord was quietly aggravated with the new accommodations; Virginia constantly apologized; Lena was vexed because someone was sleeping on the sofa and she didn't know who. Mr. Fredrick, who never complained, said something about the bathroom always being tied up, and frankly, she didn't care for the situation either.

The proverbial final straw arrived in the form of a boiled potato. Quiet had fallen on Sunday dinner and the clink and scrape of sterling against china was rarely interrupted except by muted requests for butter or salt or pepper.

She put a dab of butter on the side of her plate, passed the boiled potatoes, and took a slice of ham from the platter. Nothing but gloomy faces around the table. She shrugged to herself. Let them think what they will. She was doing her best.

Gaylord pushed his potatoes to the side and reached for a slice of bread. Virginia looked, her brow furrowed. Little Gaylord wrinkled his nose and pushed his potatoes to the side. Virginia laid down her fork and pointed to her son's plate. "Eat your potatoes, young man."

Stephen and Mr. Fredrick each took a bite of potato. Gaylord looked at Virginia and said, "They're tasteless." Virginia said, "Gaylord!"

She beheld Gaylord, a question on her face. "Is something wrong?" She put good healthy food on her table, and there was nothing wrong with boiled potatoes.

Gaylord looked at Virginia, then at her. He shook his head and smiled. "Oh, no, Mrs. H., nothing wrong at all. I guess we're just a bit tired of boiled potatoes."

Mr. Fredrick folded his napkin and stood. "Thank you, Mrs. H., wonderful dinner—as always." He turned and left the room.

Stephen cleared his throat and wiggled a finger at Virginia. "Sis, you would have loved Guam. The color of the water, the white—"

She cut her son off with a raised finger. Laying down her napkin, she contemplated her son-in-law. "Young man, I do the best I can. And while you're in my house, I'm afraid you'll have to eat what I put on the table."

Gaylord stood. "You're absolutely right, Mrs. H." He tousled his son's head. "And it *was* a good dinner." He picked up his plate and carried it to the kitchen. Moments later, the alley door opened and closed.

∞

For all she could tell Gaylord had moved out. He was not around the house; no one was up or down the stairs late, and Stephen had the cubby to himself. Young Gaylord must have moved to the bedroom with his mother and Virginia was so distraught about the incident she could barely speak.

A few days later doing dishes, she held up a plate. "Virginia, you needn't wash this one. It wasn't used." If Gaylord had stopped eating at her table, she deserved to be told just that. Her daughter didn't look up—just shrugged and muttered something unintelligible.

Laura materialized in the doorway. "Ah, Steve was right. He said you were in the kitchen." She pulled a chair back and dropped at the table. Virginia turned from the sink. "I'm sorry, Mother, I meant to tell you Laura was coming by—I forgot." Virginia shook water from a handful of silverware and reached for a towel. "I'll put water on."

Well. It was not like Laura to drop in unannounced and especially without Laura Lee and Normajean. "So, what's going on here? What are you two up to?"

"Virginia's moving out." Laura announced it matter-of-factly, as if it were common knowledge and didn't need discussing. Virginia leaned against the sink her face somber.

She turned to Virginia. "Virginia, is that true? You're moving?" After two years of living like church mice in the back bedroom, her daughter was suddenly moving? Virginia nodded, resignation showing on her face. "Really?" Her eyebrows went up. "Where are you moving?"

Laura answered. "In with me." Virginia remained silent.

She looked at Virginia. "Is that true?"

Laura spoke up. "Mother, living with you is ruining her marriage. You and Gale don't get along, you never did like him, and he won't come back in this house, and frankly, I don't blame him. And Little Gale sleeping with Steve. What did you expect? Can't you see?" She stood and put her arm around Virginia. "My dear sister needs to escape this insanity before she tears her hair out."

Virginia sniffed and swallowed. "Mother, I need to leave our stuff in the basement a bit longer. May I, please?"

She sagged. Another of Laura's impossible schemes. Laura and Donald had three bedrooms. The big one in the front, young Donald's at the top on the stairs and the girls' in back. "Have you two thought this out thoroughly?"

"We have," Laura insisted. "Don and I are going to move into the girls' room, Virginia and Gale get Donnie's room, and Laura Lee, Normajean, and Little Gale get our room."

"What about young Donald?"

"Oh, he wants to sleep on the sofa."

"So Little Gaylord, Laura Lee, and Normajean are all sleeping in the same bed?" Laura nodded. It *was* another of Laura's bizarre ideas. Virginia should know better—she must be desperate. "Well, I hope you'll reconsider this plan, for the sake of the children."

Laura waved away her concern. "School's out Friday, Mother, and Saturday morning Maury, Don and I will be by with Roche's truck to move Virginia's things to our place." She took Virginia's hand. "Come on, girl. Let's get packing."

Saturday morning, the red truck rumbled away with the children on the tailgate waving from the arms of Donald and Gaylord. The burden had been lifted, and the whole house drew a deep breath. Dinner became social again, stairs and doors went silent, and the toilet seat stayed down—mostly. She realized Stephen had spent almost four years in less than favorable social conditions and felt it prudent to turn her head when he backslid.

Blessings continued to flow. Stephen got a job in Sperry's men's shoe department at almost forty dollars a week; WTTH, the *Times Herald* radio station, hired Gaylord away from CHOK, and most gratifying, Virginia applied to be a reader.

The sorry occurrence was Herbert's passing. As glum as Maxim appeared, he handled his brother's affairs tastefully. Death was a private matter, something to keep to one's self, and he always said when his own time came, no fuss or fanfare.

But he never did get back to his old self. The gumption just went out of him, and he had trouble keeping up with the day. He eventually confided to her that he had made arrangements with the Christian Science home in Detroit. He was moving in the fall.

She vowed not to ask how things were over on Howard Street, eight people living in a one-bathroom, three-bedroom house. Both Laura and Virginia let on things were going swimmingly, although, as was not uncommon, evaluations by her daughters were motivated by pleasing her and avoiding criticism.

In truth, chaos reigned on Howard Street. Young Donald was sixteen and spent much of his time in open conflict with his parents—physically so with his father. Laura Lee was a certified terror, able to find reasons to scream and wail no matter the place or circumstance. The single bathroom was accessed on a first-come, first-serve basis and the epicenter of morning grievances. The girls and young Gaylord were allowed to travel around the block by themselves, which led to playing doctor in the overgrown lot at the corner of Howard and Eleventh. The final truth in Lena's prediction came when Laura discovered a flashlight under the children's bed. During the summer of turmoil, Donald Sr. developed a raging case of psoriasis and spent all his free time with his parents.

But out of the ruins came the decision for Virginia to find work. Two incomes would make it possible to afford a suitable place. Her daughter didn't have many skills, but her resume showed a number of typing classes, and she got a job in the front office of the high school. A week before school started, Roche's truck appeared on Ernst Court, and they moved Clara's furniture from the basement to 1134 Court Street.

The two-bedroom apartment was on the upper floor of a converted house. A covered outside stairway opened to a dim kitchen and a queer little living room with a miniscule balcony; two small bedrooms and a bath flanked the kitchen. Clara was summoned from Detroit to provide after-school supervision and slept on her own green sectional. Young Gaylord entered the fifth grade with carnal knowledge and became the envy of his peers.

Contentment reigned on Ernst Court, and under the casual eye of satisfaction, opportunity crept in. One night, after Mr. Fredrick retired to his room, she turned to her son. "I got a bank statement today, Stephen." She leaned toward him, her voice confidential. "Do you have any idea what we have in the savings account?"

His eyebrows went up. "Not in the slightest. Are we rich?"

"In many ways. But counting what you sent home, plus what I've saved, we have over $1,500. It's a shame to just let it sit idle." She held her son in loving eyes and for a moment saw David. But it was Stephen across from her, her wonderful, gorgeous son, her war hero son, everything David could have been. "I've been thinking."

Stephen leaned in, chin propped on thumbs. "Thinking of what?"

"I went to McTaggart's the other day for envelopes and noticed a for sale sign on the house behind the store—the one opposite the alley facing Court Street."

He nodded. "Why, yes. I know the one you mean. White with green trim, a big front porch, garage in back, a side yard along the alley."

"Well, Rowling Real Estate had the listing, so I called. The upstairs has been converted to apartments; three of them, each with a kitchenette and bath."

"Don't tell me you're thinking of moving?" He showed surprised. His mother was sixty-seven, an age when most women were either satisfied or resigned.

"It might be nice for us to have a little business venture—a mother-and-son company." She smiled. Stephen's face went from surprise to a grin. He raised his brows in interest. "We could take the first floor, and let out the upstairs. I think the income could be worthwhile, and our renters can take care of themselves—I'm done cooking and washing for strangers."

"A good idea, Mother." He slapped the table. "And I've got another $217 in a drawer upstairs that we can use. Let's check the place out."

"Yes, but remember, Stephen, we already have books to pack and furniture to move next week." The reading room was leaving the bank building and moving next to the Huron Theater at Military at Pine Street. "First things, first."

∞

With the reading room furniture set up and the last of the flattened boxes moved to the trash, she assessed the sky. Looked like rain was on the way—maybe not a good time to take the girls through the new house. Both Laura and Virginia wanted a tour, and it was only two blocks away. Stephen, of course, had already been through the house. Laura said she had an errand to run first and would meet them over there in a quick minute. The deal hadn't closed, but the Rowlings gave her a key.

She and Virginia stood on the sidewalk in front of the house waiting for Laura. Rowling's already had a buyer for the Ernst Court place; a gentleman named Roney. Rumor was he was planning an office park and offered a pretty penny. "Sad how change comes, isn't it?" Her feelings were bittersweet. "Knocking down Therese's house."

Virginia's face showed worry. "I wonder where Laura is." She looked to Military for the blue coupe then to Court Street. "Oh, Mother, did I tell you I talked to Marion? Little Gale just got back with Laura and Normajean. I called to see how she survived."

"The children were in Ludington?" She felt a twinge of disappointment.

"Just for two weeks. Don and Laura drove them over, then they and Donnie went to the Upper Peninsula. They picked them up on the way back. Everyone had a ball."

"Really?" She sighed inwardly. Maybe someday Marion would get over whatever it was. She hadn't seen Stephanie in ages. And Marion could have told her about the new house and what she planned to do with it. But, no, she had to hear everything from Laura or Virginia—it was so discouraging.

"Mother." Virginia held her palm up. "I felt a drop of rain. Can we go inside?"

She led her daughter up the porch steps and into a high foyer with a chandelier made of leaded glass and brass. A wide carpeted stairway with gleaming oak balusters curved upward. Past the stairway, a wainscoted corridor led to a paneled wood door with an ornate brass knob.

She pointed up the stairs. "The flats are up there—three of them. The door at the end of the hall opens to the dining room." She turned to the wood-paneled double doors and swung one open. "This is our front room." The living room was light and airy with flowered-wallpaper and carved crown moldings painted in soft mauve. A fireplace with an ornate marble mantle was to the right and, opposite, a bay with windows to the porch.

Virginia went to the bay and hooked back a curtain. "Very nice, Mother. I wonder what's keeping Laura." Her daughter was acting strange, distracted, not the least interested in the house.

She opened the door next to the fireplace. "This is the old library." She motioned Virginia into a generous room with a large cased archway in the opposite wall. "This is just right for my office. My roll top will go right here." She pointed to the archway. "My bedroom. It used to be a study—I think. That door to the side goes into the kitchen. Stephen's bedroom and the bathroom are down that little—"

Laura burst into the room. "Sorry, I got held up." She had changed from the slacks and pull-over she had on at the reading room to a cream-yellow short-sleeve sweater and gray pencil skirt.

"Va-va-voom." Virginia rolled her eyes. "Nice sweater. Is it new?"

Laura arched her back and smiled over her shoulder like Joan Crawford did in *Possessed.* "Just got it—Mother, where's the bathroom? I've got to go."

Lena pointed down the passage. "First door," she said and motioned Virginia into the kitchen. "Double sink, gas range, refrigerator, plenty of room for the table—the door goes to the back stair and the garage."

Virginia's eyes followed her mother's finger. "Mm, lot of yellow paint." She considered the motor atop the GE and opened and closed the refrigerator door.

Laura walked in pulling at her skirt. "Ah, that's better. Like the house, Sis?"

Virginia looked relieved. "Love it, especially the moldings."

What was going on? Virginia acted like she was about to be caught stealing until her sister walked in, then she brightened right up. No use asking though; she wouldn't get a straight answer. "Come through the dining room. I'll take you upstairs."

Laura shook her head. "Can't, Mother, got to scoot—Don needs the car."

Virginia agreed. "I should get going too."

∞

The morning the Ogden-Moffitt van came for the furniture, she made tuna fish sandwiches and wrapped them in wax paper. Once the van was loaded and the house locked up, she, Laura, Virginia, the children and sandwiches crammed into the blue coupe and raced to Court Street.

She stood waiting in the bay window of her new home, scowling. Where were the movers? Better than an hour had gone by; they must have stopped for lunch. Finally, an orange-and-white van swung across Court Street, stopped, and backed over the curb. A man in blue overalls at the porch steps signaled stop then threw open the rear doors and pulled a ramp up the steps. She turned toward the foyer. A terrible racket had started up and whoever was making it had to stop. The movers needed to get through.

She opened the double doors and the blare from young Donald's portable radio pounded through the opening. . . . But when he plays with bass and guitar . . . The rug was rolled back, and young Donald had Virginia by the arm and was swinging her around . . . They holler, beat me up Daddy, beat me daddy, eight to the bar. Virginia twirled out on

Donald's arm, her skirt flaring, and swung back. Laura gyrated alongside, twisting and shaking her hips like a hussy in a Quay Street dive.

She stamped her foot, "Please! Turn that thing off!" Silence swept in. Footsteps upstairs pounded through empty rooms. "Thank you. The movers are here."

Virginia was panting, her shoes off, headscarf askew. Young Donald leaned against the balusters in khakis and penny loafers, a soggy white T-shirt clinging to his belly. She frowned, and Laura frowned back. "Oh Mother, don't look so outraged."

Young Donald stopped fanning himself. "Yeah. Come on, Nana, get hip." He turned the radio on and put his arm around her waist. "The Andrew Sisters, Nana, ain't they great?"

"I'm afraid I'm hip enough, Donald." She pulled away gently and snapped off the radio.

"And *aren't* they great, Donald. You should speak properly. It shows good breeding." She stooped to put the stop under the door. "Now why doesn't someone go upstairs and ask the children to play in the yard."

A warm breeze chased excelsior between the growing stacks of flattened boxes. Screams of children playing outside echoed through open windows. She carried the cardboard box of tea cups to the dining room table and . . . was that the doorbell?

Laura called from the foyer. "Mother, someone's here," Her daughter came in the dining room leading a round-faced young woman. "I'm sorry, what was your name again?

"Hart, Ann Hart." The young woman peered around Laura, her eyes seeing boxes and stacks of china plates and teacups, each cushioned by a square of white tissue. "I apologize for interrupting, Mrs. Houston. I understand you have an apartment to rent, but I see this is not a good day. Perhaps I should come back at a more convenient time."

The woman looked to be younger than Virginia, maybe closer to Stephen's age. She had on a modest yellow and white pleated cotton skirt and a white short-sleeve top with ties down the front. She was bareheaded. Young people were so casual about going out in public.

"Oh, no, you're not interrupting a thing." She took Miss Hart's outstretched hand. "This is my daughter Laura. I have another one around here somewhere." Since when did women start offering their hand?

"I'm new to Port Huron, Mrs. Houston. But Sunday at church, Nadine Holt mentioned you might have an apartment available."

Her ears perked up. "Church, you say? Are you a Scientist?" Miss Hart was soft-spoken and had a gentle nature about her. Her shoes were sensible too: white flats with an ankle strap.

Miss. Hart nodded. "Yes, I belong to the church in Fenton. I've taken a job at the library here, and at the moment, I'm at the Harington."

Laura raised a finger. "I can show her around upstairs, Mother." She took Miss Hart's hand. "Come on, Ann. You'll love Number 3. It's got an extra window and overlooks the side yard."

She turned back to the china cabinet. A horn tooted in the alley—a McTaggart truck was blocking a green . . . oh, Stephen's green Dodge. She glanced at her watch. It was already after five. The truck pulled forward.

"Stephen's home," she announced going into the kitchen. Stephen got out of the car and swung the garage doors open. Moments later footsteps came up the back stair, and he appeared.

"Hi Sis, Mother. How's it going?" He had on his beige pinstripe suit with a peach tie and two-tone tan wingtips. She gave him a kiss on the cheek and wished he would wear a hat. Hats made men look so distinguished.

Laura came through the dining room door. "Ann wants the apartment, Mother. Said she'd call tomorrow." She looked at Stephen. "You just missed meeting your first tenant, brother dear, a really cute looking dish."

He loosened his tie. "A tenant, huh, and a dish, too? That's good."

Laura leaned against the door frame with her arms crossed. She caught Virginia's eye and wiggled a thumb at her brother. "So what do ya' think, Sis?"

Virginia eyed Stephen, her mouth bent with skepticism. "You don't think she's a little short for him?"

Laura agreed. "Yeah, probably—but she'll cut him down to size."

Virginia nodded. "No doubt."

"Enough of that, you two." She wagged a finger. "Leave your brother be. Miss Hart was a pleasant woman and doesn't deserve adolescent teasing. Stephen, I've left the beds for you to set up."

Stephen rolled his eyes at Virginia. "Ginny, how's the hubby liking his new job?"

"He's liking it. Doesn't have to take the ferry anymore. No more hassles at customs, and he's selling more airtime. Plus," she said, hugging herself, "plus, he got a company car. Can you imagine?"

Gaylord's fortunes were also on the rise. He recognized that people like to talk about themselves so he asked comfortable questions and showed interest. He dressed well and supported local events like driving the senior class king and queen in the homecoming parade or emceeing charity fundraisers and beauty contests. It was the rare proprietor in Port Huron that didn't welcome him.

"Stephen, remember, you've got voice lessons tonight." She moved the last of the sandwiches from the Tupperware bin to the table. "Come eat. I'll unpack your things for you."

She had a budding church dynasty in the making. Virginia was studying to be a reader, Stephen was on his way to being the church soloist, and young Donald had a budding interest in Science. Now if Laura would just get motivated. She started toward Stephen's room with a feeling of satisfaction. Her past struggles did hold rewards.

∞

22 July 1952

Time seemed to stand still during the years of struggle, but prosperity made seven years flash by like the tick of a clock. The flats upstairs were rented, her son was promoted to the head of the shoe department at Sperry's, *and* he was the church soloist. Virginia's family moved from the upper flat on Court Street to a duplex on Military then to an old house at Wall and Seventh. Clara returned to Detroit to help daughter Loraine with her new baby but left her furniture with Virginia. Stephen and Ann Hart, to no one's surprise, fell head over heels for each other. And to her great personal satisfaction and quiet pride, the Mother Church registered her as a Christian Science practitioner. She had built a modest following and prayed nightly for the American boys fighting in Korea.

Things were peaceful on Howard Street and the serenity was worrisome. It may be speculation over Stephen and Ann marrying eclipsed the usual pandemonium. And once it was known that Stephen and Ann *would* marry, the talk turned to *when*. For once, she didn't hear about this wedding secondhand. Stephen kept her apprised, and she loved being part of the conversation.

Ann, though, was reluctant to talk about the future. She was not entirely pleased with the library. Mother & Son was doing well, though, and if Ann's job didn't work out, she could come on board and M&S would expand.

Then out of the blue, with no warning whatsoever, Ann delivered her thirty-day notice. She was moving. And exactly thirty days later, she left for Hawaii, just like that. No reason, no explanation.

Lena sat at the kitchen table, her chin propped on palms. How could such simple things become so muddled? Ann and Stephen were so right for each other. She could not imagine what was wrong at the library, and there was no question that Port Huron was as good a place as any to raise a family. It was incomprehensible that such a nice woman like Ann Hart would leave friends and family and move almost 5,000 miles away.

Her son was so crushed, she could barely get a good morning out of him. The only thing Laura and Virginia would say was things just weren't right. Not right? What wasn't right? Both of them were lovely people, both Scientists, and both wanting the same things. How could that not be right?

Then Stephen quit Sperry's for a position with Ball Band Shoes, in Indiana. They had over 60,000 dealers and took him on to manage a territory. The job came with a big increase *and* a company car, but unfortunately, he had to move to Mishawka.

The garage door creaked open. It was only midafternoon, but Stephen's car was in the driveway. The garage door thumped closed; Stephen came through the back door with a shoebox under his arm. He dropped the box on the kitchen table, loosened his necktie and tossed his suitcoat over a chair back. He wandered aimlessly to the sink, opened the refrigerator door, scanned the shelves, then leaned against the sink counter looking glum.

She gathered his suitcoat. "You're home early, Stephen. I thought you were going out with friends." He looked like the world had ended. He had to get over her. He would meet plenty of eligible young ladies in his new job. The right girl would come along soon enough, but first, he had to realize it was over with Ann.

He stared at the shoebox. "Didn't feel up to celebrating." Stephen spilled the contents of the box on the table: coffee mug, business cards, what appeared to be a clip of sales receipts, several pencils, and a photograph. The photograph was of him and Ann in front of the tree at Christmas. He set the mug, pencils and photograph aside and tossed everything else in the trash.

She sighed. "When do you leave for Mishawaka?"

"Ten o'clock train Monday morning." He grabbed his suit coat and started for his room. "Think I'll read for a while, Mother. Call me when you start dinner. I'll give you a hand."

The door to the passageway closed.

She expected him to move out after marrying Ann, but not out of town. But no, he was leaving, and she was without a business partner, the church without a soloist, and after next weekend, she'd have to find a handyman or tend the yard herself. She should dwell on her blessings, not disappointment. For one, the Mother Church certified Virginia as a second reader.

The morning the taxi came for her son, she waved goodbye from the porch. The handyman was working in the yard next door and she hesitated with her hand on the doorknob. Maybe he was for hire.

His name was Richard, and he lived across the street in the apartment above the decorator's shop. He was a tall, thin man and judging from the wear and tear, probably years younger than he appeared. He had a gritty good nature about him and worked for cash. Plus, he had tools to sharpen the mower. He agreed to cut the lawn, rake leaves, shovel snow, and salt the walk. The porch and steps she would do herself.

Looking for a hat in the closet under the stairs, she noticed Virginia's bus stopping across the street. They were going shopping together for a gown for reading in church. Should she wear the gray scoop bonnet or the navy homburg? Her daughter modeled at Sperry's and at ladies' luncheons and would be dressed to the nines; she didn't dare look dowdy.

Virginia swept into the apartment, wearing a periwinkle-blue flared skirt with a pinched waist and hemline just below the knee; the blue shell cap she wore sat at a jaunty angle. Her shoes looked absolutely painful with pointed toes and three-inch heels. How could she walk?

She put on the navy homburg. "You look just lovely, Virginia. Are you sure you want to be seen with an old fuddy-duddy like me?"

Virginia took her arm. "I'll pretend I don't know you, Mother."

She pulled the front door closed and jiggled the brass handle. "We should go to both Sperry's and Winkleman's, but I think Sperry's will have the better selection."

The light at Pine Street turned red. Virginia took her arm at the curb. "I was thinking of a shorter gown, Mother. Just because other readers wore floor-length, doesn't mean everyone has to follow suit, does it? Perhaps something in a deep rose or mauve. What do you think?"

The light changed; they stepped off the curb in unison. A station wagon screeched to a stop, and a woman's face in the passenger seat twisted in horror.

Wide-eyed, Virginia dragged her across Pine. "Mother, come on. Really, the nerve of some people. They should learn to drive." The station wagon turned against the light and sped down Military Street.

She looked over her shoulder. "Did that look like Laura in that car?"

"Laura? No, Mother, it couldn't be." Virginia had her by the arm. "Laura's got her canasta group today. Come on. We'll go to Winkleman's first."

∞

After service Sunday, she came out of the church puffed with pride for her daughter. Virginia's reading was lovely and everyone gave her rave reviews. What a shame Stephen moved to Mishawaka. A daughter reading *and* a son soloing would have been a superb demonstration of Science.

Virginia was changing out of her gown, and she glanced at her watch. Should she wait? Her daughter wanted to stop by the house after church to talk. Why, she didn't say, but it was probably about Bible passages. Some of the names were absolute tongue-twisters, yet she made surprisingly few mistakes. It was just a shame that her husband and son weren't there to support her. Laura and her brood were absent too.

She chatted briefly with Robert and Nadine Holt, said goodbye to Clare and Florence, then decided to go home and put the kettle on. She was at the sink when Virginia came in the kitchen. Yes, she would like a cup of Sanka, but first she had to make a call.

Her daughter reappeared; the Bible was not on her mind. "Mother, Laura and Don are having problems. Laura is beside herself and needs help."

"A marital spat now and then is nothing to be concerned about." Controversy was certainly not unusual over on Howard Street. "Whatever it is, Laura will get over it."

Virginia shrugged. "Hopefully. Can we go in the front room, Mother? It's so nice there." Her daughter went to a chair in the bay and plopped. "I don't think it's a spat, Mother. Laura's unhappy with Don. He comes home, eats dinner, then he goes to his parents' house. And you know there's that psoriasis thing; he's always scratching."

Donald had put on weight too, although a few extra pounds weren't worthy of a squabble. But he did need to take better care of himself, always red-faced, out of breath. Laura Lee was still a handful, and her brother, Donald, always ran at top speed. Laura always had some grand plan in the works too. Normajean was the odd one—just a sweet eleven-year-old girl.

A station wagon slowed out front and pulled to the curb. Virginia fingered the curtain aside. "Mother, it's Laura."

Her daughter got out of the passenger side and pulled a suitcase from the backseat. The station wagon accelerated away. "Who was that with Laura?"

Virginia let the curtain fall back. "Just a friend, Mother—nobody you know." She went outside and returned with Laura in tow.

She smiled at greeting. "Laura dear, we missed you at church today. Virginia's reading was wonderful." Laura avoided her eyes, a gray suitcase sat in the foyer doorway.

"What's this all about?" Another of Laura's grand plans gone awry?

"Mother, I'm leaving Don." Laura glowered wild-eyed, as if possessed.

"You're leaving Donald?" So what Virginia said was true.

"I'm out. I've had it, Mother." Anger rang in her voice. "I'm through—through with all of them. There's nothing to explain. It's over."

Virginia pulled her sister down on the sofa. "Mother, Laura needs a place to stay." She held her sister's hand. Laura pulled away.

Lena sagged in the wingback, dumfounded. Good lord, she was seventy years old. Wasn't she entitled to be excused from this childish tomfoolery? "Virginia, you know I've got tenants and leases. I can't just ask someone to leave."

Virginia shook her head. "Can't she can use Steve's room; it won't be forever." Laura nodded sullen agreement. "Just this once, Mother, please don't be judgmental. Laura needs help."

What could she do? She took Virginia and her family in when they didn't have a place to stay. She sighed. "Well. . . ."

Her daughter was like a ghost in the house, her presence more felt than observed. She was either in Stephen's room, on the telephone, or gone. Every night, she left the house, saying she was meeting a girlfriend at Manis' Restaurant on Military Street for dinner. Laura seemed far too composed for a woman who left three children and husband of nineteen years. It was all so strange. How could she leave home? She had no job, she hadn't worked in years, but nevertheless, she was walking out on Donald. Was there someone else? The thought was speculation, but each night she left the porch light on as well as the floor lamp in the front room. In bed, she fell asleep trying to keep Laura's whereabouts from her thoughts.

∞

About a month later, the sound of the front door slamming jerked her awake. It was Laura and it was well after midnight. The dining room door slammed, and then the bathroom door. After a long moment, Stephen's door slammed. Silence recaptured the house.

In the morning, Virginia showed up early and unannounced. She came through the dining room to the kitchen, apologizing for not calling. "Don't get up, Mother. I just want to see how Laura is doing."

Virginia went into the hall and rapped on Stephen's door then let herself in.

Sometime later—she'd read the paper and watered the plants—the girls materialized. Virginia led her sister through the front room. Laura was red-eyed and sullen. "Mother, Laura and I are walking to Manis' for breakfast. We'll be back in a bit." She patted Laura's arm. "Come on, Sis, a walk will feel good."

Virginia came to see Laura the next few days, and the two spent a good deal of time in Stephen's room. The afternoon she returned from the reading room, Laura was in the front room on the sofa, her gray suitcase alongside. Laura stood and hugged her. "Thank you, Mother. I guess things worked out for the better between Don and me." She was contrite, the epitome of defeat. She had lost weight and stopped wearing makeup. Lena glanced through the bay window; a blue coupe waited at the curb.

About the time her daughter and Donald reconciled, young Donald quit college and joined the army. To her relief, he wasn't assigned to combat in Korea, but she prayed for him anyway. Once the Armistice was signed, he studied to be a first reader and was certified by the Mother Church in 1954.

Virginia moved again. This time to a small rental on Tenth Street where it ended at Military. The house was their ninth address and she worried young Gaylord might not be able to find his way home.

They bought a car too, their first. The car seemed an extravagance when they lived across from the bus stop and Gaylord had the use of a company car. The money would have been better spent on a down payment for a house. Her daughter could be a better planner.

She heard little from Marion except for a Christmas or birthday card, although Virginia said she had quit the Church of Christ and gone back to Science. That gave her hope; perhaps her daughter would finally put her animosity behind her.

The big news, however, was about Stephen and Ann Hart. Metaphorically, Ann did cut him down to size. For four years she'd left him twisting over the decision to be a son or a husband. After he decided on spouse, Ann secured an ironclad agreement that they would never live in Port Huron, and they married. Pittsburg, Stephen's region, was close enough. But her son was married to the right woman, and he promised her the holidays.

The one disappointment was the neighborhood had gotten old—like she had. In just four short years, the change was remarkable. The Black & Koerber Agency now occupied the first floor of the yellow house across Court Street. A family of foreigners—stocky people with short necks and black hair—moved into the brown house on the corner. And Richard moved from the apartment above the decorator's shop, although he still did her yard. He said the new place wasn't so blasted hot and far quieter.

Power's Drive-In was a blight. Teenagers roaring through the alley all hours of the night, squealing tires, and blowing horns. When the wind was just so, the stench of hot grease and engine exhaust hung in the air. The city council wouldn't hear her complaints about the drive-in; said

Military Street was zoned for that kind of business. The alley was public, and Power's customers were entitled.

Despite small aggravations, the weather was too nice to sit inside. She pushed the screen door open and took a deep breath of a morning only the Good Lord could make. Gossamer rays pierced soft haze under the elms, the silence broken only by sparrows cheeping in the spirea along the porch rail. Court Street was empty, save a stooped figure in a faded robe, picking up hamburger wrappers and half-filled French fry bags in the alley. The lady lived in the yellow house above the insurance agency.

She bent for the *Times Herald* on the steps and eased onto the glider. A perfect time to answer Stephen's last letter. She folded the paper on her knee and uncapped her Parker. Mm . . . ask what Ann needed for the baby? Or, better, tell him she was going to crochet a bonnet—white would be fine for a boy or girl. He knew his niece Stephanie was getting married. No doubt, he found out before she did; she got the news second-hand from Laura. Marion was in a snit over her daughter getting married at seventeen. But Stephanie didn't let her mother forget that Marion got married at the same age. When Stephanie threatened to elope, Marion gave in. Laura called the squabble deliciously ironic.

A cream-and-blue convertible swung on to Court Street. Virginia already? Yes, it was their car. Chrome slashes along the side, top down, young Gaylord at the wheel. Virginia was coming by to pick up an old lesson plan for reading on Sundays.

The Ford pulled to the curb and tooted—her grandson waved. Seniors Class of '56 was painted across the trunk in red watercolor. Her daughter came up the walk in outsized sunglasses and a bright floral-print dress and matching scarf. The woman across in the alley stared. Virginia wiggled her fingers good morning.

Virginia came up the steps and watched the Ford disappearing down Court Street. "Little Gale's picking me up after his baseball practice. Big game Friday, I can hardly wait."

"Sit." She patted the glider cushion then stood. "I've got water on; would you like some toast?" Virginia shook her head and picked up the paper and pointed to a photograph of Grace Kelly and Prince Rainer on the front page. "Some people have all the luck." She sighed. "I'd love to marry a prince." Virginia pumped the glider, bitterness showing; Lena went for Sanka. Such a lovely morning and her daughter was in the dumps.

She set the tray and two mugs on the swing. "Don't push so hard, dear, you'll have Sanka all over." The glider came to rest. "Now think if you were a princess, you wouldn't be sitting here with me enjoying this beautiful day."

"Sorry, Mother. You know what I mean. I'd just like to get ahead for a change, get people off our backs, have some freedom for once."

"Didn't I see you get out of a fine new car? You have a lovely home and young Gaylord is off to study architecture at Michigan this fall. Now that's something."

Virginia shrugged resignation. "Little Gale hasn't been accepted yet, and if he is, Clare Sperry is paying for his first year—the car's not new either, Mother." Her daughter was thin as a rail and looked as if she had been working too hard for too long. "We can't afford to send Little Gale anywhere, let alone to college. We can barely make ends meet as it is, and now we've got car payments."

A car skidded from the alley and squealed on to Court Street. A wadded bag bounced across the pavement. Virginia got up from the glider and moved to the railing.

"Mother." She hesitated, rocking back on the rail then swallowed hard. "Mother, I've decided to leave Gaylord." She pulled on her lip and turned away. A woman and a small boy came out of the brown house and stood at the corner. A long braid hung down the woman's back.

She was stunned. "I didn't realize you were unhappy with Gaylord." She knew of the gossip and innuendos surrounding his gambling and drinking. Everyone in town did. Still, she chose not to put stock in rumors and allegations and besides, her daughter never let on either. "Did something happen?"

Virginia swallowed and studied the white-painted overhead. "No, Mother, nothing happened. That's the problem. Nothing ever happens."

Her daughter brushed a finger under an eye and dabbed her nose with a Kleenex. "It's hopeless. We can't talk. We always end up fighting. Married for almost twenty-one years and nothing to show for it except bills—and I've been working for nine of those years. We're nowhere except further behind." She moved from the rail to the glider.

She patted her daughter's knee. "Nothing is hopeless, dear." Virginia's leg felt gaunt.

"I can't go on like this, Mother." A tear gleamed on her cheek. "I can't believe a thing he tells me. He's at that pool hall all the time, and what I make just disappears. People hound us day and night about money." She sniffed into the Kleenex and picked up the *Times Herald*. "I'm ashamed to be seen in public." She threw the paper down.

"I need to get away, have my own place, just take care of myself—and Little Gale."

"Have you told young Gaylord?"

"Not yet. He won't be surprised though." Her eyes brimmed. "He's . . . he's disgusted with us. Disgusted with me, disgusted with his father, disgusted with everything. He thinks he can handle finances better than we can—and probably could."

A tear ran down her cheek and she pulled out another tissue.

"I just can't tell him and spoil his senior year." She wiped her eyes. "I'm going to wait until after he's left for college. He'll probably be relieved anyway. All his dad and I do is fight."

"Where will you go? Do you have plans?"

Her daughter stared across Court Street lost in the question. "Is Richard's apartment still empty?"

"Apparently so." Lena motioned at the "For Rent" sign in the window. "Richard never had anything good to say about his apartment, except that it was cheap. Hot, all that noise from Powers, guess."

Virginia wasn't listening; she touched her daughter's arm. "You know you're welcome to come here, Virginia. You may have Stephen's room."

"No, Mother." She composed herself. "But thank you. I need to be on my own, stand on my own two feet. I'm sorry. It's all too complicated to explain."

Brakes sounded across the street. Virginia turned; a bus stopped for the woman and boy. The bus toot-tooted, a blue-clad arm waved out the driver's window.

"*Stan Szyman.*" Virginia's voice dripped with disgust. "What a scumbag."

EPILOGUE

23 June 2010

My mother moved into Richard's old apartment the first semester I was at Michigan. Her letter with the new address arrived just before Thanksgiving; she didn't want me hitchhiking home to the wrong place. A five-dollar bill accompanied the letter. Every time she wrote during my four and a half years in Ann Arbor, she enclosed a five-dollar bill.

Thanksgiving weekend, I arrived home to a small vestibule draped in dusty yellow-and-white striped fabric. The stripes swooped up a narrow, open stairway to my mother's apartment. A kitchenette crowded with our kitchen table, two chairs and ironing board was to the left of the landing. A railed walkway doubled-back to the front room and Clara's green sectional sofa, two mauve chairs, and blond end tables. The bedroom and bath were wedged between the front room and kitchen. My room was straightaway back to an enclosed rear porch with a wood plank floor that sloped to a door at the top of a rickety wood stairway. Peeling wood storm windows overlooked Powers Drive-in.

The apartment became my mother's sanctuary. She often remarked that no one had ever gone beyond the downstairs entry, not even her best friend, Florence Sperry. She cared for her privacy, Nana's well-being and pared the outside world to work, church and the reading room. Another man never entered her life, and she was quite proud of it.

The whereabouts of my father was never discussed. She wasn't responsible and said he could take care of himself. The day she moved out, I eventually learned, he came home to a dark house. The light in the small entry cast a dim glow over bare wood floors and blank walls. A tidy pile of folded suits and shirts sat in the middle of the front room along with a Tupperware of razors, shaving cream, aftershave, and an unopened box of Trojans still in a cellophane wrapper. I imagined he deemed my mother's move just another of life's recurring setbacks.

The last time I saw him, we met at Roche's Bar to have a drink. He had gone back to the boats and was a deckhand for the Interlake Steamship Company. His boat, the *Herbert C. Jackson*, was laying over and he called me wondering if we could get together. At Roche's, he related a murky tale of a recent misfortune and was strapped for cash. It was a temporary situation; could I help? I did, and when we parted, he promised to stay in touch.

I didn't hear a thing from him until some years later when I got a call from the manager of the YMCA in Detroit. My father was at the Y at the foot of the Ambassador Bridge. Somehow, he had managed to sneak his social security check from the office and drank the money away. He had nothing left for food, could I help? I did, and each time the manager called, we agreed to keep our arrangement silent. A squad car found him on the Fort Street sidewalk with three cents and my phone number in his pocket. He died in 1986, seventy-five years old.

With my father out of her life, my mother found new confidence. She had an affordable place to live, a good job, and I was in college through Clare's generosity. She also arranged—through Carol French's husband, Roy, who was a partner in Chas. M. Valentine Associates in Marysville—my first job in the architectural profession. She always attributed her blessings to Christian Science.

Science, though, was not for everyone. Aunt Laura's outbursts intensified and her illusions overcame reality. Uncle Don and Normajean checked her into the Chestnut Hill Benevolent Association, a Christian Science nursing home in Boston. The Association could not control her, and she was taken to the restraint ward at Henry Ford Hospital in Detroit where she was discovered to be bipolar. The doctors prescribed electroshock treatments, which permanently addled her mind. She was committed to Pontiac State Hospital, an institution my office was later awarded contracts to retrofit.

Originally, the Eastern Asylum for the Insane, the Pontiac Psychiatric Hospital was a dark, multi-floored medical warehouse built in 1876 to supplement the state's insane asylum in Kalamazoo. Doddering and muddled residents were held captive in gray, dungeon-like rooms.

Aunt Laura eventually recovered enough to return home, but in 1977 things went a-skelter again when Uncle Don died. She was moved to a small apartment on Military Street under the rotating watch of Normajean and my mother. Two years later, playing cards at a senior center, she met Clint Cooper, an amicable man about her age with a bum arm. They eventually married.

A year or so later, while Aunt Laura and Clint were in Ludington visiting Aunt Marion, Laura suffered a stroke. As both she and Marion were Scientists, EMS was not summoned. Laura fell into a coma from which she never recovered and spent the last eleven and a half years of her life in the Evangelical Nursing Home on North Gratiot, on her back, unresponsive. She died in 1998.

Laura's stroke raised questions; why *wasn't* EMS called? The discussion became more pointed a year later when Marion discovered a lump in her breast.

Marion called for help. Practitioners arrived, and reading and praying began. Wholehearted support came from her daughters Stephanie and Karol, as well as prayers from church members and my mother and Stephen. In short months the cancer proved unstoppable, and in desperation, Marin submitted to chemotherapy. The practitioners bowed out. But it was too late. Marion died in November of 1989, five months after her seventy-fifth birthday.

Barely two years later, Uncle Steve died. Word of his passing traveled slowly, but the whispers were that he died at home in Ann's arms, the two of them reciting the *Scientific Statement of Being.*

While Steve was being mourned, Marion's daughter Karol discovered a lump of her own. Like her mother, she was surrounded and supported by a loving family, members of the church, and practitioners. She died in September of 1992.

Cousin Karol's death came just four months after Uncle Steve's and was the final blow that cleaved the family. Opposing sides emerged. Some were bitter and resentful over decisions consecrated by belief and condemned those decisions as foolish. Others felt ostracized and personally damned because of their faith and what they believed. My cousin Don quit the church and then Stephanie, who became a Methodist the year after her sister died. The rift widened, and cousins became distant. Years later, I heard Ann had died. Writing about my people brought questions to mind if others in the family had passed.

Christian Science was the preeminent rift between me and my mother. The pain of strep throat or mumps or measles was not an illusion. Nor did I believe, when the dentist ground rot from my teeth, that there was no need for Novocain. My infirmities were all real, all-consuming and totally immune to Scientific Belief. When the dentist said open and the drilling started, tears ran down both our faces. The conflict endured decades.

Still, I was not one to scoff at Science. There was too much evidence to the contrary. Nana's healing in Branch when she delivered baby James, for one, and the accident where she about killed herself.

The accident happened in 1959, my junior year at Michigan: After Stephen moved to Mishawaka, the sight of his green Dodge sitting fallow in her garage wore on her; it was a waste of an investment. Unable to abide sloth, she decided seventy-seven was not too old to learn to drive. I was home for the summer. Would I teach her?

My mother and Aunt Laura raised multiple objections, each one reasonable. Nana had never driven a thing, she wouldn't be able to manage the complexities of an automobile, and had precious little experience even being *in* one. Protests only strengthened her resolve.

Sunday afternoons became a standing date. We started in the alley behind McTaggart's, jerking back and forth, testing the clutch and brake, trying reverse, and understanding why not to pump the gas pedal when restarting the engine. She was a quick learner and soon we were tentatively cruising along back streets, exploring parking lots and occasionally—the ultimate test—stopping on a hill. By the end of August, we were cruising through Lakeside Park and driving out to Fort Gratiot for ice cream. Over her daughters' objections, she was awarded a driver's license.

Then in December, despite more vehement objections, Nana decided to drive to Ludington to spend the holidays with Ben and his family. She also intended to see Marion and her granddaughters, Stephanie and Karol. The first three hours of the drive were uneventful. But where Route 20 curved north around Mt. Pleasant, she hit a patch of ice and put an end to the green Dodge—and nearly herself.

I got a message she was seriously injured and in the Mt. Pleasant hospital. After borrowing a car for the 130-mile drive from Ann Arbor, I arrived at the emergency ward ahead of my mother and aunt.

At first, I wasn't sure the bandage-swathed lump on the gurney was my grandmother. The doctors had stemmed the bleeding, but their carefully guarded words and expressions showed no one expected her to live. Lying there motionless with her eyes closed, she looked to be unconscious. But as I watched, her dirt-crusted hand slowly inched toward mine. I took her hand and held it, dumbstruck. Her lips moved silently.

That she survived astounded the hospital staff, and as soon she was allowed, moved to the Christian Science nursing home in Howell. Nana soon returned home, feisty as ever, and promptly rented her garage.

Nana passed in 1973 after spending three weeks in the Christian Science home in Detroit. Conscious of her mother's wishes, Virginia called Smith's Funeral Home and once Nana's remains were lain beside her mother's, she bought headstones for both graves.

My mother retired from the school district when she was sixty-five and moved to a second-floor apartment in an old Victorian on Pine Grove. The apartment came with a garage and the front room overlooked Palmer Park and the St. Clair River. She bought a new Chevrolet and devoted her days to the church, the reading room, and spending time in Birmingham with me and Gina, my wife.

Her routine changed on a rain-filled afternoon in 1990, when she left the reading room with her umbrella pulled low and dashed between parked cars and into the side of a northbound Pontiac. The doctors at the hospital said her heart rate was far too low to risk surgery and urged a pacemaker. My mother wouldn't hear of it.

Fortunately, she was not as resolute as her mother and eventually succumbed to common sense. A pacemaker would make her feel better, but would it change how she felt about Christian Science? Or would a pacemaker change how the Good Lord looked upon her? Of course not. She finally agreed that accepting knowledgeable advice was wise—despite it coming from doctors.

My discussion with the Christian Science nursing home in Howell a few days later widened the distance between believer and observer. The voice on the other end of the line was adamant. Virginia was under a doctor's care. She had a medical device implant, and they were not a medical facility. No, they would not take her. No difference that she had been a Scientist all her life, a First Church board member and a second reader. So Gina and I made arrangements with the Harrington Hotel to equip a room with a hospital bed and bring in nursing care. In retrospect, the decision was a good one. She was within a block of the reading room and her small circle of friends visited regularly.

She healed well for a seventy-eight-year-old and attributed her rapid and prescription-free recovery to the unending power of Science. Her deep belief in Christian Science was a defining characteristic. But she was not one to pray for help or a windfall, a team to win, or good weather for a special day. "Know the Truth and the Truth will make you free," was her hymn.

She returned to her place on Pine Grove and her routine of church, reading room, and modeling for an occasional local fashion show. Misfortune descended again in 2000 at a high school graduation party when she tumbled into Bob and Nadine Holt's sunken living room. At eighty-nine, her broken hip ended all hopes of navigating steps and stairs.

After touring senior centers in Port Huron with Gina and me, my mother selected the Manor, a former Catholic dormitory, at Bard and Fort Streets, right downtown. My mother never had much, but what she did fit nicely into her new place, including the new secretary, a gift from Gina, my wife, who bought it to keep her records and pay her bills. Between Gina's weekly visits for lunch and shopping, she got to know the local cab drivers riding between church, the reading room and her hairdresser. The one thing she didn't like about the Manor was the people were all old.

∞

The final months of 2009 brought my mother's generation to an end. Her downhill slide continued and shopping with Gina, her weekly cab rides to the hairdresser, and attending church became impossible.

Mother and I had discussed the *Big Question* earlier that summer and had gone to Arthur Smith & Son to make arrangements. Her decision was cremation: no funeral, no announcement, no nothing. "Just throw my ashes to the wind," she said. Gina said absolutely not.

One afternoon, driving back to the Manor after having lunch with

Normajean, she asked to turn into the cemetery. We bumped over chuckholes and past age-pitted headstones and granite memorials evincing the growth of Port Huron. Old sections, the smallest, were crowded with simple limestone slabs, long eroded and leaning. Stone monuments, obelisks, memorial benches, and carvings of the later sections showed the expectations of the lumbering era. The newer sections, sparsely occupied and with practical headstones, awaited the return of those who saw I-94 as an escape to greener pastures.

On the second pass around Section G, Gina spotted the four pink stones. The Houston plot was not much more than a small adjunct to much larger memorials. I shut the car off and toggled down the windows. Silence, except for the chattering of a distant squirrel and an occasional ping from the engine. Across Gratiot, Lake Huron was a swath of blue under leafy maples.

Gina pointed from the back seat. "Can you see the headstones, Grammie? Nana's on the left, then Grandma Anna's, Jimmy and Norma are on the right." The four markers were identical: breadbox-size, the name, date, and dash carved in pink granite and adorned by an unpretentious *fleur-de-lis*. Jimmy's and Norma's stones were gray with moss; Great gramma Anna and Nana's graves still showed polish. A black squirrel hopped atop Jimmy's and eyed the car, tail flicking warily.

Gina put a hand on my shoulder. "Where is Uncle Steve?"

"At his mother's feet." His government-issued bronze plate was inscribed *Stephen Russell Houston, RM3 US Navy, World War II, May 2 1992*, and was all but invisible in uneven grass.

I had no idea how Steve's ashes came to be at the foot of Nana's grave; any talk of death was always carefully avoided. But Ann's decision to relinquish her husband to his mother for eternity did come to mind. She had a strong sense of irony.

By February, my mother was bedridden, and not long after, accepted into hospice. But her heart ticked reliably along, and she exceeded her allotted hospice time. Fortunately, Normajean was a hospice volunteer and was able to extend her time in the program. My mother's heart ticked reliably well into the New Year.

Mid-October, Christine Edie, the Manor's owner, called to say my mother was failing and suggested we take a hotel room nearby.

The following morning, we backed out of the driveway in our

seven-house subdivision. A doe munching on our neighbor's asters eyed us nonchalantly. I stopped for a pair of bikers racing south on Kensington and turned north. It was an hour and a quarter drive to Port Huron—no longer a two-and-a-half-hour trek up Gratiot Avenue. The old four-corner towns were still there, but empty and abandoned, erased by progress and the freeway.

Our exit appeared ahead, and I snapped off the cruise control. Getting through downtown Port Huron was a lot easier than it used to be. The storefronts on Military Street and Huron Avenue were mostly blank, sidewalks devoid of foot traffic. Sperry's had a large For Sale sign in the front window, and curbside parking was abundant.

Christine Edie and Normajean were with my mother when we arrived at the Manor. The mood was somber, the TV off, voices hushed. I stepped past my cousin to Virginia's vanity bench. My mother's chest heaved and collapsed under a thin blanket and a crisp white sheet. A green oxygen machine whirred confidently amid circled yards of clear plastic. Her eyes were open but uncomprehending.

Christine held up a vial. "We're giving her morphine now; it makes her more comfortable." She stroked my mother's tangled hair and gently eased her mouth open. "Just a drop under her tongue."

Gina was on the edge of the bed holding my mother's hand; Normajean made a note of the morphine in the hospice records.

"What's with the morphine?" I asked. Our last visit she was getting Tylenol.

"She can't swallow the pill," Christine replied.

"Can't you crush it up?" She didn't answer. I persisted. "Crush it in water?"

Christine looked at me, sadness showing. "She can't swallow." Christine was stoic; she had been through this before. It was part of the job—the bad part. Be sad but strong—strong for the last one, strong for the next one. I looked to my cousin. Normajean dropped her eyes and thumbed papers.

"So the plan is she starves to death?" I tried not to sound testy. "If she can't even swallow, wouldn't it be far more humane to bump up the morphine rather than let her starve? Can't we get the nurse or her doctor to help her along?"

Christine shook her head. "She doesn't know."

Normajean nodded.

I hoped they were right. But it made sense. Her mind was gone, only unfeeling flesh remained. Perhaps it was a rare agreement between medicine and Christian Science. Once the spirit departed, neither was interested in leftovers.

By seven o'clock, Christine and Normajean had gone home, but my mother continued to breathe with great difficulty. Gina said she was hungry, so we found Pat, the Manor's nurse's aide, and told her we were going to run up to the Palms Chrystal Bar for a quick bite. Gina gave her our cell number just in case.

We were back in forty-five minutes and found Pat with Virginia. "No change." My mother's chest heaved under the blanket—each breath seemed her last. Pat left to do rounds and Gina went to sit with my mother. I snapped on the TV and muted a college football game. Just before ten o'clock, Gina called from the bedroom. "Listen" She bent over the bed.

My mother was mumbling, weak, barely a whisper. "It's her hymn."

I leaned over. *Ore waiting harp strings of the mind, there sweeps a strain.* Mary Baker Eddy's, "Christ My Refuge." How many times had I heard it? Certainly every bout of mumps or chicken pox or measles and every fever or ache or pain.

Gina opened Virginia's hymnal and slid her finger to the bookmark, then began to read along. *Low, sad, and sweet, whose measures bind.* She glanced at Virginia. *The power of pain. And wake a white-winged angel . . .* The air was thick with religion and death. I retreated to the living room. The day I often pondered had arrived.

∞

In the morning, we were back early. Christine was in the bedroom holding my mother's hand. "No change." She got up, and Gina sat down. The electric clock on the bed stand slowly swept away time.

I was in the living room staring out the window when Gina beckoned from the bedroom. "Honey." Tears streamed down her cheeks. "I think she's going."

My mother's chest no longer heaved. Her mouth and eyes were open, her jaw moved imperceptibly, rested, then moved again. I bent over the bed and listened. Gina held her hand.

"Is she gone?" Gina's voice was a whisper.

"Can't tell." I leaned closer; no sign of breath. "I guess so. Yes, it's over."

My mother had taken her leave; I brushed her eyes closed.

Gina looked at her watch. "11:11." It was Sunday morning, October 24, 2010, eleven days after her ninety-eighth birthday.

Gina sniffed and wiped her eyes. "She believed right to the end, didn't she?"

"Yes, she did. They all did." We hugged silently beside what was once my mother.

∞

My Mother's ashes spent the winter on our fireplace hearth in a garish urn we acquired decades ago at a fundraiser. She and the urn accompanied us to a small luncheon we hosted at the Edison Inn for family and friends and members of the church; my mother was the guest of honor.

The urn rose above a table replete with her favorite photographs: my 8 X 10 high school graduation picture, special letters, and cards of condolence. Tia, my thirteen-year-old granddaughter and daughter Christine's youngest, sang *Christ My Refuge,* a capella.

When spring came and life again stirred the earth to jubilance and color, Gina and I went to the Lakeside Cemetery and placed her alongside her brother Stephen beneath a small pink headstone adorned by a sprig of *fleur-de-lis.*

Finis

Lena and Laura in 1912, with Virginia on Lena's knee.

Lena and sister, Little Anna, c. 1901–02.

The Branch, Michigan, house with Lena and Benhart on the porch, c. 1893–94.

Anna in front of the house, the barn in the background, c. 1893–94.

Laura and Lena, c. 1901–02.

Lena and David in 1908. It is not a wedding picture, as they never married, and the expressions appear more aloof than joyous.

Sister Anna, Benhart, Ed, Carl, and Lena, c. 1915.

Normajean, Laura Lee, the author, and Karol, c. 1949.

ABOUT THE AUTHOR

A self-admitted old fart with children, grandchildren and great grandchildren, Gale Forbes readily concedes to having struggled with freshman English at the University of Michigan. During his 50-year career in architecture, he wrote essays for trade magazines, joined writing groups and attended workshops. He discovered in the art of writing fiction an essential aid in preparing technical reports: show, never tell. After finishing his first book, *Exercises for Miss Melodie*, a small collection of essays, an itch to discover his family roots eventually led to *Mother's People.* Stand by for his third book of historical fiction, *Changing Time*, which explores the impact of progress on a small 19th-century fishing village.

ACKNOWLEDGEMENTS

The genesis of *Mother's People* came from cousin Sandy Houston. Sandy was bent on preserving family history and had put together a rough family tree, unearthed old letters and personal histories and enlisted my support.

Cousin Stephanie Thompson, nee Hawley, got wind of Sandy's project and contributed *The History of Mason County*, a county-produced tome with a trove of details that included Ed Anderson and family, and the fire that wiped out Branch.

Little Anna's birth on August 8, 1874, anchored the story timeline, as did other key events. Family lore was an important source of detail, as was the Mason County clerk's office and internet posting of the era. During my formative years, certain topics were forbidden. The skeletons stayed in the closet. But as I became of age, certain stories made little sense, so I began to pry additional facts from Aunt Marion, who had an ingrained sense of reality. In time, my mother reluctantly realized the truth had been outed and the closet door opened.

Did Anna err with the lord's son? Most likely. Helena had no money. If Anna did the deed with a stable hand or someone else of her stature, she would have wound up in prison and there would have been no Sister, Lena, Laura . . . or even me?

Deduction filled in blanks. The essential question was what would I do given the same situation, what would logically happen next? International departures from Sweden in 1874 departed from Goteborg and went to either Liverpool, England, or Hamburg, Germany. In that Edward Stark, my great grandfather, was German and one industry in Germany at the time was taking in unwanted illegitimate children of the well-to-do in Europe, the story went to Hamburg. Herr Muhlback is a figment of imagination, and a foil for Helena.

From the early 1920s, the storyline is generally factual. My mother and her sisters were not reluctant to talk about many details of their childhoods. My cousins provided additional background information, and once the 1940s arrived, I was present.

And God bless beta readers, especially mine who read and read again to enrich the manuscript. Many thanks to Janet Kleinhardt, Eve Schwartz, Dick Davis, and my wife, Gina. And special thanks to my lovely lady of Letters, Melodie Monahan, who for years prodded me gently along the road to better writing. Thank you all.

G.

Made in United States
Orlando, FL
06 February 2023